Author's Request

This story is entirely fictitious, but the theft of Native American artifacts is all too real. The increased interest in Native American art and art objects has given rise to an illegal black market in stolen antiquities on an unprecedented scale. Grave desecrations in search of jewelry and other personal items and the plunder of ancient sites to steal artifacts are, unfortunately, an all too common occurrence. The author would ask collectors and buyers to be certain of the provenance or origin of any Native American art, art objects, and artifacts purchased from an unusual source. If you don't know the source, please check it out. Help put an end to these thefts and desecrations.

Author's Note

The term *Kushtikaw* (pronounced kush-ti-kaw) is Tlingit for a shape-shifter. In the Tlingit culture, Kushtikaws, shape-shifters, lure children and the unwitting into the forest where they are never seen or heard from again. In many cases, the stories of the Kushtikaw, like the boogeyman, are told to frighten children into behaving and staying near home. That is, unless, of course, you believe in Kushtikaws—and many do!

To make the mystery flow, the author borrowed the legend of the Raven, the great transformer and trickster, from the Pacific Northwest native culture. Since the Raven is full of mystical and magical powers and driven by insatiable greed, it was easy to weave the Raven's story into the tribal legend of the Kushtikaw. No disrespect was intended. The author hopes that, in some small way, the story will raise a curiosity in the reader to explore the wonderful Native American cultures and histories of the Pacific Northwest and Alaska tribes and clans.

Finally, this book takes place in Southeast Alaska, from Ketchikan to the remote Dall Island, off the southwest coast of Prince of Wales Island. However, because it is a work of fiction and to safeguard privacy, the author created places which do not exist, changed the names of places which do, created Tlingit-sounding words to disguise locations, and entirely fabricated Twasaan and the village of Twasaan. The raw beauty of Southeast Alaska rainforest is, of course, real.

This book is dedicated to Carol: my wife, my soul mate, my best friend, and ultimate riding companion. Without her insistence, this novel never would have come to fruition.

That which does not kill us, makes us stronger

—Nietzsche

CHAPTER ONE
1983

A harried Lt. Julie Sykes glanced in the rearview mirror and turned on the right blinker. A few moments later, her patrol car exited I-5 South at the SEATAC off-ramp in a stream of mist. She adjusted the wiper speed for the oncoming downpour. A few miles to the west, she could make out yet another band of dark rain clouds approaching. Seattle and rain seemed to go together, especially this time of year. Too early for snow and too late for sunshine, autumn in the Pacific Northwest could be depressingly dreary. She glanced at the speedometer as she decelerated to a reasonable rate, preparing to negotiate the tight curve ahead. Julie was running late, but not so late that his highness, the VIP at the airport, couldn't wait just a bit longer. With less than a year to go before consideration for promotion within the prestigious Washington State Police, Julie Sykes wanted no more trouble. *Just do your job, keep a low profile, and maintain a positive attitude*. It was the very lack of a positive attitude that had gotten her into trouble with the brass and, hence, this wonderful assignment. How could she know the captain was standing right behind her when she remarked to another supervisor that even though the department recently became accredited through the Commission on Accreditation for Law Enforcement Agencies, it was still becoming a Mickey Mouse outfit? Julie felt the blood rise to her cheeks as she thought about her vocalization.

She scanned the traffic, flicked on the right blinker again, and took another hairpin turn onto State Hwy 99. SEATAC Airport was a mere 5 minutes away. She smiled to herself as she watched a speeding minivan driver in front of her brake after seeing the patrol car. *What is it about male minivan drivers? Are they trying to compensate for something? Some university should get a grant to study the male minivan phenomenon.* Then her mind shifted back to her most recent pet peeve. *It IS a Mickey Mouse outfit. We have replaced commonsense and good judgment with policies and procedures ... just because we have too many policies, and too many of them poorly written doesn't mean I'm disloyal.* "No matter what Herr Captain Godfrey thinks," she said under her breath. *God, I hope this isn't the first stage of burnout.*

A soft sigh escaped, and then a wiry smile crossed her lips. She took the lane directing drivers to passenger arrivals. Lt. Sykes weaved around the congested traffic near the airport and proceeded toward the Alaska Airlines baggage claim, negotiating the usual chaos of hotel vans, rental car shuttles, and passenger vehicles. She scanned the sidewalk for someone who appeared like a cop in need of a ride. In her haste to leave the office, she had forgotten to ask what this guy looked like, but she was sure she could pick him out. *Funny how one cop can spot another. What is it? The eye contact, self-confidence ... something. Okay! Here we go!* Julie sighted her suspect VIP in a gray three-piece suit complete with maroon tie. She guided the patrol vehicle to the curb just in front of a Jeep being driven by some kid who looked perturbed but said nothing.

Standing under the Alaska Airlines baggage claim 3 sign,

Sergeant Danski of the Alaska Department of Public Safety made eye contact with Julie and then nodded his head. He reached down, picking up his garment bag and attaché case, then walked briskly over to the patrol car. She noticed he was about 5'8", light complexion, with short, dark hair, and appeared in fairly good shape. *Good dresser, looks like a Ralph Lauren polo shirt aficionado.*

Popping the trunk lid with the button on the key fob, Julie exited the vehicle, briefly straightened her suit, and closed the middle button on her navy blue jacket over her duty weapon. Walking around to the back of the vehicle, she smiled and stretched out her hand.

"I'm Lt. Julie Sykes from the Washington State Police," she said. "Welcome to autumn in Seattle."

"Glad to be off the plane. I'm Sgt. Skip Danski with the Alaska Department of Public Safety. Thanks for meeting me," he said as they shook hands. His immediate impression of Lt. Sykes was that she was about 5'11", obviously a career professional from the way she wore her suit with minimum makeup and a no-nonsense hair style. He liked that.

"Just throw your bags in there anywhere, the trunk is a mess," she said. It wasn't really, but that was just shop talk to explain away all the police equipment required to be carried in patrol cars nowadays.

Sgt. Danski carefully opened clips on the sides of the garment bag and laid it flat across the top of the gear. As he arranged the luggage, Julie noticed he wore a shoulder holster and kept the briefcase with him as she closed the trunk lid.

Once they got settled into the car, Julie called dispatch and informed them that she had made the pickup. As she cautiously pulled out into traffic, Julie turned to Skip. "I didn't get much information about you or your trip, Sergeant. Where are you from?" she asked.

"Anchorage via Ketchikan," he replied.

"Ketchikan? I heard you really get some rain up there, nothing like our paltry 29 inches," she said noticing the gentle mist had now upgraded to a downpour.

"Just a tad more, about 150 inches a year. You learn to live with it. The weather will drive you crazy or right out of the country," he replied.

"So what is it? You crazy or leaving? What brings you to Seattle, if I might ask?" Julie said smiling. She noticed Skip Danski maintained a military bearing and good eye contact during their conversation. *He's a little on the stiff side and seems on edge. I wonder if he's like that all the time.*

"They didn't tell you?" Sgt. Danski looked genuinely surprised.

"Tell me what?"

"I'm with Internal Affairs. I'm here to do an investigation on one of our troopers who landed in the maximum security ward at Swedish Hospital about a month ago. He's been unconscious but finally came around a day or 2 ago. As I understand it from my boss who spoke to a Captain Godfrey, your honchos feel like they have a vested interest in this case and wanted to be part of the investigation. Especially since at least one of the victims apparently was a grad student at the University of Washington. In fact, you're supposed to—"

"Whoa ..." Julie said, tilting her head down and peering over the top of her thin round-rimmed glasses at the passenger. A moment later, she had the patrol car pulled over at a nearby Chevron gas station.

"Okay, Sergeant, go over this one more time. Captain Godfrey *is* my supervisor, and he didn't say shit, excuse me, about working with you, only that I was to pick you up at the airport and take you wherever you wanted to go."

"Well, maybe you aren't the detective assigned to assist me while I'm here, but someone sure was. Captain Godfrey made that point very clear to my boss," he said.

"Alright, just stand by a second," Julie said a little perturbed as she picked up the microphone and called dispatch.

"Alpha-90, this 5-Sierra-71," she said.

"5-Sierra-71, this is Alpha-90, go ahead."

"10-4. Alpha-90 is 5-Sierra-4 available?" she asked.

"5-Sierra-71, stand by, one."

"10-4." *This is just like him to do that! One week before my vacation, and I get this. Well, if he thinks I am going to screw up my plans, he's got another thing coming.*

A deep voice interrupted her train of thought.

"5-Sierra-71, 5-Sierra-4."

God, Godfrey's voice even sounds authoritative.

"5-Sierra-4, this is 5-Sierra-71. I currently have our VIP with me. He has informed me someone from our office is going to assist him while he is here. With whom do I need to coordinate?" she asked. Julie hoped she phrased the question so as not to draw attention to herself. She wanted—no—needed—this vacation. Danski was not in her plans.

The deep voice came back. "5-Sierra-71, 5-Sierra-4, negative. You are to assist until further notice. Contact me Lima-Lima before 1700 this afternoon."

Julie flushed. She was furious but kept her composure.

"10-4, will call on land line in about 20."

"Well, I guess I'm it for now, Sergeant," she said as pleasantly as possible, trying to mask her feelings.

"You can probably call in from Swedish Hospital. Surely they have a payphone," Skip Danski offered. He felt a little awkward since it was obvious Lt. Sykes hadn't planned on this assignment and then to overhear the conversation between her and Captain Godfrey.

Reading his thoughts, Julie wanted to put everything straight. "Look, I'll be frank with you. I thought I was given the assignment to pick you up and to provide transportation because I embarrassed myself in front of my boss. No one said anything about assisting you in an investigation. And to tell you the truth, Godfrey knows I'm about to go on vacation in a week."

"*Were*, you mean," Skip Danski replied. "It sounds like you might be in for the duration."

"We'll see," she said pensively.

Heading up I-5 North, Julie asked about the case. "Since we may be working together, can you bring up to speed on how I can be of assistance?" she asked.

"Not certain. At least not until after I have a chance to interview him," he replied.

"Mind explaining how your trooper landed in the psycho ward?"

"We're not really sure. I mean we *know* how he got to Seattle. We just don't know what happened to him in the old-growth forest. He was found by a search and rescue party about a month ago next to a lake in a remote part of Misty Fiords National Monument ... in really tough shape ... too critical to talk. The search and rescue folks did what they could, then bundled him up, heloed him to a logging camp about 30 miles away. As I understand it, he almost died at the camp. MedFlight Northwest brought him here because Ketchikan doesn't have the medical facilities to treat his injuries, which apparently are quite extensive ... both mental and physical."

"If he was hurt in the line of duty, why are you down here on an IA?" she queried.

Lt. Sykes knew the answer before she finished the question ... more Mickey Mouse policies. In most police departments, it was standard operating procedure when an officer was involved in a shooting or any traumatic incident, sometimes even as minor as a traffic accident, Internal Affairs had to be summoned to investigate the incident and clear the officer. It was done mostly to protect the department from liability suits possibly stemming from an officer's negligence or misconduct. Sometimes the brass even used the unit as a means of control and intimidation. But usually the "holier than thou" IA investigators attempted to sell it to the officers as an investigation for their own protection and their careers ... even though a copy of the IA results went in one's personnel file. *Get promoted after an IA investigation? Whoever falls for that shit should quit while they're ahead.*

Then she heard a reply she never expected.

"I was sent down here because we suspect he might have killed at least four people over the past year. One theory holds that he is a ritualistic killer who was almost killed by his latest victim, the aforementioned grad student ... given the current evidence," Skip Danski said. "In fact, I was with him on the early stages of the investigation. Keep asking myself what I missed."

"I haven't heard anything about the case in the news."

"Not surprising. We have only recently connected the victims through link analysis; otherwise, the murders would appear as though they were unique and actually separated from one another by distance and circumstance."

"Does that really make sense? I mean a theory about a state trooper who runs around murdering people in the woods?"

"This is a special case; *he* is a special case." He looked away and then stared back at Julie. She felt something which gave her an uneasy feeling. Julie knew from experience when the IA was used as a method of intimidation, the outcome of anything, even a minor infraction, could be made into a firing offense. It was one reason officers hated and despised Internal Affairs. *So, Sergeant, which is it? Are you here for the truth, or are you just an errand boy for the tight-ass brass?*

Sgt. Danski continued. "At this point, nothing is clear; at least, not in my mind. We're hoping to get some answers to the evidence thus far and begin piecing together what happened." Skip Danski blew out a hard sigh. "Like I said, your office is covering the grad student ... I have his file with me ... I ... we ... suspect there is much more to all this."

Julie let off the accelerator and reduced speed near the outskirts of downtown Seattle, then exited onto a roadway taking them up into the hills overlooking Puget Sound. A few minutes later, the patrol car pulled into a parking slot reserved for on-duty police officers. Sgt. Danski sat and waited while Lt. Sykes radioed their location to dispatch. Exiting the vehicle, they quickly walked across the wet pavement avoiding several large puddles in the process and arrived at the automated, double glass doors of the hospital. Stepping inside, they looked around for directions. A black-and-white sign stating "Admissions," with a pointing arrow, directed them across a highly polished floor to a brightly lit receiving station.

CHAPTER TWO
A year earlier

From a distance, the primeval forest rose abruptly from the rocky shoreline like an obsidian wall. The long, graceful boughs of towering cedars, hemlocks, and pines interlaced at the trunks to create an illusion of dark impenetrability. In places, the branches were so interwoven it seemed they could absorb sound, daylight, and even preclude rain from reaching the ground. The visual light of the forest's inner sanctum, even at noon in the long hours of summer, was never more than a green translucence which changed imperceptibly, deepening as the day wore on from shades of gray to finally pitch-black. In the heart of the ancient forest, any trace of light was often gone an hour before dusk. This natural barrier had stood for centuries guarding the upper reaches of Twasaan Bay, breached only by periodic streams of cold, fast-flowing water. For the eagles, perched like guardians in snow-covered trees, the old-growth forest stretched into the interior for as far as their eyes could see. Accessible only by water or air, this remote, pristine area was commonly referred to as the "crown jewel" of the National Park Service's management program in Lower Southeast Alaska.

Even though midday, the pale winter light had already begun to surrender to an approaching Arctic gale racing across the Alexander Archipelago, dropping temperatures and abundant snowfall in its wake. In this part of the country, the prevailing winds came from the west and southwest, but sometimes during winter, fierce Arctic gales would drive in from the northwest, blanketing the terrain with a foot of wet, heavy snow and the forest would instantly fall silent. All around, the tall cedars began to sway periodically as light gusts of wind moved across the bay, the first signs of the advancing storm.

Then something happened ... a shift in the natural order. Mallards and red-breasted mergansers paddling peacefully along the frozen shoreline first sensed the change and hurriedly took to flight in a flurry of wing beats and calls. Moments later, the quiet solitude of the Alaskan winter afternoon was abruptly shattered when a disheveled figure burst pell-mell from the deep recesses of the ancient forest and began running along the rocky, secluded beach. The man ran as fast as he could until he finally stumbled over an ice-encrusted boulder, crashing to his knees. He knelt there a minute, gulping in huge volumes of salty bay air which were immediately spewed back out in forceful gusts of vapor. Anyone who happened across him would have been terrified by what they witnessed: a body drenched with fresh blood only partially concealed beneath a tight, ill-fitting wool jacket and pants. Charcoal paint was drawn across his face in thin lines forming an ancient, mystic, Indian pattern which accentuated wild eyes. Takqua slowly tilted his head back, extending his strong arms to the sky and mumbled a brief chant to one of his beloved deities. Transfixed in this position, Takqua's eyes rolled back into his head, the whites of his eyes exposed and a strange grin affixed to his face. After several more minutes had elapsed, he began slowly returning to the present from whatever insane nirvana he had lapsed into. Recognition of his surroundings dawned over him, and he hurriedly looked around once more, his eyes searching the wilderness around him, making sure he was still alone on this remote beach in Southeast Alaska. Exhausted and emotionally spent, he dropped his arms to his sides and lowered his head to his chest. Eventually, after catching his breath, he rocked back on his heels and rose from the snow like a demon from a frozen hell, leaving small pools of dripping blood in the white snow.

Takqua was tall and had a naturally athletic build which allowed him to maintain his weight at about 200 lbs. His facial features were fine and angular. Dark, menacing eyes peered out from under a sweat-soaked brow. The blood had already begun to mat his thick, straight, black hair which clung in strands to the sides of his face and neck. Lines of sweat mixed with specks of blood ran down his face in thin streams, partially washing away the black charcoal face paint. His perspiration seeped through his bloodstained clothing, turning into wisps of steam rising unsteadily from his body, only to disappear as if by magic. Reaching down, he grabbed the green plastic garbage bag filled with his most recent treasures, slung it across his shoulders, and staggered down the snow-covered shoreline. There was much work to be done before nightfall. He glanced around again at the solitude and smiled, observing to himself that several inches of snow had fallen the previous day, obliterating all sign of his earlier arrival. His previous, prominent, tracks were now merely obscured depressions in the freshly fallen snow.

Looking toward the horizon, he saw the approaching storm and howled a long wolf call in relief. Takqua knew the next heavy snowfall would erase even the smallest traces of his ever having been there. No one would ever know. No one, that is, except the

Indian spirits, of course, and they were elated with his most recent offerings. The spirits of the dead Kushtikaws ... the shaman shape-shifters ... they told him so. *They* had given him his freedom to carry on his work without fear of reprisals from avenging dead warrior spirits who protected the ancient villages and roamed the dark forests. He laughed to himself at how clever he had become: like the Raven. The Raven ... the symbol of the shape-shifters.

He began to feel revived as he approached the general location of an old, battered, red, aluminum canoe he had sequestered beneath the tall hemlocks at the edge of the bay. He began walking faster, then, picking up the pace, almost running. Immediately he realized he was making a lot of rapid movements while exposed on the beach. Someone from the tiny village of New Twasaan, a few miles across the bay, might be in the area and spot him! Frantically, he spun completely around to see if anyone was watching him now, but knew that he was safe. No one would be out in the bay in weather like this. He breathed a long sigh of relief, and, then, facing the wind, inhaled deeply, tasting the cold air, and surveyed his isolated surroundings.

Takqua felt entirely at home in this environment. An avid outdoorsman all his life, he knew Indian woodlore and crafts and often spent days in the wilderness, living off the land and perfecting his skills. He could think like an animal, act like an animal, sound like an animal, and, soon, even be an animal. The thought made him laugh aloud. As far as his eye could see, there were dark, choppy waters and snow squalls moving steadily across the wide bay. Not a soul in sight. He marveled at the deafening silence of winter around him. All that could be heard was the rustling of the tree branches and lapping of the water against the shore ice along the beach. In the background, he could hear the screech of seagulls as they gracefully skimmed across the bay, just inches from the water, searching for food. He was instantly struck by the awesome beauty and total solitude of the wilderness. He was in his element and truly free.

Finally at his destination, he set his bloody bundle down beside the boat. Takqua grasped the ice-bound wooden shaft of the paddle. With a sudden jerk, he broke the utensil free from the frozen snow and ice which secured it. Resurrecting the ice-encrusted paddle from the belly of the boat, he had to stop his labor momentarily and hold his throbbing head to keep it from exploding. He scooped up handfuls of snow and held them to his forehead and temple. The recent events were coming back to him now, and though he tried to think of something else—anything else—the gruesome thoughts would not go away. He sat back under the fir tree and rested while his eyes rolled back in his head. The memories began flooding back in bits and pieces.

He remembered having discovered an old couple quite by accident, shortly after he had located the ancient village called Twasaan. Their appearance was entirely unexpected and, in fact, had surprised and angered him. He had almost walked into them while strolling through the ancient village, but seeing them at the last moment, he had managed to duck behind a large hemlock and avoid detection. It had taken Takqua months of research to even confirm the existence of the long-abandoned site, and 2 more years of sleuthing before finally locating the old totems which guarded the village. He dreamed about slowly excavating the nearby graves at his leisure, looking for shaman talismans. *Now, it was too late! How did they get here? Was it by accident or design?*

He spent the next couple of hours anxiously spying on them from his hiding place in the woods as they slowly investigated the village. They were not tourists; they had a purpose. First, the couple would photograph a grave which appeared more like a depression in the thick moss-covered ground. Then, methodically, one or the other would peel back the natural covering of the tomb and superficially excavate the site. Some graves were not buried but had been fashioned by putting a wooden coffin in large, hollowed-out fir trees. These were usually the sites of Indian royalty. Every grave, once discovered and exposed, was photographed from multiple angles. Then the old couple would mark certain locations and carefully conceal the find. *Are they archeologists with a university or the government? No, it appears to be just the two of them.*

Even now as he sat near his canoe, breathing short rapid breathes to calm himself, the thought infuriated him! *How dare they disturb those graves! He had spent months going over old records in Seattle and Juneau, researching all the details to make certain this was one of the legendary villages; a very special village. It had been one of only four Indian communities that had a shaman reputed to have been a Kushtikaw ... shaman shape-changer. Tlingit lore held that to be a true shape-changer, you needed to have the shaman powers. You needed the talismans and the knowledge to perform the sacred rituals. He knew this well. An old Haida shaman he met in the Queen Charlotte Islands had confirmed the story. To acquire the power, he would need the sacred amulets, talisman, and necklaces from the shamans, and maybe the high chiefs located at the four sacred villages. The power was his for the taking, but they were stealing it before his eyes!*

Making full use of the immense fir trees, thorny devil's club, and scrawny berry bushes for concealment, he methodically stalked the couple throughout the day, moving quietly among dead ferns and walking on pine needle beds wherever possible, all the while observing them from the perimeter of the ruins. He watched their every move. Periodically, their dog, Fritz, a white toy poodle in a red sweater, would sense Takqua and bark at the ominous forest until the old man yelled at Fritz to stop. Hearing the stern threats from his owner, the little dog would lie on the ground facing Takqua's direction, wagging its tail and whining. By moving to different locations in the woods surrounding the ancient village, Takqua could observe what they were doing.

It soon became apparent the two were not amateurs. They were too adept, too knowledgeable, and too precise in carrying out their activities to be just tourists stumbling on an old village in the middle of nowhere. Overhearing snatches of their conversations, he often heard the woman respectfully refer to the man with long, thick, gray hair and glasses as "professor." As time wore on, the shadows deepened in the forest and light began to fade. The professor and his wife quit their toil, left the decayed ruins, their arms full of equipment, while Fritz ran along the narrow small-game trail ahead of them.

Takqua, curious to know if they had taken anything from the village, had continued to follow them closely. He observed the couple make their way up river for a quarter mile where they arrived at some shallow rapids. Here, they forded the Shakan River without having water come over the tops of their calf-high rubber boots. The professor picked up Fritz, and the couple helped each other over the slippery rocks. Once safely on the other side, they dropped their utensils by the trail and strode hand-in-hand toward an old trapper's cabin located a short distance away. Takqua was surprised and angered by the cabin. *How could he not have known it was there? It couldn't be a U.S. Forest Service cabin or it would have been on the maps he studied. A trapper's or prospector's cabin perhaps …*

He waited impatiently in the numbing cold of the Alaska night, praying to the gods of the forest for invisibility and stealth until they sent the next snowfall. Then, with the cover of darkness, he cut off a 3-foot branch from a nearby Hemlock tree and crept up to the cabin, carefully avoiding the pale yellow light spilling onto the snow through a large, picture window. Hiding in the dark recesses of the porch, Takqua peered into the log cabin. His eyes took in everything at once. The old woman was reading at the small wooden table, sipping a cup of tea. The professor was dozing on one of the narrow bunks, covered by a gray wool trapper's blanket. What he failed to noticed, however, was the small dog resting near the black metal wood stove. Seeing Takqua's face through the windowpane, the dog instantly jumped up on all fours, barking and growling, its legs stiff and the hair on its back standing on end. Startled from a deep sleep, the professor bolted up in bed, cursed at the animal, and threw his magazine at it. Takqua smiled and used the diversion to quietly slip back into the black sanctuary of the night, erasing his steps by brushing the snow with his Hemlock branch.

The next day, he rose before dawn and found an observation point in the forest, impatiently waiting for the others to wake up. As the minutes passed, he noticed that the freshly fallen snow had begun to glimmer, like minuscule shards of broken crystal in the increasing daylight. Takqua was determined to track their every move, from the time the couple left the cabin and crossed the river in the morning to the time they returned for supper at night, afraid that if he left them, they would find what he was looking for, what he needed.

Then, as if on command, the cabin door suddenly swung open, and he heard the couple talking in loud voices on the front porch while looking at the forest and their surroundings. He could see the old man was wearing a holster and pistol on the outside of his parka. *Why was that? Did the dog barking make them feel they needed protection?* A few minutes later, they left the cabin, wearing colorful daypacks, and headed back toward the river. There, they picked up their tools once more and recrossed.

Once on the other side, the white poodle bounced ahead of them, making fresh tracks in the snow. Takqua hid like an animal in the dark shadows, almost afraid to breathe until they had passed his position. Then, he adeptly followed them back to the ancient village, careful not to leave any tracks of his own.

Settled comfortably on a thick bed of pine needles under a large cedar tree, he observed the couple systematically excavate the gravesites identified from the previous day. Takqua could see that with each tomb the couple discovered, they would follow a certain pattern. First, they opened and photographed the coffin and remains in the original position, cataloging any jewelry or other artifacts in the tomb. Next, they would take only the best examples of the native art they found. Then, the professor and his wife would carefully rebury the site again, covering the surface of the tomb with earth and dead branches. It wouldn't fool a good woodsman or a tracker, but anyone accidentally finding the ruins in a month or 2 wouldn't be able to tell if any of the gravesites were ever disturbed ... if they could even find the sites at all.

After two freezing days hiding in the woods watching the couple explore the Tlingit gravesites, their excited voices told him they finally stumbled across what Takqua had been searching for: the burial treasures of the village shaman. His heart began to pound. These treasures, he knew, were different. The shaman was believed to be a Kushtikaw. *The power of the Kushtikaw was his. With the power of the shape-shifters, he could walk in two worlds: this world and the spirit world. In this world, he could walk the forests and beaches of the ancients in the form of wild animal luring unsuspecting villagers into following him, where he could physically capture their souls and send them to the spirit world. Then, he could change back into his human form and simply walk away, or change into a raven and fly to another village. In the spirit world, he would have power, strength, and the souls he took to serve him as slaves and do his bidding. But to have the power, he required the talismans. These things were not just artifacts, to him, they held a power, and were destined to be his ... even if he had to kill for them.*

Coming back to the present, he regained his composure although his mind continued to inject him with heavy emotions of anger, fear, and frustration. His mind slipped, and he began remembering, again, just how impatient he was when they found the shaman tomb, the same one he, himself, had been searching for, for months. He could tell by their excited comments it was a treasure trove. The professor remarked how he had never seen anything like this before. His wife wondered aloud how much they would get when they sold the artifacts to the Metropolitan Museum. Thinking quickly, Takqua reached down and retrieved his hunting knife with a brightly beaded handle from his sheath at his side. He stripped to the waist, taking off his wool coat, thick sweater, and undershirt. Then he dragged the razor-sharp edge of the knife across his muscular chest in four long strokes. The wounds were very superficial, but bloody. He smeared the blood over his chest and the wounds looked even worse. Next, he dug into the hard earth, grabbing dirt and twigs which he rubbed over his hair and face. With a few more handfuls of soil, he smeared the dirt mixed with blood down to his waist. That done, he wiped blood and dirt over his face and arms. He was ready. The makeup applied, Takqua now carried out the ruse of pretending to stagger out of the woods half-naked and dirty, shivering in the cold, and crying hysterically that he was a camper being chased by a crazed brown bear.

The couple, at first in total shock and disbelief that someone—anyone—would be in these woods in winter, quickly recovered. With the looming threat of a bear attack, the professor fumbled with the holster, drew his revolver, and looked around worriedly. Takqua sensed immediately the old man did not know how to use the weapon and smiled to himself. Then, under the protection of the professor, they hurried back to the safety of the cabin.

Once inside, they bolted the cabin door, warmed him, tended to his wounds, and then wrapped him in a blanket. They introduced themselves as the Toddwells on a late vacation before the bay froze over for winter. Professor Toddwell explained that he was a nature photographer and his wife was a naturalist. Takqua listened to their lies and smiled, pretending to be grateful. Then the old man noticed something he hadn't seen before, Takqua's necklace. Instantly the old man's suspicions were aroused.

"That is an interesting necklace you have, young man. May I see it?" The professor walked closer to Takqua to examine the jewelry.

"No, I haven't seen anything quite like this. Most unusual. Janet, look at this necklace, would you?" Takqua stood perfectly still as if frozen to the ground.

Janet, finishing tiding up the kitchen, came over, wiping her hands on a dish towel.

"Oh my, that *is* an interesting item there. Did you find it or buy it?"

The words had barely left her lips when he sprang like a mountain lion, overpowering them and tying their hands behind them to the wooden chairs in the cabin with their own belts. They had cried and pleaded for their lives as they witnessed the person they saved being transformed into an ancient demon before their eyes. He had prayed briefly to his Indian spirits and when that ceremony was completed, he took charcoal from the fireplace making large circles around his eyes and lines down his cheeks and chin. Then, deliberately, methodically, he drew life from the their old, writhing, bodies, one at a time, with his own knife, as they squirmed and screamed in horror and pain for hours, their dog running around and barking helplessly outside. When he was sure he had all the information they knew about the ancient village and all the artifacts, he cut off their heads and disposed of the bodies outside, culminating his revenge by killing the little white dog.

The grisly task completed, he squeezed into the professor's jacket and boots and then tore the small cabin apart, searching for any additional artifacts the Toddwells may have secreted from the village. Finally satisfied that he had recovered everything, he grabbed a large green garbage bag from under the old porcelain sink. Opening the plastic bag with one bloody hand, he stuffed the artifacts into the bottom. Then he picked up the professor's head by the hair and dropped it unceremoniously into the depths of the sack with a loud thump. The woman's head followed. The heads struck each other in the bottom of the garbage sack, sounding like two ripe coconuts being hit together. They belonged to him now.

CHAPTER THREE
Seattle

Standing at the admitting station, Lt. Sykes identified herself and Sgt. Danski to a Mrs. Michaels, according to her name tag, and requested to speak to the head nurse. Fifteen minutes later, they were ushered into the office of the chief physician, Dr. Wang, on the psychiatric ward of the Swedish Hospital. A very young Dr. Wang, dressed in green scrubs, invited them to sit down on small institutional chairs of fabric and chrome. He listened intently as Sgt. Danski explained his assignment. When Skip had finished, the doctor looked at him intently for a few moments.

"Ummm. No, he is not well enough for ... that ... an interview. He is heavily sedated and keeps going in an out of consciousness. If he could talk, I doubt that anything he said now would be of any use to you or admissible in a court of law."

"Well," Julie cut in, "can we at least see him?"

"That depends on what you want to do."

"Just see him, Doctor, nothing more," Sgt. Danski replied.

"OK, but no interviews, nothing stressful. You can tell your supervisors I think it will be several more weeks before he is able to remember anything and communicate coherently."

Dr. Wang escorted the two state troopers past the guards, the heavily secured entrance, and finally down a long, poorly lit hall with yellowing tile flooring to a locked metal door with a thick reinforced glass window. The painted sign below the window identified the room as 804.

Lt. Sykes looked around and then over at Dr. Wang. "Damn, this place is depressing."

"It's the best we have, maybe the best in Seattle," the doctor responded.

"Can we see him now?" Sgt. Danski asked a little impatiently.

"Sure, let's see how the patient is doing." Dr. Wang looked through the glass portal. Satisfied that all was well inside, the doctor unlocked the heavy metal door and entered the dimly lit room.

Julie Sykes turned to Skip Danski. "What did you say his name was again?"

Doctor Wang replied, "Cody O'Keefe."

Sgt. Danski looked at the patient in bed and was shocked by what he saw. It didn't even look like the Cody O'Keefe he remembered. The trooper was obviously in bad shape and had lost a lot of weight. Skip walked up closer to Cody, reached over, and held his hand. Clear plastic tubes were running in and out of the trooper's body, which still had dressings over obviously deep wounds. Blood was beginning to show through the bandages. The dressings needed changing. All the while, monitoring machines in the room hummed in the background with quiet efficiency. The doctor picked up the bed chart and flipped through the pages.

"Hummm. He is still heavily sedated but improving."

Sgt. Danski was about to say something when his hand was suddenly gripped tightly. He looked down at a bruised and disfigured face, his puffy, bloodshot eyes barely opened. Sgt. Danski could see the veins on Cody's neck extended. Surprised by the strength and suddenness of the action, Skip's immediate reaction was to pull his hand away, but he couldn't.

"Doctor Wang! Doctor Wang!" he repeated in a raised voice. "Your patient ... Cody ... I think he's awake!" Looking down, Skip saw O'Keefe glaring at him with a look of bitter hatred. He couldn't talk, but he was speaking volumes.

CHAPTER FOUR

The vivid recollection of the recent events continued to unfold in Takqua's mind in short clips of time punctuated by exploding flashes of sharp, colorful images. He grabbed another handful of snow and rubbed it over his face; he still felt dizzy. He recalled how he had glanced around the interior of the bloody room and then retraced his steps back along the small-game trail to the Indian ruins, leaving drops of blood along the way. Before long, he could make out the silhouette of the totems guarding the old village. Silently, reverently, he walked past the rotten totems and the collapsed, decayed beams of the longhouse before finally stopping at the burial grounds. He knew what he was looking for; the professor and his wife had already found it for him.

Takqua solemnly approached the unique tomb, peeled back the green moss cover, and stood, staring down into the shallow depression. The coffin was constructed of bent cedar, carefully carved and painted with symbols. Now, however, the paint was faded, making the symbols hard to decipher, and the wooden box had surrendered to the continual eroding power of the rain forest. A drop of blood splattered the top to the tomb. He knelt down quickly and wiped the spot with his finger, leaving an elongated smear across the wood surface.

Opening the casket, he could see it contained a number of interesting artifacts which were scattered about the skeleton, including strands of burial beads, a type of ceremonial wand or club, a number of carved effigies in the shape of animals, and a small bow with a quiver containing intricately fashioned arrows. But he was not here for those. He carefully moved them aside and reaching down, Takqua ceremoniously retrieved a verdigris skull from the grave, bedecked with native burial jewelry denoting a shaman. The skull was protected by an ornate wooden helmet made with bits of abalone shell, metal, and feathers. As he picked up the skull, he couldn't help but admire the carved wooden covering which was elaborately fashioned in the shape of a raven with large abalone eyes that appeared to shine an incandescent blue in the dim light of the forest. Takqua knew that in Indian mythology, the raven was called the trickster, the Tlingit symbol used by the shaman, and sometimes denoted magical and mythical qualities.

He removed the massive helmet from the skull and placed it on his own head ... and slowly began dancing the dance of an ancient ritual. After awhile, he took the helmet off and set it down. Grabbing a handful of burial bead necklaces from the coffin, he draped them about his neck.

He located the green plastic bag he had left near one of the totems for safekeeping and returned to the shaman's tomb. Then he reached in to the bottom and felt around. His hand found what it was searching for, and he pulled out the bloody head of Dr. Toddwell. Methodically, he placed the head of the professor on the skeleton where the shaman's skull had been previously. The professor's eyes were open and mouth agape, a testimony to the last moments of brutal horror he had experienced before he died. Gazing on the face, he noticed with cold disinterest that the professor had bitten off his tongue sometime during the death ceremony.

Takqua straightened the head, stood up, and admired his handiwork. Then he laughed, thinking about what the next discoverer might say when they reopened the gravesite. He covered everything back over and even added a few more branches to further hide the tomb.

Walking over to the totems marking the entrance to the burial grounds, Takqua knelt before the main village totem. Reaching back into the bloody bag, he retrieved the head of the woman by her hair. Holding it up, he placed the head in the outstretched arms of one of the carved figures. Her open eyes were set into a stark, bloodless face, contrasting with the dried blood smeared on her cheeks and corners of her mouth. Then Takqua prayed. He prayed that the spirits would forgive his incursion into their burial grounds. He prayed his offerings would appease them. He prayed for the spirits of the good professor and Mrs. Toddwell to serve as slaves to the deities and do the spirits' bidding ... just as any Kushtikaw would do. He would soon be Takqua the Kushtikaw, the powerful servant of the shaman spirits!

He lapsed back into the present moment from his self-induced trance, revitalized and renewed. A smile played at the corners of his mouth. He looked down at himself, realizing he was still dressed in Dr. Toddwell's clothing. He especially liked the fact that he was wearing Dr. Toddwell's ... Harry's ... boots, even if they didn't fit him very well. Takqua thought that part was very clever. Even if the oncoming snowstorm didn't cover all his tracks, no one would be able to figure who committed the crime, not even search dogs!

It was low tide and Takqua's canoe was more than three times the distance from the water's edge as when he first set foot ashore. He went about the chore of launching the canoe in silence. The wind had picked up and whitecaps were beginning to appear on the surface of the water. With the help of adrenalin, Takqua barely noticed the cold seeping into his body. Finally removing the accumulated snow from inside the boat, Takqua leaned into the canoe, trying to push the square-ended aluminum boat into the cold water. It was more difficult than he expected. It simply wouldn't budge. He tried again. It was stuck!

"No!" he screamed. "Not now!"

In desperation, he began to rock the boat from side to side, slowly at first and then faster.

You are too smart to let this happen, his brain screamed. *Think of something!*

He became relieved when he saw that the canoe moved down the beach a little each time he rocked it. He tried getting behind and pushing the boat next, but it wouldn't move. Finally, he tried rocking the canoe and pulling the boat toward the icy water at the same time. Between the combination of rocking and pulling, the boat finally broke free from the rocky shore, and banging against the random boulder, slid the rest of the way down the beach and into the bay. By now, Takqua was sweating profusely, streams of perspiration mixed with deposits of dried blood and dirt on his face. He wiped the sweat from his eyes with the back of his sleeve. It came away bloody. Wading into the brackish water up to his waist, he quickly washed his face and long hair as best he could.

That task completed, he ran cold fingers through his wet hair then waded back to the canoe. Hurriedly, Takqua climbed into the aluminum boat, pushed away from the shore with one motion, and lowered the small black Mercury outboard motor off the stern. Setting the motor in place, he began pulling on the starter cord. Then he saw that he had left the plastic sack on the beach. With a startled cry of disbelief, he grabbed a paddle and using it like a pole, frantically propelled the drifting canoe back to shore. Before the bow had even touched the beach, Takqua jumped out. Running through the icy water while kicking the water ahead of him into a white froth, he dashed up the beach to retrieve his possessions. Grabbing the bag and slinging it over his powerful shoulders, he raced back to the waiting canoe drifting near shore. Without further difficulties, he started the engine and Takqua set off, the little motor propelling the canoe swiftly through the water. He steered the boat as close to shore as he dared, hugging the icy rim of the southern shoreline to ensure he wouldn't be noticed. Using this tactic, he worked his way around the spit of narrow land protruding from the western shore of Twasaan Bay and continued to follow the contour of the shoreline. Even if he wanted to go faster, speed was very risky since ice patches forming near the mouths of streams could damage his boat, and cutting through slush ice might leave a trail that would be obvious even after the ice froze.

After about 30 minutes, he spotted his destination, a natural nook in the shoreline marked by two broken branches in the form of an upside-down V secured to a bare tree branch which hung out over the water. Takqua moved the lever of the outboard motor over to the far left and steered the aluminum canoe toward shore. The indentation in the land was almost imperceptible, a tiny but very deep, rocky cove. Above the steep embankment was a flat space about 10-foot square, which he had found more than suitable for camping. Overall, the entire area was naturally concealed by the thick branches of the evergreen trees which hung over the edges, providing a perfect camouflage. Takqua had chosen this spot more than a week ago and had intended on using it as a temporary base of operations. As the canoe bounced up on the narrow beach, he stepped into the cold water and unloaded the bag, then pulled the boat up onto the bank as best he could. Although he was miles from the cabin by water, he knew that he was just over a high ridge from the Shakan River which flowed past the cabin to the bay. High in the hills above him was the source of the river, and his escape route.

Takqua was just beginning to twist the clamping screws of the motor bracket to unbolt the small outboard engine from the skiff's transom when he first heard it, and the sound stopped him dead in his tracks. He looked out over the water but saw nothing. He listened intently for a few minutes but the noise didn't reoccur. He dismissed the sound and so returned to his task. Suddenly, an electric bolt of fear surged through his body. He heard the noise again! This time there was no mistaking the distinct sound. *Could it be? Is there another boat coming to the cabin?*

Quickly Takqua ran to the edge of his lair, scrambling out on all fours until he found a vantage point from which to scan the bay. Lying prone, he could barely see a gray motorboat with one occupant as it glided slowly through the water, sending up small bits of spray. The boat engine noise stopped, and the vessel drifted in the rising swells only a half mile from his position! He could see the boat operator begin to methodically scan the beach with his binoculars. Unconsciously, Takqua ducked and caught his breath, wondering if his hiding place would be detected.

Watching intently, Takqua made out details of the boat in the decreasing light. It was a Department of Public Safety patrol boat. For a second, Takqua panicked, wondering how he could have been discovered so soon. *Someone must have seen me,* his brain screamed, *but how? No one was around! How else could they know so quickly? Think! Think! Think!* Takqua's brain tried to sort everything out but it was too much too soon. He held his head in his hands, remaining frozen in fear that he would be discovered. He wanted to curl up in a ball, but all he could do was watch. He unconsciously reached to stroke the special beaded shaman necklace he constantly wore as protection and a means to communicate with the shaman. His fingers found nothing. His necklace and talisman was gone!

Heart pounding, Takqua watched as the boat cautiously worked around the skim ice in the bay until it finally disappeared from view around a bend in the shoreline. Then he jumped up nearly hysterical and began searching for the necklace by crawling on his hands and knees across the rocks and working his way back to the canoe ... nothing. He searched the camp ... nothing. He looked in the canoe ... nothing. He panicked. It must be at the cabin. He had to find the necklace. Without it, he was lost. Takqua made up his mind. He couldn't wait any longer. He knew what he had to do. He had to find the necklace before the trooper found it. He was in a race for time.

For the trooper in the patrol boat his day began hours earlier. The last thing Cody O'Keefe imagined when he answered the telephone at "o-dark-thirty" was to be told to report for duty. For one thing, it was his day off. The brass never wanted to call someone out on their day off; it cost too much in overtime.

"Sure, Marsha," he told the dispatcher, "no problem. I'll be right in."

Of course, it *was* a problem—it was his day off. He had planned to pick up around the small apartment and then, later that afternoon, grab a bite to eat at one of the restaurants downtown where the locals hung out and just read. Instead, he opened the bedroom closet and, selecting a freshly pressed uniform, and got ready for work. Less than an hour later, he reported for duty at the Department of Public Safety, Ketchikan Post, located on the Tongass Highway.

"Morning, Marsha," he said to the busy receptionist as he pushed through the glass door.

She looked up from her switchboard situated behind a long wooden counter, and cradling the telephone between her chin and shoulder, continued to talk to someone at the other end of the line while she waved with her hand for him to come over. He always marveled how secretaries and dispatchers became so good at doing 10 things at once. Multitasking, they called it nowadays. Marsha Johnson was an old-time veteran who had been with the Department of Public Safety for over 30 years, if memory served him correctly. She looked liked anybody's grandmother but under that thin, soft veneer lay a true battle ax, he knew ... he had watched her in action. She was in charge of all support staff and had a way of straightening out any trooper who got out of line with "her" dispatchers. The experience for the offending trooper, usually one of the new recruits just fresh from the academy, was totally humiliating. Fortunately, it rarely happened.

Marsha's family had been pioneers in Alaska well before the turn of the century. One of her ancestors had taken part in the Stikine River gold rush, a fact she always reminded any macho trooper recruit. She had grown up in rural Alaska, Ketchikan mostly. She loved her life. The rest of her family was engaged in the commercial fishing industry and lived in the tiny community of Pelican, about 35 air miles east of Sitka.

As Cody strode over to the massive wooden counter, he could see she had a fist full of pastel green telephone message notes waiting for him. She was just finishing her conversation and motioned him to stay.

"Yes sir, that's correct, Ketchikan is on an island. Yes, that's right ... water or air access only. Air or water access *only* means that you need an airplane or a boat to get you here. Why can't you drive from Fairbanks? Well sir, because we are located on an island." Marsha looked at Cody and rolled her eyes. "No sir, Southeast Alaska is not like the Cape Hatteras or the Florida Keys, where most islands are accessible by interisland roads. Southeast Alaska is part of the Alexander Archipelago, consisting of almost a thousand islands, most all are remote and uninhabited. Uh-huh, well, you can drive the ALCAN highway. Yes ... Uh-huh... Yes sir, some islands are inhabited by bears."

There was another long pause during which she began to doodle on a notepad close to her. "Yes, it's very safe here. Bears can be a problem if you don't take precautions. No, no one I know has been eaten by a bear."

Cody could tell she was starting to get impatient. If she didn't get off the phone soon, he'd call her from the squad room located in the back of the building. Seeing his discomfort, Marsha concluded the conversation with "Sir, this is Alaska. It is a fifth the size of the continental U.S., mostly consisting of miles and miles of pristine wilderness. One might logically expect wild animals to live in a wilderness."

Cody had heard her make the statement before, but he was never quite sure whether she was referring to four-legged animals or the two-legged variety.

Hanging up the phone, she swiveled in her chair and walked over to the counter. "Sorry, Cody, I didn't know it would take so long."

"That's OK, what's up?"

"Well," Marsha paused, "you've got several messages here, but the new lieutenant is the one who called you out. He wants to see you before you get settled in."

"He's here at 0600? Is he in his office?"

Cody wasn't much looking forward to any meeting with the "brass" and had hoped to keep a low profile around the office until he found out more about the new boss. Now events had overtaken him.

As he walked by the open office door belonging to the new resident lieutenant, a loud voice rang out. "Hey, you! Cody O'Keefe?"

"Guilty as charged," he said. "Are you the new post commander?"

"Yep," Bob Blocker said, shoving a big hand forward.

Cody noticed that the lieutenant conformed to the old-style management philosophy of the troopers. A good trooper was over 6' tall and 200 lbs, and even better if he was the size of a linebacker. In the territorial days, troopers were often selected for their physical appearance as much as anything. *Command presence was everything*. The lieutenant had straight, coarse black hair that was cut short, with wide eyebrows, a broad forehead, and a square jaw. The uniform was a tailored fit. Even the seams were sewn in to sharpen the creases. His brass and shoes were spotless. *Yep, command presence is everything,* he restated mentally.

Lt. Blocker was sizing Cody up too. He was staring into steel-gray eyes set in a face which combined sharp facial features with a ruddy complexion and closely cropped brown hair that was thinning on top and whitened at the temples. The intensity of the trooper's gaze and apparent intelligence somehow reminded the lieutenant of a wolf. *He's been around for awhile. Some good experience and a few "attaboys" in his file and a few "aw shits" too, but he can take care of himself*, he thought. *Just the person to take on this assignment.* At just a tad over 6' and weighing about 185, Cody looked like what he was, a bush trooper. His uniform could use a better pressing and boots needed a shine, but his leather gun belt was well oiled and polished and his duty weapon looked clean. All in all, the lieutenant liked what he saw.

Grasping his hand, Cody's new supervisor said, "I understand you have quite a reputation for operating in the bush, and as a pretty good tracker too, I might add."

"It takes continual practice. Not so much a skill as a lifestyle."

"Well, I think that's great, so long as you understand that no job is finished until the paperwork is done."

"No problem, Lieutenant. I always try to do my best."

Cody noticed Bob had a big warm smile and a friendly demeanor, the kind supervisors always used when they wanted something and hoped they didn't piss you off.

"Welcome aboard, Lieutenant," Cody said, although he wasn't sure yet that he really meant it.

"Say, why don't we grab a cup of coffee and come back to my office. I'd like to discuss something with you."

"Sounds good, I haven't had any coffee this morning." *I wonder what's on his mind.* Cody mulled that thought over as they got their coffee and walked back into the lieutenant's office.

At the lieutenant's suggestion, Cody obediently sat down in a hard-backed chair. Sitting across the large wooden desk from Lt. Blocker, he noticed that the lieutenant was obviously well organized and very structured, with a penchant for pushing paper ... something he himself was always hoping to avoid. It wasn't that Cody didn't want a promotion beyond the rank of trooper, it was just that he didn't want all the management headaches that went along with the rank. Cody liked being out on patrol, and ultimately, being responsible only for himself.

"I need someone to make a run to a cabin on the Shakan River, in Twasaan Bay," the lieutenant began. "As I understand it, you're about the most skilled boat operator I have. There's a bad gale heading this way. It's bad out there now and will likely get worse, but this may actually be an emergency."

"What about the Coast Guard?"

"It's too bad to fly, and their patrol boat won't leave unless it is a confirmed emergency. Their boat is on standby to assist any fishing vessels that may get trapped by the storm."

Then Lt. Bob Blocker laid out the details. "Mr. Toddwell, or rather, Dr. Harry Toddwell, is a well-known professor of archeology and mythology at a small college in upstate New York. He and his wife had arrived in Ketchikan in December, just after Christmas, and rented an old cabin on the Shakan River ... I understand there is only one there. Near as we know, they bought a bunch of groceries and hired a floatplane to fly them to the river. You know this area like the back of your hand, Trooper O'Keefe. I don't have to tell you about Twasaan Bay. You know how remote it is ... anyway ... so the couple flew in with enough food and supplies to last them a month, maybe 2, a VHF radio capable of transmitting and receiving messages. Their dog 'Fritz' was with them."

Very few people had seen Lower Southeast Alaska the way Cody had. He was literally in the rain forest all year long. And he could conjure up those images anytime—the old-growth forests, wild rivers, clear, cold streams, and especially the ragged, snow-capped mountains. He had been in the mountains and knew them for what they were: foreboding and dangerous with broad granite faces which were constantly wet or icy. Angry, tumultuous waterfalls originating somewhere in the swirling, gray-misted heavens cascaded off the mountains, freefalling to earth in a white, frothing rush hundreds of feet below, giving birth to the raging rivers and silver streams. These natal waters, Cody had observed firsthand in the field, would mature and grow with the terrain into crystal clear streams winding through miles of deep verdant valleys of red alder, black cottonwood, lodge pole pine, and devil's club, a thorny, unpleasant plant with large stalks and leaves, which can grow over 5 feet in height.

Continuing onward, the waters travel through dense dark forests of red and yellow cedar, Sitka spruce, and western hemlock, where the moist forest floor was covered by a thick carpet of moss accentuated by green bushy ferns. The streams, creeks, and rivers grow as they meander through the wet, flat, honey-colored muskegs bordered by blueberry, willow, huckleberry, and low bush cranberry and herbs. Eventually, they find their freedom, spilling into the coves, bays, inlets, and sounds. He was intimately familiar with the marine environment; waters alive with crabs, shrimp, clams, sea urchins, mussels, abalone, and a variety of fish, including the famous Pacific salmon species: chinook, coho, sockeye, chum, and pink.

He felt at home here. Southeast Alaska had some of the most magnificent old-growth forests in the world. The mountains were all densely forested below 3,000 feet; tall majestic conifers and white-barked deciduous trees thrived in the rich, black earth. Gracefully curving branches of the fir trees would often lace together so intricately that daylight is rarely more than a dim glow. Most of Southeast Alaska is in the Tongass National Forest, the largest such forest in the United States. Cody knew that a map or chart would tell you this area is also part of the Alexander Archipelago. Over a thousand named islands and numerous unnamed islets and reefs make up Southeast. Prince of Wales Island was the largest among these magnificent islands and the third largest island in the United States. Each island, large or small, was more of the same, etched in rocky shorelines decorated with log-strewn beaches and bordered by the towering conifers of cedar, hemlock, and spruce.

Now Cody mentally drew on what he remembered about the bay. Twasaan area was on the east side of Prince of Wales Island. He read somewhere that the large island was home to the ancients long before the advent of European civilization. They made their homes along the few sandy beaches next to the dense forests of the islands, gathered clams, abalone, and black seaweed from the shores, fished in the saltwater bays and inlets and the cold, silver streams filled with salmon and trout, and hunted and killed the mighty brown and black bears.

When Cody was on patrol, he often came across petroglyphs, the signs of ancient civilizations. These messages, carved in stone, were still standing, located at the secluded mouths of bays and inlets in the more remote recesses of Prince of Wales and the neighboring islands. A native belief was that these carved symbols were believed to have marked strategic borders which protected old burial grounds and sacred sites, and perhaps even provided guidance and messages to the ancient traveler passing through on his way north or south. Cody knew Twasaan Bay had such markers; he had found several while on patrol.

What troubled Cody was that most people rent cabins during the summer when the days are longer and the salmon and berries are everywhere. But the Toddwells had chosen to rent the cabin in mid-winter for their own reasons. The local resident who owned the cabin didn't really care when the cabin was rented so long as it stayed occupied the majority of the time. In recent years, the cabin was often broken into and shot up by vandals out having a good time. Keeping the cabin rented kept the vandals at bay and provided a much-appreciated cash flow for the owner, especially during the slow winter economy.

He tuned the lieutenant back in as his superior continued. "As far as anyone knew, the last message sent by the Toddwells via the marine radio operator was almost a week ago. They had called their daughter in Arizona and had made plans to meet her at the airport in Ketchikan sometime in the middle of March."

"So what's the problem?"

"The problem is that their daughter, Alice, had a change in plans and has tried to reach them for the past several days, but can't. She got worried and called us. Apparently, neither one of the Toddwells have any outdoor skills at all. And there isn't a New York deli behind every cedar tree out there."

"So we don't really know that they are, in fact, in trouble?"

"No, but they're old. If they are in trouble, they might not be able to call for help. It's been so damned cold lately that I'm afraid that if anything is wrong, they won't be able to take care of themselves."

Cody saw the look of concern on the lieutenant's face.

"There's a severe storm brewing out in the Gulf of Alaska, and it's building fast. As I said, the winds are too high for a helo or floatplane anyway. Nope, this is a boat patrol. If you start within the next couple of hours, you probably have enough time to get to Twasaan before the storm hits. But if you get out there and think it's too rough, turn back. We'll just have to wait out the storm."

Cody looked at the lieutenant. "The trip to Twasaan Bay can be rough, but if I can get out past Guard Island, I can make it all the way. There is a Forest Service cabin at Skowl Inlet. I can duck in there if things get too bad."

The lieutenant looked appreciative. "If these people are in trouble, do whatever you can to help them out. If necessary, stay with them and then call for a helo when the weather clears, no ifs ands or buts. The last thing I want is some East Coast nature lovers freezing to death on my watch because they couldn't take care of themselves. If they have any problems at all that can't be fixed right away, let's get them back to Ketchikan where they can talk up their great adventure with their daughter in the lobby of the Ingersoll Hotel."

Following a very complete briefing from Lt. Blocker, which included the standard manager's admonishment to not "burn up a lot of overtime," Cody had gone home to his still-unkempt apartment and threw some provisions and his gear into large waterproof seabags. He would have taken more time to pack properly, but he didn't have time to waste. Cody knew that the seas habitually calm down just after dawn for about an hour ... he wanted to be on the other side of Guard Island when, or if, that happened.

After hurrying through town to the public dock in the cold silence of morning darkness, he stowed all his gear carefully aboard the Whaler, ensuring the equipment was lashed down tightly for the trip ahead of him. Then he ran up the walkway, checking with the harbor master's office for a recording of the long-range forecast. Receiving the news, he headed out the door. *Sounds to me like what I would have guessed*, he thought. *Dismal, deteriorating to shit.*

He performed a final inventory while warming up the twin outboards. Then he quietly cast off from Bar Harbor, a modern, well lit dock located on the north end of Ketchikan proper. On board, he had brought enough supplies to stretch for a week ... if things got tough. Whenever he needed supplies, they were usually purchased at Sea Stores Plus, a local grocery store with a Lower 48 attitude and high Alaskan prices. He hadn't planned on staying out for a week, but then, you never knew what to expect. Cody was well aware that one radio call from his supervisor and his entire assignment could immediately change to something else. And supervisors didn't want to hear that you hadn't planned for the unexpected, especially when you were on overtime.

As his patrol boat raced down the protected waters of Tongass Narrows, thin needles of colored light from Ketchikan bounced off the rippling surface. Ketchikan, his home and duty post for the past several years, was a fairly good-sized community, at least by Alaskan standards, with just over 15,000 residents. Located on the banks of the Tongass Narrows on Revillagigedo Island, it supported logging, fishing, and the tourism industries. Unlike Sitka to the north, which is a community planned and laid out by Russian fur traders, Ketchikan just seemed to materialize. Some of the residents said that any planning that took place over the years more or less resembled flotsam and jetsam, which just took hold along the beach and grew into a community. Known as the "Gateway City," Ketchikan is about 36 miles north of the Canadian border and is the first town you see when entering the state by boat or ferry. Other islands in close proximity to Ketchikan are Gravina Island, which boasts the Ketchikan International Airport, and Annette Island, the Indian reservation.

Cody inquired about the regional history when he first arrived. The original community of Ketchikan first began as a summer fishing camp for a small band of Tlingits who fished along the shores of the Tongass Narrows. The camp was known to the Indians as *Kitschk-him*, which literally means "thundering wings of an eagle." In the early days, the downtown creek was filled with wild runs of chinook, or king salmon, but with the advent of civilization and overharvesting, the river was now kept supplied by an active, state-run, fish hatchery.

Supposedly, the name of the town was coined by the natives who observed large flocks of eagles feeding on the spawning salmon in the creek. According to local lore, the missionaries, sailors, and Yankee traders arrived one summer, and finding the Indians camped along the shores, began the customary social and commercial intercourse. Soon, the Indians left for their permanent winter camp, but the small group of white settlers remained. A muddy tent city was erected on the banks of Fish Creek, at the location the natives called Kitschk-him. The white settlers changed the name to something they could pronounce, hence, the name Ketchikan. To date, the Indians continue to play a role in the local community. Just to the south of the city of Ketchikan is the native community of Saxman, and across the Narrows is the Annette Island reservation.

Cody tried to stay out of town as much as possible in the summer. The narrow, rain-soaked streets of the town were crammed with rusted cars, dented trucks, and a wide variety of humanity. This rather unique stew of drunken loggers, rowdy fishermen, solemn Indians, vacationing students, and townspeople, blended with an equally large number of gawking tourists wrapped in cruise ship issued, clear plastic packaging, to protect them from the rain. The whole eclectic mixture was sprinkled with just a dash of crazies and criminals for local color. In Ketchikan, as the saying goes, "anything can and will happen." Summer was a hectic time for the local police.

Law and order in the city of Ketchikan was maintained by a small, but highly professional police force superbly adapted to sorting out the "crazies and the criminals" from the general population when the ferries and boats arrived from the Lower 48. Most of the nuts were easy to detect among the throngs of tourists and students because of their garb, which ran from the ridiculous to the sublime. Weird combinations of fringed buckskin jackets and laced leather knee-high buckskin moccasins were accented by Oakley reflective sport glasses and colorful goose down ski vests. Others arrived in wool trapper blanket coats and designer blue jeans. Some carried rifles in leather cases lashed to their brightly colored state-of-the-art backpacks, others strapped large hunting or Bowie knives to their legs. Most of the homeless appeared to be in a state of transition, searching for the meaning of life. Others had come looking for trouble.

In the old days before the Ketchikan Police Department was fully staffed, the state troopers would meet the ferries and boats and perform a valuable culling service, sending anyone even looking suspicious back aboard the ferry to continue northward to the next stop, or putting them on the next southbound ferry for Seattle. Since many of these eccentric individuals arrived in Alaska indigent, the Alaska Marine Highway System began losing money. The ferry administrators began petitioning the Commissioner of Public Safety to put a halt to the practice. The troopers, not to be undone by a simple bureaucratic misunderstanding, began to purchase the reprobates tickets to the next nearest port, usually Wrangell or Petersburg, where the ticket purchasing process would repeat itself yet again by another trooper who didn't want the undesirables in his community either. But all good things must come to an end, and the end of the line in this case was Haines, Alaska. Haines was known as a small, quiet, artistic community. Nestled at the base of the cloud-covered Wrangell Mountains just a few miles away from Skagway, of Klondike fame, it was the northernmost stop of the Alaska Marine Highway system. To reach central Alaska from Haines requires travel by road—through Canada. And this is where the troopers' best efforts failed to meet the Royal Canadian Mounted Police test.

Over the years, the Royal Canadian Mounted Police, too, have perfected the sorting-out process. The Mounties, as they are often referred to, also have a long history of stopping transients and miscreants from entering Canada thus preventing trouble in the Yukon and Northwest Territories stretching back well before the days of the famous Klondike Gold Rush. During the gold rush era, the RCMP would turn back anyone not entering Canada with at least 1 year's supply of food and gear—about one thousand pounds. Many a disappointed miner found himself permanently marooned in Skagway because he was found wanting by the RCMP. Clearly aware of the ongoing efforts by the Alaska State Troopers, the RCMP would simply intercept the derelicts and turn them back at the U.S./Canada border on the Haines Highway. These hopeless individuals would then slowly straggle back along the road to Haines, looking for food and shelter. A public outcry from the good citizens of Haines ensued, likely led by the local trooper stationed there who was now responsible for all these castaways. A new decree came down from on high in Juneau, the Governor's Office to be exact, and the practice was abolished. So now, the historic responsibility of the culling process, such as it was, fell on the shoulders of the Police Department of the Gateway City. In winter, though, it is much different. The real Alaska emerges from beneath the snowy mantle. A peace and tranquility descends over the town, the wet-soaked streets are empty of tourists, and the residents smile and say hello to one another. The locals say that you know when winter has arrived because the grocery-store clerks quit asking for identification when customers write a check, the parking lots are less than half full, and the motor homes and travel trailers are conspicuous by their absence.

CHAPTER FIVE

Cody reached the end of the Tongass Narrows, entering Clarence Strait. He was just passing Guard Island at daybreak, and from what he saw, conditions looked bad, but still passable. Due to the vast open bodies of water and the wind, he saw that the seas were beginning to stack. Cody turned and glanced back one last time at Guard Island, and the automated lighthouse, and got his final bearings. It felt comforting to know that, at this point, he had little difficulty in making out the pulsating flashes which could guide lost and confused mariners into the protected waters of Tongass Narrows and Ketchikan harbor. As he nosed the boat forward into the ominous, turbulent waters of Clarence Strait, the wind speeds pushed to 25 knots, with gusts to 30. *From now on, it's dead reckoning and good luck*, he thought to himself grimly.

Three hours later he hadn't made much progress against the mounting waves. Cody cursed under his breath and instinctively braced himself. He fought the helm to gain control of the small patrol boat. On the horizon, if he dared to take his eyes off the turbulent waters long enough to look, the thin line between sky and sea had melded together, forming an ominous snowstorm. Time and again, menacing 10-foot, jade-green seas capped with white, frothing waves would hammer at the low stern of the craft, making steering extremely difficult. No matter how skillfully he handled the small boat, every now and then, the challenger would win the contest as a rogue wave poured over the transom, gaining access to the open cockpit of the 24-foot Boston Whaler. When that occurred, the deck became awash in foam and cold saltwater, which swirled around his heavy, insulated rubber boots until the large electric bilge pump dutifully jettisoned the sloshing water with a high-pitched, intermittent whine. Cody knew that to leave the cold metal helm unattended under these conditions, for even a split second, would invite catastrophe. Any large wave could easily push the stern around, forcing the craft sideways down the face of the swell and into the trough, parallel to the rough seas. The boat, vulnerable in that position, would be at the mercy of the elements, and likely capsize in a frigid coup d'gras administered by the next successive wave.

The wide, fiberglass boat was powered by massive, twin, steel-gray 125 horsepower Johnson outboard engines securely bolted to the thick transom and providing more than ample power. The now-ice-coated chrome throttles on the broad, sturdy, console were positioned ahead, the starboard throttle slightly forward of the port to compensate for existing sea conditions ... the dual outboards dutifully responding to Cody's throttle commands by emitting a low pulsating hum. At the base of the out-drives, twin stainless steel propellers slowly churned up the water, leaving a detectable wake of discolored water, bubbles, and steaming exhaust which floated to the surface only to be carried away by the wind.

The twin engines easily provided sufficient power to control the patrol vessel in the turbulent seas and maintain the critical attitude of the craft on the top of the swell; however, the actual distance covered under such adverse conditions was minimal. The forward speed and distance traveled by the small boat was determined more by the general speed of the seas than by anything else. For Cody, controlling the bucking boat in the windswept waters was becoming increasingly difficult as time went by. His sweating palms had started tingling from trying to firmly grip the thin helm through a pair of olive-drab wool gloves sheathed inside an even larger pair of insulated Arctic parka mittens constructed of waterproofed leather and heavy nylon.

Periodically, the precarious balance of the small craft tittering on the apex of a large foaming crest would be broken, and the haze-gray fiberglass Boston Whaler would surf down into the trough. During those times, there was nothing Cody could do but hang on and steer straight. As the heavy patrol vessel plowed forward, spray droplets from each wave mixed with the dropping air temperatures to form a thin row of icy tails along the metal bow rails. Where the water and ice were protected from the rising wind, long icicles had begun to form. He had watched the slow metamorphosis for a couple of hours now.

"If my luck holds out," he muttered to himself, "I will be anchored in Twasaan Bay before the icing becomes too bad." He had reason for concern. Icing conditions while frustrating for mariners in the Southeast, can often be fatal in the Arctic. In the distant waters of the Bering Sea, fishing ships, their decks and superstructure coated with ice from similar weather conditions, can easily become top heavy and unstable in the rough seas. Unable to recover from the rolling motion of the rough seas due to the treacherous weight attributed to icing, the ships would simply continue to heel over and slip underwater—instantly sinking with all hands on board.

Experienced mariners all knew about the hazards of ice in the rigging and superstructure, yet every year, another crab vessel fishing the black, frigid Arctic waters would disappear leaving no trace—except for the families back home. In Cody's case, the ice might play more subtle, insidious tricks, like freezing the bilge pump closed or icing up the exposed fuel lines and shutting down fuel-starved engines—each with its own potentially fatal consequences. This sobering thought brought him back to his own reality—and his immediate environmental conditions.

Wiping the cold sea spray from the yellow plastic lens of his goggles with the back of his mitten, Cody checked the fuel gauges on the console once more and half-turned to visually inspect the large white bilge pump to ensure it was still working. Then he reassessed sea conditions.

"Just another SNAFU—situation normal all fucked up," he admitted to himself, muttering the words between clenched teeth while wrenching the helm to starboard, compensating for an unusually large wave.

For all of the complaining, Cody was proud to be a commissioned officer in the Alaska Department of Public Safety. As a state trooper, he was authorized to enforce all the laws of the great State of Alaska, a jurisdiction which consisted of a geographic area one-fifth the size of the continental United States and out into the Pacific ocean to the three-mile limit. Disbursed across this vast area were less than 400 personnel accounting for most all of the field force in the Department of Public Safety—the Division of Alaska State Troopers and the Division of Fish and Wildlife Protection. Cody really loved his work. He liked being "in the bush" and prided himself on his self-reliance. That is one reason he declined what most of his classmates thought was a plum assignment to the Division of Alaska State Troopers, in Anchorage, upon graduating from the academy in Sitka. Instead, he chose to be posted to the Fish and Wildlife Protection Division, affording him the maximum opportunity for routine travel throughout lower Southeast Alaska. All in all, Trooper O'Keefe considered himself fortunate enough to be doing what he really wanted to do—fight crime, his way, on his terms, on the Last Frontier.

O'Keefe was in his current predicament because he was assigned to an exceptionally large geographic area. His patrol zone was immense and almost totally remote, most of it accessible only by air or water. Instead of patrolling by car or truck, like his urban law enforcement counterparts, Cody's patrol vehicle was the fiberglass Boston Whaler. Week after week, he loaded the 24-foot patrol craft with supplies and survival gear and headed out on patrol, sometimes to the Dixon Entrance, sometimes north toward Wrangell and Petersburg, other times around stormy Cape Chacon to Craig, or Hydaburg, or any other far-flung community which clung to the rugged shoreline on verdant Prince of Wales Island. He prided himself as an old-fashioned law enforcement officer, always on patrol, always looking for outlaws. He believed in the department's unofficial motto of "*one riot, one trooper.*"

And Cody was one of the few who knew how much truth there was in that terse statement. The troopers worked on the edge. Things that other law enforcement officers throughout the United States took for granted were luxuries for the likes of him. Where he and other bush troopers routinely operated, there was no backup in the event of an emergency, no one to respond if extra assistance was required, and no ambulance. Once he was more than a few miles out of town, he was definitely on his own. When on patrol, these troopers had to rely entirely upon themselves to get the job done—and that also meant knowing how to stay alive.

Still almost 10 miles away and separated by increasingly turbulent waters lay Twasaan Bay, Cody's intended destination. The long, narrow bay lies like a giant snake among the mighty mountains and forested hills that make up the remote eastern edge of Prince of Wales Island in Southeast Alaska. "Southeast," as it is called by most residents, is Alaska's panhandle and is comprised of over 600 miles of primeval, rugged wilderness stretching from Icy Bay north of Yakutat, to the Dixon entrance and the Canadian border. This mountainous territory is renowned for its deep fjords, majestic glaciers, and pristine forests. The panhandle is a small part of a large-scale ecosystem known as the Pacific Northwest Rain Forest Belt. Here, the relatively warm waters of the Pacific Ocean and prevailing southeasterly winds combine to create the moist climate that supports the lush forest. Along the coast, mountains rise up from the mist of pounding surf-lines and stretch toward the sky, the peaks often lost in the gloomy twilight of rising fog and rain-filled clouds and, in winter, snow.

Cody O'Keefe let his mind drift just a little from the work at hand. He knew Twasaan Bay was the ancestral home of the Twasaan Indians, members of the Tlingit tribe, one of three Indian tribes which now inhabit Southeast Alaska. At the time of the Purchase in 1867, Alaska was divided into three separate ethnic and linguistic cultures—the Indians, Aleuts, and Eskimos. Three Indian tribes have traditionally made their home in the panhandle: the Tlingit, the Haida, the Tshimsian, and a few Aleuts.

Although recorded history in Alaska covers less than 300 years, its prehistory dates back many thousands of years. Historians and archaeologists have described the tribes of Southeast as the most aristocratic of all Indian tribes north of Mexico, perhaps rivaled only by the Pueblo Indians of Arizona and New Mexico. The native societies of Southeast Alaska had many commonalities but subtle cultural differences. Each tribe, for instance, spoke a distinct and unrelated language, yet the three tribes were a maritime culture of fishermen, whalers, traders, and warriors. Their total dependence on the sea for their very existence is reflected in the tools, religion, and society of their colorful culture.

For thousands of years before any white man set foot in the region, the Indians routinely traveled throughout Southeast by wooden canoe. Fashioned from the trunks of huge cedar trees, these sturdy vessels varied in sizes and shapes. The smaller vessels, usually 7 or 8 feet long, and quite plain, were used for fishing and traveling. Their massive war canoes, however, were something entirely different. These boats were often in excess of 30 feet long, with sharp bows and sterns festooned with ornate carvings and painted in brilliant primary colors of red, aqua blue, yellow, black, and white and were paddled by war parties, often for hundreds of miles, along the coastal waters of the Pacific Northwest.

Although their art and technique varied, these tribes did have many similarities drawn from the harsh environment. Clan symbols such as the Raven, Wolf, Killer Whale, and the Bear adorned their longhouses, totems, and boats. Collectively, the influence of these three tribes in the Pacific Northwest extended as far north and west as the Aleutian Chain, as far east as the Mackenzie River, and as far south as California. It is estimated that at the beginning of the historical period, approximately 150,000 Pacific Northwest Indians lived in a 176,000 square mile area from above Yakutat, Alaska, to Mendocino, California.

Most all tribal members lived in permanent communities which had well constructed abodes. Their governments were aristocracies, with descendants recognized through their mother's lineage. These ancient societies were quite orderly and governed by unwritten laws. The laws and tribal customs proven effective over time and governed the Indian societies for centuries. Each tribe was subdivided into major clans. Among the Haida, tribal members were either a Raven or an Eagle. Tlingits were divided into Ravens and Wolves, and the Tshimsian had four clans, the Eagles, Wolves, Ravens, and the Killer Whales. In most cases, each clan was further divided geographically into a number of small villages. Since good beaches are scarce along this rugged coastline, wherever there was a delta, or a spit of land with a sandy beach to land a canoe and ample open space, a village or camp would be established. Since the ancient tribal lands virtually enveloped his designated patrol zone, Cody held a certain fascination and curiosity concerning the natives of Southeast.

He began to feel the cold and fatigue setting in. After several hours of battling the elements, whenever the large gray patrol boat periodically slipped off the apex of a crest and slid bow-first into the trough, Cody's immediate response would be to instantly jam the throttles forward. By now, this maneuver had become more a reflex than a conscious thought. Plumes of white sea spray blanketed the boat as the powerful engines would come to life, and the vessel leapt forward again, clawing up the back of the cold, green swell like a mountain lion climbing a steep, grassy incline. As the boat reached the precarious crest, he would throttle back the engines and ride the wave until the careful balance was somehow broken and the tiring struggle pitting man and machine against the violence of nature began once more.

Through increasing snow squalls and rising seas, Cody could just faintly make out the landmarks identifying the approach to Twasaan

Bay, but he still had to cross Clarence Strait. Clarence Strait is a long body of water connecting the open sea to the Inside Passage. The strait also acts as a natural venturi, funneling the strong prevailing winds from the turbulent Gulf of Alaska, often at gale force velocities, directly into the inside waters ... much to the consternation of vessels transiting the area. As near as Cody could figure, he was currently at the approximate intersection of Clarence Strait, Behm Canal, and Tongass Narrows. At the confluence of the three bodies of water, the wind, tides, and opposing currents all came together in a witches' brew, creating a rough stretch of water which demanded constant attention to seamanship.

Cody checked the bilge pump once again and after looking over his gear to make sure the constant pounding had not loosened anything, he wrestled the boat farther into the violent waters and toward his ultimate destination. Eyes straining against the icy mist and salt spray, he quickly scanned the horizon for a landmark identifying the entrance to the bay.

Although it was now midmorning, he knew that he had less than 5 hours of daylight remaining. In Alaska, winter daylight hours are scarce, and with the heightening storm, he knew he would lose the "working light" sooner than normal. He forced open the stainless steel latch, securing the hatch on the short console. Bending forward quickly and grabbing the microphone, he brought it close to his lips. The communication range of his dilapidated radio equipment was limited, and he wanted to report in before he lost all communications.

"Ketchikan A-2, Ketchikan A-2, this is 5-A-19." Each number of his call sign was pronounced separately so that it sounded like five-A-nineteen. He tried once more. "Ketchikan A-2, Ketchikan A-2, this is 5-A-19."

The response from the Ketchikan dispatcher was an incoherent hail of static. While the static was frustrating, the lack of communication was not unusual. The Boston Whaler had been equipped with an old Motorola radio stripped from a surplus state trooper patrol vehicle before it went to auction. The radio was of marginal use, but with the help of the Communications Support Section, he had the relic patched up. To save costs, he had installed it himself, but it never really worked well; too many wires, too much water, too much corrosion. The best he could hope for was a 10-mile radius from the dispatcher at the Ketchikan Post. *I must be well beyond that now*, he thought.

Cody had initially installed the radio to assist him in his monitoring of the numerous salmon purse seine and gillnet vessels fishing throughout lower Alaska during the summer. One of the channels was VHF channel 16, the U.S. Coast Guard emergency channel, which he used most often to contact fishing vessels. Most crews monitored that frequency and the Alaska Department of Fish and Game channel 8 to communicate with fisheries' biologists working on the fishing grounds. And then there was a secured channel he could use to contact the dispatcher at the DPS office to run routine criminal history checks on fishermen while patrolling the fisheries.

Although some vessels have an all-Alaskan crew, most fleets are comprised of fishermen from communities up and down the West Coast ... Washington and Oregon mostly ... who fish Alaska all summer, then return south for the winter. Many of those vessel operators employed crews consisting of both professional fishermen and especially college kids. But every now and then, a skipper would make the mistake of hiring someone "off the docks" when exigent circumstances arose and without checking them out. "Off the docks" was code for someone from the local mission, on parole, or just out of a halfway house. The commercial fishing industry has long been used by criminals on the run to avoid the law. Nowhere else can a wanted felon travel so freely, and remain so anonymous, as within commercial fishing industry. This is especially true on the West Coast, where small commercial vessels routinely fish the most remote regions of the United States for 6 months out of the year. And an inadequate background check on the fishing grounds, Cody soon realized, could have fatal implications for a lone law enforcement officer.

After installing the radio, he always made it a habit to run identification checks on all crew members he had not seen before. Occasionally, he would hit pay dirt with an outstanding felony warrant on a crew member or skipper, and he would haul the surprised criminal off to jail, much to the consternation of the rest of crew. But the radio was of limited value outside Ketchikan, and often, he would patrol the remote regions of Southeast Alaska for days without radio contact of any kind. Cody tried the radio one last time.

He manually changed frequencies to channel 16.

"Ketchikan A-2, Ketchikan A-2, this is 5-A-19, can you read me?" After a few seconds he tried again. "USCG Ketchikan, this is unit 5-A-19, can you read me? Over."

Hearing nothing but static, he said, "U.S. Coast Guard Ketchikan and Ketchikan A-2, I don't know if you can hear me, but my position is approximately 5 nautical miles south of Twasaan Bay, weather conditions are deteriorating. ETA (estimated time of arrival) at the cabin is 1500 hours. Can you copy? Over."

Hearing no response, Cody tried once more.

"Ketchikan A-2, this is 5-A-19, nothing heard—out," and reaching down, he replaced the black plastic mike in its retaining clip, turned off the radio, and fumbling with the chrome metal catch through his mittens, finally secured the fiberglass hatch.

After enduring about another hour of intense, abusive, wet, and extreme cold, he saw he had made some meager progress. When the patrol craft was on the crest of a large swell, he could definitely make out the small prominent islands of jagged stone which thrust out into the water from both sides, like sentinels guarding the entrance of the bay. Every now and then, he saw volumes of cold seawater being hurled 20 or more feet in the air as the massive waves rolling up Clarence Strait smashed full force into the rocks, the power of nature's fury culminating in a roar and violent white explosion. In good weather, he would have been able to locate the entrance of the bay from the outskirts of Ketchikan by taking a visual sighting on the snowcapped peak that had an unusual characteristic of a radical drop on the prominent side, leaving a jagged white tooth to scrape the sky. Usually the very tops of the mountain peaks would be obscured by the omnipresent clouds of Southeast Alaska. Hence, the term "skyscrapers" that he gave them. These mountains which formed the range ran almost the length of Prince of Wales. Now, with the low clouds obscuring all of the landmark except its verdant dark-green base, what remained most visible were the base of the islands and the extending rocky shoreline peering though a thin veil of haze. Slightly farther beyond the wide mouth of the bay, Cody knew that the waters would begin to narrow, eventually terminating at a small hidden cove and the clear waters of the Shakan River. On one side of the mouth of the Shakan River, he would find the small Alaskan log cabin and, hopefully, the Toddwells. *Just 2 hours to go maybe ... maybe a little more,* he thought, *depending on the weather.*

The ominous clouds continued to increase and darken, indicating a severe snowstorm was approaching. Foreboding, swirling somber clouds etched in slate gray stretched across the horizon, pummeling toward him at about 30 miles per hour—judging by the wind and sea conditions. The thought of how he got himself into this mess passed quickly through his head. He cursed again and wiped away the freezing droplets on his goggles.

"Even if I am fortunate enough to make to landfall before dusk, I sure as hell am not going anywhere until this damn weather improves," Cody promised himself aloud. He had been through this type of weather before; he knew what to expect. There was a distinct possibility that he would simply have to sit tight and ride it out for a day or 2. For a split second, Cody thought about turning around, but then dismissed the thought almost immediately. The idea of trying to turn around and fight 8- to 10-foot seas with deteriorating weather conditions was a fool's errand ... a lot like the one he was on now, he mused.

Cody was marginally protected from the cold seas by a stubby waist-high console equipped with a smoke-tinted plastic wind screen. Still, with the rising wind and decreasing temperatures, spray from the pounding seas flew back from the bow, blowing over the ice-coated windscreen and adhering to the chest, shoulders, and upper arms of his heavily insulated brown nylon parka. There, the moisture collected and grew with each successive wave, eventually forming into large icy patches until the wet material of the parka flexed or creased, expelling bits and chunks of icy buildup. Even with the well-made parka, Cody felt the chilly dampness beginning to seep down from the neck of the wet parka and slowly work through the front of his wool shirt, soaking his thermal underwear.

A small cough and sputter from one of the engines immediately returned Cody's attention to the present task of controlling the twisting patrol boat in heightening seas. He glanced briefly at the instruments in the console and once more listened intently to the steady hum of the twin outboards. Turning around, he visually checked to see if the overboard discharge pumps were still functioning. With his large insulted hood with wolf fur trim covering his head and partially obscuring his face, it was difficult to hear the familiar electric whine of the pumps indicating they were operating properly. Satisfied that nothing was amiss, he slipped back into thought as his body reacted automatically to the sea's conditions. Cody pulled the fur-trimmed hood out slightly from his face and breathed down into the body of the parka. The warmth from his breath felt good on his neck and chest. After two more breaths, he readjusted his garments and focused on his assignment. To Cody, hypothermia posed a much greater threat than the rough seas or a severe winter snowstorm. Wet clothes meant loss of body heat. Heat loss could lead to hypothermia. Left uncorrected, hypothermia can kill. Dressing properly, he knew, was the key.

During his training at the State Trooper Academy, outdoor survival experts advocated the layering effect in which clothing could be taken off, or added, depending on weather conditions. That was in dry climate. In the wet environment of the rain forest where precipitation amounted to more than 150 inches a year, staying completely dry was next to impossible. Cody's clothing choice was first and foremost designed to protect him on his long patrols. His thermal underwear was constructed of a wool and silk blend. Although many mountaineers and explorers espouse the thermal and weight advantages of synthetic fibers, he found that synthetics were decidedly ineffective at lower temperatures when combined with high humidity—essentially the environment of Southeast Alaska. He knew the trend in modern outdoor wear over the past few years gravitated toward nylon and other synthetic fibers. The pundits all swore by it. The new fibers are lightweight, wick away moisture, dry quickly, and can be machine-washed and dried. He had tried a number of these products and was dissatisfied with all of them; wool was still his favorite. After the underwear would come the wool shirt and either heavy wool bib overalls or baggy military surplus pants with suspenders. This was definitely not issued gear, but essential to survive the rigors of law enforcement in the Alaska bush.

Over the years, he had developed his own set of rules for officer safety and survival and broke one department regulation after another in the process. In fact, Cody routinely broke several regulations every time he got ready for a bush patrol. Any one of those protocol violations, he knew, could get him suspended or worse. He never wore his uniform in the bush, preferring the wool bib overalls and Alaskan wool shirt. It provided extra thermal protection in the thoracic region. In one deep buttoned shirt pocket was a small survival kit, the size of a hard sided package of cigarettes, which contained a space blanket, plenty of fire-starter, first aid supplies for minor injuries, and a lightweight, bright orange, plastic garbage bag. In the opposite shirt pocket, he kept a sharp triple-blade folding knife and a small military strobe light. This constituted his personal survival equipment for the rather unique life-threatening conditions in Southeast.

Cody was trained to live off the land. It was easy to find good water to drink and plenty to eat ... if you knew where and what to look for. The litmus test in a survival situation in the rain forest was keeping warm and dry; hypothermia was the big killer. The onset of hypothermia is often very slow but in the event the boat capsized, Cody knew his chances of survival, even with a float coat, was simply a matter of minutes. Immersed in cold water, the body rapidly begins to lose heat.

The saltwater temperatures in January in Southeast Alaska

hover around 38 degrees. Constantly calculating the probabilities, Cody estimated his chances of survival in these waters would be less than 30 minutes. Cody had already decided that when he reached shore, he would make the time to dry out and "mug up." This is an old Arctic term referring to drinking something hot, usually tea, from a tin cup. He always tried to carry a large thermos of steaming hot tea in the console of the boat.

Trooper O'Keefe clearly understood the Alaska Department of Public Safety was an autocratic, paramilitary organization; creativity and self-resourcefulness were often viewed with disdain. Adherence to regulations was seen as a sign of a team player. The trouble was that Cody was in continual conflict with the *Operating Procedures Manual* ... the troopers' bible. The firearms policy was one he broke with impunity. The issued side arm of the Department of Public Safety is the Smith & Wesson .357 caliber. He would routinely leave his duty weapon at home in favor of his .44 Magnum revolver. It wasn't that he didn't like his duty weapon ... it was just that the .44 Magnum provided more flexibility.

Cody was an avid hand-loader, so he normally carried hand-loaded .44 Special ammunition designed for combat shooting. The special ammunition was of a much lower velocity than Magnum rounds but loaded with a soft nose bullet, it provided excellent anti-personnel ballistics. Since the .44 Special is essentially a downsized version of the .44 Magnum round, the .44 Special ammunition can safely be fired from any weapon chambered for .44 Magnum. The final result was that Cody was equipped with an excellent anti-personnel round that provided good penetration, adequate knock-down power, and excellent recoil control.

In his leather ammo pouch on his belt, he carried 12 rounds of .44 Magnum ammunition loaded to maximum velocity and topped with hard alloy bullets, made by Barnes. These bullets are constructed of a specially designed metal compound providing deep penetration and expansion, ample protection against hostile bears, if the need ever arose.

Another regulation he broke concerned the use of long arms. Each patrol vehicle was issued a Remington 870 pump shotgun. Instead, he would take his parkerized Marlin 1886 lever action chambered for .44 Magnum and equipped with a flat black synthetic stock. In his rifle, he carried six rounds of the high-velocity hand-loaded ammunition. The rifle was capable of carrying more, but six rounds kept everything consistent, since his revolver also held six rounds. He knew from his training at the Public Safety Academy in Sitka that consistency and training are critical elements of survival in any shootout.

Most important, however, the combination of rifle and revolver just made more sense in the woods than a shotgun that held five rounds and then became useless, or the lack of interchangeable ammunition should the duty pistol become inoperable. He was firmly convinced the rifle/revolver combination provided flexibility, reliability, dependability, and life-saving qualities.

When he intended to patrol ashore, Cody made it a habit of always taking his small brown Cordura nylon rucksack with extra thick, foam-padded shoulder straps. In his pack, he routinely carried a spare set of thermal underwear, extra matches, fire-starter, several heavy-gauge plastic trash bags, 20 yards of green parachute cord, binoculars, a tin cup, tea, a topographic map of the area, his lunch, and at least two extra meals of survival rations, along with an assorted number of regulation books, evidence tags, ammunition, and other required tools of the trade. His only rule on what to carry was to keep the total weight of the pack down to between 15 and

20 pounds. Cody tried to carry just what he needed and no more. His experience in Vietnam had taught him that combat survival often depended upon proper equipment and the ability to maneuver.

It was early afternoon when he finally approached the islands marking the entrance to the bay. An intermittent sun, only a pale yellow glow behind fast-moving clouds, was suspended just above the horizon. By now, he could clearly hear the roar of the waves as they expended their fury against the rocks. Turning the helm to port slightly, he lined up the bow of the vessel with the center of the entrance. Cody was glad that he had less than a quarter mile to go before reaching the sanctuary of the inner bay. Fighting the seas was beginning to take its toll. His back was already aching from standing for hours in a half-crouched position, knees slightly bent and hands tightly gripping the wheel, while the deck under him bucked and plunged with each new wave. He wanted to rest, but with the winter storm on his heels and still a good distance to go, he knew he would never make the log cabin at Twasaan Bay before nightfall if he stopped. He had no choice—he had to press on. Cody turned once more to see the dark, menacing storm clouds already heading up Clarence Strait. The snowstorm was bearing down on him fast.

Once in the relative safety of Twasaan Bay, he began to unwind a little. As the seas began to die down, he eased the throttles forward slightly and the patrol boat picked up speed. Suddenly he spotted a thick white layer of skim ice blocking the passage to the furthermost reaches of the snow-covered bay. Cody instinctively reached for the chrome throttles on the open console and slammed back on the levers, instantly muzzling the screaming twin Johnson 125 horsepower outboards. The fiberglass patrol craft immediately responded to the decreased power, the nose of the craft dramatically dropping and rising again. The wake created by the rapid de-escalation formed a long, deep blue-green swell, etched in white foam. The wave lifted the stern of the patrol boat briefly, providing a forward push and then gently settled down.

"Damn, damn, damn!" Cursing under his breath, Cody slammed his fist down on the console, ripped the frost-lined ski goggles off his face, and pulled back his hood for a better look. Reaching for his armor-coated binoculars secured in a wooden box on the side of the open console, he removed the lens caps and adjusted the focusing rings, placing the instrument to his face. He hadn't expected to see ice along the shore of the bay, but he only had himself to blame.

"Shit! I should have known better," he said aloud to himself. After more than 7 years in Southeast Alaska, he had come to expect the unexpected. He gave the multiple black-faced gauges set in the open console one last look and turned the ignition key. The engines died and the cold quiet of late winter blanketed the surroundings. Cody plopped down on the hard, frozen, ice-covered, pleated vinyl seat cushions covering the small bench seat and cradled the binoculars in his arms. Fumbling around in the pocket of his issued parka, he pulled out a clean chamois cloth rag. He blew on the lenses, carefully wiping each in turn. Satisfied that the 10 x 50 binoculars could now be employed once again, he checked the settings and began to closely survey his surroundings. Surface ice was a serious impediment to his mission.

For a moment he felt trapped. He couldn't go back to Ketchikan; the storm would catch him in the middle of the strait. But he also couldn't go forward because of the ice. Cody was contemplating an alternative location to weather out the storm when along the ice edge he made out what appeared to be a narrow, black river set in an all-white landscape. He realized he had found a route through the main channel of Twasaan Bay! From this distance, the passage looked extremely narrow but marginally navigable. He had to check it out. Cody put his gear back on and fired up both engines. Putting the low throbbing engines in gear, the patrol boat surged forward and seconds later, was planing across the choppy water, providing a bumpy ride.

"Keep a sharp lookout," he muttered under his breath as he zigzagged around small patches of slush ice. As he entered the thin passage leading to the back of the bay, he slowed the vessel down. In confined space, floating ice, debris, and logs became his chief nemeses. Cody's experience had taught him that running into a thick sheet of floating ice could have severe consequences for a fiberglass hull. A barely submerged log might instantly puncture a hull or destroy one of the out-drives, leaving the vessel totally disabled.

The biggest problem with surface ice is its transparency. The ice sheets float at or near the surface, often with a thin coating of water on top, deceptively disguising the ice as flat calm water. Even an old trapper or fisherman, traveling in a small boat, could easily be deceived into thinking these sheets of ice were actually safe and navigable waters. Running aground on this treacherous ice often resulted in irreparable damage to the hull and dire consequences to the occupants.

Cody kept pushing forward. While the narrow strip of deep water was still navigable, the entire shoreline of the bay appeared coated with ice and snow. Slowly, the narrow passage began to widen, giving way to the warmer waters of the bay. Within a mile, Cody noticed that the surface ice had receded almost to the shoreline. Breathing a sigh of relief, he urged the patrol vessel forward and soon was racing toward the Shakan River and the Toddwells' cabin.

Several miles ahead, he spotted the small village of New Twasaan on the starboard side. He allowed himself only a brief glance in the direction of the Indian community. Everything there appeared so tranquil and quiet under the blanket of snow. With the aid of diminishing daylight, he could barely discern the amber glow of lights shining through drawn windows. Most of the homes had their wood stoves going. The gray smoke from the chimneys drifted and swirled lazily above the village. The little community's boats were all moored at the dock, and the entire village and surrounding area were covered in a deep blanket of snow. He was not encouraged by the smoke patterns floating about the village. Cody O'Keefe had come to realize that he could predict what the weather was going to be by watching the smoke from a fire. If the smoke went straight up, chances were very good that the weather would clear within 24 hours. But if the smoke swirled over the chimney and drifted back down to earth, poor weather ... often rain or snow ...resulted. He wasn't a meteorologist, but he was well versed in bush craft and outdoor survival skills. He checked the fuel gauges once more and fixed his eyes on his destination.

Almost an hour later, Cody was as close to the mouth of the Shakan River as he dared go. The fresh water from the river had frozen at the mouth, creating huge chucks of floating ice which spilled into the back of the bay. From his vantage point, he could see the swirling mist rising slowly from the fast-moving water as it flowed toward the frosty bay. The trooper reached down and cut the power on the twin outboards and drifted in silence as the dark, brackish water gently lapped at the sides of the hull. From his position, he could readily make out the Toddwells' cabin, solitary and dark on the frozen banks of the Shakan River. He pulled off his mittens and checked the time on the luminous face of his Swiss Army watch. There was probably no more than an hour or 2 of daylight remaining ... at the most. With the dropping temperatures, Cody figured the icing would probably get worse. With the storm closing in on him, he figured he would have to spend at least one night with the Toddwells.

Cody flipped open the latch securing the fiberglass console door and again pulled out his armor-coated Nikon binoculars. For several minutes, he surveyed the cabin and the surrounding area attempting to take in all the details. The old cabin appeared cold and dark; there was no sign of activity. No smoke could be seen coming from the small metal chimney at the end of the cabin's steeply pitched roof. He didn't like the looks of this one bit.

"Now where the hell would two people from the East Coast go in weather like this?" Cody grumbled to himself. "If this thing turns into a damned search and rescue ..." Perturbed, he reached into the console and turned the radio on, moving the selector switch over to channel 16 VHS, the open channel that the Toddwells would be on. Channel 16 is the channel monitored by the U.S. Coast Guard for emergencies, but in Alaska, it is also serves as the common contact channel. However, "bush radio" etiquette requires that once communication is established, the two parties must immediately shift to another frequency in order to not tie up the emergency network. Stretching out the coiled plastic cable and pulling the black plastic mike up to his lips, Cody attempted to contact someone at the cabin.

"Toddwells, Toddwells, this is Trooper Cody O'Keefe. Over." He waited a moment, but there was no response. Cody waited a few more seconds before trying again.

"Toddwells, Toddwells, this is Trooper Cody O'Keefe, come in please. Over." Again, no response. Suddenly the radio crackled and the static was broken by a familiar voice.

"Hey, Trooper O'Keefe, this is VPSO Whitefeather. Over." Cody smiled, immediately recognizing the slow, deep voice of Officer Tom Whitefeather, the Village Public Safety Officer from Twasaan.

"This is Trooper O'Keefe. Over."

"Yeah, hi, Cody, let's switch to one-one."

"Roger, one-one it is."

Moments later, Cody was establishing contact on the alternate frequency channel 11.

"This is Trooper O'Keefe on one-one, how copy? Over."

"Yeah, Cody, I got you loud and clear. Say, what are you doing in my neck of the woods and in god-awful weather like this? Over."

It seemed a long time ago that Cody first met Tom. He knew immediately that Tom was an Indian, a Native American. He had a stout build, in a muscular way, with a barrel chest and a dark, smooth complexion which never seemed to fade ... even in the cloudy and rainy Southeast Alaska environment. Cody guessed his weight to be over 215 and standing close to 5'8" ... a little taller with his cowboy boots on ... he could look over 6' when he needed to summon a commanding presence. Tom had a large, round face, dark eyes peering from under a set brow, and a jovial attitude. He was known throughout Twasaan for his quick wit, good humor, and a broad smile that exposed rows of white, uneven teeth. Cody guessed Tom's age between 35 and 45; his black hair was already well streaked with white. Usually it was shaggy and hung well below the collar of his khaki uniform shirt.

Tom had been in his office preparing some papers for court when his scanner picked up Cody's transmission. He hadn't spoken with him for several months, so he was interested in getting caught up on the latest goings-on in law enforcement. His radio equipment sat atop a small, faded, tan metal credenza in the corner of the office. On one wall was an oil painting of an attractive Indian maiden dressed in white doe skin with beaded fringe trim, sitting bareback on a large gray Appaloosa. The rough-wood framed picture was one of the few reminders of his former days on the Oklahoma reservation. On another wall were his police certificates that he had received from training with the Bureau of Indian Affairs, the BIA as it was known, and his Village Public Safety Officer certificate from the Alaska Department of Public Safety and other professional accolades, all carefully displayed in a row. Below the picture of the Indian maiden was Tom's electronic equipment, consisting of an outdated police radio equipped by the state with several restricted frequencies which enabled him to directly contact the troopers in Ketchikan. Next to it was a large, but archaic, VHS radio and scanner. Whenever he was in the office, he made it a habit of monitoring radio traffic. "Crime is like prairie lightning. You never can tell when, or where, it might strike," he was fond of saying.

His office was so small that he could literally swivel around from his desk to the radio equipment and reach the microphone without stretching. It was convenient, but very cramped. Tom liked to prop his "rundown at the heels" cowboy boots upon the desk, lean back, and take full command of the small room. The tribal elders, upon presenting him with the tiny office, remarked that he was very lucky, indeed, to have such a spacious office with a view of both the harbor and the bay. He wasn't at all surprised later to discover that all the rest of the offices in the elongated building were not only much larger, but all had terrific views of the harbor and the bay, too. He was only mildly amused, however, when he discovered that his office was, in fact, a converted janitorial supplies closet with a window cut out by the use of a chainsaw. If he were less experienced, it might have become a point of contention. But Tom had been in tribal law enforcement far too long to let it bother him; besides, he had already accepted the job. Putting his own spin on things, he simply referred to the operation as "lean and mean" and "crushing crime on a dime."

Trooper Cody O'Keefe had more than a passing interest in tribal cultures, especially after a terrifying mystery at Naha Cove. However, from his very first assignment to lower Southeast Alaska, he was interested in native customs and especially wanted to understand the realm of tribal law and bush justice. Cody had studied Alaska law at the academy, was fairly knowledgeable about the U.S. Constitution, and knew a little about the history of Anglo-Saxon law; but his real interest was in making a comparative study of tribal justice and law ways. Periodically, when on patrol, he would stop in at the small villages and spend time with the local authority, usually the Village Public Safety Officer (VPSO), or the village police chief. He knew that the Indian villages in Alaska, with the exception of Metlakatla located on Annette Island, were not reservations at all, and did not fall under the auspices of the Bureau of Indian Affairs. So every now and then, when a crime was committed in the village or involved a village member and a trooper was to be detailed to the scene, he would volunteer to respond or assist—in order to learn more about how the tribal law and justice worked in a remote setting.

One of the first things he learned when he started working in the native villages was that tribal authority and tribal law are distinctly different from the Anglo-Saxon authority and Anglo-Saxon law. Tribal law and law ways more closely follow the concept of Anglo-Saxon common law and are based upon long-standing traditions and social mores similar to that developed in Europe following the medieval period. It was, simply put, the known law of the people.

Cody knew that most native villages are microcosms unto themselves, and behavior which might seem unacceptable by Anglo-Saxon standards is often acceptable within the social fabric of a native community. It had only been within the last 20 years or so that most of these villages received more than cursory attention from the State of Alaska. Prior to that time, the villages were simply "on their own" to administer state and tribal law as they saw fit. The Alaska State Troopers were most often turned to only as a last resort, because it frequently meant that the culpable village member would likely be arrested and removed by the troopers—an action the inhabitants viewed as tribal banishment by proxy. And banishment from the tribe was the harshest sentence that could be administered for a crime. So what often was viewed as a simple pretrial arrest by the Alaska State Troopers had a profound effect on the natives who viewed the procedure as cruel and unusual punishment.

Over the past couple of decades, however, significant improvements in tribal relations had taken place and villages were provided law enforcement officers through the Village Public Safety Officer program. Cody thought the changes were both progressive and needed. The State of Alaska had initiated the Village Public Safety Officer program as a resurrection of a much older concept called the Alaska Native Police Force, which came into existence during the U.S. Navy occupation in Alaska in 1897 which followed close on the heels of U.S. Army occupation.

The Native Police Force had a short, but very honorable, and productive history. Whether it was the botched occupation by the U.S. Army, which resulted in the bombardment of the native village in Wrangell, or the general lawlessness of the frontier, the top-ranking naval officer in Alaska, Commander Beardslee, formed a small

Native Police Force in Wrangell to maintain law and order. The program was so successful that, shortly thereafter, the commander also formed another native police unit in Sitka, which, at the time, was Beardslee's base of operations. Cody believed the reason the Native Police Force was so effective lay in the selection process—only tribal chieftains or counselors were initially selected. Therefore, these officers could "walk in two worlds," able to enforce both tribal law and territorial law, and knew how to strike a balance between the two.

O'Keefe knew, however, that times had changed; the Native Police Force was dissolved, and during the intervening 60 years before the VPSO program was initiated, history had set its own course. It was inevitable that there would always be disagreements between Anglo-Saxon law and tribal law.

The state-sponsored VPSO often became fodder for personal political ambitions due to the heated internal political structure of most tribal governments. Unfortunately, like most good things involving public welfare, politics often gets in the way. The political structure of most native tribes provided for the extensive use of councils whose authorities frequently overlap. Members within these councils often vie for power, and it was not uncommon to have a VPSO officer finish police training and start to become familiar with the responsibilities of office, only to be fired with a turnover in tribal government. A new officer, who could better reflect the politics of the newly appointed council members, would then be hired when this occurred. It was as much a frustration to the VPSOs as it was to the State of Alaska and the state trooper assigned to the area, but little could be done.

Tom Whitefeather was the VPSO of the new village of Twasaan, sometimes referred to as New Twasaan. Long ago, there was another historic Indian village located on the other side of the bay near the entrance to Clarence Strait. It had been deserted for decades, but in the 1960s, a group of Twasaan natives petitioned the State of Alaska for the right to inhabit their old ancestral grounds. A new Twasaan emerged further back in the bay for more weather protection and on the sunny side for better growing as well. It was not only much larger, but it was also located on a spit of fertile land carved from the wilderness with bulldozers and explosives. The roads were all graded and modern homes, trailers mostly, sat in predominant locations overlooking the bay, each with a satellite dish attached. The village had a large number of fishing boats and pleasure craft which were now tied up at a new concrete dock and breakwater, replacing the need for sandy beaches. On the hill, above the village, a bright yellow building housed a huge Japanese power plant and generator which provided electricity to the community and the fish processing plant. Both civic operations employed almost anyone in the village who was not a commercial fisherman and wanted to work. ATVs, all-terrain vehicles, were the most common form of transportation because of their versatility for work or play. Cody O'Keefe had watched the new village become a prosperous community over the last several years, growing slowly under the guidance of a progressive tribal council.

When he was there last autumn, he introduced himself to the recently hired VPSO for Twasaan, Officer Tom Whitefeather. Tom had just graduated from the advanced Municipal Police Officers Program, a 6-week program at the State Trooper Academy in Sitka, designed specifically to train city police officers and VPSOs. The Public Safety Academy had the distinction of teaching and training most officers in Alaska, with the exception of Anchorage, Alaska's largest community with a population of over 250,000 residents. The Anchorage Police Department had their own training academy, which closely reflected the modern training regime of most large police departments on the West Coast. Cody liked Tom immediately. The officer was easy to get to know and unpretentious. He had come to Alaska the previous year from a Cherokee reservation in Oklahoma, where he worked for 4 years as a police captain for the BIA. He remembered sitting in the small dank office located at the far end of the community hall as Tom reminisced.

"A tough beat," Tom had told him shaking his head and smiling. "You wouldn't believe the problems. Each tribe has at least one tribal council. Most tribes have more," he said, "so everything becomes so political." Tom leaned back in his wood chair and glanced at his law enforcement certificates arranged on the wall with military precision.

"The supreme council is usually the Executive Tribal Committee Council which establishes subcouncils and ad hoc panels, adopts regulations, and creates jobs and allocates the fiscal budgets. I guess it's like anything else; if the Executive Council is good at administration, there is enough to go around. If they aren't, then the whole tribe suffers. In defense of the councils, however, there really isn't enough money to go around on most reservations or the councils aren't business-oriented. Hell, my last 6 months, I worked without pay because someone screwed up the operating budget. One day I decided to move on ... it just wasn't worth it." Tom Whitefeather looked down, slowly shaking his head again.

Cody had gotten the distinct impression there was more to the story, but didn't feel right in pushing. After attaining the rank of captain, as Tom had put it, more from attrition than his qualifications, he decided he wanted a change in his life before he burned out on law enforcement entirely ... hence his job in Twasaan. He had told Cody that his roots were actually Seminole from Florida.

During the 1800s when the federal government established reservations in Oklahoma, Andrew Jackson, then president, gave the U.S. Army the orders which forced a multitude of different tribes into the Oklahoma Territory, or "Indian Country," as it was legally defined at the time. The U.S. Congress called this directive good for the nation—the fulfillment of Manifest Destiny. The Indians called this action an illegal seizure, a violation of the Fourth Amendment of the U.S. Constitution. But since most Indians at the time were not considered citizens of the United States, the Constitution—and so the Forth Amendment—was interpreted as being not applicable. Tribes from as far away as the Eastern Seaboard made the fateful, forced migration of thousands of miles. In some instances, it took over a year of constant traveling to reach Oklahoma. Most tribes were broken and decimated, the old and very young dying daily along the trail. The march became known to the Indians who traveled it as the Trail of Tears.

As for the new job, Tom didn't expect much trouble, at least none that he couldn't handle or hadn't seen many times before. Cody remembered they had spent the rest of the afternoon talking "cop shop," exchanging information and discussing various crimes and criminals. Tom's uniform consisted of the tan-colored poplin uniform VPSO shirt tucked into his favorite pair of faded blue jeans and scruffy cowboy boots. A dark brown ball cap with the VPSO logo embroidered on the front was jammed down over his hair. Cody noticed that around his neck he wore a turquoise necklace with an ornate sterling silver eagle feather in the center. It wasn't the authorized State of Alaska uniform by a long shot, but it was comfortable and certainly suited Tom. Cody smiled to himself whenever he thought about that ... they must be kindred souls.

Cody keyed the mike, responding to Tom's initial inquiry.

"Nothing special going on, Tom; just checking up on a couple called the Toddwells who are supposed to being staying at the Shakan River cabin for a few months. You haven't seen them have you? Over."

"No, sure haven't," Tom replied, stretched back in his chair, feet propped on the desk and looking at the opposite wall through well-worn tips of his crossed cowboy boots.

"You know," he said pensively, "I was over in that area about 2 days ago and everything looked OK then. I mean, I didn't stop by and say hello or anything, but the Shakan cabin was lit up and there was smoke from the wood stove. As I passed by I also saw an old, dented-up, red aluminum canoe with what looked like a black trolling motor or something pulled up on the beach about 2 or 3 miles from the cabin. It could be theirs or maybe someone is working a trapline in the area. Anyways, whoever it was must have wanted to get to shore real bad, 'cause they had to break through the ice to get it up the beach. Did the Toddwells have a canoe? Over."

"Not that I know of, Tom. They were pretty much fixed to stay at the cabin. They had worked out a deal with Ketchikan Air Taxi to keep them supplied, over."

"Yeah, well, do you need any help, or can you handle it? No, wait, don't tell me—one riot, one trooper, right?"

"You got it," Cody said laughingly. "Say, Tom, you could do me a favor and telephone Ketchikan Dispatch and tell them I am on scene and not to expect me back tonight."

"Yah, no problem. By the way, if you get a chance, why don't you stop by for a cup after you get finished over there? There's something I'd like to bounce off you."

"Coffee sounds real good, Tom. You got a deal. Probably be

sometime early tomorrow morning. I'll call if I get delayed, over," Cody responded.

"OK, tomorrow it is. Out," Tom replied.

Cody officially terminated the transmission. "This is Trooper O'Keefe, out."

Cody stowed the radio and brought the binoculars up to his eyes once more, systematically scanning the beach in an attempt to locate the canoe. He didn't find the boat Tom had described, but he could easily make out some long marks in the snow along the shoreline where a canoe could have been dragged along the rocky beach. Fortunately, it hadn't snowed hard yet, so nothing had obliterated the disturbed marks in the snow. With the light-gathering capabilities of the Nikon binoculars, Cody could just make out a trail of footprints leading from the beach into the woods. He scanned the shoreline one last time for any sign of human activity then put away his binoculars and pressed the starter button on the starboard engine. Putting the vessel in gear, he turned the helm to compensate for the single engine and began slowly motoring toward shore.

About 50 feet from shore, the sheet ice became thick enough to damage the hull. Cody turned off the engine and stripped off his orange Mustang float suit and jacket. Once that feat was accomplished, he grabbed a large wooden oar from its cradle in the boat and, leaning over the bow, began hitting the sheet ice with the oar, breaking the ice into small negotiable chunks. It scarred the oak oar, but Cody didn't care—better the oar than the hull.

When the ice was sufficiently dispersed, he paddled the boat forward a few feet, repeating the entire process. It was slow, back-breaking, and tedious work. Nevertheless, there was an urgency to his mission. Cody could see that time was running out. Daylight, his greatest ally in the wilderness, was rapidly surrendering to evening. A deep darkness had already begun descending into the valleys and ravines of high mountains in this remote landscape when Cody finally gained the shore. He had deliberately beached the bow of the patrol boat down several yards from the where the marks were made in the snow. He was curious about the tracks he had seen earlier and wanted to examine them more closely.

"The Toddwells could simply be out for an afternoon hike," he said to himself, "or they could be in real trouble out here somewhere." Search and rescue is serious business in Alaska; in fact, it is the primary directive of the Department of Public Safety. He wanted to carefully examine the signs left in the snow to see if they would tell him anything. But first, he had to see to the safety of his patrol boat.

CHAPTER SIX

Takqua watched as the trooper put the patrol boat in gear and headed toward the Shakan River. Once the vessel was out of sight, he bounded down the rock face of the stubby cliff to the red canoe. Reaching into the stern, he quickly pulled the drain plug on the aluminum boat. He watched it fill with water until it finally became unstable, then twisting the canoe on its side, allowed it to fill, then with a strong shove, pushed it out into the bay. The canoe rolled slightly and sank stern first, the weight of the engine dragging the boat down into the deep pocket of water. Satisfied that the canoe would never be found, he climbed back to the campsite, picked up a fallen branch and swept the 10 x 10 foot area clean of any sign to disguise his presence. He tossed what few essentials he had at the camp into the green plastic bag and headed in the direction of the cabin.

With daylight edging to dusk and still a mile or so from the log cabin, Cody made a conscious decision to spend the night away from the boat. Hopefully, he would be invited to spend the evening at the cabin with the Toddwells. If not, well, he could always have an uncomfortable bivouac in the forest. Walking forward to the bow of the patrol boat, he broke out the ground tackle he had carefully stowed for this operation and set about rigging a complex anchoring system. First, the Danforth anchor was balanced at the tip of the bow, with the shank of the anchor pointing toward the console. Next, he set the attached anchor chain and 50 feet of ½ inch anchor line carefully on the tip of the bow flaying the line carefully with the terminal end shackled into the pad eye on the deck. Then he took a second section of 200 feet ½ inch diameter line and tied it carefully to the base of the anchor, using a bowline knot. That task completed, Cody gathered up his .44 Magnum Marlin lever action rifle, faded brown Cordura backpack, and tobacco-colored nylon parka. He carefully lashed his rubber boots to the outside of the pack with bungee cords. As a matter of habit, Trooper O'Keefe would always put his credentials and badge into the front pouch pocket of his bib overalls so they would not get lost in the myriad of pockets which normally festoons outdoor clothing. He checked to make sure his identification was still there. Then he pulled on his insulated rubber waders over the outside of the wool overalls and prepared to depart the boat. Around his waist he wore a wide leather belt with a Velcro closure. The plain brown leather belt carried other essentials. A medium-sized hunting knife with a bone handle and sharpening steel on one side and a leather pouch with a brass snap closure containing 12 rounds of .44 Magnum ammunition on the other. In front was a buckskin pouch containing a sophisticated forester's lensatic compass.

Cody slipped back into his jacket and rucksack and then visually checked the boat over a final time. He was ready. A few feet from the bank, he switched off the ignition, killing the outboard motor. The patrol boat lightly touched the rocky shore. He swiftly lowered himself off the bow and into the shallow water. It was cold. Firmly gripping the bow rail with one hand, he reached into the boat, gathering his rifle and remaining possessions and placing them on snow-covered rocks. Next came the difficult part. Holding one end of the yellow 200 ft. ½ inch line, he walked swiftly to the tree line. Finding a suitable fir tree he could enlist as an anchor, he secured one end of the line around the base of the tree trunk and then returned to the boat. Walking out into the frigid water, he again grabbed the bow, this time gently pushing the vessel ahead of him. When, at last, the cold water reached his thighs and the top of his tan waders, he gave the vessel one last powerful shove, sending the boat out past the shore ice. He continued to watch the line tied to the tree and the anchor perched on the bow play out as the vessel drifted out in the bay.

When the patrol craft finally reached the end of the 200-foot line, the travel momentum of the boat pulled the anchor off the bow. With a loud splash, the anchor and chain spilled into the water. The anchor was now set in about 20 feet of water, well away from the shore. The anchor line carefully secured to the pad eye and looped around the base of the anchor while the bitter end was tied to the trunk of the fir tree using a bowline knot. Cody would be able to retrieve the boat in any tide condition, unless the bay froze over. He watched the boat rock back and forth slowly for a few minutes to ensure the anchor was holding, then turned and waded back to shore.

Reaching down, he gathered his gear off the rocks and walked the line back to the fir tree to check the terminal end of the line. Satisfied that everything was properly secured, he found a tall fir tree that had a dry bed of pine needles beneath the boughs and peeled off his waders, replacing them with his rubber boots. When that task was completed, he checked his rifle and pack and located his flashlight. Next, he rolled up his canvas and rubber waders, placing them beneath the tree. The lengthening shadows told Cody that darkness was rapidly closing in. He pulled the liquid-filled compass out of his leather pouch and took a bearing toward the general direction of the cabin. He wasn't far away and if he had the time he would have simply walked along the beach. As it was, it would be near dark before he arrived at the Shakan cabin ... if he traveled cross-country.

He adjusted the padded straps on his pack, checked the sling on his rifle, and set off down the beach to where he first observed the tracks in the snow. He was careful when approaching the area since he only wanted to make one path to the tracks he first saw on the beach. When he was close enough to the footprints, Cody knelt down close to the ground and used his police flashlight to sidelight the tracks and trampled snow. It only took him several seconds to read the sign, but he didn't like what he saw.

The tracks were made by one individual, probably a male judging by the size and depth of the footprints. The person was likely under 6 feet tall since the tracks were about size 9 or 10. The lugged soles told Cody that the person was probably not from the Southeast area, since most lugged soles are found on leather-sided shoes and boots. The trappers and fishermen in this region used rubber boots which had several distinctive patterns ... none of them lugged soles. He closely examined the lugs to discern a pattern and any variations in the pattern, such as a gouge in a lug. Since Vibram lug soles are created with different patterns for different purposes, he thought he might see more, but the snow had filled in between the lugs and a distinct pattern was hard to determine. His eyes continued to strain over the crushed snow and shadows as he came across large spots of what appeared to be bloodstains in a long line toward the water.

He also found a depression indicating the point where a smooth bag, maybe a plastic garbage sack or duffle bag, was placed in the snow. Judging by the diameter and depth of the depression, the bag was filled with something weighing around 20 to 40 lbs. The tracks also revealed the person obviously knew where best to beach a boat using the contours of the shoreline to the best advantage. Could one of the Toddwells have been here? If not, who? A trapper? And where was that person now?

Cody was worried about the deteriorating weather and decided he had better not waste too much more time. Rummaging through the outside pocket of his pack, he located the small Olympus 99 camera. Using the flashlight for backlighting, he took several photographs of the boot prints. The red stains and smudges in the snow were too small to capture with his camera. Pulling off his mittens, Cody carefully used his pocket knife to cut out several small samples and placed each into separate, small, manila paper envelopes he carried to gather evidence when he was in the field. The blood was mixed with snow and likely contaminated, but it would tell him whether the blood was human or animal in origin. The manila packets were then hastily numbered, labeled, sealed, and placed in an outer pocket of his pack. He made some quick notes in his field diary and drew a rough sketch of the footprints. The rest he filed in the back of his mind. If he had more daylight, he would have liked to follow the tracks leading back into the woods, but he was severely pressed for time.

Standing up, Cody glanced around for anything else out of the ordinary and seeing nothing in particular, loaded up his gear and slipped quietly into the dense black forest, switching on his flashlight to negotiate natural obstacles that might block his way. Periodically, he would pull the folded map out of his pocket and consult his compass to make sure he was still on track to the cabin.

CHAPTER SEVEN

Now in a race to the cabin to search for his necklace, Takqua's breath spewed from his mouth and nose in small violent puffs of vapor. Sweat dripped from his brow as he literally clawed at the hillside, his feet slipping on the frozen terrain. Every now and then he would lose his grip and slide back down the slick hill until he could grab a bush or tree trunk to stop his slow descent. He had already lost a fingernail in the process, ripped off when a strong root was forced under the nail and failed to give way. Takqua barely noticed the excruciating pain. He was more intent on retrieving the necklace, the only piece of evidence that might link him to the murders. He might have made better time if he didn't have to carry the plastic bag with him. What he estimated would be an easy climb had now turned into an agonizingly slow effort made all the more painful by the pending darkness.

Dragging the sack with his artifacts, helmet, and shaman skull, he finally reached the ridge and tracked along the spine until he could make out the snowbanked river. Then he began his descent. After about an hour of bursting through brush and pushing aside devil's club, he backtracked cross-country through the woods until he came to a small-animal trail which led him to a shallow, gravel-bottomed stream. There, he followed the stream as it led him to the river.

Takqua walked quickly through the woods paralleling the river until he saw the familiar path which led to the cabin. Here he stopped and found a place to hide the plastic bag. Finishing that task, he hurried down the trail toward the cabin, trying to beat the fading light and the trooper he had seen on the boat. He caught sight of the cabin about the same time he perceived, or rather sensed, a movement in the forest, and ducked behind a tree.

For what had to be only several minutes but felt like an eternity, he watched from behind the tree, only one eye and a bit of his head exposed. Carefully watching the woods for an as yet unseen presence, he detected nothing. Wet and shivering from the dropping temperatures, he wrapped his arms around his chest breathing through his nose and exhaling slowly and quietly through clenched teeth so as not to be discovered. Minutes passed and he was about half convinced that it was his mind playing tricks on him when he saw it. This time, the movement was real. In the dimming light, Takqua could make out the figure of the trooper moving slowly through the woods, the beam of his flashlight scanning the ground, as if he were tracking or stalking. Takqua might have risked a surprise attack if he were armed, but he was not. All he could do is wait and watch—and hope he wasn't detected.

Nearly an hour had elapsed when Cody crested a small frozen, brush-covered hill where he could see the outline of the snowcapped cabin on the other side of the river. As he approached the river, he turned and went upstream in hopes of finding a place to cross. The river wasn't deep, but it was wide at the terminal end and would get much deeper when the tide came back in. It wasn't long before he caught sight of a place to ford the river. Holding his rifle in both hands for balance, he stepped into the river, adjusted his balance, and cautiously waded across. Once on the other side, he slipped into the woods to a point where he could observe the cabin in the last few minutes of waning dusk, and sat down. From the tree line, he could look almost directly at the cabin, which was partly visible through the surrounding evergreens.

Cody never minded "going it alone." In fact, he preferred it. But working solo in law enforcement in Alaska dictated a different set of rules ... if you wanted to stay alive. One of the first rules he learned was that you *never, ever* approach a cabin, boat, campsite, or individuals without first waiting a few minutes to survey the surroundings. By standing perfectly still and observing, he often gathered a wealth of information, better preparing himself for the initial contact. He could, for example, determine if any resource crimes had been committed in the near vicinity, how many individuals were in the close proximity of his intended contact point, who was armed, and if they were, what type of weapons and where the weapons were located and so forth. Like in combat, Cody learned that surveillance meant intelligence, and good intelligence increased your chances of survival, in addition to being an important step in the investigation and evidence-gathering of a crime. It was a good officer survival and safety practice.

From his vantage point, his eyes missed nothing, but there was very little to see. The cabin was either not occupied, or they were running a "cold camp" judging by the lack of smoke from the black metal chimney stack, which protruded above the cabin roof. There was no sign of the Toddwells nor their dog ... although they could have been out for a day hike. That idea seemed unlikely, he thought, since the weather was so dismal and obviously getting worse. All in all, it didn't look good, and he was beginning to get a bad feeling. Waiting several more minutes and seeing nothing out of the ordinary, Cody quietly broke cover and slowly headed for the cabin, employing the trees in the vicinity to conceal his approach. He methodically worked around to the back of the cabin, the only side that had no windows. When he was in position, he ran quickly toward the log home in a combat crouch.

Stopping to rest at the back of the rustic cabin, he took a moment to make certain his .44 Magnum stainless steel revolver was loaded and readily available. The adrenaline was pumping now, coursing rapidly through his veins. Moving cautiously along the rough exterior of the darkened cabin, his shoulder rubbing the side of the exterior wall, Cody carefully avoided detection by concealing himself well below any windowsills. Reaching the front of the cabin and the porch, he peeked around the corner and seeing nothing, quietly jettisoned his gear and rifle. His revolver at the ready and holding his flashlight in his other hand, Cody carefully crawled toward the closest window and peered quickly into the main room of the cabin. He couldn't a thing; the cabin was pitch-black. He didn't want to shine his flashlight into the cabin just yet. The beam from the light might reflect off the pane, removing any advantage of surprise and clearly identifying his position.

Cody now backed away from the window, retracing his steps. Then, using the high, wooden porch for partial cover, he quickly ran to the steps leading to the front door. He cautiously approached the steps to the front door trying not to make any noise. Standing to one side of the entrance, he knocked loudly.

"This is State Trooper O'Keefe. Is anyone home?" he said. There was no answer. He tried again.

"This is State Trooper O'Keefe. Is anyone home?"

Hearing no response, he crouched down and tried the doorknob. It wasn't locked. With his stainless .44 Magnum revolver in his strong hand and holding his six-cell aluminum flashlight in his left hand, he threw open the door, and in the process, rolled the flashlight in a wide arc so the beam could shine across the cabin floor.

Cody watched from his half-hidden position at the base of the door frame as the powerful beam from the flashlight lit up the room. The place was a mess, but no one was home. He quickly entered the room, his back to the interior wall, and reaching out, retrieved his flashlight. His police training had taught him that anyone standing in the doorway of a darkened room with backlighting made an easy target. With a bright flashlight in his hands, a trooper was sending the message "here I am, shoot me." By learning to roll the flashlight properly across the floor, he eliminated the possibility of revealing his position, while at the same time seeing everything inside a room. The technique wouldn't work in a big room, but it was excellent for this small, one-room log cabin.

The beam of his flashlight trained on an old, green Coleman lantern on a nearby table. Cody grabbed the light and primed the fuel tank using the slender brass plunger. Turning the knob on the side of the green metal lantern, he heard a recognizable hiss as the gas began to escape into the main chamber. Locating his wooden matches in his shirt pocket, he struck the head on the rough wood table. Holding the lit match to the interior glass chamber of the lantern, the silk sock erupted in flames, the room soaking up the light. Within seconds, he had adjusted the flame and set the lantern on a hook.

Then he looked about the room and was shocked by what he

saw! He noticed almost immediately that the large VHF radio had been totally and, apparently, deliberately destroyed. The small table which served a multitude of purposes was overturned. The chairs lay on their sides and research papers were scattered about. Clothes were thrown everywhere. Sensing foul play, he began to systematically take into account the placement of everything in the room. When he saw the dishes, however, his blood went cold. Clearly, the Toddwells had company at one time, because there were three overturned cups on the rustic cabin floor.

Not wanting to destroy any evidence, Cody began to back out slowly when he slipped, nearly losing his balance. Looking down at what he had at first mistaken as a shadow from the lantern across the room, he saw what was actually a large blood trail leading to one of the side windows. He would have seen it immediately if he had come up that side of the house, but he hadn't. The pool led to a point in the center of the cabin. Drag marks on the floor lead to the blood-soaked chairs. Resting in the darkening pool was a white washbowl filled with bits of fat and translucent strips of meat. Cody didn't pick it up; he didn't need to. The metal bowl was filled with strips of human skin. He didn't know whose blood and flesh was in the cabin, or if it was even connected somehow to the bloodstains found on the beach, but he now suspected the Toddwells had been recently murdered. The realization of this made his hair stand on end and his pulse quickened.

Backing slowly onto the front porch, Cody retrieved his pack and rifle, and using the flashlight, began carefully walking around the house to pick up the trail of blood from the cabin. The beam from the flashlight illuminated the snow on the ground. He noticed the same Vibram tracks as the ones found on the beach. So the two scenes were somehow connected! How they were connected, however, he wasn't sure. Moving around to the side of the cabin, the horror continued to unfold in slow, graphic detail. It was easy to follow the blood trail from the side window. His flashlight picked up a long, deep, red smear down the side of the cabin wall and across the snow-covered ground. Following that trail was easy. Someone in Vibram boots, maybe the same as he had seen on the beach, had dragged something heavy to what appeared to be the outhouse, in the process, leaving a deep blood path in the snow. The blood trail ended ominously at the outhouse door.

Cody couldn't overcome the feeling that he was being watched, yet the events of the moment and his curiosity overshadowed this feeling. Walking carefully around behind the outhouse, he flashed the beam of his light into the dark surrounding woods to see if he could catch a glimmer of anyone, or anything. He jumped back suddenly in surprise and fear. Looming out of the darkness just inches from his face, the beam from the flashlight illuminated the white fur of a small dog in the blackness of night. It had caught him off guard because he had been looking down at the snow for evidence. The animal hung by the neck from the bare limb of an alder tree with what appeared to be an old, rusty, wolf snare wire. The dog's eyes bulged and its tongue protruded grotesquely from its mouth as it swung slowly back and forth. Cody photographed the dog and felt the carcass. It was cold.

Cody still couldn't shake the strange sensation he was being watched as these macabre scenes unfolded, but he saw no evidence that anyone was around. Turning his attention to the faded wooden structure, he carefully approached the weather-beaten door. All his senses told him not to open the door, but he knew he had no choice. With his flashlight in one hand and revolver in the other, Cody tugged slightly on the wooden latch of the old door. The response was instantaneous. As though the door were spring-loaded, it flew open as a naked carcass tumbled out into the snow. He could see now that there was a second carcass still inside the tiny outhouse. Both were decapitated, partially skinned, and painted in blood.

For a moment, his mind deceived him, not wanting to believe the bodies were human. They looked more like skinned bears. Then the realization of what he was looking at hit him hard. He was shocked and would have dropped his flashlight had the scene not paralyzed him. The bodies where in such bad shape he couldn't tell who was who. It was too much for him. Cody felt the burning bile rise in his throat in a violent rush. Instinctively, he turned to one side, gagged briefly, and then vomited several times.

For the next few minutes, Cody was stuck between the horror of the gruesome deaths and his duty. He knew he had to do something, but his mind was frozen. Repeatedly, he kept casting the beam of his flashlight from one mutilated body to the next, and then dragging the beam across the woods, half expecting to illuminate some demonic attacker. Finally getting himself under control, Cody began to methodically survey the entire scene and get his mind working again. He deduced that the bodies must belong to the Toddwells since they were near the cabin, but no one could be sure until autopsies were performed.

Meanwhile, Takqua had reached the river in time to see Cody enter the woods on the other side, and then he lost sight of him until he saw the flickering flashlight beam at the cabin door and then finally the lantern go on in the tiny cabin. He watched mesmerized as the figure he had seen earlier became silhouetted by the cabin light walking back and forth. For a brief moment, he thought that the crime would go undetected, the person would get scared and leave. Any hopes he had evaporated when he saw the figure from the cabin, or rather the telltale flashlight beam being held by someone in the darkness, bounce along the snow until it arrived at the front of the outhouse door. Takqua knew he had lost the race. The crime was about to be discovered. The idea of searching for the necklace at the ruins crossed his mind, but without a flashlight, there didn't seem to be much use; he was wasting time. Anyway, he reasoned, if the magic necklace were found at the old village, it would likely be mistaken for just another beaded necklace. If the police were to find his necklace at the cabin, well, it was evidence of his presence. Takqua quietly picked up his possessions and walked swiftly along the riverbank, heading upstream, following his now-altered plan of escape.

The loss of the necklace was significant, but Takqua knew that there was still one abandoned village he had not found, one village where reputedly the most powerful Kushtikaw had lived and practiced his evil. That place was Sha'te. Very little was ever written about the village. No missionaries ever visited the place. All reference to the old village was through stories passed down from generation to generation by word of mouth. He had been searching for Sha'te, the most powerful village of the Kushtikaws, but now, in losing his necklace, he felt vulnerable and weak. In Takqua's mind, the solution was clear. He had to find Sha'te now more than ever, and the grave of the most powerful Indian shaman that ever lived.

Several minutes later, he was finally able to wade out into water that was shallow enough for crossing. Even though it was dark, Takqua estimated that it must be close to seven o'clock. He could still barely make out the outline of the top of the mountain through the trees. Over the ridge was safety. A sense of urgency briefly overtook him, and for a second, he wanted to run away. Takqua quickly put those feelings behind him. He knew he had time now and must go slowly to avoid making any more mistakes.

Sitting down to rest, he opened the plastic garbage bag and pulled out the Raven helmet which he set on his head. He felt his power returning to him as the spiritual strength of the dead shaman entered his body. He began feeling omnipotent again.

After a while, Takqua slowly took off the helmet and all his wet wool clothing. He soaked the clothing in the shallows of the stream, weighing the bloody clothes down with rocks. The water was so cold it burned his skin and numbed his head. He almost could see the stream turn a bloody red as he rinsed the final particles of dried flesh, skin, and blood from his body, while rubbing small grains of sand and gravel over his entire body. Finally, holding fine bits of sand and gravel in one hand, Takqua worked the crude pumice under his fingernails and around his cuticles. It took almost a half hour of shivering and washing in the cold water before he pronounced himself totally clean.

Gathering up the clothing belonging to the former Dr. Toddwell, he waded across the stream to the opposite bank. There, he shoved the wet clothing under water, allowing a few moments for all the air to escape from within the folds of the clothing. Then he weighted the entire bundle down with stones. He knew that the clothes could only be concealed from a casual observer. If a real search took place, they would eventually find the jacket, pants, and boots. By then, however, Takqua hoped that he would be a thousand miles away.

The first snow squall finally reached the back of the bay as Cody began going over the crime scene. During the next several hours, he fought snowstorm, darkness, and increasingly colder temperatures as he worked frantically to record as much information and evidence as possible before the snow covered everything. At first he wanted to return to the vessel and call for help, but then he dismissed the idea since he knew that unless he worked quickly, the snow would cover all valuable trace evidence outside. He was also concerned that if he left the area for too long, mink and marten might decide to feed on the corpses before additional help could arrive. How was he going to protect the crime scene and the corpses? Too many decisions and too little time.

After what seemed like an eternity, Cody glanced at his watch. It was almost eleven o'clock. He had been working outside for more than 3 hours now. All his best intentions of warming up or turning in early had long since vanished. He was tired and cold but somehow drew on an inner strength to keep going. Cody realized that although he had tried not to miss anything, still all the elements were against him and there was a good chance he was likely missing crucial evidence. Mentally, he went over his list of crime-scene duties. He had diagramed the crime scene, including the cabin and surrounding area, the outhouse and its surrounding area ... including the dog, and had photographed all important evidence except the bodies. Above all, he tried not to disturb anything.

Finally satisfied, he gathered all the blankets in the cabin and returned to the mutilated corpses. There was a certain risk he took in bringing the blankets out of the cabin and covering the bodies. Wool blankets trap hair and fibers and there could be valuable trace evidence that might be destroyed or improperly transferred to the bodies, but he had no choice. Leaving the bodies uncovered would expose them to the elements and the animals of the forest. He lay the blankets down next to the bodies and photographed each one.

As the last flash went off recording one of the arms, he noticed there was something resting in a pool of blood at the base of the body. He took a small twig and poked around until he could pick it up. Trooper Cody O'Keefe had found an odd-looking Indian necklace. *Not the usual Alaska native necklace,* he thought. *No, maybe something from a Southwest Indian culture.*

It appeared to be broken on one side, most likely when the killer dropped one of the bodies in the outhouse. The necklace was unusual. It was made of rough turquoise stones, carved bone, and black jet beads. The center piece was a large triangular bead ... he had never seen anything like it ... consisting of individual bands of abalone shell, turquoise, and black stone. At first he was just going to leave it, but then changed his mind.

"Tom might be able to tell me what this is, or what it means," he wondered aloud, and wiping it off as best he could, stuffed the necklace into the deep breast pocket of his coarse wool shirt. Then he unfolded the wool blankets and covered the bodies where they lay in the cold snow.

By midnight, the winter storm hit in earnest. Cody knew that he needed to call Ketchikan Post and report the gruesome homicides as soon as possible, and that meant getting back to the boat and trying to radio. Cody held no illusions. The double homicide was clearly something for which he had not been trained. This was something which needed to get passed to the elite homicide investigation unit, the Criminal Investigation Bureau, commonly referred to by the initials CIB, which handled complex criminal investigations. When he made contact with the Ketchikan dispatcher, Cody would request CIB assistance as soon as possible. If he could make contact within the next couple of hours, CIB might be on scene before noon tomorrow.

He gathered up his gear and prepared to head out. He was determined that if he couldn't reach Ketchikan, he could at least relay his call for help through VPSO Tom Whitefeather at Twasaan. Using the radio at the cabin was out of the question, of course, as it had been totally destroyed.

Takqua was beginning to get numb from the cold. Rubbing his arms repeatedly, he generated little warmth. He knew that if he did not get some heat soon, he would likely be dead before morning. Beginning to get impatient, he was afraid that if he didn't start walking soon, he might be in serious trouble. His feet were already numb and painful. He could feel the cold air beginning to sap his energy and steal his core body temperature with every breath he took.

Takqua paused one last time to look around and listen to determine if he were alone. All that could be heard was the rustling of wind-blown branches at the top of the hill. The total darkness confirmed his solitude. With a grunt, he hoisted the cold, wet plastic sack over one shoulder, and satisfied that there was no evidence that could be directly traced to him, began to walk upstream.

At some point along the agonizing trek, he began slipping on ice and stumbling over slick round river stones while moving further upstream. Takqua knew hypothermia was setting in. Shivering uncontrollably, he left the gurgling water and briskly walked into the black forest, the vines and brush scratching his skin. There was almost no snow here. The long branches of the massive trees blocked everything from the sky, including light. Here, the forest floor was covered with brown, dried pine needles and felt soft to his bare feet.

At last, he found the place he was looking for, a natural grotto surrounded by towering cedars. Any smoke from a fire would be trapped in the escalating series of overlapping branches from the massive trees. With the wind and the snow, his location would be virtually undetectable.

Secure in these surroundings, Takqua lowered his burden from his shoulders. Digging around in the large garbage bag, he found what he was looking for in the very bottom of it. He wiped off the blood and looked at the plastic cigarette case he had thrown in the bag as he was leaving his lair. Now he was glad he did because inside, it held matches and fire-starter. He opened it and found the plastic container with the starter kit. Using a dead branch as an implement, he began to dig a small hole, a depression really, in the frozen earth. The exercise felt good and warmed him up a bit, but he knew that unless he did something soon to protect himself from the cold, he would be likely be dead from hypothermia before first light.

Shaking uncontrollably, he opened the clear plastic cigarette case, dropping the contents on the ground. Scooping up dried pine needles, moss, and small twigs in his violently trembling hands, Takqua methodically lined the bottom of the tiny fire pit. Next, he hastily gathered thin dead branches from the forest floor and stacked them in a bundle alongside the depression. Taking the fire-starter, he laid a ribbon of the flammable substance in the bottom of the makeshift fire pit. After adding dried twigs and old moss, he then attentively touched a flame to the alchemy. The substance smoked for a second, then burst into flames as a frail wisp of smoke rose from the infant campfire.

Now becoming impatient with the sense of impending death and a primitive instinct to survive, he placed more dried moss on the fire and watched as the flames grew. Next, he added dried twigs and small branches to the hungry fire. Flames danced across each piece of wood as the heat began to increase. Finally satisfied that the fire had matured to a point where it could not be smothered, he broke off larger pieces of dead branches and thrust them end-first into the earth on the sides of the pit, forming a primitive wooden cone over the strengthening fire.

Takqua lay down on the pine needle-covered ground and curled his body around the small campfire, feeding the fire more twigs and warming his head, arms, torso, and thighs. His shivering numbness turned to burning pain, then a warm glow. Finally, the pain began to subside. After about an hour or so, he knew he needed to move on. Takqua painfully stood up and, moving stiffly, smothered the little campfire with a small amount of the freshly dug earth. Trampling down the soil to make it appear natural, Takqua blanketed the entire area with armfuls of dried pine needles taken from under the nearby conifers.

Convinced the immediate area appeared undisturbed, he prepared for the last part of his journey. He forced himself up the side of yet another hill covered by old-growth forest. Finally at the top of the mountain, he looked down and saw what he was looking for, the logging road where he had left the faded blue '60 Ford pickup truck several days earlier. Standing in the middle of the unpaved road, he threw his head back and howled a long wolf cry of victory, and then ran naked down the road.

Cody had just crossed the Shakan River and was about to enter the woods when he heard the long cry. It made his blood run cold! From somewhere high in the valley far above the woods, the long chilling howl floated through the air. He knew this wasn't a wolf or even a wild animal of any sort. In the dark recesses of his mind, the thought exploded: he had heard the bloodcurdling cry before—it was human!

CHAPTER EIGHT

Snowflakes the size of silver dollars fell gently to earth in the omnipresent winter darkness. The quiet serenity of the falling snow was disrupted by the abrupt appearance of a dirty, naked man running, staggering, down the abandoned logging road toward a rusty, pale-blue Ford pickup truck with a dented cab and cracked windshield. Half hidden from the road in a small cluster of fir trees and covered with a light dusting of snow, it was barely visible from the road. Far from the snow-covered truck, he could barely make out the narrow strip of snow which marked the shoreline and the smooth icy edge of Twasaan Bay. It seemed a thousand years since he launched his canoe just days before. What then took several hours of travel by canoe along the thick tree-lined shore to his hide-out would have been impossible on foot. The shoreline was littered with rocky drop-offs, log-strewn beaches, and heavy brush. Now, with the shallow coves of the bay frozen over and skim ice forming even in the deeper water, travel by canoe was impossible. He had almost been trapped by the weather.

Following the river up into the mountains had been his only

option for escape. Crossing the 4,000-foot mountain was a testament to his stamina and determination. And more importantly, no search team would even think it plausible. Takqua was beginning to feel safe again and, in relaxing, brought back the excruciating pain racking his body. His dirty feet were bloody and scraped, the bottoms cut on the sharp rocks that formed the foundation for most logging roads in the Tongass National Forest. Streaks of sweat and dirt lined his face, and his body was marred with numerous welts and scratches. The long, irregular, self-inflicted knife cuts across his chest had become slightly infected over the intervening hours, and it hurt to breathe deeply. Takqua hobbled and limped to the truck, and steadying himself by grasping the side of the truck bed, opened the door. After a few long seconds in which he thought the keys were missing, Takqua heaved a sigh of relief when he located them tucked under the front floor mat, where he had left them days before. Shaking uncontrollably, he inserted the well-worn chrome key into the ignition slot and turned it. It took several tries before he finally coaxed the engine to life, sputtering and coughing as all the cylinders came on line.

Relieved that he would indeed survive after all, Takqua let out a long, painful groan as he pushed himself back gingerly across the frayed and cracked bench seat of the old truck, his naked body racked with pain and cold. Forcing his arm forward, he brushed his cold, numb fingers against the control on the dashboard of the old truck. If he hadn't managed to flick the worn plastic knob up, he would have died little by little over the next few hours. As it was, his efforts turned the heater in the truck on full blast. Fully exhausted, he lay across the ragged bench seat and fell asleep.

After a few minutes, he was jolted to reality by the realization that fatigue was his worst enemy. It was only a matter of time before the state troopers began looking for the person who killed the Toddwells. Any hours wasted now meant the safety margin between him and the troopers would be significantly reduced. Although Takqua believed he was far too smart to ever be captured, there was no need to tempt fate. He mustered his courage and calling on his sacred deities for strength, found the energy to move on.

Takqua forced himself fully awake and slowly began putting on the raincoat he had left earlier in the pickup. It wasn't much, but better than nothing. Still shivering even though the heat in the cab of the truck was now approaching maximum, Takqua unscrewed the cap off his stainless steel thermos and began slowly sipping its contents. He wished the apple cider could have been hot, but he knew that after several days in winter temperatures, hot was a luxury not to be expected. With the addition of the liquid nourishment, he could tell his body temperature was beginning to rise. As this renewal of life progressed, his muscles ached and his head began to pound. He could spend the night here, on the side of the road, but knew he shouldn't. He didn't have a minute to spare.

Pulling together all the remaining energy he possessed, Takqua put the truck in gear and in a moment, the dented Ford truck with rattling, rusty fenders was spinning its bald tires. He twisted the steering wheel violently, making a sharp U-turn, and then headed down the snow-covered road for the Craig Sportsmen's Lodge and Resort.

Twice en route to the lodge, he stopped the truck at natural vantage points and surveyed the area around him to see if he had been followed. Takqua knew he hadn't but he had to be sure. Now totally convinced that he had thwarted any law enforcement, he turned onto the main logging road, put on his headlights, and drove hard toward the lodge. The truck rattled, slipped, and slid as he negotiated the slick, snow-covered logging roads, working his way slowly toward the opposite side of the large island.

It was well after three in the morning when he barely made out the lodge through the increased cascade of descending snowflakes caught in the high beams of the old Ford. The hotel was located some 7 miles outside the quaint fishing village of Craig, Alaska, and had been an excellent base of operations. He had found the place quite by accident on one of his previous explorations looking for old Indian ruins on the islands of Sea Otter Sound. The area was remote, and no one asked you about your business, and, even better, being gone from the hotel on fishing or hunting trips for a few days at a time seemed entirely plausible. With the exception of polite conversation at the lodge, he had been pleasantly left alone.

Craig, located in southwestern Prince of Wales, the ninth largest island in the United States, was once an Indian summer fish camp. Over the years, Craig developed as a major western fishing port for the salmon purse seine and troll fishermen who plied their trade in the azure, turbulent waters of the North Pacific. The fishing community was named for its founder, Craig Miller, an Alaskan visionary and chief employer in the region, who hired local Haida and Tlingit Indians to pack salmon for Hyman H. Bergman, an agent for the German company Lindenberger Brothers of Hamburg at the turn of the century. Although salmon continued to remain Craig's chief industry, today, the town was well supported by logging and tourists, as well as investments emanating from the native corporations.

Some of the roads in Craig were paved, but most were not. Several years earlier, the highway department paved the road between Craig and Klawock some 7 miles distant. He saw Klawock just briefly when he had first arrived on the island. His first impression of the village was that of a rustic Indian fishing community trying desperately to gain a commercial foothold in the waning years of the twentieth century. The road between the two small towns was lined with towering cedar and hemlock trees on one side and a beautiful view of the water on the other. Bald eagles were plentiful. They could be seen daily, flying low over the water in search of a quick meal or perched conspicuously atop the tall pines that border the water, their white heads looking like candles on a Christmas tree.

The citizens of Craig and Klawock consist mostly of Alaska natives, with a strong Anglo presence from old-time Alaskan sourdoughs, made up mostly of fishermen, loggers, and trappers. There is also a strong contingent of U.S. Forest Service reprobates who came into the country looking for the "last frontier" lifestyle, found what they were looking for, quit their jobs and hung on. What they, and most everyone else, find so endearing about the last frontier is the astounding, rugged remoteness and independent attitude. This concept of forced solitude naturally reinforces the thought that in all this awesome natural freedom, one can do as one pleases. No one will find out, because no one is around. As the saying goes, "Alaska is the land of the individual and other endangered species." In this and other remote corners of the world, however, all the locals know each other, their past sins, the indiscretions of their parents and grandparents. Somehow, all was forgiven in time and the communities continued to function, to the casual observer, at a pace which deceptively inferred that nothing ever happened. All in all, not a bad place to live ... or hide.

The rusty blue truck shook and rattled as it weaved around the last bend, the headlights finally illuminating the north-side of the lodge with its rustic, brown-stained siding and tired yellow trim. He punched in the headlight switch, killing the lights, and twisted the ignition key, shutting off the engine. Using the momentum of the vehicle, he put the transmission in neutral and quietly coasted to the far end of a large snow patch that constituted the Sportsmen's parking lot. He hoped these precautions would preclude anyone from waking up; he certainly did not feel like explaining himself, or his bizarre appearance, at this hour of the night.

After setting the brake and retrieving his plastic sack, Takqua, or "Willem Tuttle" as he was known at the lodge, bit his lip to keep from crying out in pain and slowly exited the truck. Trying to appear casual in the event he was confronted by the owners or other patrons, he quietly opened the front door and walked confidently into the lodge sitting room, trying to hide his ubiquitous pain.

The dank interior of the lodge was dark except for a small light on a table next to a heavy overstuffed chair. The interior of the lodge was what he termed "vintage Alaskan predictable": a river stone wall at one end of the lodge housed a massive fireplace which still burned brightly. Scattered with little regard as to design, or eye appeal, were trophies of stuffed fish or animals which festooned the other walls constructed of natural pine and then stained a smokey golden oak to give the appearance of age. There were so many trophies, in fact, that the casual visitor might ponder if the abode were a lodge or a taxidermy shop.

Interspersed beneath the lifelike trophies with their piercing glass eyes focused on everything and nothing, were a slew of cheaply framed action photographs littering the walls and end tables. When he first saw the pictures, he was amused that they were almost all black-and-whites of the owner, Mr. Johann Freese, with some celebrity who visited the lodge in the distant past. He mused to himself that the photographs were also Alaskan predictable, depicting some notable or a celebrity with the cause célèbre: a large fish, bear, mountain goat, or Sitka black-tailed deer. The owner and the client-guest crouching bravely next to some huge Boone and Crockett animal laid out prone on the ground. In each photograph, the great white hunter is holding a large caliber rifle and grinning from ear to ear. Mr. Freese was usually on the other side of the animal, opposite the hunter, with a fixed smile denoting the knowing and benevolent big-game guide. Willem did not miss the fact that most all were signed, especially the ones of politicians, senators, and congressmen who had visited the lodge over the past three decades. Why did politicians always sign their name with their titles? *Fame is fleeting*, he thought to himself.

The opposite wall was the most impressive. It was devoted entirely to a huge glass window, which ran the entire length and height of the wall from floor to ceiling. The huge panes of glass were reinforced and supported by two massive oak beams formed in the shape of a cross. Now appearing ominous and obsidian black due to the darkness and the snowstorm, during the day, the window was an eye to the world, overlooking the entrance to the sea. A guest could easily spend all day gazing at shore and sea, watching gray, foreboding winter storms approach or the seals, whales, eagles, and seabirds perform a carefully choreographed ballet of survival within the ocean's ecosystem.

The floor of the lodge was almost entirely carpeted in a gray, heather, or a tweed commercial-grade pile, with little or no padding. The tough, coarse carpeting was essential in helping keep the lodge warm and, of course, to add the air of sophistication. By contrast, his room was covered with carpet tiles which clashed with the wallpaper design.

To his immediate right on a small wooden stand was a squat glass pot containing warmed-over coffee, long since past the point of "fit for human consumption." He looked around the room, and finding himself entirely alone, quietly crept up the stairs that led to his bedroom. He immediately noticed, stuck to the door, a small yellow square post-it note with a brief scribbled note from Johann Freese, the owner, asking him to confirm his departure date as soon as possible.

Upon opening the door to his small well-kept room, he observed another similar-sized note placed on his small television set from Gerta Freese, the owner's wife. Mrs. Freese was apparently worried that he had not been in the lodge, nor had he called for several days. She asked that he notify her upon his return. Under other circumstances, Takqua might have been alarmed over this concern posed by the owners. However, tonight, he was just too tired to care.

Stashing the plastic sack containing his bloody possessions in the closet under a pile of dirty laundry, he searched through the drawers until he found a pencil. He scribbled a brief note on the back of the original from Gerta. He explained briefly that he was fine but that he had an accident with the rental canoe and engine and he would pay for everything when he settled his bill. Then he dropped the raincoat and put on a pair of blue jeans after which he hobbled painfully downstairs and placed the note on the cash register in the lobby, where it would be found immediately by the proprietress in the morning. He certainly did not want to become the subject of a misguided search and rescue effort. Barely able to keep his eyes open, he returned upstairs and just made it into bed when he passed into a deep, trancelike sleep.

CHAPTER NINE

Cody glanced briefly back at the old cabin one last time and then set off into the woods, retracing his footsteps back to the boat. There was nothing else he could do…for now. Although nighttime, it was much easier going back. The strong, bright beam from his black metal Maglight flashlight easily illuminated the tracks he had made earlier. Cody moved through the forest as fast as he dared go. In his haste to report the crime, he wanted to ensure he didn't overlook any potential clues or evidence while walking through the woods on his return trip to the patrol boat.

Nothing made any sense to him at this point, but his mind was working on a puzzle of life-and-death proportions. He systematically reviewed what he did know, trying to put it all together. Apparently, the Toddwells had been killed earlier, but the exact time of death was an unknown. In fact, he wondered if it would ever be known. The cold temperatures could easily mask the exact time of death. They had been slain in the cabin by at least one person in Vibram boots who had trussed them to the chairs, and then tortured them to death. The bloody pool on the floor and thin strips of skin in the washbowl were a more realistic indicator of the time of death. The blood was still liquid, not fully congealed, and the skin had not frozen in place. Whoever did this crime was obviously very good with a skinning knife. The fact that they left so few clues indicated that they were obviously an expert woodsman too.

After the Toddwells were murdered, the killer dragged their bodies to the outhouse and shoved the door closed. The whys were beginning to build in his mind. Why were the Toddwells here in the first place? Why had the radio equipment been destroyed? Why had the crime taken place in the cabin, why not in the woods? Why were they tortured? Why had the bodies been decapitated? Why had the dog been killed? Why the necklace in the pool of blood? What was the howling he had heard in the hills? He just couldn't place it all together, not yet. It was all too new; too large a crime scene; too much evidence; too weird; and too remote. Solving the murders, he knew was going to be difficult ... maybe even impossible.

The return trek was uneventful and before long, he was back at the trees near where his boat was tied up offshore. Pulling on the yellow anchor line, the base of the anchor broke free of the icy water and soon the bow of the boat was nudging the shore. Cody gripped the bow rail with one hand and threw his gear onto the deck with the other, then quickly scrambled aboard. Not bothering to push the boat away from shore, Cody opened the control panel, activated the batteries and radio, and grabbed the microphone.

"Ketchikan A-2, Ketchikan A-2, this is 5-A-19, over."

After a few seconds he repeated his call. "Ketchikan, Ketchikan, this is 5-A-19. How copy? Over."

After a brief pause, he tried Tom Whitefeather.

"Twasaan, Twasaan, this is Trooper O'Keefe. How copy? Over."

The silence was eerie. Alone on a dark night in a remote area of Alaska, he might as well have been on the dark side of the moon with two corpses. The temperature was well below freezing. Putting down the mike and rubbing his cold hands together, Cody blew warm air from his breath into the cup his fingers formed and put his mitts back on. It helped a little, but not much. He had been outside for many hours now, and even properly clothed, he was beginning to feel the effects of the damp cold air and lack of food and water. He picked the mike back up and began once more, trying not to think of his personal discomfort.

"Twasaan, Twasaan, this is Trooper O'Keefe, over."

Again, there was no answer. *Tom must be asleep*, Cody thought to himself as he looked at his watch. Convinced that Tom was either asleep or the radio on the boat was out again, he made the decision to get underway for Twasaan. Minutes later, with the boat safely out in the bay and away from the shore ice, he lowered the outboard engines and cranked over the motors. The engines erupted into life and without a second thought, Cody threw the engines into gear and started for Twasaan across the bay and some 5 miles away.

The snow had been falling hard for several hours, the huge silver flakes affixing themselves to everything. He wiped his goggles again and turned on the dual spotlights to see the surface in an attempt to avoid hitting any floating ice or partially submerged logs. Even going as fast as he thought safe, it was well after 3 a.m. before he docked the patrol boat in Twasaan. Working through the ice patches was difficult enough, but finding an ice-free slip was almost impossible. He saw one at the end and headed for the slip.

As he approached the dock, he quickly cut the engine, tied the craft to the mooring cleats, and hopped out. He should have been more careful. In his haste, he lost his balance on the walkway coated with ice and snow. Cody slipped, landing on his back with a loud thump. Lying partially on the dock and partially on the low railing of the patrol boat, he tried to breathe. Pain shot through his body each time he inhaled.

O'Keefe lay there for a few minutes under the pier lights. Bright white spots like sparklers were jumping in front of his eyes. He closed his eyes and waited. Finally gathering his wits as he lay there, he mentally checked himself over. He knew he couldn't stay in that position. He had to get himself onto the pier. He started to move his extremities. Toes and fingers first, then arms and legs, lastly his neck and head. Finding nothing apparently wrong, he rolled on to his stomach, brought his knees up under his body, and unsteadily raised himself to a standing position. Severely shaken but otherwise unhurt, he picked up his gear strewn across the icy walkway of the pier and gingerly made his way up the ramp toward Tom Whitefeather's house. It had been a bad 24 hours, and it didn't look like things were getting any better.

Tom's house was actually an old mobile home, rundown even by Res standards. It was a relic of the North Slope pipeline days, so it had seen years of hard use. The village had purchased several during an auction at a great price. To keep from freezing to death in the winter, Tom had installed thick Visqueen plastic sheeting over the windows and door to help keep out the cold. Cody saw a rusty stovepipe protruding from the top of the mobile home, a white plume of smoke steadily rising into the night. Almost without conscious thought, he surmised the smoke rising straight up into the air meant a change in barometric pressure and that the weather would likely improve within the next 24 hours.

That might be the first good break we get on this case.

Just a short distance from Tom's mobile home was the community center and Tom's office, which made it convenient in winter. It took less than 5 minutes to walk there. Cody continued to labor up the steep slope from the dock to the trailer, his back still smarting from the fall. When at last he trudged up to Tom's faded light blue mobile home, he took a couple of deep breaths and knocked loudly.

"Tom, this is Cody. You in there?" He waited several seconds before trying again.

"Tom, wake up. It's me, Cody."

"Tom, you in there?"

Still nothing. At the risk of waking up one of Tom's neighbors, he tried once more ... loudly this time.

"Tom, Tom, com'on, it's me. Wake up, dammit."

This time he heard a sleepy voice ... an obviously female Indian voice.

"Go away, Tom's not here. Come back in the morn'." It said in a heavy Tlingit accent.

Cody ignored the voice. "C'mon, Tom, open up. It's me. It's an emergency. I've got to talk to you. I'm freezing out here."

Before the sentence was finished, Tom, in jockey shorts, T-shirt, and cowboy boots, opened the flimsy rust-stained metal door of the trailer. Holding the door open wide with one hand, he motioned Cody to come inside the trailer.

"Alright, alright. Jesus Christ, what the hell are you doing here at this hour of the night? I thought you'd never get here. What's happened?" followed with "Are you OK?"

"I tried to call you on the radio, but I couldn't raise you or Ketchikan," Cody replied, involuntarily shivering. He entered the home and glancing around the room, immediately found what he was looking for. The black, metal wood stove in the corner of the living room. Peeling off his parka and outer shirt, he turned his back to the huge wood stove and placed his hands behind his back to better feel the heat. Then turning around, he warmed the front of his body. It was the first real heat he had experienced in almost a day. He relished the moment, letting the heat from the stove revitalize his half-frozen body.

"Alright, this better be good," Tom said, dropping his stocky body onto the vinyl upholstered couch covered in several Chief Joseph wool blankets.

"What's up? You said it was an emergency."

Cody turned and stared at Tom. For a moment, he couldn't speak, then thoughts of the cabin scene flooded his brain.

"It's an emergency alright ... multiple homicide. Someone killed the Toddwells. At least, I *think* they were the Toddwells. This was the worse I have ever seen ... Nothing this bad before. They were tortured ... butchered and mutilated. And the worst thing is we may never know who or why. Tom, are you sure you didn't see anyone in the bay the last day or so?"

"Nope, just that red boat I told you about. Do you think whoever used the canoe was part of the crime, Cody?"

"I saw the drag marks on the shore that must have belonged to the canoe, some footprints in the immediate area. Vibram soles. Took photos and picked up what looks like blood evidence along the beach, but the canoe was long gone. There could be another explanation too, maybe a trapper. The location of the canoe was almost 2-3 miles, maybe more, from the cabin. There might not be any connection whatsoever. Does anyone in Twasaan own a canoe like that?"

Officer Tom Whitefeather thought about it a moment. "Do have some canoes around, sure, but none that color. This time of year no one goes out in a canoe. They know better. They get caught when the bay is freezing over, and they'll die. You can't paddle or push through the slush ice, and it is too thin to walk on. If someone doesn't see you stranded out there, you die from the cold."

Trooper O'Keefe rubbed his forehead and thought a minute. "Well, that might explain the Vibram soles though. Vibram soles would not be worn by an Alaskan around here. Maybe the outsider wouldn't know that. An outsider wouldn't know not to use Vibram-soled hiking boots around here "

Now Tom threw out a possibility. "Cody, Twasaan is on the longest, widest arm of the bay. On the other arm, the west arm, there is a lot of logging activity and the logging roads run all over the place. Eventually, those roads lead back to Craig, Klawock, hell, even Haidaburg. Maybe the canoe belonged to a logger? Loggers wear vibram soled boots when they work. What about that?"

"Hell, I don't know anything except it was bad. I have to get word to Ketchikan on this immediately. Can I use your radio?" Then looking around the room, Cody spied the phone next to the couch. "Better yet, how about the phone? Can I call in from here?"

"Sure, but you are going to need some privacy or the whole village will know what is going on. Let me see if I can get rid of the Indian Princess." Tom got up from the couch and yelled down the hall in the direction of the bedroom.

"Dorothy, I'm sorry, something important's come up. You're going to have to leave now. I'll stop by your place first thing in the morning."

"Screw you," a returning female voice said. "It's already morning. It's almost four-fucking o'clock in the goddamn morning. Have you looked outside? It's cold as hell and snow'n. Are you crazy?"

Tom glanced over at Cody who was now sitting on the couch

and who just looked back with his eyebrows raised. Finding no sympathy, Tom returned to his mission with a little bit more diplomacy.

"C'mon, Dot, please. This is an urgent police matter."

"Hey, dammit, I told you, I'm going to leave in the morning. Your friend can stay. It's OK with me." Dorothy slammed the bedroom door.

"Dorothy, uhhh, Dot, com'on now. Be reeasoonable ... pleeasee."

A moment later, Dot opened the bedroom door and strutted out buck-naked down the short, narrow hallway to the living room. Her presence took both Cody and Tom by surprise. As she entered the living room, Cody estimated that Dot was probably in her late twenties to early thirties, medium height, and had an athletic build for a native ... most native women ran naturally to the heavy side. He also couldn't help noticing she was well ... attractive.

Being nude, of course, didn't hurt, but Dorothy sure wasn't embarrassed either. Her facial features were aquiline, complimented by high cheekbones and brown skin that appeared to be tanned. Her eyes were as dark as midnight and flashed angrily. Her long, straight, black hair was rumpled and casually pushed back from her forehead, where it fell down around her shoulders, stopping just above her small, firm breasts.

Walking into the living room, Dot's arms were crossed around her rib cage adding support and forcing her nipples to be extended. What really piqued Cody's attention, though, was an ornate tattoo depicting a colorful bald eagle, claws and all. It was about 10–12 inches tall in total length from wing tip to the claws and ran from above her hip to her thigh. The art work was superb. Cody's first impression of Dorothy was of someone who was used to the night life, a stripper or hooker maybe, with a beauty that would soon disappear like night fading to dawn if she didn't change her lifestyle.

And she was probably, well ... cold too, without her clothes.

Seeing Dot enter the room, Tom glanced up in surprise and was about to say something, but she spoke first.

"Hey, who's this asshole?" she said pointing at Cody.

"Dorothy ... Dot, this is Trooper Cody O'Keefe from the Ketchikan Post. He has some important business, and he needs to use the phone," Tom responded.

She turned to Cody on the couch, her hands on her hips. Then looking directly at him with a piercing stare, she said testily, "So, you like the eagle, huh? Got it in Anchorage. I'm from the Eagle clan, you know ... born in Hoonah."

In Cody O'Keefe's mind, it confirmed the stripper theory. With that, Dot turned sideways, jutting out her hip, showing Cody the full eagle which wrapped around her upper leg. The carefully drawn raptor had shaded brown feathers and white wing tips which reached toward her waist. The rest of the bald eagle was just as exquisitely tattooed, the colors flowing down her body in various shades and hues of brown, cream, beige, and ebony. It was hard for Cody to ignore the fierce outstretched claws of the big bird which reached forward across her thigh, sharp, well-detailed talons fully exposed.

"See ... here," she said pointing as she moved seductively closer toward him, dropping her hand to the tattoo. Now Cody's face was not more than a couple of feet from the triangle of her pubic hair. "The eagle has its wings back, 'cause it's comin' home. It's goin' to land soon."

As she spoke, her slender index finger with a carefully painted red fingernail traced the outline of the tattoo, finally stopping at the very end of one of the extended claws. Then, very slowly, she began to move her finger from the pointed tip of the yellow and orange talons toward her inner thigh. Stopping at about the inner bikini line, she looked at Cody and hissed, "and I just bet you can't fuck'n wait for me to show you the eagle's nest down there, huh?"

Cody blushed and looked at her apologetically. "Sorry, I didn't mean to stare," he said as he got up from the couch and walked back to the stove. *This room is suddenly getting awfully small. I'm over forty and should know better,* he thought.

"Jesus H. Christ, Dot, what the hell do you think you're doing!?" Tom looked at her angrily. She knew Tom was in no mood for her games, but she defiantly stood her ground. Frustrated, Tom turned to Cody, obviously uncomfortable.

"Shit, Cody, let's just go over to the damn office where we can talk in private. Never mind, Dot, thanks for nothing."

Dot grinned smugly. She had won. The place was hers until morning, maybe until noon.

Cody looked over briefly at Dot. "Nice meeting you, I guess." He was still nonplussed. He could see in that brief moment Dot was still smiling but her glaring stare sent him a different message.

"No, it's not," she replied pointedly.

Cody noticed Tom had already grabbed his wrinkled denim jeans off the floor and had started putting them on. Dorothy turned around and walked back into the bedroom, slamming the door so hard the whole mobile home shook. The bedroom lights were out a second later. By now, Tom, fully dressed, was cinching his large, colorful beaded belt buckle with a Southwest Indian pattern on the face. He grabbed his weapon and holster off a hook near a tiny kitchen table which was festooned with a half-empty plastic milk container, dirty glasses, a half-filled bottle of Southern Comfort, and two plates holding the cold remnants of steak, rice, and beans. He wrapped the heavy leather Sam Browne gun belt with a stamped, basket-weave pattern around his waist and adjusted his pistol and the load. Cody, looking around the small home, saw pieces of rare meat and coagulated blood on the dinner plates from the last meal and almost vomited.

Opening the front door, Tom called to the back of the trailer, "When I come back, you better have this damn place cleaned up, Dot." Tom knew the chances of that happening were slim to none, but he wanted to get his digs in anyway.

"Fuck you, Lawman!" resounded from the back of the darkened trailer.

The cold, crisp air cut like a knife as the two law enforcement officers stepped out into the winter, negotiating their way down the narrow, and now frozen slick, path which led to the office. On the way, Tom filled Cody in on Dot.

"Don't be too critical of her," he said, shaking his head apologetically. "Life's been pretty hard for someone her age."

Tom explained how he had first met Dorothy, or Dot, as she sometimes called herself, when he first arrived in Twasaan. They seemed to hit it off right from the start. They were both considered different by the community. He was the outsider, and she was the outlaw, at least as far as tribal elders were concerned. Tom was immediately moved when she told him about herself, but she wanted none of his sympathy. She was tough and independent. Her story was typical but with an unusual twist.

"She lost touch with the culture when she became a teenager. Too wild, too crazy ... another rock 'n' roll rebel."

Tom spoke without glancing over at Cody. "The story's pretty tragic," he said his breath forming vapor plumes as he pronounced each word. "Her parents really had a hard time taking care of her, so they sent her from Hoonah to some relatives in Ketchikan for high school. There wasn't a whole lot of parental guidance. Dot lasted 2 or 3 years, then dropped out or was kicked out. Her parents were mad as hell and brought her back home, but as soon as she turned 18, she left home for Anchorage ... just lived by slumming around. You know the routine, sex, drugs, and rock 'n' roll. Partying all the time with oil-field workers, loggers, military ... anyone with money and looking for a good time."

"Yeah, I know. Hell, I've seen it. Anchorage can be one tough town," the trooper replied.

"Well," Tom continued while readjusting the hood on his parka, "the story gets a lot worse. She got into some abusive relationships with these party guys, whites mostly. One of her supposed boyfriends, a drug dealer, got her hooked on coke so she could start turning tricks for him. She began dancing at one of the sleazy strip joints and taking johns on C Street to pay for her habit. Eventually, she got herself arrested, which probably saved her life, and did 30 days in the Anchorage Correctional Facility, and another month of mandatory detoxification and education. When she finally got out, she left town."

"Where'd she go, back to Hoonah?" Cody asked, hands thrust deep in his coat pockets and trying to keep warm.

"Yep, but just long enough to grab a bag, fresh change of clothes, and catch the next jet for Seattle ... said she wanted to start a new life. The problem was that she didn't know anybody and had no education ..."

"So she starts right back into the sex, drugs, and the rock 'n' roll scene," Cody finished the sentence.

"You got it. Started drinking heavily and doing drugs with the GIs from Ft. Lewis. When she finally hit bottom, she was dancing in one of the big nude clubs off SEATAC and hooking tourists and

GIs on the side. It was only a matter of time before the city cops or the MPs busted her again," Tom said, shaking his head.

"Anyway, she eventually gets arrested. This time, though, she draws a female public defender, who, fortunately, turns out to be an Alaskan native with a family in Juneau. The attorney is a well respected person in the Alaska Native Sisterhood and the Alaska Federation of Natives. The judge wants to sentence Dot to 2 years in King County jail for prostitution and possession, and a mandatory completion of detoxification at the Native Public Health Clinic. Thing is, this public defender talks to the judge and convinces him it is in the best interest of the community if she could have another chance. So the judge tells Dot that he will suspend all but the detox time and time served, if Dot writes a 50-page paper on the history of Hoonah, her clan, and the Southeast Alaska native culture."

"What happened?"

"It changed her life, Cody," Tom said. "While in detox, Dot started researching Alaska native history during the Russian-American period, the Tlingits ... the whole bit. Gets totally involved in her roots and tribal culture. She finished her paper, got clean, got released, and looked for a safe haven to pull herself together. Dot has relatives here in Twasaan, so she moved in with them for a time and then got a place of her own. Around here, they say she probably knows more about the Native American culture in general, and the Tlingit culture in Southeast, specifically, than do most scholars and university professors. Speaks quite a bit of the Tlingit language too. But the experience really hardened her, Cody. She hardly ever leaves the village. Doesn't drink or do drugs anymore. Says alcohol and drugs are the worst diseases brought by the whites to subjugate the Indians; chemical warfare. The combination of the self-education process and total emersion in Indian culture left her very bitter and extremely anti-white."

"Really? I hadn't noticed, Tom," Cody looked over at him. He could see Tom was smiling. Cody was smiling too.

Arriving at the community business office building, Tom pulled off his gloves and, reaching into the deep front pocket of his thick parka, and pulled out a large key ring. Working the brass lock, they entered the building through the side door. Tom flicked on the dim florescent hallway lights. Seconds later, the two men stood in front of the scarred wooden door marked *Tribal Law Enforcement* in black plastic adhesive lettering and, just beneath, the words *Tom Whitefeather, VPSO.* They entered the brightly lit room and turned on the police radios. Tom left to get water for coffee; it was going to be a long day. After a few moments to let the radio warm up, Cody tried Ketchikan once again.

"Ketchikan A-2, Ketchikan A-2, this is 5-A-19, over."

The response crackled back immediately. "This is Ketchikan, 5-A-19."

"Ketchikan A-2, this is 5-A-19. Be advised there has been a multiple 10-94 at the cabin on Twasaan Bay." Cody used the 10 code for homicide to convey what had transpired.

"10-4, 5-A-19. Understood. Can you be contacted by land line?"

"10-4, Ketchikan, I'll try in a couple of minutes."

"5-A-19, understood. We'll be standing by."

"Ketchikan A-2, 5-A-19. 10-4."

Tom Whitefeather already had the phone at the ready. Cody quickly dialed the telephone number of the Ketchikan Post. A few minutes later, he was connected to dispatch. Fortunately, Lorie Henderson, one of the oldest and most experienced dispatchers, was on duty.

"Cody what happened? Can you talk?"

"Yeah, but I don't know how much we can rely on the line not being compromised. Here's what I need. You have to wake up our new lieutenant and tell him I am at the VPSO office in Twasaan. Tell him that I followed up on his assignment from yesterday morning. Everyone at the cabin, including the dog, is dead. It's real bad, and we're going to need help from the Criminal Investigation Bureau here as soon as possible. In the meantime, I could use some help with security and photography in the morning. I will ask Tom Whitefeather if he can assist until CIB arrives. I haven't had any sleep, so I might try and grab some sleep here at the VPSO office until you call back."

"OK, Cody, I'll get back to you as soon as possible."

Hanging up, Cody turned to Tom. "Let me fill you in on all the details. You're not going to believe it." Cody went on to explain what he found at the cabin, the blood all over the cabin floor, and the mutilated corpses of the old couple, Dr. and Mrs. Toddwell.

"It was weird. Looks to me like they were actually skinned alive! Tom, it was incredible. Their bodies had been flayed, the strips of flesh placed in a washbowl. Sometime in the process, they were both decapitated."

"Jesus! And the maniac or maniacs are still out there."

"He, she, or they are not only out there, I'm not sure we're going to solve this one. Everything is against us. It's in a remote location, no witnesses, no weapon, and no apparent motive. Hell, even Nature is working against us on this one."

Tom watched Cody in silence as he continued. "The really sick thing is that it looks to me like he tortured one to death before he started working on the other. I've never seen anything like it. It must have taken a long time for those folks to die."

Tom asked some preliminary questions, the routine cop talk of who, what, why, when, where, and how. Cody gave him what he knew, including the necklace he had found. Then, reaching into his pocket, he retrieved the blood-coated necklace and held it to the light.

"Look at this, Tom. I found it in a pool of blood. It looks like an Indian necklace to me," Cody said as he passed the jewelry over to Tom.

"Whoaa! Isn't this evidence? You should have left it there," Officer Whitefeather admonished.

"Yeah, I know, but there is something about this thing, and besides, I had already photographed the scene with the necklace in it," Trooper O'Keefe responded.

"Well, it could be Southwest Indian, maybe Navajo or Hopi, but I don't think so. This thing is different somehow. The triangular shape of the center bead, the broad bands of color, and then there are these strange carved bone beads on either side of the triangular bead, they're different too," Tom opined.

"Is there some meaning?"

"There has to be a meaning to this one. It's about as authentic as it gets. This isn't tourist shop stuff, this is the real McCoy. Only thing is, I don't have a clue what it could mean." Tom pensively continued to massage the bead between his thumb and index finger. It was smooth to the touch. "I should probably have more knowledge about these things, but I don't. When I was a kid growing up on the reservation, we really weren't encouraged to study native culture. The teachers all focused on how to prepare us Indians to assimilate into society. As I got older, I just wanted to forget the all traditions and get on with life."

Cody shifted in his chair. He was well aware of the long-term effects of the massive cultural eradication efforts undertaken by well-meaning missionaries in the nineteenth century and the continuing effect that groundwork has on tribal life today.

"Tom, what about Dot? Do you think she might know something about a necklace like this?"

CHAPTER TEN

After 30 minutes of impatiently waiting for Ketchikan to call back, Cody was almost ready to call dispatch again when the phone rang. Tom reached over, picked up the black receiver, and held it out to Cody.

"I'm sure it's for you."

It was.

Cody brought the phone to his ear and said, "Trooper O'Keefe."

"Trooper O'Keefe, this is Lt. Blocker here."

"Yes sir," Cody said, waiting.

"Tell me again what is going on. Dispatch called and said that you discovered the Toddwells have been murdered."

"Yes sir, well, that's probably correct. I have two bodies at the cabin and they are probably the Toddwells. That's correct." Cody spent the next few minutes briefly filling in the lieutenant on all the details over the last hours beginning from his initial assignment to finally making the call to Ketchikan. He purposefully omitted the part about the Indian necklace.

"OK, Trooper, here's what we're going to do. I'm not able to send anyone over there this morning in this weather. It's already crappy and may be deteriorating. But I will call CID now. They should be able to get to Ketchikan by midafternoon, 1500 or so. That means that if the weather settles down, and with refueling and all that, the best I can do is to have a full investigative team there by late afternoon ... *if* we get a break in the weather."

"Yes sir. I understand. The area is remote and with the winter storms and all, I'm sure the crime scene will be safe until CID gets to it. As for the team, it would probably be best if they flew into the village of NewTwasaan. The bay is iced over on the cabin side, and so the floatplane won't be able to reach shore anyway. If they come here first, I can use the patrol boat to shuttle them over."

"OK. Let's use that as the plan for now. And Trooper, don't go back over and start messing around. The Fish and Wildlife Division doesn't do this sort of thing very often. I don't want any mistakes on this investigation. It's bad enough that it's in the middle of nowhere. The forensics on this will probably be shit. Call back at 0800, and I should have an update."

"Lieutenant, I understand. But I have more experience investigating crimes in the bush than almost anyone in the detachment. I'd like to stay around and help the CID investigators."

"O'Keefe, look, they have their job, we have ours. This isn't a search and rescue anymore; it's a body recovery and homicide case. I'll offer your help, but that's all. CID has a good track record."

Cody could tell by the voice that the lieutenant was stressed. As a newly promoted supervisor, Cody knew that he wanted to make a good impression on his first big-crime case.

Cody chose to ignore the barb, and instead, responded with another "Yes sir."

"Alright, everything clear? Is there anything else?"

"Got it, Lieutenant. When the trooper notifies the next of kin, we probably should try and find out exactly what the professor and his wife were doing here in the middle of winter, because they sure as hell weren't vacationing."

"I'll do what I can and pass on anything I know. That's it for now, Trooper O'Keefe. I appreciate all your work and effort. Let's let the professionals take over from here. You remain available to answer their questions and provide area support."

The last sounded a little too patronizing to Cody. He was pissed but kept his cool, responding with yet another "Yes sir."

Then he added, "I will call back at 0800." Cody passed the phone back to Tom, who hung it up slowly.

"Cody, what did he say?" Tom looked concerned. "All I got on this end was a bunch of 'yes sirs' and then your face turned real red."

"Well, for one thing, he told me I was one hell of an investigator, best he's ever seen and he's certain I'll have this thing wrapped up in no time."

"Yeah, right." The stress of the moment made the comment somehow comical to the two lawmen, and they both broke out laughing.

"OK, so now what, Cody?" Tom left his chair and in two steps had reached the coffee pot. He poured a large cup of coffee into a plastic thermal cup, the kind you get in the major gas stations.

Tom extended his arm and passed the cup over to Cody saying, "Does your lieutenant want you to stay here? Is there anything I can do to help?" Tom sat back down in his chair and propped his cowboy boots on top of the desk.

"We're pretty much free until 0800. The CID won't arrive until this afternoon, if at all." Glancing at his watch, Cody noted that it was now well after 5 a.m., but the adrenaline of the moment and the coffee was working. He was tired but not sleepy. Cody took another long draw from his coffee cup and looked at Tom. "What do you say we wake up your sleeping Indian Princess and ask her about the necklace?"

They drained the last of the coffee from their cups and left the office, leaving the radio gear and the lights in the building on. Then the two lawmen renegotiated the slippery traverse back to Tom's mobile home. The walk back through the snow and ice was made in silence. Only their footsteps could be heard crunching through the fresh snow; each lawman deep in his own thoughts. Arriving at the mobile home, they noticed that the lights were back on in the small trailer and a heavy smoke was escaping the chimney. Dot was awake.

Tom entered the home quietly first and saw Dot, now fully dressed, in tight blue jeans and a baggy beige sweatshirt with an Indian bead motif embroidered on the front and shoulders. Sitting at the small dinette table, her hands wrapped around a cup of coffee, she looked up as they entered.

"Hey, Dot, how come you're up?" Tom asked cheerfully.

"Who isn't? As soon as you guys turned on the lights at the community center, the phone started ring'n. Everyone wanted to know what was go'n on."

"What did you say?" Tom asked, concerned.

"Hell, didn't say anyth'n. They all knew more than I did. They told me that there is a state patrol boat tied at the dock and wanted to know what the Alaska State Troopers were do'n in town."

"So what did you say?" he asked again.

By now, Cody had also entered the room, which constituted the living room and dining nook. Dripping melted snow on the blue heather-colored shag carpet, he busied himself with taking off his brown nylon parka and leather palmed mittens.

"I told'em that was your business, I didn't know anyth'n ... yet. What is going on anyway?" she asked.

Tom, unzipping his heavy olive green nylon parka with wolverine trimmed hood and taking off his boots by the door, looked over at Cody. The trooper had hooked his brown nylon parka on a peg near the door and glanced over at Dot.

"Is it Dorothy or Dot?" he said, evading the question.

"Dot, to my friends."

"I hope someday we can be friends," Trooper O'Keefe replied. Then he continued. "Something happened to a couple of folks across the bay, and we may need your help."

"Help? How can I help you?" she asked. Her glance and body language signaled to Cody that she still hadn't warmed up to him. O'Keefe pulled out a scratched chrome metal chair with thin vinyl padding from the dining table and sat down across from Dorothy.

"I have something I want to show you. Tom says that you are an acknowledged expert in native cultures, especially Southeast Alaska native cultures."

"Well, not an expert by white standards. I don't have a formal education, noth'n like that. But I have studied the culture of our people and learned the ways of our forefathers and ... mothers. Did you know that the Tlingits were a matriarchal society before being 'civilized' by the white man?"

"Yes, I did," he responded. He could detect the look on Dorothy's face soften a little.

Reaching into his pocket, Cody withdrew the necklace and passed it over to her. He could feel the electricity of the moment immediately fill the air. She held the necklace gently in the open palm of her hand, then closed her eyes while running her index finger across the surface of the center bead. Then she opened her eyes and examined the edges of the triangular bead and the row of unusual beads carved with the shape of animals on either side.

"Where did you get this? What is this goop all over the necklace? It looks like dried blood." Then realizing what she had just said, her eyes widened. "What shaman died?"

"Shaman!?" Cody and Tom both exclaimed in unison.

Tom Whitefeather had already unbuckled his gear, took off his coat, and hung it up in its usual place on a hook next to the door. He pulled another chrome chair up to the tiny metal dining table with a yellow vinyl top.

"Dot, why do you think a shaman died?"

"Because this is the real thing. See, you can run your finger across the bead. There is no seam. It's perfectly smooth. The design is like a burial bead necklace, only a different kind. It's not like the ones the royalty were buried with when they died. This one is special. It was used by a shaman in ceremonies to walk in the land of the dead. You know ... talk to the spirits of the dead shamans and for shape-shifting ceremonies."

Cody looked over at Tom Whitefeather and then began. "Dorothy, we want to keep this information just between us, OK? The blood on the necklace is real, but it came from an old couple that were murdered, probably yesterday or the day before, across the bay at the old trapper cabin on the river. They were just tourists or campers. I found the necklace at the cabin but cannot figure out what it has to do with the homicides. It just doesn't make sense. Maybe there is no connection at all," he surmised.

"So this necklace is more like some sort of a talisman, but for what?" Tom asked, looking at the triangular bead.

"Like a telephone to the spirit world."

Cody raised his eyebrows and shot her a questioning look. "A telephone?"

"You asked me, alright!?" she said angrily. "I'm trying to help you. To explain the symbolism to you in a way that you'll understand. Now, do you want to know about the necklace or not?" Dot was visibly upset at the implication that her credibility might be challenged.

Officer Whitefeather intervened. "Hey, hey, take it easy, Dot. He doesn't mean anything by it. We're just asking, OK? You're the expert, and we're just here learning. Hell, when I first saw the damn thing, I thought it might be Hopi or Navajo."

"OK, then listen to me ... both of you idiots. This isn't Navajo, Hopi, or Arapaho, or any other known tribe. This necklace is more than a talisman. It doesn't ward off evil spirits. This is different, more powerful; it helps you talk, or communicate, with the spirits of dead shamans who can help to change the wearer from human form to animal form. The wearer can walk in the spirit world.

She held the centerpiece of the necklace up to the exposed lightbulb hanging above the cramped table. "See, look at the bead in the middle. It's like a burial bead ... triangular. See these bands? The first black band signifies the void before conception and birth. The second band made from white abalone shell signifies coming to the light. Birth, youth, and innocence. That sort of thing. The turquoise band, the third one, means maturity and wisdom. And the last black band means death, and a return to the void from which we came ... the journey between the eternities. Now, the other beads signify movement when traveling between the eternities. Not reincarnation, but the ability to enter and exit the spirit world," she explained.

"Do you understand what I am trying to say?" she finally asked.

"Nope," the lawmen replied together shaking their heads.

Tom leaned over the table to get a better look at the necklace. He thought for a moment before he responded. Cody was at a loss for words. He just stared at Dot, not knowing what to think.

Cody broke the silence by asking Dorothy the question which would change the way he viewed this entire investigation.

"What do you know about shamans?" he queried Dorothy.

"What do *you* know?" she challenged in reply.

Trooper O'Keefe gave Dorothy and Tom a thumbnail sketch. "Historically, all the cultures in Alaska had ceremonies and believed in spirits. All had a 'shaman,' a medicine man, incorporated into their beliefs. Many Indian cultures still believe in the ancient spirits—both good and bad." He also knew that Indian beliefs had collided with Christianity and that missionaries were responsible for systematically eradicating the ancient belief structure from the villages they preached in until it ceased to be a religion at all. He didn't mention that part to Dot.

"And you are sure this necklace was used by, or belonged to, a shaman?" Tom inquired of Dot.

"There is no other explanation. The two beads on either side of the triangle, see? Each is exactly the same. Special carved bone beads with black ends. Most likely human. Wisdom from the dead. The other beads in the necklace in the shape of animals, they look a lot like a fetish and tell a story too. They are the special ceremonial beads. I've heard about necklaces like this before but never knew they really existed until now."

Cody took the necklace back and examined it closely. "Are you sure, Dorothy? I mean, why can't this be just another Indian beaded necklace?"

Dot's temper flared again. "You don't get it do you? Do you

think I'd make this up? Look for yourself! The beads are real; they are authentic. No, Trooper Cody, whatever your last name is, this necklace, and what it means, and is as real as the dried blood all over the necklace. Just because this is the only one I've ever seen don't mean I don't know what I'm looking at." Dot's lips tightened to a thin line, and her jaw muscles tensed as she looked at Cody.

"Dorothy, chill, OK?" Cody said. "I'm just asking questions. You are really helping us ... really."

Tom took the necklace and slid it across the table top back to Dot, who picked it up and started to examine the piece of jewelry again. She explained that she first began her studies by learning from the tribal elders who, after they got to know her better, would also teach her about theology and the natural order of the universe. She learned things that could not be found behind the cool glass panes in educational institutions in the cities like Anchorage, Juneau, and Ketchikan, or even museums like the Smithsonian. There are some things that only an insider who was totally submerged in the culture could understand. This was the part of tribal history which was more elusive ... more intangible.

As she explained it, the shamans of the Pacific Northwest and Alaska tribes were herbalists, spiritualists, magicians, psychics, and psychologists. Each shaman was special and had a sacred duty to the village, the clan, and the tribe. She tried to explain to Tom and Cody in so many words that the beliefs of the Indians were based in an archaic, primitive religion, consisting of a complex alchemy between the natural and the supernatural, the physical and the spiritual. There wasn't the separation of the two worlds like the Christian beliefs. The old religion was alive, something so strong that it mocked the concept of time and space. She believed that spiritual entities could live quietly in the deep, dark recesses of the old-growth forests and the subconsciousness of the Tlingit, Haida, and Tshimsian. And by bringing the living religion to the tribe, a shaman was held in high regard. They were more powerful than a priest or a holy man from the plains tribes.

This strong underlying belief structure—a spirituality brought to this wilderness eons ago from some unknown region ... has been quietly kept alive for thousands of years. A boreal chronology captured centuries before Western civilization in the tales of heroes, heroines, and deeds of bravery, mythical kingdoms, and common folklore. The feats of daring and arduous journeys by warriors and heroes of the tribes were recorded forever in carvings of wood and verbal history and always based in these strong spiritual beliefs. Part of these beliefs included these mystical, mythical demigods and half-human animals which haunt the dim forest floors, float the solitary rivers, and permeate the aura in the vast tracks of this primeval wilderness. The shaman connected the tribe to these gods and explained natural phenomenon.

As Dot continued speaking, Cody instinctively understood. *You don't have to argue the existence of their beliefs—it instantly becomes apparent in the overwhelming solitude when you are alone in the rain forest. You feel the power of the spirits on the small hairs at the nape of your neck, hear their breathing in the heavy raindrops and screeching cries of the eagles, smell their presence in the moss and the decaying hulks of the fall trees, taste their existence in the clear mountain streams, and see them walk in the form of wisps of mist rising from the forest floor*, he thought. Time faded away as Dot told the two lawmen about how the Indians viewed shamans as the bridge or the link between the animal, spirit, and human worlds. She gave examples of how the ancient shaman could induce deathlike states, kill enemies, and make slaves hemorrhage, unravel the mystery of dreams and even have out-of-body experiences. A shaman would impress the villagers with incredible feats of self-torment and pain control, such as sticking knives through their sides, then walking around the longhouse singing war songs.

"A shaman can control his body temperature, foresee the future, experience an incredible amount of pain, and never show it. Most of all, the shaman had great powers, or at least could create illusions of great powers," Dot had summed up her discussion.

"Are you saying that this happens even today?" Officer Whitefeather asked.

"No, of course not," Dot replied. "The white man ruined all that. Christianity replaced the worship of nature and natural phenomena. The real shamans were killed or discredited by missionaries and their converts. Today, a shaman, if he is even known, is more like a tribal counselor. They have lost their real power."

"Did these shamans ever have evil practices, you know, devil worship or something?" Cody asked.

"No," she replied pensively, "not like what you are thinking. But like all holy men, they sought power from the spirit world. Only a very few, and only the most powerful, were reputed to be shape-changers, the only ones who could move in both worlds. These few eventually became the legend of the Kushtikaws."

"What do you know about Kushtikaws? Do you believe they ever existed?" Tom Whitefeather asked.

"That's a difficult question to answer. In Indian mythology, Kushtikaws are represented by the symbol of the Raven, the trickster. The Raven, as seen by the clans, is a gregarious spirit who often plays tricks on the people to get his way. The Raven can also be a comical character when his tricks backfire on him. There is a darker side to the Raven though. The Raven can also play tricks by changing shape or taking on human or animal forms and appearing real. Because of this, Kushtikaws use the Raven to denote shape-changing power. Is it true? Who knows enough to speak of such things? That knowledge and power were lost to us forever."

Trooper Cody O'Keefe looked over at Dorothy and then back at Tom. "Why are you so sure? Couldn't someone still study the old ways?"

"It is not that easy," Dot explained. "To understand the significance in Tlingit culture, you have to hold the deep belief many of us have about Kushtikaws, the shaman shape-changers. There are many well documented stories about men, women, and children who are seen walking by themselves on a deserted stretch of beach where they see an unusual animal who entices them into the woods and then steals their souls. Once their soul is stolen, they never leave the forest and return home. Some say the animals even talk to their victims because they are actually shape-shifters in disguise. Today, mothers often warn their children not to walk far from home or play in the woods by themselves because the Kushtikaws might get them. There is mystery within this myth because no one has ever seen a Kushtikaw change shape. Although through oral history there have been one or two evil shamans who have been expelled from a tribe, usually, as the story goes, the Kushtikaw changes shape to an animal and they go live in the forest forever," she responded.

Dot glanced over at Cody O'Keefe. "Your name is Irish, right?"

The trooper nodded.

"Well, did you know that in the Celtic culture, many of your Druids were considered to be shape-changers that could change to night birds and fly great distances, ride dreams into the future, and even communicate by mental telepathy to another person miles away? Shape-changing isn't just some aboriginal tale thought up by ignorant Indians in remote parts of the world."

"I believe you," Cody said.

"Why? Because of the Druids?" Dot asked skeptically.

"No, because I believe not everything can be easily explained. There are forces of good and evil in this world that transcend religion. Let me share something with you. Once on patrol I had something strange happen to me. Maybe it was a Kushtikaw."

Dot scoffed, "Kushtikaw? And you're still here to talk about it?"

"Hold on a minute, Dot," Tom said, also skeptically. "This ought to be good."

"OK, I know what you are thinking, but you want me to have an open mind, and I want you to have one too. There could be a connection to the murders at the cabin." Trooper Cody O'Keefe set the stage. "I patrol all over lower Southeast. Most of my time is in the rain forest, miles from any town or Indian village. And I will agree with Dot that strange things, unexplainable things, can happen when you are out by yourself. Just being a nonbeliever will not protect you. It makes you more vulnerable because you are ignorant."

Cody then began to describe his own strange experience months before. He didn't want to talk about it, but at the same time, he thought it might be important. He hoped that by analyzing what happened, he could somehow rationalize what had transpired. The *incident* as he preferred to call it, happened during a patrol to Naha Cove ... if it wasn't so real he could almost believe he dreamt it up ... almost.

"There is a lot to this, but here is what happened. I was on a patrol near the Canadian border ... Dixon Entrance ... the day was much like this one—the weather was deplorable and the winds were high," he said, getting into the story. Cody explained that a fierce gale had brewed up in the icy waters of the Gulf of Alaska and, picking up momentum along the Queen Charlotte Islands, had swiftly moved across the Dixon Entrance, slamming full force into lower Southeast Alaska. After fighting the seas for several hours trying to get back home to Ketchikan, I began to look for a place to bivouac until the storm abated. "I was at least 45 miles south of Ketchikan, the closest city in Alaska, and about the same distance north from Prince Rupert, the closest city in Canada. Traveling that distance in my patrol boat during a full gale was simply out of the question. I had never entered the cove before, but checking the chart, I knew the waters would be deep enough to navigate the patrol vessel to safety.

It was early afternoon when I located the small tranquil body of water identified on the chart by a light blue indentation in the beige topography. The waters of Naha Cove are shallow and deemed not navigable by most mariners. But I surmised that this would keep most boats from using the cove for refuge. However, my patrol vessel needed less than 2 feet of water depth to maneuver, and there was plenty of water for that. The cove also posed other natural barriers to would-be explorers and fishermen. It was totally protected from the outside world by a shallow rocky reef running across the entire length of the mouth of the remote cove. At extreme low tides, the mouth would actually dry up. Anyone in the small cove during a spring tide would be a prisoner of the time and tide for hours until the incoming tide submerged the rocky entrance once again."

Cody remembered well nudging the patrol vessel over the natural breakwater constructed of rocks and sand, and watching the bottom abruptly rise to meet his boat and then submerge quickly as he breached the barrier and floated quietly into Naha Cove. It was only after he had positioned the craft in the middle of the tiny cove and turned off the engine that he began to notice an eerie silence that was so pervasive it seemed to envelope the area. This unsettling pall was so acute that Cody could actually hear the low waves lapping the shore, although the beach was more than 25 yards away. Dismissing all this as fatigue, he poured himself a cup of tea from the rust-spotted Stanley steel thermos lying on the bench seat of the boat, then settled down to eat lunch in the light, cold rain. At first, he tried paying a little less attention to his surroundings and more to his sandwich, consisting of a thick slice of Jarlsberg cheese between two slices of dry German black bread which he washed down with the strong, hot tea, however, he still could not shake this uneasy feeling that something was amiss.

Casually glancing at the shoreline, nothing really looked out of place. The day was misty, and a light drizzle continued to fall slowly to earth, soaking everything not protected. From his vantage, Cody could see the tall conifers that encircled the cove and marveled as he watched the treetops being whipped and torn by the forceful gusts of wind that barely rippled the water in the tiny protected cove. Sitting back on the bench seat, Cody poured another cup of tea and surveyed the beach. He noticed that like most of the coastal areas, seaweed draped over slick black rocks which littered the cove. Further inshore, the boulders gave way to a coarse, brown, sandy beach which was bordered by the ubiquitous wall of massive fir trees with long sweeping boughs. He was sitting in the boat, staring at nothing in particular, when the hair on the back of his neck began to tingle. Cody vividly remembered feeling he was being watched. Resorting to logic, he tried to dismiss this sensation by turning his thoughts to the details of the pending bivouac, the trip home, official reports ... anything at all. However, the persistent feeling gradually permeated his subconscious until he could think of nothing else. There was no way he could bivouac comfortably, knowing someone, or something, was watching him. In exasperation, he dug through the messy console in front of him until he found his gray Nikon 10 x 50 armor-coated binoculars and began to carefully scan the tree line.

Cody spent the next several minutes trying to detect anything out of the ordinary, but the tall trees were not immune to the howling wind high above the storm-protected cove which sent the trees gently swaying, effectively concealing sight and sound. As his mind and eyes adjusted to the natural pattern of the forest, he spotted an animal stealthily traveling between the large rocks scattered along the shoreline. Raising the binoculars to his eyes, he identified the little furry animal as an otter, it's shiny, sleek, ebony coat blending with the deep colors of the mussels and the dark shadows of the large boulders.

Cody continued to closely monitor the otter's progress with his binoculars, watching as it hunted for food between two large barnacle-encrusted boulders. Then he saw—or thought he saw—two blue orbs of light in the deep recesses of the tree line above the otter. He refocused the binoculars to try and sharpen the image. Now Cody could faintly make out the distinct specks of color periodically hidden by the graceful swaying of the trees. His curiosity heightened, and he moved the binoculars back and forth across the area, trying to identify the source of the lights. The area was too remote for humans; besides, he would have seen a boat, a fire, a tent, or some other sign of human occupation. There wasn't any. His methodical search of the tree line picked up the two specks of light again, and he quickly focused the rings on the binoculars, trying to concentrate on just the glimmer of luminescence. He instantly felt a shot of electric adrenaline course through his body. They weren't lights at all—they were more like eyes!

Increasing curiosity rapidly replaced the surge of surprise as his mind scrambled for a logical explanation. The eyes, if they were eyes, were too high off the ground to be a bear and certainly were not human! *Deer maybe? No, not in this wind; the deer are all bedded down*, he thought, dismissing that idea. He knew animals' eyes would shine white at night when caught in the beam of a bright light, but this was daylight and the orbs were blue! He kept the binoculars trained on the phenomenon when he noticed the otter heading directly toward the bluish orbs. He watched in fascination as the sleek animal worked its way slowly into the tree line directly below the peering blue eyes. While Cody watched, both the otter and the blue orbs simultaneously disappeared. He was in awe. He couldn't even put down the binoculars. Cody had never seen anything like this before, and he remained transfixed, staring at the spot for almost a half hour more, but neither the otter nor the blue orbs reappeared.

Patrolling in the remote Alaska wilderness can affect one's sensibilities, especially if you are all by yourself, Cody knew that. He was aware that in nature often things weren't at all as they first appeared and behind each mystery there was usually a logical explanation. He knew that what could present itself as menacing or threatening was often just an anomaly.

His curiosity getting the better of him, he resigned himself to exploring the area after lunch. He was about to turn his attention to finishing his sandwich and tea when suddenly the acid feeling in the pit of his stomach returned. Now he was sure he was being watched! Grabbing the binoculars, Cody searched the tree line once more. They were there again, in the same spot, the blue eyes steadily peering back at him. His investigative curiosity peaked. It now had the better of him. He lowered the binoculars slowly while watching the general area and, feeling for the ignition keys, cranked over the twin outboards. Still looking directly at the spot in the woods where he had last seen the eyes, he turned and headed the patrol boat for shore.

Cody remembered how he had quickly planned his moves. The tide was coming in so he didn't need to worry about beaching the boat. This enabled him to gently run the vessel aground a short distance from where he had last seen the glowing eyes in the deep forest. When the vessel had just lightly touched the shore, he jumped off the bow, playing out several fathoms of 3/4 inch anchor line as he quickly walked up the beach, his sight fixed on the spot where he had seen the phenomenon. Running out of anchor line, Cody planted the sharp splayed metal flukes of the 30 lb Danforth anchor into the beach and headed toward the dark woods. The closer he came to the forest, the more difficult it became to see the eyes. Finally, when he was close to the fir trees bordering the shore, he couldn't see the bluish orbs at all.

CHAPTER ELEVEN

Cody continued telling his story to Tom and Dot in the tiny space that served as the breakfast/dinner nook. "I worked my way slowly, carefully, into the old-growth forest looking for tracks or any other kind of sign. Then I just froze. I couldn't believe my eyes. Close by were several ancient carved totem poles. Their once-brilliant colors had long since faded into dull, muted patches of pastel. The faces carved on the poles were unlike any I had ever seen. Smiling heads with human characteristics sat atop squat, artistic wolf, beaver, and otter bodies, one on top of the other. Weather and time-worn with moss growing along the north side of each pole, they still faithfully stood vigilant over the entrance of an old Indian village, long since abandoned and in total disrepair. Feeling somehow even more threatened with this discovery, I slowly reached into my wool coat, found my leather shoulder holster, thumbed the snap, releasing the leather retaining strap securing my revolver and lightly pulled on the weapon to free it in the holster. I didn't know what to expect but I sure as hell wanted to be ready."

Then Trooper O'Keefe paused and looked over at Tom and Dot.

"So what happened next?" Officer Whitefeather queried.

"Well, then it got really strange," the trooper replied. He recounted how his officer survival training took over, his senses trying to take in everything at once. Cody's eyes looked for movement, his ears strained to hear footsteps on the mossy forest floor, and his nose tested the humid pungent air for animal or human scent. Nothing! He might as well have been deaf, dumb, and blind. He could detect nothing ... nothing tangible, that is. Yet, the feeling of imminent danger was all around him. He explained how looking toward the ruins of the village, he thought he could make out the azure-colored eyes now peering at him from the darkness of the old doorway in a partially collapsed longhouse.

Cody quickly drew out his weapon and holding the revolver at the ready with both hands, moved through the woods as he had been trained. Slowly, he stalked in a half crouch, picking his route, moving carefully from cover to cover, all senses on full alert, working his way quickly and quietly toward the dark doorway where he had last seen the dim orbs. Heart pounding and adrenaline surging, he stopped at one side of the opening and positioning himself in a combat stance, did a quick peek inside.

Seeing nothing, Cody darted to the other side of the portal. Again, he quickly looked into the vast darkness of the room, and again, nothing. Satisfied, at least in part that he wouldn't be surprised, he now cautiously stepped through the portal and into the derelict longhouse. The interior of the building was cool and dank. Part of the roof had long since collapsed, the rotten timbers having given way to the elements of time and nature. Where parts of the roof still held in place, dim shafts of gray translucent light carried a wet drizzle through the gaping holes. The air was thick and smelled damp and musty. Looking around, he could vaguely make out ritualistic paintings on the walls. Similar to the totems, grotesque animals with human heads and clawed arms and legs were attacking humans. On another wall was painted a huge drab green frog with faded white spots and large black eyes leading a long string of warriors.

Now he smelled something or, more likely, felt something strange. Cody turned abruptly. A stench of decayed flesh filled the air. He sensed more than saw, an evil presence very close to him. In a crouch, he spun around in a complete circle, his weapon trained waist high at the perimeter, his finger already applying pressure to the trigger and ready to fire in a split second. *There!* his mind screamed, *over there. At the doorway!* Through the portal, Cody briefly caught sight of a human form painted in black designs and thin stripes darting behind an old cedar tree. What happened next continued to haunt him to this day.

He had shouted out, identifying himself as a trooper and calling to the person to stop running. Whoever it was, whatever it was, looked back and then ran off, taking a deer trail through the old forest. Cody instantly took up the chase, determined to end the mystery. Every now and then, he managed a brief glimpse of the fleeing figure, but it revealed little. The apparition was naked except for a carved wooden mask shaped like a raven's head. Strange designs and stripes of black were painted on the entire length of his torso and down his arms and legs—and it had a powerful effect. The form moved swiftly through the devil's club and fern, darting around fir trees and leaping over fallen logs. Cody chased the figure for what seemed like an eternity when the moss-covered forest floor suddenly gave way.

Cody explained to Tom and Dot how he remembered pitching forward, unable to stop his momentum. He fell hard into an old grave. Even now, almost a year later, his mind played back the scenario with all the terror his emotions were capable of delivering. Cody still visualized himself falling in slow motion, the force of the fall knocking the air out of his lungs, the weight of his body crushing his skeletal rib cage in a series of sharp crackling noises. A verdigris-covered skull had bounced around in the soft moss of the shallow tomb, the lower jaw separating from the skull. Cody was cognizant of being wedged facedown, in the grave, unable to move and gasping for breath. Suddenly, he sensed someone standing over him at the edge of the grave. He tried to look up, but all he could see from his perspective was a pair of bare legs, painted from the shins on down. Then he felt powerful hands on the back of his head pushing his face down into the soft earth of the grave. Reflexively, he tried to struggle for air but could not lift his head to gain a breath. Fear shot through his body like a frigid electrical current as the adrenaline surged through while he fought for his life. Just before losing consciousness, Cody heard a distant howl, not quite wolf and not quite animal.

"Now here is the part that starts to sound like I'm losing my mind. I swear I heard that same howl last night in the hills above the trapper's cabin!" Cody looked at their faces and saw the Tom and Dot were having a hard time believing him.

After a few awkward moments, Tom broke the silence. "Now what is that line in the Robert Service poem...*strange deeds are done under the midnight sun*?"

Dot was more curious than credulous. "I have never heard any'ting like that. Hell I never read any'ting like that. You sure you aren't just making this up?"

"Anyway, it is a great story go ahead and tell us what happened. You got killed right?" Tom said grinning.

Cody had no choice but to reluctantly finish the story. “Ok,” he said, “but it ends here, in this room. So here is what happended next…”

When he came to the following morning, he was no longer face down. He climbed painfully out of the shallow mossy depression and sat at its edge and pulled himself together. He was unhurt and still had his weapon, but as he stood up and looked around, Cody noticed that the grave had been desecrated. The skull was missing, and who knew what else? Cody searched the area around the ruins, but whoever robbed the gravesite had already left with artifacts belonging to the primeval tribe that once occupied this remote stretch of shoreline.

A week later, his patrol finished, Cody had returned to Ketchikan and filed the usual activity reports. He kept it brief and only mentioned he had found evidence of desecration in Naha Cove, omitting all of the bizarre events of his encounter. How could he explain what happened? Hell, if he could explain what happened, no one would believe him anyway!

When Cody finished his narrative, Tom whistled lowly, breaking the overpowering spell of the story. Dot sat quietly. Trooper O’Keefe sensed a shift in her attitude toward him now. After a long pause in which nothing was said, she looked pensively at the trooper.

Dot knew the history of the village at Naha Cove and explained it to the lawmen. It had once been prosperous and healthy. Then, some time during the late 1870s, the entire village had been suddenly decimated when one of the tribal members returned from an extended trading expedition to the white settlement called Prince Rupert with gifts and trading goods.

“One of the gifts was influenza. No one asked for that. In the end, what few Indians remained after the plague had to move on to other, larger villages or cease to exist."

"OK, but leaving the history alone for a moment, couldn't what I have seen at the village have been a shape-changer?" Cody asked, hoping for some logical explanation of an illogical event.

"You might have seen a Kushtikaw, but you are still alive, so I don't think so. Kushtikaws get their power by taking over the spirits of the living and offering them as slaves to our gods in exchange for spiritual power. Of course, having your soul stolen means slavery for eternity. Most Indians will tell you they don't believe in Kushtikaws. But some, especially the older ones, still believe in Kushtikaw legends and rarely go into the woods by themselves. They just don't talk about it to whites." Dot looked intently at Cody for a few moments. "In mythology, real Kushtikaws are the very heart of evil," she said as she took another sip of coffee, "but I never heard of Kushtikaws stealing from our ancestors' graves. Only the whites do that."

Cody knew that grave desecrations were often guised in the righteous cloth of learned archaeology. Professor Toddwell was supposedly an archeologist, and the necklace was authentic. *Is this a coincidence? Or is there perhaps another connection?* he wondered.

"Could this necklace possibly have belonged to a living Kushtikaw shaman?" Cody asked.

"Maybe," she responded deep in thought.

"But if the couple had it at the cabin, maybe they just found it in the woods. The Kushtikaw bit matches the necklace but nothing else. Of course, if they did find it, where did it come from?" Tom Whitefeather asked.

"Exactly," Cody finished.

"That is what doesn't make any sense," Dot said. "I can't tell you about the necklace, only what the necklace means. I'm just telling you, guys, that if, IF, there were a real shaman walking around with the power of the Kushtikaw, he is one, the only one, and one of our people would know about it. He would not rob graves, and he would not kill people in a cabin. Besides, no one today knows that much about the old shaman ways anyway, not even me."

Tom and Dot looked over at Cody, who was busy scribbling a long series of notes in his daily diary. He put his ballpoint pen down for a moment.

"So," he said, "let's just say for the moment that the necklace is simply an Indian artifact. Where would it have come from? It was found at the cabin, so supposedly it came from one of the victims. Is it possible that it came from that area? It doesn't appear as though the necklace was left behind on purpose; it wasn't prominently displayed ... like, perhaps, draped over a body.

"OK, listen. We know the professor was an archeologist. He chose to come here in the dead of winter. Why?"

Tom looked over at him hesitantly ... "We're not sure...."

"Right," Trooper O'Keefe replied. "But the archeologist died, and a very special Indian necklace was found at the scene of the murders. Either he had it with him from before he got there, he found it there, or someone else brought it there. Just for argument's sake, let's explore the possibility that he brought it with him."

Tom answered first. "When I worked on the reservations down south, one of the biggest problems we had was with grave robbers. People out exploring would come across an old gravesite and desecrate it, just to take any artifacts that were buried with the body."

"The same is true here in Alaska," Dot said bitterly. "Most of our ancestors moved from a winter camp to a summer camp. Sometimes the whole village was destroyed by disease or warfare.

When this happened, the village and the sacred burial grounds were slowly overgrown by the forest.

"Amateur historians, hikers, and hunters will sometimes come across these old villages. They will take whatever they can find to keep for themselves or sell. Look at all the old pieces of totem poles in front of stores and souvenir shops from Alaska to Washington, D.C. Hell, Seattle is full of 'em. Most people don't know what the shops have. I was disgusted to see a souvenir shop in downtown Ketchikan selling burial necklaces as trading beads. They were definitely old. Those necklaces could only have come from a gravesite ... or someone's private collection," she added.

"So there is a real market in authentic native jewelry?"

"You better believe there is, Cody," Tom interjected. "Especially now that the Indian collectibles are in style. The money this stuff brings has convinced a lot of folks to get into the business. Have you ever heard of the Antiquities Act?"

Cody shook his head.

"The Antiquities Act was passed at the turn of the century specifically to stop would-be explorers from destroying the Native American culture by desecrating old gravesites and selling off the artifacts." Tom pushed back his chair and walked over to the cupboard.

"How about some coffee? Dot, you want a refill?"

Cody made some more notes and looked over at Dot.

"You said you thought you saw authentic burial necklaces in Ketchikan. Did they look like this one?"

"No, burial necklaces usually have round or oval-shaped glass beads; the ones I've seen are long strands of deep royal blue and black-colored glass beads. Sometimes they also have other beads mixed in with them, but I am not sure if that really means anything." Dot pushed her plastic coffee cup over in Tom's general direction, asking for a refill.

Cody peered outside through the opaque, Visqueen-covered windows. It was still dark, but wolfdawn wasn't far behind.

"Where did you see those other burial necklaces in Ketchikan, Dot?" O'Keefe was getting familiar with Dot, and she didn't seem to mind.

"Over at the Sourdough Provisions Company, on Tongass Avenue ... they had them in the window. It's been a while since I was in town, but I'm sure I saw them there the last time. Sometimes they even try to pass them off as antique trading beads. It's enough to make you sick."

"Alright, then I guess it would be safe to say that someone like the professor and his wife wouldn't just bring something like that out into the woods. It apparently is rare, and that means it has a high commercial value beyond cultural considerations. The professor likely would have put that jewelry in safekeeping, maybe at his university. That leaves us with two other possibilities."

"Right," Dot said speaking up. "He found it, or whoever killed him wore it."

"Right," Tom echoed.

"So that leaves us with, did the killer wear it, and why did the killer wear it? We don't know the answer to either question yet. So, let's explore the possibility the professor found it. Wasn't there once an old village over there, Dot?"

Dot glanced at both of them before answering. "Yeah, there was a village over there, the old village of Twasaan."

"How come I never heard about it?" Officer Whitefeather asked.

Dot ignored the question. Cody O'Keefe asked if many people knew about the old village.

"Well, it's not a guarded secret, if that's what you mean; it's just difficult to find is all. Twasaan was a small village ... not much else to say," Dot answered.

"Would it draw someone like the professor to it, for archeological reasons?" Tom asked.

"Who knows? We don't even know what he was look'n for, or even if he was look'n for any'ting."

"Great, we've now come full circle," Cody injected.

Tom spoke up. "Let's just say that there was something he wanted, whatever that was ... would a necklace like that be the reason for his search?"

"Definitely not," Dot replied strongly. "The old village of Twasaan had a shaman, sure. Almost all the villages did. But not a powerful one like what you are talk'n about, not someone who would wear the necklace, and certainly not a Kushtikaw. The elders have never spoken of someone ... anyone like that here."

"OK, Cody, any more ideas? Where do we go from here?" Tom asked.

"Well, you both made some good points. There is a village over there; *that* could have attracted the professor ... maybe, yes ... maybe, no ... we just don't know. But what we are fairly certain of is that a necklace like this one here is something that would not likely be found in old Twasaan," Cody looked over at Dot.

"Right," Dot replied nodding her head at both of them.

"Then, you are suggesting that the killer likely wore this necklace?" Tom asked Cody.

"That's what the events and the evidence seem to be saying, *if* we are correct in our assumptions."

"Then another unanswered question which would support this theory is whether the graves at the old village have been desecrated," Tom thought aloud.

"Right, and if they have, is there anything in common with my experience at Naha Cove?"

Dot was surprised. "You still think then that the two might be somehow connected and that a Kushtikaw was responsible for the murders? Is that what you are saying?"

"I'm certainly not dismissing the possibility that anyone, including an Indian shaman, could have committed those gruesome crimes, especially since the necklace was found at the scene."

The conversation died down a bit. Cody turned and looked at the electric clock on the wall. "We're going to have to get over to your office pretty soon. I'm going to need to check in."

Then turning to Dot he said, "Thanks for all your help, Dot, I really appreciate it. Do me a favor though. Please keep this information between the three of us for now."

Tom laughed. "Dot keeping a secret will be harder than her giving up smoking."

"I can keep a secret," she said quietly to herself, deep in thought.

CHAPTER TWELVE

The gray translucent light of a midday snowstorm had already filled his room before anyone bothered to knock on his door.

"Mr. Tuttle? Mr. Tuttle? Would you care for something to eat? We didn't see you at lunch." The nasal voice belonged to Mrs. Freese, the wife of the owner of the Sportsmen's Lodge.

"Mr. Tuttle? Are you alright?"

Opening his eyes, he could barely form the words he heard himself utter. "Yes, yes, I am quite alright, thank you, Mrs. Freese, just a little tired. I will be down shortly."

"OK, well, I will get started then. Can I bring you some tea?"

"No, not now. Thank you," the voice replied.

He could hear Mrs. Freese's heavy footsteps fade away. He had determined, almost instantly, that Mrs. Freese was an overweight and overcaring frustrated figure who sought to mother her guests rather than cater to them. Since his arrival 2 weeks earlier, he had ascertained in a rather short period of time that she was nosey and somewhat pushy, especially about her cooking, which she obviously equated to enjoyment judging by the girth of both she and her husband. Takqua tolerated her unsolicited attention only because it suited his needs and made for an excellent cover. He estimated she must be in her early sixties, although her ample body hid the wrinkles normally prevalent at that age, so that she actually appeared years younger. She usually could be seen in a large patterned dress with some floral designs and often had on heavy wool socks pulled up midcalf and brown clogs, a possible hint at her Scandinavian ancestry. She wore her light gray hair twisted into a bun which sat perched on the back of her head, several strands of hair hanging loose across her forehead. Despite her funny appearance, he could see that she was the true force behind the operation of the lodge, overseeing virtually everything from the books to the cooking, cleaning and reservations.

Mr. Johann Freese, an overweight, aging country boy-turned-professional hunting guide, barely managed his guiding responsibilities, but kept the guests amused by telling hunting stories by the hour in the great room of the lodge while consuming copious amount of bourbon. They were quite the pair.

Takqua lay in bed for a time, collecting his thoughts and trying to sort things out. His head hurt, and his body ached all over. He needed time to plan every detail with total accuracy or it would jeopardize his cover ... and escape. Takqua was, even now, transforming mentally into the role of Willem Tuttle, the avid sportsman from California with a penchant for wilderness photography, who often spent days in the woods alone to capture that "special photograph." He portrayed himself to be the Ernest Hemingway of the 35mm camera, taking on challenging photographic assignments for major magazines with worldwide circulation.

He slowly propped himself up on his elbows, brushed his long, black hair from his forehead, and glanced around the room carefully and then down at himself. Willem was amused by what he saw. His body was bruised, battered, scraped, and cut. His mind began to concoct a believable story. He fell back into bed and closed his eyes. After a moment, convinced that he had all the details worked out satisfactorily, he rehearsed the scenario in his mind several times as he slowly showered and got ready for dinner. Before he put on a fresh change of clothes, he pulled the bed sheet off the bed and tore it into strips, creating long cloth bandages which he wrapped tightly around his chest, upper arms, and legs.

He was currently the only true guest in at the lodge. The other residents were actually a group of engineers employed by the U.S.Forest Service, who were allocated certain rooms under a government contract with the Sportsmen's Lodge during the winter when things got slow. The government contract worked well for Johann and Gerta. Leasing the rooms helped pay for the upkeep during the long, lean winters. Not having to worry about cooking any special meals provided them time to themselves to work on small projects around the place. This morning, the engineers had left early with another road crew. Johann told him when he first arrived that they were usually out until well after dark.

Both Gerta and Johann were alone in the large dining room, deep in conversation, when he entered. Both stared at him, mouths open in disbelief, as he gamely limped to the massive oak dining table, sitting himself down opposite the amazed couple.

"Oh, my God, you look terrible, Mr. Tuttle, what happened?" Gerta blurted out, her hands coming to her face. She got out of her chair and flurried about, pouring his tea and fixing him something to eat.

He noticed that Mr. Freese, seated comfortably in a large dining chair, lowered the book he had been reading. Johann's reading glasses, perched on the tip of his nose, were tilted down so he could get a better look at Willem.

"You sure look like hell, Willem. What the heck did you get into?" Johann asked, obviously ignoring his wife's previous question.

Raising his right hand in a calming gesture indicating all was well, Willem said, "I had a terrible experience on Bowers River just on the back side of Hollister Mountain. I was next to the bank of the river, trying to photograph a large cinnamon-phase black bear I had found. At the time, I thought it best if I concealed my presence by using the canoe as a blind. I was crouched down, preparing to take a picture when another bear surprised me by approaching from above and behind me. With the snow and all, I didn't hear anything until he was almost on top of me. When I turned to see the bear, I lost my balance, the canoe rolled, and over I went. The river is passable, but icy. I barely managed to save myself ... lost the canoe and engine though. Sorry." He didn't know that the river was icy for sure, but it helped the story along. Then he added without a pause, "But I will certainly pay for it when I check out. Just let me know how much." Willem figured that offering to pay for the boat would allay any concerns and curiosities they might have.

He was wrong.

Johann, the hunting guide extraordinaire, showed immediate interest. "Cinnamon bears, really? I didn't know there were any on this island and out this time of year. Well, I'll be damned," he said.

"Well, I think they were cinnamon-phase bears," responded Willem Tuttle in an effort not to get pinned to a lie. "I didn't really get close enough to see them for sure. They might have been small brown bears. But I thought brown bears hibernated all winter. "

"Well, of course they had to be cinnamon bears, what else could they be? Yah, I mean, if they were big, golden colored, they had to be alright," chipped in Gerta.

Mr. Freese framed his response in an effort to be logical and think the issue through. "You see, Prince of Wales Island hasn't had, maybe never had, any brown bears. No, you got to go more toward the interior islands like the ABCs, you know, Admiralty, Baranof, and Chichagof, before a guy would see d'em big brownies. But not around here, no sir. So if you've seen golden bears, they've got to be cinnamon 'cause everything else in these parts is black, and everyone can tell the difference between a cinnamon and black." Saying this convincingly, Mr. Freese turned his head slightly to imply that Willem obviously knew too, or needed to apologize for this great error.

"Well, they were a long way off initially, and when that one came up behind me, I was so scared, I really don't remember what I saw."

"You did say you saw cinnamon bears though."

"True enough, I just didn't have time to positively identify them."

"Yep, they must have been cinnamon alright. And out in midwinter. They must have been awakened by something." Clearly, Mr. Freese was convinced.

"You're right," Willem said quietly through tight lips, his anger rising but under control.

Not one to miss an opportunity to gather more information for a future hunt, Johann pressed on. "Wait a minute while I get a topo of the area so you can show me where this happened. In case I can recover the canoe, of course."

Getting up from the heavy wooden table, Johann Freese strode over to a large cabinet and retrieved a fistful of topographical maps of Prince of Wales Island. With the advent of all the logging taking place on the island, topographical maps were accurate and plentiful. Unfolding a creased, soiled, large-scale map across the table, Johann carefully turned the map around so that it could be read easily by Willem.

"Here you go. This here is Hollister, right here, see? And ... and over here, next to the green patch of color on the map is the Bowers River, see? Now you just follow the river around to the point where you saw the bears ... and overturned the canoe." Mr. Freese had his fat finger poking repeatedly at the thin blue line indicating a river. Willem continued to feign interest, elaborating on the lie as he went along.

"OK, I think I can see can the area. It is difficult to read maps sometimes. Alright, I started from the road ... here. Then worked my way around in this direction ... no this direction ... no, well, I can't tell ... for sure ... you understand ... but I think it was around this area ... here."

"Can't be there. You would have had to paddle upriver. Maybe it was here?"

Was this idiot trying to be helpful? Probably just trying to help himself is more like it, thought Willem as he turned and smiled benignly at Johann.

"What about this place? Do the two look similar? I can't tell for sure on the map." Willem pointed out two distinct grids on the map.

"Well, sure they can look the same here, but hell, they are miles apart." Mr. Freese intended to press on, but fortune stepped in in the form of Mrs. Freese.

"Now, Johann, give poor Mr. Tuttle a break. Let him eat something and get settled in. Then you boys can talk some more." Gerta smiled down at Willem as she placed tea, soup, and a tray of crackers and cookies before him. Willem bit his tongue to keep from losing his temper then smiled back, pretending to be grateful.

Over the dinner, Johann continued with his barrage of polite questions and Willem Tuttle, "Takqua," continued to be responsive and receptive but elusive. He knew, however, that he could not withstand these questions for long before he slipped up. His opportunity for escape came none too soon. With the meal almost over, Gerta politely asked how much longer Willem intended on staying. "Not that we want to get rid of you, understand. It's just that if you are going to leave us, we need to tell Southeast Transport and Cargo to arrange for your transportation back to Ketchikan," she explained.

Working his goals into the thought process, he said, "Well, first thing in the morning would work best, if the weather permits. You don't mind scheduling a flight then, do you? I'm thinking of spending several days in Ketchikan and seeing the town. I might even do a little photography on Deer Mountain," Willem proffered.

"Then it's settled. I'll call Marge now, in Craig, and see what I can do. It's still early, yet, I am sure we can get you out sometime tomorrow ... providing we get the weather. If not, well, you just have to be our guest for a few days more, is all." Putting on her best mother smile, she turned and walked toward the small office located behind the cash register. "And please be careful on Deer Mountain. I heard that could be treacherous. We don't want you to have another spill. I am sure your company doesn't either." With that she was in the office and out of view.

A short time later, she returned with the news.

"There's a small problem with the weather," she began. "As you are aware, we had the snowstorm last night, and there is another one supposed to be here in the morning, which will supposedly give us another 8 to 10 inches of snow, so travel tomorrow is definitely out of the question."

Willem's anticipation was beginning to fade to apprehension. Gerta continued. "They have been grounded most of today because of the snow. However, there is supposed to be a short break in the weather this afternoon, and they may try and get a flight off, but it's risky. The pass between here and Ketchikan is definitely closed, so they will try to fly the long way around the southern end of the island, over Hydaburg. If all goes well, you should be in Ketchikan just before dark."

"Or?" Willem was looking for options.

"Or if the weather forces you down, you will stop over at Hydaburg or Metlakatla for the night."

Willem knew both towns were native villages and he did not want to be found carrying his artifacts in a native community. "What if I stay here tonight, can I leave first thing in the morning?"

"Marge says that a new front will be in before they have enough light to fly. So it seems, Mr. Tuttle, if we don't get you out today, it may well be several days before you can leave." Gerta brushed the strands of hair from her forehead and looked concerned. "Not much of a choice, is it?" she said sympathetically.

"No. I guess I leave this afternoon. What do we need to do?"

"I'll call Marge back right away and confirm, but you need to hurry if you intend to catch the flight. It will be leaving within a few hours. Johann can take you to Craig and see you off."

Then turning to Johann, she said, "Honey, please help Mr. Tuttle with his things while I go over his reservations. And you will need to stay until he has lifted off. Marge will tell you if they clear the south end of the island. If not, you will need to pick him back up when they return."

It was very clear to Willem who was in charge. Johann nodded at his wife and got up to put the topos away.

Lack of air traffic control and accurate weather forecasting was a significant hindrance to flying. Most small air companies that traveled in the region often determined the severity of the weather by flying into it. If it wasn't too bad, they tried to punch on through; if it was bad, hopefully, they turned around. They routinely risked sudden death from impacting a mountain in zero visibility.

The DeHavilland aircraft most Alaskan companies used were extremely sturdy and reliable, but they were equipped with little navigation gear. Although to many paying customers, the bush pilots flew by the seat of their pants, they were actually more professional than just rural barnstormers. Almost all of them had close friends who had died as a result of a stupid mistake. As the saying goes, "The clouds in Southeast Alaska often have rocks in them."

There was a flurry of activity as Willem Tuttle struggled upstairs and began packing. He threw all his laundry into a military surplus green nylon duffle bag. Then he put his camera equipment in a well padded suitcase and finally packed his most precious possessions in a large handbag he intended to hand carry to Ketchikan. With the packing accomplished, he looked around the room to ensure nothing was left behind. Then he made his bed to disguise the torn sheet and left the used towels at the foot of the bed for Mrs. Freese. Satisfied that everything was proper, he put the handbag strap around his neck and shoulder and picked up his duffle bag and hard-sided suitcase. Instantly, he was racked with pain. He suspected that the strips of bed sheeting binding his chest and leg wounds were going to give way. Taking small breaths, he paused to get himself under control and then attempted the task again. It still hurt, and the pain brought tears to his eyes, but he managed to hang on long enough to get the bags into the lobby. From there, Johann could do the rest.

Seeing Willem, Gerta called out to Johann to take care of the bags. Mr. Freese took one last gulp of coffee and rose from the table. Ambling toward Willem, he said, "Now, son, let me take care of those for you. You're in bad enough shape as it is. How about your carry-on handbag?"

"No, I'll manage, thank you, Mr. Freese." Then turning toward the cash register, William said, "Well, I suppose this is it, Mrs. Freese. How much do I owe you?"

"Room and board comes to $650 a week. Let's see; no phone calls, no faxes, I guess that's it, except for the canoe and engine."

"Of course. How much do I owe for those items?" Willem began to feel dizzy from his wounds. He certainly didn't feel comfortable standing for much longer.

"Johann? How much for that old canoe and engine? Do you remember what we paid for it?"

Johann put down the bags and thought about it for a second. "Well, let's see. The canoe was about 3 years old, but pretty beat up. The engine was almost new, if memory serves me correctly."

"Two and a half years old. It was a Grumann. The engine is a year old next month," Gerta corrected, smiling and nodding to Willem.

"Yeh, guess so. I think we paid about ... let's see ... well, maybe $1,200 for the two."

"More like $1,700 for both," Gerta corrected again. This time she glared at Johann.

"Oh, yah, $1,700; right. So with usage and all, how does $1,500 sound?" Johann looked at Willem and then sheepishly over to Gerta for confirmation.

"Johann, that's too much. That boat and engine wasn't worth more than $1,300," Gerta interjected. Both Gerta and Johann then looked over at Willem to see if there was an objection, but he was already reaching for his wallet. He started counting out hundred dollar bills, but ran short. Smiling, Willem Tuttle presented an American Express card. "This should do it, Mrs. Freese."

"Thank you, Mr. Tuttle." The bill was settled with little more fanfare than a signature.

Willem turned around and saw that Johann had already left with the bags. He said his final good-byes to Gerta and walked out into the crisp, winter afternoon. The snow had stopped, although the sun was nowhere to be seen. Johann brought the lodge van around and picked up Willem. The trip to the Craig floatplane dock was mercifully short and without conversation. The bright yellow DeHavilland Beaver on floats, with orange and fuchsia lightning streaks along the sides, was already in the process of loading up when the van arrived. It was low tide, so the ramp leading to the floatplane dock descended at a sharp angle.

"Be careful now," Johann said as he walked around and opened the double doors at the back of the Dodge Maxi-van. "The ramp is very slippery with the ice and snow. They will pick up your bags; you just need to get yourself down d'ere. Thanks for coming to the lodge. I hope we have the pleasure of seeing you again." With that, he stuck out his big hand. Willem shook his hand briefly and turned to walk down the ramp.

"Say, you want them to take down your carry-on too? Could be dangerous with that extra weight, ya know?"

"No, no, thank you, I'll manage just fine." Willem grasped the railing and half slid, half walked down the icy ramp.

Reaching the bottom of the ramp, he could overhear the pilot's conversation with the passengers on the floating dock. "We need to take off in the next few minutes if we're going to make it back. I don't like the looks of this weather at all."

CHAPTER THIRTEEN

Willem estimated the pilot was about 21 or 22, out of high school but probably never went to college. *Hell, I bet he doesn't even shave*, he thought. The kid had already loaded most of the cargo on and was about to load the passengers.

"OK, who's first? Let's see ... you," the young pilot said pointing to a fisherman dressed in an old wool jacket, grimy jeans, and rubber boots, "get in the front seat with me. And don't touch anything. You and you," he motioned to a young married couple, "I want you all the way in the back. You will have to sit on the mailbags, but the seat belts will still work OK. Now, you three," pointing to Willem and two other men, "you guys need to sit in the middle." As Willem got ready to board, the kid pilot stopped him. "Say, why don't you put that in the back with the rest of the cargo?"

"No, thank you. I'd prefer to hold on to it, if you don't mind."

The pilot was about to say something else, but he changed his mind. "Your call," he said as he shrugged his shoulders.

Once all the cargo and six passengers were loaded, the pilot ran a knowing eye over the aircraft one last time and checked to see how high the pontoons were riding in the water. It was common knowledge that all the pilots routinely overloaded the aircraft to maximize company profits. The long aluminum pontoons were the only real way of telling how much the pilots could load on and still fly. If the pontoon sat too low in the water, they would off-load some cargo or passengers. If the pontoon sat too high, they would try and take on more weight.

Willem watched the pilot through the large window of the DeHavilland and wished they would get started. The young pilot, eyeing the pontoons closely, opened a cap on each, pumped out some excess water with a small, gray, plastic manual pump, the kind designed for small recreational boats. Securing the pontoon caps again, he walked around to check the brightly painted aircraft over for the last time. Finally satisfied, Willem observed the young pilot cast off the mooring lines and pushed the floatplane away from the dock. A second later, the young pilot jumped into the cockpit with a burst of enthusiasm, donned his headset, buckled his safety harness, and then reached over and flipped up the magneto switch. The electric charge from the magneto jolted the big propeller-driven engine to life. Smoke and exhaust spewed from the exhaust manifold as the big blades began to thrash at the cold air. Waiting a few seconds, the pilot pushed the throttle forward and the engine revved up. Adjusting the propeller pitch, the kid coaxed the aircraft forward in the water.

"OK, I am required to tell you this," the kid-pilot shouted over the noise of the engine.

Willem noticed the pilot was actually trying to grow a moustache. Fine wisps of black hair stood out prominently on his upper lip.

"You all have seat belts, use'em. Don't smoke, don't drink, not even coffee. Last week, someone was drinking Black Velvet from a bottle and threw up all over the inside of the plane. In no time we all got sick from the smell. When I finally got the plane landed in Ketchikan, we were a mess and the bird was in terrible shape. Took 3 days to clean it out. So anyone drinking, or who wants to drink, needs to get out now. No takers? OK." The kid was in his element.

Willem barely listened to the rest of the guidance from the pilot. He was watching the scenery.

"On the sides of the plane are holders with your flotation vest, in case we have to make an emergency landing in water. Let's just hope that doesn't happen. OK, that's it. We're off. Next stop is in about an hour and 40 minutes." The kid was finally done. Everything had come out in one long stream of knowledge. It was apparent to all that questions would not be tolerated.

Willem watched out the window as the plane bounced along as it gained speed across the surface of the bay. As hauls of brown water flashed by, he saw the pontoons suddenly break free from clutches of gravity, confirmed by silver streams of saltwater trailing off behind the rudders. Slowly, the DeHavilland fought to gain altitude.

While the Southeast Transport and Cargo airplane lifted off, 20 miles away on the other side of the island, a light blue Grumann Goose with yellow stripes and a State Troopers emblem on the bulbous nose circled twice over the Twasaan village and, finding enough unobstructed surface to land, made a water landing in Twasaan Bay. Cody and Tom watched from the dock as the large amphibious aircraft skipped across the water, eventually reducing speed and squatting down in a wall of spray. The WWII-vintage aluminum plane turned back around and taxied over to the village dock. The investigators from CID had arrived.

CHAPTER FOURTEEN

The pilot in the shiny, twin-engine, Grumann Goose cut the power on the aircraft and quickly climbed into the back compartment and, turning the door latches, opened the large side cargo door.

"Hey, would you mind helping out?" he called to the small group on shore. "Quick, grab the edge of the wing pontoon!"

The pilot gave a series of short commands to the onlookers.

"OK. Now, walk the wing forward slowly. Watch out for the pontoon. Watch it!" Then finally with a sigh of relief, he said, "Good, good. That's great folks, thanks."

The pilot jumped out of the Grumann and scrambled to moor the aircraft to the dock. Cody and Tom walked down the pier as two residents helped to finish mooring the large aircraft. With the docking procedure finally completed, three troopers dressed in shirts, ties, and slacks, and wearing navy-blue Alaska State Trooper parkas, stepped from the plane onto the slick dock. They looked exactly like what they were ... a long way from Anchorage.

"Watch yourself," Cody said as he grabbed the first investigator.

"This dock is real slippery. I fell and busted my ass on it last night."

Cody greeted everyone in sequence as they exited the aircraft, then introduced them all to Tom. He had not worked with any of the troopers before, but he knew them by reputation as being hardworking and aggressive investigators. While Tom helped them unload their gear, Cody walked over to the pilot who was talking with a group of natives. He knew John Morgan, a veteran pilot from the Air Force, who had been with the Division of Fish and Wildlife for over 15 years. John was a likeable guy, a little on the heavy side for a trooper, but with a big smile and bushy moustache and sense of humor to match. During the time they had known each other, they had logged hundreds of hours together covering Southeast Alaska on commercial fisheries patrols, guided and sport hunting patrols, and numerous search and rescues operations. They had not seen each other since his last transfer to "D" Detachment in Anchorage a couple years ago.

"Long time no see, Cody," the pilot said with a broad grin while pumping his hand and slapping him on the shoulder.

"You got that right, you old outlaw. How the hell are you doing?" Cody replied.

"Couldn't be better; kids are in college now and the old career is finally taking off."

"Hey, I heard just last week. Congratulations on your promotion to sergeant."

"Thanks," John said, still smiling. "Say, Cody, rumor has it that you refused to apply for the sergeants' exam again."

Cody shrugged. "Just didn't seem to have the time."

Picking up his flight bag and thermos, John said, "Cody, you gotta make time. Otherwise, you're going to spend your whole career on patrol in the bush."

"There are worse things than being in the bush, John. Anyway, I'm not sure I want to give up what I'm doing, at least not just yet."

Cody walked over and made sure the forward mooring line was tied tight and returned.

Sergeant John Morgan looked at him closely. "I understand that you asked for CID to come down and take over this murder investigation?"

"John, listen, this is the worst homicide case I've ever seen. CID *should* take this one."

"What happened to the guy who said he could do it all?"

Cody laughed. "Maybe I'm getting older and wiser. And I have a new lieutenant." They both laughed.

John looked at him earnestly, "Or maybe you ought to be taking the corporal/sergeant's exam."

"Maybe."

They both strode over to where Tom and the three CID investigators were standing. The group was under the charge of Sergeant Jim Nichols, who stood almost 6'3, with broad shoulders and a narrow waist. He was a military veteran, weightlifter, and runner who kept himself in top condition. A former LAPD detective with a reputation for being bright and never mincing words, he had worked his way up through the ranks quickly. With his short blond hair, blue eyes, and good looks, he epitomized the troopers.

"Cody, you Fish and Wildlife guys turn up things in the weirdest places, but this one has to take the cake. We're miles from nowhere and miles from the crime scene," Jim said smiling.

Cody replied, "I hear you. My job's in the woods. It just so happens this murder occurred in the woods, too. I'm sorry there wasn't any place closer for the plane to land. We're about 5 miles from the cabin where the murders took place. I'll take you there in my boat when you are ready to go. You'll need to change clothes and get into something warm before we get started."

Sergeant Nichols looked around the village. "Is there someplace where can we get briefed on the crime? We need to get the information you have before we get started."

The tallest member of the trio was Don Fletcher, who stood just over 6'4 with closely cropped dark hair and a pencil-thin moustache. Don was a retired Army Special Forces type, who had come to Alaska at the close of the Vietnam War. He prided himself in being an Alaska State Trooper and considered CID the highlight of his law enforcement career.

"Cody," Investigator Don Fletcher interjected, "you did the right thing calling us in on this. We take all the tough assignments. Now I know you go through the same training as we do, but you 'fish cops' don't do this sort of thing much. Did you remember to take any notes?"

"Yes, I took notes. I would be happy to share them with you, Don." Cody replied ignoring the slight.

The term "fish cops" always galled him, although he never said so. It simply demeaned a very complex profession relating to environmental and resource law enforcement. *Some things change, some things never change*, he thought to himself. In concept, the troopers in both the Division of Alaska State Troopers and the Division of Fish and Wildlife Protection were designed to interface, overlap, and reduce escalating enforcement costs. All the troopers were trained together at the Public Safety Academy in Sitka. The troopers in both divisions were empowered with concurrent authority and jurisdiction throughout the State of Alaska.

In reality, however, animosities and counterproductive competitiveness existed between the two units which never seemed to be reconciled. While the Division of the Alaska State Troopers concentrated on crimes against the people, the Division of Fish and Wildlife Protection, as the name implies, primarily concentrated on crimes against natural resources. Cody never thought much about the "division of duties," as it was called. He simply did his job. And he liked it all, from arresting drunk drivers to arresting fish poachers. It was all the same to him. He tried to explain to any other trooper who would listen—a criminal is a criminal. Where a crime was actually committed shouldn't make a difference, it was still a crime against the peace and dignity of the State of Alaska.

The rife between the two divisions continued, however. Snide comments would surface about the Fish and Wildlife troopers not being "bona fide" troopers infuriated some in the Fish and Wildlife Protection and was simply shrugged off as ignorant comments by others. Cody, working both sides of the street, was considered the odd duck by all his coworkers. He really didn't fit in with either group, but because of his demonstrated versatility and experience, he was routinely called in when there was trouble. Since his rookie year, he had been involved in homicides, arsons, search and rescues, poachings, spotlighting, commercial fishing violations, and a host of other police-type activities. It really didn't matter much to him as long as the job got done.

Sergeant Nichols picked up his gear and looked at Cody as if to sum him up. "I also spoke to Lt. Blocker on this investigation. You will be free to return to your fish and wildlife duties as soon as we are set up and you have completed your report on the incident. The lieutenant told me you are a good field investigator, best in the bush, in fact. He also told me you'd probably be pissed about this but the edict comes from on high. We'd like to have you along on this one, especially since you called us in on it, but you know how the commissioner is on things like this; fish cops aren't bona fide."

There it was again. Not bon fide.

"Sure," Cody responded, "I understand; no problem. Tom, would you mind if we used your office again?"

"Nope, but it's a little small. You guys are going to be kinda cramped though."

The investigators loaded up as much gear as they could carry. The extra police equipment they brought with them was picked up by Tom and Cody. Fully loaded, the group laboriously trudged up the snow-covered hill to the office, under the watchful eyes of virtually the entire village. A short time later, the small group of law enforcement officers had squeezed into the small room, leaving their baggage cluttering along the narrow hallway. Blue State trooper parkas with the unique five-star pattern badge sewn to the sleeves, beaver pelt fur trooper hats, mittens, and caps were everywhere. Any hook, or anything that could conceivably be used as a hook, was employed. Even an old rodeo trophy that Tom had on the file cabinet was festooned with a beaver fur trooper hat. Cody was about to explain what had transpired when Trooper Fletcher interrupted him.

"Ah, Jim ... Cody, before we get started, let's make one thing clear. This is a matter for the State. Does Tom need to be here? No offense, Tom."

"Tom knows as much as I do, and he has been in on this investigation from the start. This is his village, and his office. Hell, yes, he needs to be here."

Sergeant Nichols spoke up. "Cody ... we may need to discuss some confidential aspects of this homicide that need to remain just within our investigative group."

Turning to Tom, Cody said, "Tom would you mind if we discussed this in private?"

"Sure, no problem. Cody, I'll be at my trailer if you need me."

If Tom was angry, he didn't show it ... but Cody was. When Tom left the room, Cody looked at the group.

"Listen, guys, Tom is the best resource you are going to have here. He may not be a State Trooper, but he is an experienced law enforcement officer and the VPSO in NewTwasaan."

Trooper Skip Danski, the last member of the investigative team, interrupted the conversation. Skip was lean, athletic, and quick-tempered. A martial arts expert, hand-to-hand combat was his specialty. Cody knew that last year Skip was named Trooper of the Year for his work in apprehending the head of a Nigerian drug organization trying to get a foothold in Anchorage. In the process of apprehending the kingpin, Skip had beaten the crap out of four knife-welding Nigerians with his PR24 baton. Cody sized him up as brash, a bit overconfident, and a genuine asshole ... but good at police work.

"Look, Cody ... we have a double homicide to investigate. We all need to work together as a team. That includes you."

"Including Tom?"

"No, we just told you! *Not* including Tom, Cody. Now we're wasting valuable time. Let's just get on with it."

Looking around the room once more, Cody shrugged and thought *Tom's not bona fide either, apparently. These guys are going to regret not having Tom on their team.* Then, he cleared off Tom's desk, telling them what he knew and drawing a map as he went. He covered all the details, except one. He wouldn't tell them about the necklace ... at least not yet.

"OK, so let's put this into perspective," Sergeant Nichols said.

"Don, you take notes."

"Right," he said taking out his pen and opening a fresh notepad.

"Skip, you think about any follow-up questions I might miss." Then turning to Cody, he said, "OK, from the beginning. The cabin where the murders took place is approximately 5 miles from here ... as the crow flies. In the middle of winter with the bay almost frozen over. There are no other cabins or people in the vicinity ... no roads, no logging camps, no nothing. In fact, the closest village and any people in this *whole* bay is Twasaan."

In speaking, he had emphasized the word *whole* and spread his arms apart, so as to imply there were no other possibilities. Cody had heard that Sergeant Nichols was famous for overstating the obvious.

"You found the mutilated bodies of the Toddwells in the outhouse and their dog hung up in a tree. To your knowledge, there were only one set of tracks leading from the cabin to the outhouse and you found a similar set of tracks at the beach where a red canoe was seen earlier in the week."

"So far that's correct," Cody confirmed.

"You also said that Tom thought there may have been a trapper working the area before you arrived, but you didn't actually see the boat."

"Right. Tom said it was an old beat-up red aluminum canoe with a black outboard. The canoe was a square-ended job ... it had a flat transom, unlike normal canoes, which are double-ended."

"You also said that the bodies had been skinned and decapitated."

"Right ..."

"Let me clarify. You just implied that a person had to be very good at skinning to have done that crime."

"I think they would have to have been, sure. And know how to cut through bone."

"So, it is logical to assume that based upon geography, weather, time, et cetera, that the person or persons who perpetrated this crime should be reasonably close. So did you ever think of finding out who in Twasaan owns a red canoe?"

"I asked Tom. He said the canoe doesn't belong to the village or anyone in the village."

"Have you asked if anyone in Twasaan is out trapping?"

"No."

"Have you asked anyone anything at all? Like who the fuck has been out of the village over the past few days? Have you asked anyone *any* fucking questions *at all*?" Then Sergeant Nichols exploded. Slamming his hand down on the table top, he jumped up, leaned across the table, and thrust his face within inches of Cody. Taken by surprise, Cody moved back a little. He could feel Nichols' breath as he spoke, each word carefully annunciated.

"This crime happened in an isolated area, in a weather-restricted environment where the scumbags can't possibly get far ... unless, of course, we sit on our hands and watch them leave. *Action*, Cody. This case cried for *immediate action*. Hell, if you did something besides think like a fish cop, we might have already solved this murder by now."

Cody stared back into the angry face but did not reply. The other two investigators looked intently at Cody.

Sergeant Nichols, now leaning very close to Cody, said through clenched teeth, "So the only fucking thing you have really done since yesterday is to share everything you found with an Indian VPSO, who is probably friends with everyone in Twasaan. Hell, he might even be good buddies with the murderer! This is *just fucking great*." Shaking his head in disgust, the sergeant sat back down and folded his arms, glaring at Cody.

"Cody, you're a real piece of work." Then looking to his right he said, "Skip, do you have any questions for Trooper O'Keefe?" He emphasized the word *trooper*.

"No, Jim, you just about said it all."

Cody sensed the charged atmosphere in the room. His friend, John, the pilot, was clearly embarrassed by the outburst. Cody looked at the three investigators and then said quietly, "Tom is a professional and a friend. If he knew anything about this, he would tell me."

With this statement, Don rolled his eyes at the other investigators. "And VPSOs are *soooo* trustworthy."

Cody chose to ignore him and continued. "No, I haven't looked for a trapper or a red aluminum canoe here in Twasaan. But I was first on the scene. *Remember*? I was there for hours. I called you! You guys haven't even been there. This homicide has a lot more to it than you think. This is more than a murder in the bush and the local native is arrested. Sure, anything is possible, but I just don't think it was a trapper from Twasaan."

"OK, we're game. You haven't even interviewed anyone, but you have a theory. Great! Who do you think did it?"

"I'm not sure yet, but my guess is maybe a shaman ... or at least some psycho who believes himself to be a shaman ... maybe a Kushtikaw."

There was a moment of silence in the room. Then Skip Danski said slowly, "A just *what* again?"

"A Kushtikaw, that's a kind of shaman," Cody said softly. Saying it now even sounded preposterous to him.

"You think these folks were killed by a witch doctor? Or whatever the hell it was. What is a Kush ... kusth ... whatever the fuck you said?"

"A Kushtikaw. An evil shaman, powerful enough to change into animal form."

This response brought about laughter from the group.

"Oh, no, we're going to have to call in the SPCA or the Humane Society 'cause we don't have authority over critters. I see now, we can throw basic police procedure out the fucking window 'cause the fish cop's got it all figured out, and you know what? The shaman dressed as a snow bunny did it. That's a new one on the old 'the butler did it' theory! This is just ... fucking great ... boy ... I hope fish cops are better at moose poaching than they are at homicides."

With obvious disgust, Jim Nichols slammed his notebook closed, as if making a statement as to the validity of the information, and said, "Well, at least we all agree on one point: an Indian probably did it. Look, Cody, we've wasted enough time here. We're going to run this investigation by the book. Now, how soon can we get to the crime scene?"

Keeping his anger under control, he answered, "It's almost dark now, so unless you guys plan on camping on the beach, I suggest we leave tomorrow morning just before daylight. The weather is supposed to improve in the next 24 hours or so. We can get a full day in."

"OK. I'll buy that. In the meantime, let's get a complete statement from the VPSO and find out who has a canoe and hunts and traps in the village."

"Sure. I'll get a hold of Tom now. You guys will also need a place to sleep tonight, so I'll see what I can arrange. The closest motel is in Ketchikan, but I might get us some space on the gym floor in the new school." Cody noticed the sergeant carefully finished putting his notebook and drawings away. He had calmed down some.

"Look, Cody, this is all probably straightforward. Chances are, this is just another robbery/murder like the one in Tanana last year, except the guy, or guys, want us to think that they are crazy. Same scam, new twist."

It was clear to Cody that Jim was used to running CID and liked being in full control. What he was not good at was abstract thinking.

John Morgan, the pilot, hung up the telephone. He had been talking to the airport control tower in Ketchikan for the latest on the weather. "Well, the tower tells me there is a small snowstorm in Ketchikan right now and it's moving this way. Should be here in about 2 hours. Ketchikan will begin to improve in about an hour, but you guys should start seeing some snow by then. I really don't want to lay over, so if you guys have all your gear off the Goose, I'll crank up and head for Juneau to refuel and stand by."

"Just like a pilot—out before things get tough," Don said. The group laughed but knew Don didn't mean it. As they left the building, Cody turned off the lights and locked the door. A light snow was already beginning to fall.

Cody and John left the group at the school gym and headed over to the trailer to pick up Tom Whitefeather. Then the threesome walked down to the dock to get John and his Grumann Goose underway.

"Any second thoughts about calling for CID?"

"No, they're a bunch of prima donnas, but they are good at what they do," Cody replied.

"I think they are a little out of their element in the bush," Tom added. "It's one thing to investigate a homicide in a trailer in Barrow and another thing entirely to investigate a homicide out here. Things have to be done differently."

Tom and Cody were acutely aware of the fundamental differences. Outdoor crime scenes were subject to changing weather and barometric pressures, fluctuating temperatures, vegetation, wild animals, including scavengers and rodents, all of which escalated the obfuscation of minute traces of evidence or could obliterate evidence entirely. Indoors, a corpse will decompose, but it remains where it fell, with all the evidence attendant to the crime scene still intact. Outdoors, a corpse not only deteriorates faster, the corpse may actually be pulled apart by both large and small animals and scavengers. This is one reason why outdoor crime scenes tended to be much larger than city crime scenes. Search patterns were often run over large tracts of surrounding area to check for trace evidence and other clues. Time, elements, animals, geography, and lack of witnesses were hurdles which needed to be surmounted if an investigation were to be successful.

Cody said what the group was thinking. "I think they know all that, and it scares the hell out of them. This case is big—real big—and the fact that the victims were, well ..."

"Not to mention tourists," Tom interjected. "Don't forget about the tourists. The last thing Alaska needs is some maniac stalking tourists in the forests and torturing them to death. Not a pretty picture."

CHAPTER FIFTEEN

Officer Whitefeather and Trooper O'Keefe stood on the float dock as John prepped the state aircraft. On his command, they cast off the lines and watched as the plane slowly taxied out into the bay, then turned into the wind and with full power and flaps extended, bounced across the icy waters until it struggled to break free and rise into the air. Walking back toward the village, Cody asked Tom to double check and see if anyone had a red canoe or a red square-ended canoe.

"Sure, no problem," Tom replied. "I'll get that to you in the morning, but like I said, I would know if there was a canoe like that around. Here, I would know who owned it."

Cody felt a spark of remorse. "I know. Thanks, I appreciate it. By the way, does this village have a shaman?"

"I know what you are thinking, and the answer is no."

"I thought so, but I needed to ask."

Tom glanced at Cody. "I would have told you."

Cody felt embarrassed, but satisfied. No one said police work was easy.

At the same time, in Ketchikan, a yellow DeHavilland Beaver floatplane circled once over the city looking for floating logs and debris, then making its final approach, skipped across the water several times before it settled gently on the Tongass Narrows near the city dock in downtown Ketchikan. Willem breathed a sigh of relief as the plane finally came to a halt and then slowly turned and picked up speed as the aircraft maneuvered on the water. He watched intently as the kid carefully brought the DeHavilland alongside the float dock. When the plane was just inches away, the pilot jumped out onto the icy platform, stopping the forward momentum of the aircraft by securing the mooring lines of the plane's left pontoon to two painted chocks' position strategically on the dock. Minutes later, Willem stepped out into the brisk Ketchikan evening just as snow began to fall.

The bags and all the cargo were delivered a short time later to the tiny but brightly lit terminal building located at street level on Tongass Avenue. As Willem limped out of the terminal and flagged a cab to the curb, he noticed the snow was thick and heavy, and smiled. Seconds later, the cabby retrieved his gear from the terminal and loaded it into the back of a late-model Chevy rental converted over to an Evergreen taxi. Willem still kept the smaller bag containing his trophies on his lap. The driver, a high-school student making a few extra dollars after school, got behind the wheel with a great deal of pride. "Where to?"

"The nearest pharmacy, then you can let me off at the Cape Fox Hotel."

"Cape Fox, good choice," the boy said as he signaled and pulled away from the curb, driving on the poorly lit streets of Ketchikan.

After a short drive through the business district, the converted taxicab pulled up into the broad, circular drive of the Cape Fox Hotel.

Reaching into his pocket, Willem paid his fare, including a respectable tip for the additional effort. Clutching his carry-on in one hand and a large paper bag containing first aid supplies purchased at the pharmacy in the other, he painfully exited the vehicle.

"Please give the bellhop my bag," was all he said entering the expansive, brightly lit lobby of Ketchikan's newest hotel.

Willem strode stiffly across the opulent lobby, biting his lip against the pain and trying not to limp. By the time he reached the long reservations counter, he felt lightheaded. He needed rest and fluids. Willem's hand touched the silver-plated service bell sitting alone on a thick and very polished speckled-brown marble countertop. The ring was answered almost immediately.

The Cape Fox Hotel sat perched on one of Ketchikan's most strategic heights, commanding a view of the downtown area, Tongass Narrows, and Gravina Island. The structure was a multistory affair, fairly nondescript on the outside. Looking around the lobby, he decided the interior of the building was a cross between modern architecture depicting a ski resort and a hunting lodge ... confused and gaudy. The only saving grace to the building at all was the high ceilings and tall outboard windows spaced informally apart and now, due to darkness, appeared like black onyx soldiers standing at attention.

The night manager emerged from the drudgery of paperwork in the depths of the back office.

"Yes sir. Can I help you?" he said smiling.

"Please. Reservation for Edgar Abbott," Willem said, now discarding this alias as smoothly as dropping-off dirty laundry.

"Thank you." The manager entered a few codes on the reservations computer. Edgar watched the green-colored screen flutter to life. "Let's see, ah yes ... have it right here. How are you going to pay for this sir? Cash or credit card?"

"Cash, two nights."

"Very good, sir. Can you fill out the registration form, please?"

After a few more uncomfortable minutes, Willem Tuttle aka Edgar Abbott was taken upstairs and shown to his room, which did not overlook the city but, the bellhop assured him, would have a splendid view of snow-covered Deer Mountain in the morning.

Edgar got settled in, took a long hot bath, and dressed his injuries. Then he put the *Do Not Disturb* sign on his door and went to sleep.

Two hours before daylight, Cody rolled out of his sleeping bag on the floor of the school gymnasium and woke up the investigators. He had slept hard and now felt fully revitalized. Looking around, he was also relieved to see that the troopers had brought outdoor clothes with them, instead of just uniforms. As the group dressed, they used their small backpacking stoves to heat water for a breakfast of instant oatmeal and coffee. Tom Whitefeather showed up about an hour later with a large thermos of coffee and some news.

"Hey, you're looking better. Yesterday you looked like shit."

"Yesterday I hadn't slept any either. Did you find out anything?"

"Cody, I checked around the village. There are at least nine canoes in all, five aluminum and four fiberglass. The fiberglass canoes are all green. Two of the aluminum are just silver-colored. Thing is, only one canoe, an aluminum canoe, has a square transom to hold a small outboard engine."

"So who owns that boat?"

"I knew you'd ask. Tommy Harold aka Tommy the Trapper."

Cody knew Tommy. In fact, he had arrested Tommy in the bush once on an outstanding warrant for assaulting a Ketchikan police officer. He vividly remembered Tommy had gone to town to pick up some trapping supplies and food and decided to stay and have a few drinks. By midafternoon Tommy was drunk ... and belligerent. The bartender tried to get Tommy to leave, but he wouldn't budge. The bartender had called the police who dispatched an officer to the scene. Things somehow got out of hand and a tussle ensued. Tommy the Trapper ended up taking the young officer's revolver and escaping town. When Cody finally tracked him down, literally, he came back to town and went to jail without any trouble at all. Alcohol will do that to some people, and, like with Tommy, had a tendency to give you a rap sheet as long as your arm.

"There's one other thing you need to know, Cody. The canoe is not red, but then Tommy has been away from the village for the last week. My guess is he's trapping. Beaver and martin season will close here in a couple more weeks."

"I'll tell Sergeant Nichols. I'm sure he'll be pleased. See if you can raise Ketchikan troopers and have dispatch run a current state and national check for wants and warrants. We'll need a copy of his fingerprint card too."

"Sure. Be back in few."

Cody walked over to where the three investigators were stowing their gear and passed them the thermos of coffee.

"Here, this may be better than the instant stuff, but no guarantees though."

"Thanks, Cody," Don said as he took the steel thermos and poured a cup.

Turning, Cody said, "Sergeant Nichols, Tom ran down all the canoes in the village last night. There is only one canoe that even remotely fits the description. It belongs to a convicted felon named Tommy Harold aka Tommy the Trapper. Tom is running a wants and warrants on him now."

"Good. Do we know where he is?"

"Not yet. Apparently he has been gone for about a week now."

"Well, looks like we have a suspect before we even get started. The troopers always get their man!"

Cody noticed that Nichols had emphasized the words "before and always" and it worried him. Cody looked at the group.

"Remember, this is a square-ended canoe, but it is the wrong color. Tom said the canoe was red."

Now Trooper Danski brought Trooper O'Keefe to task. "You know that eyewitnesses are unreliable. They see things, imagine things, visualize events. We're not saying Officer Whitefeather is wrong. All we're saying is that there is a coincidence that a square-ended canoe, fairly rare, is seen across the bay last week, and there is one here in Twasaan that is missing. By another coincidence, the one across the bay is missing. You know that Tom was passing by at, how close? A mile? Two miles? Maybe what he saw was a red wool coat draped over the side of the canoe. At the angle off the water, maybe it looked just like a red canoe."

"OK, enough," Sergeant Nichols concluded. "Cody, before we leave town, let's make sure Ketchikan Dispatch gets word to the local radio station that the state troopers need assistance in locating a red or silver aluminum square-backed canoe with a small outboard on Prince of Wales Island and Tommy Harold. Hopefully, someone might see the canoe out here somewhere and give dispatch a call." While the CID finished packing, Cody left and returned sometime later.

"Dispatch is working on the request now."

Skip Danski looked up from his gear bag. "Great. If we get lucky, we might have our man before the sun goes down."

No one said anything else. They were all thinking the same thing. *One suspect with all the right toys in a remote area during winter. What could be better than to bring the case to a swift conclusion?*

CHAPTER SIXTEEN

An hour before dawn, the troopers hauled their cumbersome gear down to the dock. Cody had already been there for some time now, preparing the boat. It had started with the ritualistic shoveling out of accumulated snow, then breaking the ice that had formed in the cockpit, along the railing, and in the transom. After pouring copious amounts of saltwater over the decks, they looked clean and acceptable for patrol. Finally, he checked the gauges to see if he had enough fuel. With the maintenance completed and safety checks done, he motioned the troopers standing on the dock to load their gear and come aboard. Tom hadn't returned from contacting Ketchikan by the time Cody started warming up the engines, but he knew Tom could raise him on the patrol boat radio, if necessary. When everything was stowed and all passengers aboard, the troopers cast off. Cody pulled up his parka hood and adjusted the snow goggles over his eyes. Then he put on his overmittens, cranked over the wheel of the patrol vessel, and pulled away from the dock, bow pointing in the general direction of the Toddwells' cabin.

The ride over was short and uneventful. The extreme cold

dampened any conversation. The investigators huddled behind the windshield, trying to break the wind and stay as warm as possible. Not much was said. As Cody and CID investigators reached the other side of the bay, they got a call from Tom on the secure frequency.

"5-A-19, 5-A-19, this VPSO Whitefeather, over."

"VPSO Whitefeather, this is 5-A-19, go ahead."

"5-A-19, be advised that the suspect has no, repeat no, outstanding warrants, over."

"Copy, no outstanding warrants. Thanks. 5-A-19, out."

Cody turned to Jim Nichols. "Did you catch that? No warrants."

Sergeant Nichols nodded his head; he understood. It was too cold for much of anything else.

Instead of anchoring up in the same spot as before, Cody maneuvered the vessel further toward the mouth of the river. Here, the ice was much thicker and more difficult to negotiate, but it was almost dawn and he could see better. The new location allowed the CID investigators to walk directly to the cabin without having to cross the Shakan River. Cody looked around while setting the anchor. There was new snow covering the ground. *The lieutenant was right*, he thought, *the forensic evidence here will be shit*.

"Damn, it's cold this morning. It has to be below 20." Trooper Danski hugged himself and tightened down on his parka hood.

"It's the humidity. This high humidity makes this cold cut through your clothes like a knife," Sergeant Nichols emphasized the word *knife*.

"Once we start hiking, we'll all warm up," said Cody. "It's wolfdawn. The sun will be up shortly."

"*Wolfdawn*?" The word again emphasized by Sergeant Nichols.

"Wolfdawn is the period of darkness just before sunrise.

Sometimes it's called false dawn."

"Never heard of it."

Cody shrugged and reached for his field notebook. He carefully went over all the details, step by step, to the investigators concerning what he had seen when he first arrived, and remembering the blood samples he collected, Cody turned them over to Trooper Danski.

"Thanks, Cody. I doubt these samples will be any good by now. The blood and water must have been thawed and frozen at least a couple of times, but we can send it in anyway and see what comes back. Is there anything else you should tell us?"

"Sure. Insist they check to determine if it is animal or human in origin," Cody responded.

"Why's that?"

"Because if it animal in origin, we may be looking for a trapper in Vibram-soled boots. On the other hand, it may also indicate that Tommy the Trapper is just that ... a trapper."

"It could also be proof that he is both a trapper and a murderer," Danski added.

"Perhaps. But the only thing we have from the area of the beach is the Vibram sole boots and these blood samples."

Jim walked up to Cody and in his best command presence said, "And a witness who saw a square-backed canoe."

The four troopers headed off into the woods toward the cabin, Cody explaining as they went. The fresh snow crunched beneath their feet, their breaths appeared like geysers originating from somewhere inside their snorkel parka hoods. Cody used his long black flashlight to guide the group through the woods to the cabin. By the time the sun was peeking over the mountaintops, they had arrived at the cabin and the scene of the homicides. He could see that all traces of his footsteps were erased. *That means that the killer's footprints are gone too*, he thought. The rest of the group was thinking the same thing.

The sun reflected radiantly off the snow-covered roof of the cabin. Cody looked for animal tracks in the snow and seeing none, breathed a small sigh of relief. A whole day had gone by without anyone here. He was momentarily concerned that a bear, wolf, mink, martin, or some other critters might have begun to gnaw on the frozen, headless corpses he left out in the yard. Glancing in the direction of the outhouse, however, he could several large ravens, their black heavy wings folded behind them, walking back and forth across the top of the two bodies. With a start, Cody leaped ahead of the group, running through the snow toward the ravens and waving his arms erratically.

"Whoaaa. Go on, get out of heeere."

The ravens watched him disdainfully, turning their heads from side to side and nervously hopping along the length of the bodies. They waited until he got within their comfort zone, then took flight, screaming and cursing, to the nearest tree limb where they stopped to watch what would happen next.

Cody turned back to the CID investigators and, panting from running so far through the deep snow, feebly motioned them to come over. "The bodies of who we think are the Toddwells are just over here, next to the outhouse. See the two mounds over there in the snow?" Even though it was daylight, the terror of the incident was still fresh in his mind and Cody suddenly felt nauseated.

Walking over and brushing away the snow, Sergeant Jim Nichols and Trooper Fletcher exposed parts of the two bodies. The wool blankets were frozen and stuck to the corpses. "Good fucking thing we got here when we did. Look at those holes in the blanket. The ravens must have been here yesterday too."

"Yeah, but they didn't do any damage."

Two of the investigators worked back enough of one blanket to see most of what had happened to the Toddwells.

"Oh, my God, look at that!"

"I've never have seen a murder without a head before."

"I saw a headless body once at a traffic accident ... in Fairbanks ... a girl in a new sports car and a BP fuel truck collided. Grrosss!"

"Shit, look here, Cody wasn't bullshitting. They really have been skinned."

Cody could hear Sergeant Nichols emphasize the word "have."

"Whoever did this is a real sicko ..."

During this exchange, Cody stood off to one side, trying not to look at the bodies. The memories were too fresh ... still too real. He felt the bile rise in his throat again, and for the next few minutes, he had dry heaves.

"Cody, sorry to interrupt your prayers," Skip said sarcastically while walking up next to him, patting him on the back. "You said there was a dog around here somewhere?"

Cody, doubled over and down on his knees, pointed in the overall direction of the woods behind the outhouse. Trooper Danski took off on his search.

"Found it. Boy, it's strangled to death with a wolf snare. I thought it was a frozen floor mop when a first saw it. Looks like more evidence against Tommy the Trapper, eh?"

Under normal conditions, the troopers would have begun by first cordoning off the entire area with crime-scene tape. Here, it wasn't necessary. There were no family, friends, onlookers, or reporters who could trample the area and destroy possible clues.

Instead, Skip Danski began by videotaping the outhouse and the bodies, including the dog. Then, he and Sergeant Nichols bagged the blood-caked hands of the victims and then carefully placed each body, still with their blankets, into a heavy rubberized body bag, finally zipping them closed. Next, they retrieved the frozen carcass of the dog and placed it into a paper sack, along with the stainless steel wolf snare. When that task was completed, Skip began videotaping the outside of the cabin, and then the porch, and finally the entrance to the cabin. That was completed about the same time Don had finished all the physical measurements of the crime scene. Then the investigators stopped briefly on the porch to confirm their data.

"OK, let's see if we can draw this scene to scale," directed Sergeant Nichols. Don quickly read off the geographic coordinates of the cabin from a topo while using a drafting stencil to place a figure of the house on a sheet of graph paper. Next, he indicated the point he had used to determine the closest point of the river in relation to the cabin, and finally, the outhouse in relation to the cabin and the point on the river. And then a prominent old fir tree some distance from the cabin and the river. The final outcome was that the investigator had accurately triangulated the position of the cabin and the outhouse in relation to natural and permanent geographic features. Next, standing on the porch, he used his compass to take a bearing on the highest visible peak in the vicinity.

"Say, Cody, what's that mountain over there?"

"Sugar Mountain. The one next to it is Saginaw."

Don jotted down the bearing, in degrees true, of the peak on Sugar Mountain in the right-hand margin of the blue graph paper. He would use that information later when he had a new topographical map. Finally, he read off the distances and the bearings in degrees true from the cabin to the outhouse, the location of the victims, and the spot where the dog was found. Although Danski had videotaped everything, Sergeant Nichols had backed up that endeavor with a complete set of photographs, carefully recording each shot, the film ASA, the F-stop, and the distance. After the diagramming had been completed, they rested on the porch for a while before tackling the interior.

Jim took the lead. "The outside of the cabin was the easy part. Now, we have to take our time and work through every piece of evidence we can find in the cabin. Let's go slowly and start from the door. Remember, it's real easy to contaminate a crime scene, especially when the area is small, like the interior of this cabin. We'll go in one at a time, initially using the same path as the person before us. Skip, you go first with the video camera. Don, you're evidence man. You're in charge of bagging and tagging. I'll take notes and photographs. Don, before you pick anything up, make sure that we have it on video and a good photograph."

Then turning to Cody, he said, "By the way, did you see anything when you were here that might have been used as a weapon? We should be looking for two items, I imagine: the ax that he cut off their heads or perhaps a sharp knife he used to skin them with?"

"It was pretty dark that night, Sergeant, and to tell you the truth, I was so stunned by what I saw, I wasn't really thinking straight. However, as I told you before, I did take a set of rudimentary photographs and wrote down some notes in my daily diary."

The sergeant turned and addressed the group. "OK, Cody, read off your notes looking through the window. We'll stand in the doorway and try to visualize what you saw that night."

Cody was surprised to find that for all the bravado the day before, he had managed to wrangle his way into the investigation. Maybe no one would notice.

"Right. Stand by." Cody swung his pack onto the porch, unzipped his parka, and took off one mitten. Then, reaching into the deep pocket of his thick, gray, wool shirt, he retrieved his small leather-bound notebook. "Here it is. OK. I entered the cabin, looked around, saw the place was a mess. The table had been overturned, and the radio was destroyed. Over in the corner—"

"Wait a minute. What radio?"

"Uh, let's see. There was a radio on the floor, a large VHS radio."

"Are you sure?"

"Sure I'm sure," Cody said, obviously perturbed.

"Well, it sure the fuck isn't here now."

"Let me see." Cody peered into the cabin, but the radio was missing. Other stuff had been misplaced as well.

"Shit. Someone *has* been here. They had to have gotten here yesterday morning, before the heavy snowfall, or we would have seen their footprints."

"Yes, or you didn't really see what you said you did, Cody," Skip said over his shoulder.

Cody looked Trooper Danski squarely in the eye, his jaws tight and working hard to keep his anger under control. "What, exactly, are you trying to say, Skip?"

"Just that you might have been spooked and run off is all. Cody ... there's no shame in being scared. You were here, you found the bodies, and you panicked."

Cody took two quick steps toward Skip Danski. "OK, let's follow that line of reasoning to its conclusion, shall we?" Cody was within inches of Skip's face. "If your assumption is correct, then what about my notes, my descriptions, my photographs, taking time to cover the bodies, etc. ... No, investigator, you are full of shit!"

Suddenly, Jim Nichols was there pulling them apart. "Break it up, both of you!" he said getting between the two troopers. "Com'on, Skip, he's right. Cody was here; he did his job; and he left. Someone must have tossed the cabin in the meantime."

"Then why aren't there any tracks in the snow?"

"Probably because the storm last night covered them over."

"Sure, but there aren't even any depressions. It didn't snow that hard."

"I don't have all the answers; let's just get on with it, OK?"

Skip glared at Cody, thinking, *There may be a truce, but this war isn't over, not by a long shot.*

Sergeant Nichols turned to Cody and gripped his sleeve. "See if you can determine if anything else out of place."

"Well," Cody replied, cooling down, "stuff has been moved, but I don't really know what, for sure ... at least ... at least not until the photographs are developed. In the meantime, while you guys go through the cabin, why don't I look around and see if I can pick up any sign of a trespasser?"

"Or the murderers, Cody. A criminal always returns to the scene of the crime. Remember Sherlock Holmes?" Sergeant Nichols reminded him and then went on. "But I gotta tell ya, this still looks to me like a double homicide was committed locally. How many people are out freezing their asses off in weather like this? Not many unless they are experienced woodsmen. My bet is that we are going to find our killers out here somewhere, living in the woods. Hell, they're probably watching us now right now, for all we know. This thing has the all the earmarks of our friend Tommy the Trapper."

"We don't know that."

"No, but I have a hunch that's the way this thing is going down. It was pretty early in my career when CID broke the Knik Arm murders back in the late seventies. Remember that? The baker did it. Took all those girls out on the flats and hunted them down. Well, I had a hunch a plane was used to commit those crimes, and guess what? It was. We found the plane, and then we found him. Well, I've got a strong hunch on this one too."

Cody looked at him and shrugged. "Whatever. I'm going to look around."

"Sure, go ahead. Let's plan on meeting back here in a couple of hours."

CHAPTER SEVENTEEN

Cody put on his gear and began by circling the cabin first and then expanding the search pattern in 10-yard increments. After an hour of methodically covering the woods, he still was no farther along than he was when he started. Tired from walking through the woods, he sat down by the edge of the river, turning his face to the sun and warming up. Everywhere around him were the signs of an early spring. The bushes next to him had just the tiniest beginnings of little buds forming from the bark. He could make out the unmistakable cries of the young eagles working the shoreline, calling out with their shrill high-pitched calls. Black ravens flew from tree to tree, crisscrossing the river in search of mischief. And if he listened very carefully, he could even hear the water gurgling under the shallow icy crust which bordered the river. On the opposite side of the bank, which was still blanketed in early morning shadows, he saw signs that an otter had recently left the swift, frigid water, negotiating the icy, snowy bank in search of food.

Cody rested for awhile, and then gathered himself together, preparing to depart, when he saw a mink come out of the woods. In its mouth was what appeared to be colored cloth. Cody jumped up and yelled. Surprised, the little mink dropped the object and scampered off. He rose and brushed himself off, looking upriver for a way to cross. Searching the riverbank, he saw the place he had used 2 days earlier, a bend where the water ran over a set of multiple rapids.

Picking up a small-game trail running adjacent to the river, he followed it upstream to the wide, shallow rapids. He stopped, unzipped his parka, and took off his socks and boots in preparation to cross. Then, scanning the immediate area around him, he found just what he was looking for. Walking over to a fallen tree, he tore off a stout branch from the mossy trunk which he could employ in crossing the river.

After judging the depth and current and selecting a place to cross, he waded out into the swift water, and using the makeshift staff for support, negotiated the slick, round rocks. After some near spills, Cody reached the other side, sat down in the sun, and carefully dried his feet in the cold air. Then he put his socks and boots back on and, readjusting his parka and weapon, walked over to the small item on the ground that had caught his interest, careful not to walk on the trail. Reaching down, he picked it up. It was a gnawed-on scrap of a red-colored paper, a receipt. On one side the name "Ketchikan Marine Electronics" was printed across the top in black. The sides and bottom portion of the paper tag were missing but, at this point, it really didn't matter. What did matter was the receipt was not faded and not wet with snow. It hadn't been out in the weather very long.

Cody looked at the animal tracks in the area and decided that the mink had picked up the receipt somewhere downriver. Cody began following the animal tracks in the fresh snow. He could imagine the mink bouncing along the game trail, red paper tag firmly held in place by rows of small, sharp-pointed teeth. The game trail closely followed the river for another 50 yards, then veered suddenly toward the woods.

Cody turned and followed the small-animal tracks, the possibility of a Kushtikaw waiting for him briefly crossing his mind. Once in the woods, the trail became harder to follow. The ground was frozen and without snow, Cody could only guess he was still on the tracks. Then as sometimes happens, the small-game trail simply disappeared. He looked around to try and pick up the tracks again, but it was no use. Cody began a concentric circular search of the area in hopes of picking up the mink track again when he found something else instead. A fresh boot print or part of a print actually. Cody could clearly make out a partial boot print imprinted on the fragile soil at the apex of the undefined path. Even though the track was in the woods, he could tell the track was fresh, no more than 3 days old. Tiny bits of fresh debris still filled in around the track. The frost had not distorted the regularity of the edge of the boot print. No doubt this was recent ... very recent.

Taking off his pack, Cody took out his flashlight and kneeling down, placed his face just inches away from the partial print and then used the strong beam of the flashlight to sidelight the track. The shadows caused by sidelighting highlighted the partial print, revealing its secrets. He could make out that the track was of the side and edge of the toe of a boot, a rubber boot to be precise. He knew the track well; he had seen it countless numbers of times. It was made by a rubber boot, a Uniroyal, commonly worn throughout Southeast Alaska by just about everyone. The dimensions of the toe led him to believe that the person making the track wore a man's size nine, meaning the wearer probably stood about 5'7 to

5'9. This could easily fit Tommy the Trapper's description. Only one thing bothered him; this was not at all the same track he had seen the first day when he landed on the beach. The print on the beach was made by a man's size 9 or 10 but had a lugged Vibram sole. Cody carefully left the trail so as not to disturb any other undiscovered tracks. Then he retrieved his notebook. Examining his drawing of the first track, there was no mistake. They were not made by the same boot or the same person.

Cody made a subsequent sketch of the new print and then marked the print with a stick stuck into the ground. Picking up a skinny branch from the base of a nearby alder, he cut a groove around the outer circumference of the stick. Then he cut two more rings, one 2 feet from the first ring and another 3 feet from the first ring. Walking over to the partial print, Cody lay the tracking stick down next to the print, matching the bottommost ring to the toe of the boot. Slowly, he moved the stick in an arc until he caught sight of another print, barely visible in the frost on the ground. He smiled to himself as he realized that the second ring on the stick picked up a new track, a heel print. Cody marked the heel and toe of the latest track and started forward. *Whoever made these tracks was certainly not in a hurry,* he thought. He continued to follow the tracks for a few more minutes, carefully marking the location of each print.

He was just beginning to mark another footprint when he suddenly froze in position. Although he couldn't see anything, Cody could smell smoke from a campfire. Quickly, he drew his .44 revolver and cautiously made his way toward the source of the smoke, using any available trees for cover and careful not to brush against bushes or step on dead branches. After what seemed like an eternity of stalking through the woods, Cody could just make out a small lean-to and campfire through the trees. There was a blackened metal pot hanging over the fire, and over to one side lay at least three recently killed martins and a beaver. Cody waited patiently to get a glimpse of the trapper, but no one was there. The camp was empty. He had just about given up surprising Tommy the Trapper when he caught a movement out of the corner of his eye. To his surprise, Tommy stood up from behind a large group of bushes, toilet paper in hand , only a few yards from where Cody was watching the camp. Tommy wasn't tall, but he was big, well over 225 pounds. He noticed that Tommy didn't even have his pants pulled up all the way. The crack of his butt showed above his belt and his T-shirt stretched tight over a large beer belly. Cody couldn't resist.

"Psssst."

Tommy froze, his big outstretched arms half extended in the air.

"Psssst. Over here. Tommy, keep your arms in the air. You're under arrest," Cody said in a half whisper.

Tommy instantly turned, and he and Cody locked eyes at the same instant. He could see the surprise and wild fear in Tommy's wide eyes.

"Ahhhhhhhhh." Tommy let out a long scream and charged, pants beginning to slide perilously down, while the T-shirt rose over his mountainous beer belly, arms outstretched like a sumo wrestler.

Cody only had a split second to sidestep Tommy before both bodies collided with a loud thump and crashed to the ground. Cody lost his balance, the impact dislodging his weapon from his hand and bouncing into the bushes. Not encumbered by outer clothing or equipment, Tommy had the clear advantage. The momentum carried him, and he climbed on top of Cody, grabbing at his collar and neck.

Tommy sat astride him, pushing the full weight of his body down on Cody and choking him. He screamed "you're not going to arrest me again! No more!"

Fear radiated throughout Cody's body as he felt the intense pressure on his throat and weight on his chest. Cody couldn't speak, and he couldn't breath. He tried to pry Tommy's hands off his neck, but it was impossible. The animal fat and blood on Tommy's hands and arms left from skinning trapped animals forestalled any possibility of a good grip. Then suddenly, he heard a loud crack. Tommy stiffened, and his eyes rolled back in his head. He loosened his grip and fell heavily on top of him.

Cody almost passed out by the time Trooper Danski pulled Tommy off him. Standing over both of them with his collapsible baton in his hand, he said, "You OK?" Then he used his boot to push Tommy's unconscious body over, face down.

"Yeah, I think so. Thanks," Cody managed between gasps of air and choking. He was clearly shaken.

"What the hell happened?" By now, Skip had Tommy cuffed and lying face down in the ground.

"A prank gone bad, and a whole new twist on the flight or fight syndrome, I think," Cody said, still coughing and massaging his neck. "I thought he would run, but I never thought he would attack," he said before another coughing spell hit him.

"He's lucky you didn't blow his ass away."

"He wasn't armed." More coughing and wheezing.

"So what? If I wasn't looking for you, you might be dead by now. Lucky for you I saw you on this side of the river and thought that you might be on to something. This guy's killed before, and he probably would have killed you now."

Cody didn't want to get into an argument about what he found just yet, so he let the comment pass. Tommy was moaning, beginning to come to. There was a short gash just behind his ear, and it was bleeding profusely.

"Let me see if I have something to stop the bleeding," Cody said looking through his pack.

"If I were you, I'd let that dumb son-of-a-bitch bleed to death."

"Well, I'm not you. I don't have anything in my gear that will work. I'll try and find something I can use as a compression bandage in his camp."

Cody picked up his weapon and after checking it over, holstered the revolver and strolled into camp, his eyes searching for something usable. When he reached the small green camouflage lean-to, he pulled back the flap of the tent and whistled. He could tell immediately it was Tommy who ransacked the Toddwells' cabin. A large cardboard box of canned food, the outmoded VHS radio, and even some of the professor's Orvis outdoor clothing were clearly visible. The shirts even had his monogram on the cuffs and were folded and stacked neatly to one side of the tent. *Probably took them out of the drawers in the same condition*. Cody found one of Tommy's old faded flannel shirts and cut a long strip, then located some twine near the dead animals.

When he returned to the woods, he found that Skip now had Tommy sitting upright. He was having difficulty thinking and was muttering incoherently, but he was alive.

"Looks like you really whacked him," Cody said to Skip as he bandaged Tommy's head wound. Because of the location of the wound, he had to wrap the bandage over his ear at an angle and then tie a knot directly over the injury. Tommy winced but said nothing.

Then Cody added more twine holding a flat piece of wood directly over the wound. It seemed to work OK.

"Well, if anyone asks, and I'm sure they won't under the circumstances, I tried to hit his collar bone and the baton glanced off his shoulder and hit him in the head."

Cody looked up at Skip Danski. "All the stuff from the cabin is in his tent, including the professor's clothes. There's no doubt Tommy broke into the cabin and took off with their stuff," he said changing the subject.

"There's no doubt Tommy killed the Toddwells, you mean."

"Tommy didn't kill the Toddwells."

"So you say."

"So the evidence says."

Shaking Tommy, Trooper Danski said, "OK, Tommy where's your fucking canoe?" The Indian trapper said nothing but pointed in a general easterly direction with his head.

"Stay here with this bozo, Cody, and I'll check it out." Skip stored his collapsible baton in his large blue fanny pack and headed off into the woods.

"Say, there aren't any bears around here, are there?" Trooper Danski yelled over his shoulder.

"Only black bears, and they do move about this time of year."

A look of apprehension crossed Skip's face. "I thought bears hibernate in winter?"

"No, only brown bears hibernate."

"Uh."

After Danski left, Cody looked over at the prisoner. "Tommy, is all that stuff from the cabin?"

Tommy nodded.

"How long have you been trapping?"

"Now or ever?" Tommy looked up at Trooper O'Keefe through the strip of makeshift bandage wrapped around his head.

"Now."

"Ugh. Been out about 2 weeks, maybe. You lose track of time.

Don't wear a watch. Anyways, I can't remember ... my head hurts."

"Yeah, well, this is important, Tommy, so think on it hard. Did you see anyone out here this last week?"

Tommy shook his head. "Just the old farts from the cabin one day."

"What about another boat?"

Tommy shook his head again. "No, nothing. Didn't see nothing, hear nothing, don't *know* nothing."

"Listen, asshole, you don't tell me the truth and you will be trying to remember what happened to your sorry ass for the rest of your life ... from a tiny cell in the Seward penitentiary."

"Trooper, I stole some shit out the cabin, sure. The damn cabin was wide open, and no one was there. Door was wide open ... anyway, the people staying there left the cabin and all their stuff. Place was a mess. They really trashed it. So maybe that's a felony, maybe not. But that's it. That's worth a year max. Your fucking white man threats don't do nothing to me."

"Yeah, well, if you're such a smart asshole, what's max incarceration time for multiple homicides?"

"Murder? Man, I can't do that kind of time. Not now, not ever."

Trooper Danski arrived back at Tommy's camp about a half hour later. "Found the canoe, just as Tom Whitefeather described it, black motor and all. Boat has a lot of blood in it and a bunch of traps and some bait. Could be animal blood, but who knows. We better get back to the cabin with Tommy-the-fucking-trapper and report in to Jim. Then we can return and take this place apart. I'm willing to bet we find enough evidence by lunch to wrap this murder investigation up."

"I told you. I didn't kill anybody, really." Tommy was getting scared. "I just heard about it for the first time a few minutes ago."

"Shut up, asshole. I'm going to read you your Miranda rights, and then we can talk all you want." Danski pulled a well-worn manila card from his wallet and went through the litany ... "You have the right to remain silent. Anything you say can and will be used against you in a court of law. You have a right to an attorney and to have him present when you are questioned. If you can't afford an attorney, the court will appoint one for you before any questioning. Do you understand your rights?"

Tommy dropped his head and nodded solemnly.

"We're going back to the cabin. If you have anything to say, tell it to Sergeant Nichols."

About 40 minutes later, they were back at the cabin with Tommy in custody. Skip was more convinced than ever they had their murderer. Cody was equally convinced they hadn't.

"Hey, Jim, look who we found in the woods. Tommy the Trapper," Danski called out as they neared the cabin. Everyone stopped what they were doing and looked. Jim Nichols broke into a big grin.

"Well, well, well. Good work. Where you find him?"

Skip answered first. "About a mile from the river. Had a tent full of all kinds of goodies from the cabin. I also found the canoe with some blood in it ... matches the description the VPSO gave us. To top it off, he even tried to kill Cody."

"You OK, Cody?"

"Yeah, I'm fine. Tommy has a bump or two, though."

"I had to settle him down with my collapsible baton. He was choking the shit out of Cody here." Trooper Danski sent an icy look at Cody.

Jim Nichols looked over at the prisoner. "Tommy, has anyone read you your rights?" Tommy nodded. "OK, good. Well, I'm going to read them to you one more time. Pay attention, partner, you never know, there might be a test on this at the end of the week." Sergeant Nichols read him his rights one more time.

"Now, Tommy, do you want to tell me anything?"

"I didn't kill anybody. I was trapping."

"How long you been a trapper?"

"Most of my life. My grandfather, he taught me."

"You have a trapline?"

"Yeah, three traplines. They run about a half mile each. I got over sixty traps."

"You skin everything you trap?"

"Everything I'm going to keep."

"So you must be very good at skinning?"

Tommy nodded, wondering where this questioning was going.

"Where's your skinning knife?" Jim asked.

"In camp, with the rest of my stuff. You guys arrested me, and I need to get my stuff. I can't leave it out here."

"Yeah," Cody interjected, "got that right. Someone might think he abandoned his camp and would steal all his stuff."

The group chuckled. Jim was less amused. He shot Cody a glance, then looked over at Tommy. "You must be real busy then?"

"Yeah, pretty much. I'm about through ... the season will be ending soon."

"Well, if you are so busy, how come you ended up with the Toddwells' possessions in your tent?"

"Look, I already told the other troopers this. I took the stuff from the cabin ... I admit it. Hell, they're rich. Besides the door was wide open, and the place was trashed. But that's all. Just some food, the radio, some ammunition, and clothing. I figured the owners weren't coming back anyway."

"Did you ever meet or see the Toddwells?"

"No."

"Why did you come over here in the first place?"

"I came to ask them why they were digging up the graves of my ancestors in the old village. I was going to tell them to put back anything they found or I'd call the state troopers."

Don interrupted, "Well, that's one for the books, a thief calling the cops on an archeologist."

Sergeant Nichols raised his hand slightly to establish order in the group and refocused the line of questioning.

"Tommy, why did you come over here? Why did you think these folks were doing that?"

"I was on my trapline across the bay early on the first day out and saw smoke coming from the wood stove, so I knew someone was here. It was cold as hell, so I thought maybe they would give me a cup of coffee or something to warm up. I took the canoe over here to say 'hello,' only they were leaving when I got here. They had shovels and backpacks and were wading across the river toward the old village."

"What old village?"

"Old Twasaan is just a couple of miles over that hill from here," he said, pointing to the nearest rise.

"Did you talk to them at all?" Jim was looking closely at him for body language.

"No, they were too far away. I thought maybe I would come back later. Then about 2 days ago when I set up my camp where you guys jumped me, I walked over to the old village to see what they had done. That's when I saw where those people had been robbing the graves of our ancestors."

"So you got mad, came over here, and killed them," Trooper Danski surmised.

Jim Nichols looked over at him sternly. "Let him tell his own story, Skip."

Tommy continued. "Yes ... No ... I mean, I was coming here to talk only. I was mad. Anyone would be. You know, if someone digs up a grave in a white cemetery, it's called grave robbing. But someone digs up the grave of an Indian and its called archeology. In the old days, before the white invasion, Indians never robbed the graves of another Indian. Burial grounds were as sacred as one of your churches. Anyway, when I got here, the fucking place was empty, except for the junk in the cabin. I thought they must have cleared out in a hurry, so I helped myself."

"Oh, bullshit. Cut the crap, Tommy, and come clean before I smack you again." Danski was losing patience.

"I told you true! I only took some stuff from the cabin."

Cody stood up and stretched. "Jim, can I ask Tommy a couple of questions?"

"Sure, as long as they are in keeping with what we're doing here," Jim replied.

"Tommy, you say they were robbing the graves, but you never saw them robbing the graves, right?"

"Yeah, that's right. But I know they did."

"OK, let's say they did desecrate the graves ...."

Tommy looked at him uncomprehendingly.

"Let's say they robbed the graves. Where are the artifacts? Did you find anything during the time you were in the cabin?"

"No," he said quietly.

"But you saw where they had dug up graves in the old village of Twasaan?"

"Yes, the earth was fresh."

"How did you know the earth was fresh?"

"Because that morning it was real cold, and there wasn't any frost on the moss covering the graves."

"OK, Tommy. Did you look to see if anything was disturbed?"

"No, I was too scared. I just got close enough to see what happened, but I didn't look into the graves."

"OK," Jim said. "How do we get to the old village?"

A few minutes later, Tommy had explained what he knew. Jim instructed Skip to start a fire in the front yard where Tommy could stay warm until he, Cody, and Don returned. Then the trio packed up their gear and headed into the woods, leaving Tommy in Skip's care. The troopers forded the river and headed back toward Tommy's camp. At about the halfway point, they marked the trail and headed off into the woods for almost an hour. After picking up a small-game trail for 50 yards, they ran straight into the village. It was only a few yards from the beach, but was so concealed with underbrush and cedar trees that the whole place was naturally protected from view. Jim Nichols gave directions.

"Don, get the camera, shoot everything. Cody, we're going to go through this place systematically. Use your compass to get bearings on this place and start working up the coordinates. And don't anyone touch anything until I say so."

CHAPTER EIGHTEEN

Cody headed off toward the beach where he could get bearings on the surrounding mountains and other geographical features. The other investigators first circled the site to pick up any prints leading in or out of the village, but the snow and hard ground had erased everything. Don was walking around in back of the gravesites when he called out.

"Hey, I found some clothes ... a shirt and jacket ... over here."

"OK, Don," Jim replied, "mark it and let's go on."

Don took a piece of international orange plastic surveyor's tape and marked and photographed the location. When the group was satisfied that there were no other clues to be found, they moved into the village from a single direction.

"This is the way in and the way out," Jim explained. "We don't want tracks all over the place. Before we get started, Don, how about photographing the bottoms of all our shoes in case we run into any footprints."

Cody had just finished up and rejoined the group. "Let Don take photographs of your boot prints so we don't get them confused with any other prints out here."

In a few minutes, each of them had had both their shoes photographed. Don kept a photograph log of each shot taken. Jim was carefully checking a path which ran through the village when a large totem pole loomed up ahead.

"Oh, fuck, look at that!" Don and Cody turned to see what Jim was pointing at. There, resting obscenely in the arms of the large carved totem pole was the sightless, blood-soaked head of Mrs. Toddwell. Don photographed the head in place and tied a strip of plastic tape to one of the outstretched arms on the totem which held the macabre trophy. They moved through the ruins of the village in silence, now looking for the head of Professor Toddwell. It took about an hour before they located his head, perched on top one of the skeletons in a shallow grave. It took over 4 hours of methodically searching the village before they felt like there was little more that could be done. The heads were gathered up, as was the clothing, and all trace evidence was "tagged and bagged" according to procedure. Then they headed back to the cabin.

Don broke the silence first. "Well, Tommy's story just doesn't check out. I think we can make a pretty good case on an Indian who was pissed that two whites were poking around the ruins of an old village and desecrating the gravesites, so he kills them and steals their stuff. He was certainly capable, has knowledge, motive, and opportunity. A nonnative wouldn't care if a gravesite was explored, but an Indian would. And Tommy was pretty vocal about it."

Cody spoke up. "I don't think he did it. This is too bizarre for Tommy. I know him. He's a little crazy, sure, but he's not capable of a crime like this."

"So you know who did it then?" the sergeant asked.

"No, I don't. But I have a feeling we're about to make the wrong case on the wrong criminal."

"Well, the evidence says you're flat-wrong, Cody. We'll confront Tommy back at the cabin, and I bet he breaks and gives us a confession. In the meantime, whichever way this thing goes, keep your comments to yourself. The last thing we need is some fuckin' attorney calling you as the star witness for the defense."

Once back at the Toddwells' cabin, the investigators collected mutilated bodies and body parts, including the bowl containing skin and a sample of fluid it contained. The carcass of the little dog was kept separately, but next to its masters. Jim dispatched Skip and Don to survey Tommy's camp and gather the evidence and the canoe. Jim instructed Cody to return to the vessel and call Tom Whitefeather in Twasaan to see if they could raise Ketchikan. They would need a prisoner transport as soon as possible.

"OK, we'll meet back here in about 2 hours. Any longer and it'll be pitch-dark. We'll pick up Tommy's canoe and tow it to Twasaan, so you guys can just place any additional evidence in the canoe. Wrap it so it doesn't become contaminated with whatever was in the boat. We need to keep our trace evidence as clean as possible. We'll have a relative or friend of Tommy's break down his camp for him. And, Cody, keep the radio traffic to Twasaan down to a minimum. We don't want the whole world to know what we're doing out here."

As Don and Skip headed back across the river to Tommy's campsite, Cody departed for the boat. He was glad to get some time to himself. He had to think and sort things out. Things just didn't add up.

When he arrived at the patrol boat, the tide was out. He pulled on the line with a little tug and brought the vessel in close enough to shore to pull himself up over the bow. The boat appeared in good shape. He checked the batteries and then called Tom Whitefeather, the Village Public Safety Officer in Twasaan. Tom answered immediately.

"Cody, good to hear from you. I was just wondering if you guys would be returning tonight or if you were going to bivouac over there? The temperatures are going way down tonight ... might hit the single digits the forecast says."

"No, we're coming back tonight with one in tow."

Tom Whitefeather understood immediately. "Roger, one in tow. Want me to contact Ketchikan for transport? Over."

"Roger that, I don't think there is much we can do about returning today, so let's say first thing in the morning. Over."

"Is the transport for who we thought it was?" Another cryptic question. "Over."

"Roger. We'll also need some place to keep him for the night."

"Roger that. I'll get started. Stand by while I call Ketchikan lima-lima."

After about 30 minutes Tom Whitefeather called back. Cody heard the radio static broken with the familiar "5-A-19, 5-A-19, this is Twasaan VPSO, over."

"Roger, Tom. Got any good news? Over."

"Sure do. The professor was a specialist in North American Indian cultures. Very knowledgeable and respected in his field. He had told colleagues before he left New York that he thought he might have located the site of a very important Indian village."

"Well, that sure clears up what he was doing here, doesn't it?"

"Yeah, looks like."

"We have a pickup scheduled for 0800 tomorrow morning. The Grumann Goose will come in from Juneau and pick up CID and cargo, over."

"Roger, thanks, Tom. I'll see you tonight. Over."

"This is Twasaan VPSO, out."

Cody finished checking the gray fiberglass patrol boat in preparation to depart for Twasaan as soon as possible. It had been a long day, and the team hadn't even stopped for lunch. He estimated that it would be dark within an hour, and they needed to get things wrapped up. *At this rate, it's going to be well after midnight before we turn in.*

Cody returned to the Toddwells' cabin before the two-hour deadline only to find total pandemonium. He saw the investigators in the woods near the cabin and walked over to see what the commotion was all about. On the ground was Tommy the Trapper, dead. His face half-blown off. Sergeant Nichols was pale and shaken by the experience. Everyone was talking at once.

"What happened!?" Cody exclaimed.

"It's my fault," Jim Nichols replied ashen-faced. "I'm to blame. I started interrogating him as soon as everyone left. Tommy kept denying anything to do with the murders, but I kept after him, trying to break him down. I presented him with all the evidence, the canoe, him being a trapper, the stuff at his campsite ... everything we had on him, leaning on him hard. I sure didn't paint a pretty picture of his life after he was found guilty. Tommy began crying and still kept denying everything but the thefts. Finally, he told me he didn't want to discuss it anymore, he wanted an attorney. I said fine, and that was it. After a while, Tommy asked if he could just sit on the porch for awhile. I said sure. Apparently, he had somehow worked his way out of the restraining cuffs and when he got to the top stair, he turned and jumped on me. The next thing I know is we're fighting for my weapon. I had my finger on the trigger, and when he tried to pull my hand away, there was a shot. I rolled away from him, and he was lying like he is now, with half his face blown away."

"Oh, fuck."

"There could be another interpretation," Trooper Danski proffered testily, his breath visible in the decreasing temperatures. He raised his gloved hands to count off the reasons on his fingers. "One, this guy has been the number-one subject from the get-go. He has a record. Are we surprised given his propensity to physical violence? Hell, this guy almost kills Cody this morning! He's violent. He's assaulted a police officer in the past. Two, let's not forget that the fuckin' bay is almost totally iced over. It's the middle of fuckin' winter. The closest settlement of any kind is Twasaan ... where he lives. It's not like there are lots of other people are out and about. Three, he had the right boat and outboard, seen near here just before the murders. How many other aluminum canoes with square sterns and black outboard motors are there around here? None! Four, he was a trapper ... and the victims ... let's not forget them ... they were skinned alive! A real professional job. How many people even know how to skin an animal? Not many ... how many can skin well enough to do a human body? Even less, I would imagine ... don't forget that either!" Skip was waving his arms and getting more and more passionate as he went along.

"Five, by his own admissions and statements, he was here, he saw them. He knew what they were doing. He saw the fresh diggings. He was mad as hell that they supposedly were robbing his ancestors' graves ... and, by golly gee ... guess what? Dead bodies here at the cabin and the heads of the Toddwells turn up in the village. Six, we find the Toddwells' stuff in his camp. We find his canoe, full of blood."

Danski paced around the group. "Read the goddamn evidence!

Isn't that what we're taught? He had motive, opportunity, intent, and plenty of ability. I think what really happened here was Jim lays it all out for him. Everything. It finally starts sinking into this dumb son-of-a-bitch that he's made some serious mistakes in committing this crime. Incriminating evidence is everywhere. The last thing he was probably thinking was that the crime would be discovered so soon ... he just wasn't expecting us. So now Jim's talking to him, not about a little evidence supporting probable cause for arrest, Jim's talking about a hell of a lot of evidence ... proof beyond reasonable doubt, in fact, enough for any jury to convict him of two homicides!

"So Tommy starts thinking the chances are real good he'll likely be locked up in some cell in prison so deep they'll have to pump him sunshine every day so he can get his 10 minutes of exercise. He gets real scared imagining his freedom's slip-sliding away. He panics and is willing to commit another murder to keep his freedom. It's no one's fucking fault. Show me one piece of evidence that doesn't point to this Indian trapper ... just one piece of evidence."

Cody spoke up. "How about the Vibram tracks I found? He's wearing rubber boots."

"So what? He wore one set of boots to commit the crime and then changed. Is that so difficult to grasp? Hell, where are the fucking the clothes he wore? They must have been covered in blood. What did he use to behead the Toddwells? We haven't found an ax or a saw. No boots? You're worrying about no boots? We may never get any of that stuff. Stick to the evidence we have and you'll come to the same conclusion. Bye-bye, Tommy ... end of case. Now let's get the fuck out of these woods and get back to Twasaan before we all freeze to death."

Jim and Don were both nodding their heads in agreement.

Cody couldn't believe it, but then, no one took his Kushtikaw theory very seriously either. "You guys have your theories, and I have mine, but I'll tell you this. Tommy's death is going to be difficult for the Native American community to accept."

Don glared at Cody and said icily, "Well, shit happens."

It was several hours after dark before the bodies of the Toddwells and Tommy the Trapper could be loaded into the boat, along with the evidence and all the other gear the investigators and Cody brought with them to the crime scene. Finally, after checking to make sure everything was aboard, Cody started the engines and turning on the dual spotlights, began to slowly motor down the shore to where Tommy's canoe was beached. The few minutes it took to arrive at the canoe were passed in silence. Everyone was deep in thought, especially Cody. He was saddened by the unfortunate death of Tommy and deeply disturbed that nothing would ever be done to apprehend the real murderer.

As the spotlights illuminated the aluminum canoe, the lights reflected off the water and the trees along the shore. Cody was startled, seeing two spots of blue light staring back at him through the darkness. For a second, his mind jumped to the conclusion that it was the Kushtikaw, but the shining eyes turned out to be no more than patches of snow on a tree bough. He breathed an inward sigh of relief and refocused his attention on maneuvering the patrol boat close enough so that Don could reach over the bow and grab the upturned motor on the end of the canoe.

"Got it! You can pull back now."

Reversing the engines, Cody backed away from shore. Once in deeper water, the canoe was brought alongside and a tow bridle fashioned for the stern of the patrol craft. Then, turning the craft around, they headed slowly back to Twasaan, negotiating patches of thick floating ice.

CHAPTER NINETEEN

It was close to 7 p.m. by the time the troopers arrived at the dock in Twasaan. If it hadn't been so cold or maybe a little earlier, there might have been more people on the dock to see what was going on. As it was, the single metal post with a halogen light illuminated only Tom Whitefeather and Dot, standing there huddled close together, their parka hoods pulled tight and hands thrust deep in their pockets. Cody used the twin engines to maneuver the patrol vessel alongside the dock, reversing one throttle and putting the other forward, "walking" the patrol boat sideways until it came alongside the dock directly under the lights. Tom could see in Cody's face that something was wrong. He saw that Tommy was missing. There wasn't a lot to figure out.

"Say, Dot, Cody is going to have to get the boat squared away before he stops for the night. How about you bring us some coffee down here?"

Dot was going to make a snide reply, but she saw the look on Tom's face. It worried her. "Sure," she said, "I'll be back in awhile."

When she was out of earshot, Tom turned to Cody. "Where's Tommy?" he asked.

"Dead. He tried to kill the sergeant, and they fought over his weapon. It went off killing Tommy."

"Shhiitt!"

"That about says it all."

The troopers discussed their next move. "Might as well leave the bodies here for the night. It will be easier for us move them to the plane in the morning," Don thought out loud.

"Well, if we do, we need to post a guard to make sure nothing disappears. No offense, Tom."

"No offense taken."

"OK, well, then, let's just leave everything here for tonight. Who wants to take the first watch?" Jim looked around for volunteers. Seeing that no one was going to volunteer, Cody half-heartedly raised his hand.

"I'll do it," Cody said tiredly. "When will I be relieved?"

"Let's see," Jim said as he glanced at his watch. "It's just after 2000, and we need to go until 0800 tomorrow; that's 12 hours. Each of us will need to stand a three-hour watch. Skip, you will relieve Cody at 2300, Don will relieve Skip at 0200, and I will take the final watch of 0500 to 0800."

Everyone sluggishly filed off the dock and slowly made their way to the gymnasium to prepare something warm to eat. Sergeant Nichols walked off with Tom to use the telephone and report to the Ketchikan Post about the day's events and the death of Tommy the Trapper. It had been a very long and very cold day.

When the sergeant was through at the office, Tom walked back down to the docks to speak with Cody. "What happened out there?"

"There's not much more to the story than you already know. He tried to escape and was killed."

"While in *custody*?" Tom looked angry.

"Look, Tom, it's not what you think. Sure he was in custody, but he somehow slipped out of his restraints. There was a fight between him and Sergeant Nichols, and now he's dead."

Tom looked disturbed, his breath jetting out from somewhere behind the wolverine ruff on his hood. "The tribal attorneys are really going to have a field day with this one, Cody. You know that."

"Yep. Well, there's not a lot that can be done about it now."

There was a long silence. Then Officer Whitefeather spoke up.

"So do you think that Tommy really did it?"

"Do you?"

"Nope."

"Me either."

They both stood there in silence under the lamppost as the snow began to fall again in tiny flecks mixed with ice. It was so cold and dry that the snow could be brushed from their parkas like beach sand.

After a while, Dot mercifully reappeared with a large thermos of coffee and several sandwiches. "I looked out the trailer window and saw you guys standing here by yourselves, so I figured you'd be here for a while. I hope this helps."

"This is great, Dot," Cody said. "I haven't eaten all day. Thanks."

Tom unscrewed the thermos top. "I'll have some coffee, if you don't mind."

"Uh-huh, help yourself," Cody barely managed to say, his mouth was already stuffed with part of the first sandwich.

Dot turned to leave. "I'll be up at the trailer if you need anything."

"Thanks, Dot," they both responded. Tom stayed with him for awhile longer, then headed off to the trailer. Cody spent the rest of his shift trying to sort things out.

CHAPTER TWENTY

Morning broke with bad news all around. John Morgan, the pilot for the Department of Public Safety, would not be able to fly the Grumann Goose down to retrieve the investigators and the bodies. Juneau was socked in with snow squalls and a thick fog. Most recent forecast showed that it might be days before the weather lifted. In the meantime, Ketchikan Dispatch, under orders from Lt. Blocker, had arranged for a charter aircraft from the Inter-Island Flight Service. A DeHavilland Twin Otter on floats would be landing before 0900 to make the pickup.

Trooper O'Keefe had called Lt. Blocker earlier from VPSO Whitefeather's office to report in, only to get chewed out for not following orders by getting out of the way and allowing the investigators to do their work.

"Great, just great," Cody heard the lieutenant say. "You were supposed to be their transportation and support. Instead, you are the one who found Tommy Harold and are now one of the witnesses in his death."

"Sorry, Lieutenant, but they needed help. It isn't their normal working environment. I only did what they asked me to do."

"Well, I'm asking—no—telling you—to get the troopers on the charter aircraft, wrap it up, and come back. While you are waiting around, get Officer Whitefeather to write up a statement or investigative report concerning his involvement in any of this and bring the paperwork back with you. We'll need this for the shooting board and the grand jury, if there is one, investigating the death. If you leave before noon, you should be back at the Ketchikan Post before dark."

"Yes sir."

"Has the community found out about Tommy the Trapper yet?"

"No sir, not yet."

"I can tell you this," Lt. Blocker pronounced. "When they find out, the shit is going to hit the fan. The fact the investigators caught him red-handed ... so to speak ... is the only thing that will help quiet this down."

Cody gave him the news. "Lieutenant, sir, I might as well tell you, because the investigators will soon enough, I don't think he did it."

"O'Keefe," the lieutenant said raising his voice, "that's counterproductive, speculative bullshit. You are a team member. Just shut up about your views and let this thing play out on its own. This is the last I want to hear about it."

"Yes sir. I'll get the investigative details in writing from Tom and head back as soon as possible."

"Check with me when you get in."

"Yes sir."

Officer Whitefeather walked into the office as Cody finished his conversation with Ketchikan. "What's the plan for today?"

"A charter aircraft is going to pick up the guys and the bodies and transport them back to town. The lieutenant wants me to get a supplemental statement from you on your activities supporting the investigation and bring it back with me when I return to Ketchikan."

"You going back today?" Tom asked. He stretched his arms to get the circulation going.

"Yep, this morning after the plane takes off."

"That's going to be a long trip for you," Officer Whitefeather opined.

"Sure, but better than the other day. At least I won't have to fight the weather."

"That may be the only break you have," Tom replied as he started flipped on the switch to the Mr. Coffee. Soon, the smell of fresh brewing coffee filled the room.

An hour, later the village was buzzed by a red- and yellow-painted aircraft. The loud noise confirmed it was a twin engine DeHavilland. The plane banked over the end of the community and flew parallel to the shoreline looking for debris in the water. Hitting sheet ice or a semisubmerged log could have serious consequences for the aircraft and crew. The pilot made two more passes. Apparently satisfied that landing posed a minimum risk, he turned into the wind and gently brought the bird down. The aircraft skipped along the surface of the water for about a quarter mile before slowly coming to rest on the buoyant, aluminum pontoons which looked like long, inverted kayaks. Then the pilot turned toward the floating dock and shut down the engine which would come over the top of the wooden platform. As the aircraft neared the dock, the pilot slid out of his door, walked gingerly forward on the slick pontoon, and threw a polypropylene tie-up line to one of the investigators.

"Don't tie it to anything yet; just hang on a minute." The pilot tied off to the forward-most cleat on the left pontoon. "OK, walk the plane forward slowly, that's it. Now tie off the line to the cleat over there on the dock but not too tight."

As the front of the left pontoon touched the floating dock, the pilot jumped off sliding slightly but otherwise staying upright. In his hand was the second line which was secured to the back of the pontoon. The pilot pulled the aircraft into position and then adjusted both lines so that the left pontoon rested gently against the beams of the dock. When the task was completed, the pilot climbed back into the aircraft and finished securing the plane. Then the experienced bush pilot came ashore and introduced himself as Matt Thomline. When introductions were completed, Tom and Cody helped load the bodies while much of the village stood watching from a distance.

"Do you think they know anything yet?" asked Cody.

"No, we've kept this whole this pretty well under wraps," Tom said. Then continuing on, "When you get to Ketchikan though, you will need to call me before it gets into the press so I can tell the village council what happened to Tommy Harold."

"Sure will, but this has all the earmarkings of a shit storm," Trooper O'Keefe replied, loading the last body into the side door of the twin Otter. Once the plane was loaded with passengers and cargo, Cody and Tom set the canoe inside the aircraft and closed the door. Then they cast off the tie-up lines and pulled the floatplane away from the dock. The pilot cranked off the magneto and first one engine then the other erupted in a ball of smoke and a roar as the propellers of the large motors gained momentum. Revving up the engines, the pilot slowly guided the aircraft out into safe waters, turned into the wind, and threw the throttles forward. The plane rattled and shook, picking up speed. Soon, it was bouncing off the tops of the swells, leaving long white streamers of water in the bay. Then it was airborne and on its way to Ketchikan, a mere 40 minutes away. The silence on the dock was deafening.

Tom Whitefeather watched the plane disappear in the distance and then turned to Cody. "Might as well get breakfast before taking off. Dot has volunteered to cook, God help us."

O'Keefe glanced over at Tom and smiled. "I need to say goodbye to her and the village council, and you need to write a summary of your actions during the investigation before I leave anyway. Let's go, I could use something to eat."

The pair walked through the crunchy snow to the trailer in silence, each lost in his own thoughts. They were stopped by a couple of village elders who wanted to know what was going on. There was an investigation concerning some missing people across the bay, Tom told them. Because it was an active investigation there wasn't anything else he could say right now but as soon as he could, he would brief the council.

Arriving at Tom's rundown trailer, Tom called to Dot. "Here we are, ready or not."

Dot opened the door and said smiling, "It's almost done. Come in and start with coffee."

The two lawmen didn't have to be asked a second time. They kicked their boots to dislodge any excess snow, wiped the soles on an outside rug at the base of the stairs, and stepped up into the trailer. Surprisingly, it smelled wonderful. The aroma of eggs, bacon, and toast all blended together in the small kitchen. They hung their gear up near the door and then sat down at the dinette while Dot brought over the pot of coffee and two mugs.

Tom and Cody looked like they wanted to talk about the case, but they didn't want Dot to pick up on the details. Dot, sensing the awkward moment, broke the silence.

"Hey, it's OK you two talk'n. I know more than you think," she said, turning the eggs in the cast-iron skillet. Then she continued. "You told me about the murders, and the investigators told me about the details, includ'n poor Tommy Harold."

Tom Whitefeather looked incredulous. "They *told* you *everything*?"

"Ummm, not exactly," Dot confessed. "But they do like to impress a lady bring'n 'em sandwiches and coffee. I heard more by just stand'n around talk'n to them and overhear'n what they were say'n."

"And you haven't told anyone?" Cody asked.

"No, I wanted to see what you two were go'n to do first," she replied.

"Well, *if* you know what's going on, you know that they think they have solved the case with Tommy the Trapper," Tom said. "Cody and me think that this isn't over yet. They got the wrong guy."

"Who can't defend himself 'cause he's dead," Dot added.

"You heard that too?" Tom exclaimed. "Damn."

"I told you they were trying to impress me by elud'n to certain things, ya know. All you had to do was listen."

Cody O'Keefe turned in his chair to face Dot, who was putting the finishing touches on the fried potatoes. "Dot, please keep all this to yourself. The village doesn't know about Tommy. Tom and I are going to explain everything to the council as soon as we can. If I am not here, then Tom will do it himself. We are not going to keep them in the dark."

"You guys better think of someth'n quick then 'cause this isn't gonna stay quiet much longer."

Cody replied, “Dot, there’s nothing we can do until we get authorization from Ketchikan and Lt. Blocker. If I were to say something now, I would be disobeying orders.”

“Out here, authorization from Ketchikan don’t count for shit,” she mumbled under her breath.

Tom Whitefeather spoke up. “Dot, we want to talk to you about the rest of this case as Cody and me see it.” Over breakfast, the two lawmen filled Dot in on the developing Kushtikaw theory, as it was now being called. Tommy had been shocked by the grave desecrations. As a trapper, he knew the village was there for years and said nothing, and more importantly, took nothing. He wore the wrong type boots. They didn’t have Vibram soles. Tommy Harold might have been in trouble from time to time, but he respected his clan. So, dismissing Tommy the Trapper as a suspect, that left them with the necklace, the only solid connection to ancient gravesites and the Toddwells and a lot of questions.

Cody took up the discussion of what to do next. There were two maybe three approaches to the investigation. First, the person, or persons, who committed the murders was still free somewhere. It was doubtful that he, she, or they, would stay around with the investigators tromping through the woods, so where did the murderer or murderers go? If Tom actually saw the canoe that belonged to Tommy, how did this person or persons get to the Toddwells in the first place? Second, who was or were these criminals and what did they want? Third, assuming grave desecrations played a major role in the murders, as evidenced by the heads on display in the ancient village, what was the connection between the Toddwells, their murders, and the graves?

The three discussed the conundrum over breakfast and by the last cup of coffee were no further along than when they started.

"So, where do we go from here?" asked Officer Whitefeather.

"Let's just say, for a moment, that the common connection between the Toddwells and their murderer is the graves," Cody began. "Assume that archeology was only part of what they were doing. What else could be done under the guise of archeology?"

"Sell'n artifacts is the only thing," Dot allowed.

"OK, if they were collecting artifacts under all the authorized permits, could they be keeping and selling less valuable pieces on the black market?" Tom asked.

"Dot has said there are stores in Ketchikan that sell burial beads as authentic antique trade beads and such, isn't that right?" Cody asked.

"Ya, there are three I can think of right now. The Sourdough Provisions Company, Rainforest Antiques, and the Totem Store," she said as she touched each finger and named them off.

"So, you're thinking, Cody, that the Toddwells may have sold lesser quality artifacts to the antique stores and kept the rest for the university or a museum?" Tom asked.

"That's just a thought. If the killer or killers are still around somewhere, would they go to one of the shops and sell the artifacts they had?"

Officer Whitefeather spoke up. "So you're saying the motive for the murders was robbery?"

"I'll admit it is far-fetched, but a thought nonetheless."

"What about the placement of the heads of the Toddwells in the old village? That doesn't sound like robbery to me," challenged Tom.

"I agree with you, along with the way the Toddwells were murdered. It sounds ritualistic," admitted Trooper O'Keefe. "How about we go back to the necklace. Would a shaman have committed a ritualistic murder like that, Dot?" he asked.

"Never," said Dot.

"Never say never," chimed in Tom Whitefeather.

"Think about this angle for a moment," said Cody O'Keefe. "Tommy said he only saw the Toddwells. They were murdered by someone unseen by anyone, including an experienced trapper, who not only committed the murders in a ritualistic fashion, but was good enough to slip by undetected and used the weather to his or their advantage. Meaning they are not just good in the woods, they are an expert. They may have left behind the necklace which is connected to a dead shaman who might have been a Kushtikaw. Again, the association between grave robbing and Toddwells. Let's look at the shaman theory again."

"That's native history and Dot's department," said Tom, looking over at Dot.

"True. And I've been think'n. How many ancient villages had a Kushtikaw shaman?"

"And I wonder if the Toddwells explored those too," added Cody.

CHAPTER TWENTY-ONE

Soon Trooper O'Keefe would have to head back to Ketchikan. The weather would only hold for so long. Tom promised to look into Forest Service permits to see if anyone was using another cabin in the area. Dot would research reports and stories of villages of where Kushtikaws might have lived nearby.

While Tom wrote up his investigative report, deliberately leaving out the Kushtikaw theory, Trooper O'Keefe stopped by the council office and after some small talk broke the news he had nothing to share but anything that became public information he would pass on to Tom. The village elders were concerned about the recent activities and Cody O'Keefe made as many apologies as was necessary to maintain decorum. An hour later, he met Tom and Dot on the way back to the trailer. Tom handed him his report in a large envelope.

"Don't worry. The envelope is larger than my report," Tom said smiling broadly and showing his white teeth. "You know us VPSOs hate to write anything down anyway. It's a cultural thing."

Cody laughed and placed the packet in the inside pocket of his parka. Once back on his patrol boat, he tested his radio, which thankfully was operational, and called in to tell dispatch he was underway. Leaving Tom and Dot on the dock, he spun the helm and was soon maneuvering through the skim ice and on his return trip home.

Four hours later, Cody was skimming down Tongass Narrows toward Ketchikan. The protected waters were smooth and a change from all the rough weather and ice he had experienced in recent days. He turned into the fuel docks, cut the engines, and tied up. The trooper took on one hundred gallons of gas before maneuvering his vessel over to the city docks. When all the gear was unloaded and stowed in his truck, and the patrol boat scrubbed down and secured, Trooper O'Keefe drove to the Ketchikan Post on the north side of town. He arrived amidst the hubbub of news reporters and television cameras. Someone must have leaked something to the media he mused. He hoped that someone was not Dorothy. He parked on the side of the building to avoid the small but avid crush of reporters. No such luck.

"Excuse me. Are you with the state troopers? Were you part of the murder investigation? Can you comment to our viewers about the case?" All this came rapid-fire from a female television reporter dressed in an aqua-colored rain suit who was covering the story for the evening news.

"Nothing to say, sorry."

Turning and talking over her shoulder, the news reporter called to her cameraman. "Jerry, get the camera lights on. Over here quick!" Now she stuck the microphone in Cody's face. "So, what can you tell us about Twasaan Bay?" she asked.

Cody never missed a beat. "Well, ma'am, the weather is terrible, lowering temperatures are starting to create slush ice, and the much of the near-shore area has become frozen over, especially near the freshwater streams."

"That's *it*? That's *all* you have to say?" The reporter was incensed.

"No, one other thing. It is snowing on and off too. That's about it." And with a low voice, Cody excused himself and entered the law enforcement building through the side entrance, leaving the cameraman running footage on the closing door.

"Shut off the damn camera, you idiot," he heard a female voice say as the door closed behind him.

The squad room was filled to capacity with the Anchorage CID team, the on-duty evidence custodian, off-duty troopers, and, of course, Lt. Blocker. The returning investigators had laid all the evidence out into three distinct areas on the floor. One pile consisted of evidence taken from the cabin and the Toddwell homicides; the second section of evidence comprised items taken during the arrest of Tommy Harold aka Tommy the Trapper. His aluminum canoe was even outside, stored next to a maintenance shed. The last group was the small pile of evidence from the shooting. That evidence was being kept on the side for the team being sent to investigate the shooting. Cody noticed the evidence custodian working through the Toddwells' possessions.

"Where are the bodies?" he asked no one in particular.

"The coroner met us at the terminal and had them transported to the funeral home," Skip replied.

"The Toddwells' next of kin, Alice Toddwell, has been notified and is on her way from Arizona. She should be in Seattle tonight and here on the first Alaska Airlines flight in the morning. The on-duty trooper will meet her at the airport and escort her here," Trooper Danski added to indicate all the details were being looked after.

Lt. Blocker was in his office when Cody O'Keefe arrived to check in. Cody handed Tom's report to his supervisor, who peeled back the edge of the yellow, legal size envelope and carefully extracted exactly one sheet of paper.

"That's it? A one-page report?"

"What's the problem?" Cody asked.

"This," the lieutenant said, holding up the report. "A person can't die on a single sheet of paper, much less three deaths."

"I understand, but you know how VPSOs are, Lieutenant ... minimalists."

"Is that supposed to be funny?"

"No sir, just factual."

Leaning back in his chair, the lieutenant rubbed the top of his close-cropped hair with both hands, obviously frustrated. "OK, O'Keefe, take this *missive* with you and write up the circumstances of your investigation. Be sure to fold in all the activities mentioned by Officer Whitefeather so that the reports corroborate each other."

"Can do, Lt. Blocker," Cody said as he reached for Tom's report.

"And Trooper," the lieutenant added, "it better be more than one page long when you're finished."

Seizing the opportunity, Trooper O'Keefe said, "Lt. Blocker, I am going to need access to the evidence so I can refer to each item correctly and in consecutive order in my report."

"Talk to the evidence custodian and tell him to give you whatever time you need."

"Yes sir. Thank you."

"And close the door on your way out."

"Yes sir," Trooper O'Keefe said as he turned to leave the office.

Back in the squad room, Cody approached the evidence custodian, a female trooper, with his request.

"Sure thing, Cody. No problem. I just finished listing all the items and attaching chain of custody forms to most of them. I don't know if the FBI lab will be able to make heads or tails out of your blood samples. They left by special delivery an hour ago, along with some skin samples and blood from the cabin and the victims. As for what's here, you can examine each piece as it is laid out. When you're through, I'll secure each piece in the evidence room. Until then, I'm responsible for all evidence and your shadow."

"Sure, thanks," Cody replied.

"Aren't you forgetting something?" she asked.

"Uh, what's that? Wash my hands?" he asked.

"Don't be funny, your photographs. Jim Nichols said you took photographs. Where are they?" she demanded.

"Oh, yeh … those. Hang on and I'll get my camera. You can have the film."

"I want the negatives. You need to have the film developed." Then she said, "Give the rolls to me and I'll ask the duty trooper to run them over to the camera store."

Cody rummaged around in the bottom of his rucksack until he retrieved his camera and the rolls of expended film. A few minutes later, he handed the items over to the evidence custodian, who listed each roll separately on a chain of custody form before obtaining the proper signatures and giving the on-duty trooper the photographic evidence and the mission.

In the meantime, Trooper O'Keefe had turned his attention back to the physical evidence laid out on the squad-room floor. He sighted the red tag with black lettering he had found on the bank of the Shakan River. Picking up the plastic bag which contained the tag, he turned it over in his hand. One side was clearly marked with the words "Ketchikan Motors," with an identification number and telephone number. *That's easy enough*, he thought. Turning the paper tag over in his hand, he barely could make out some type of name and address. Cody wrote down the telephone number and placed a call to Ketchikan Motors. He got a recording. It was after hours and the shop would be closed until nine o'clock in the morning. He filed the information away in his daily diary and continued to examine the evidence.

By 1900, seven o'clock in the evening, things started to die down. It was Friday evening, and everyone was getting tired. The reporters had left after being promised that a public relations spokesperson would have a press conference first thing Saturday morning. The evidence custodian told Cody she needed to go home and fix dinner and would meet him back at the office in the morning. The investigators and Lt. Blocker had taken off for dinner, and Cody found himself alone in the squad room. Just then, dispatch called back.

"Call for you on line three."

"Who is it?" Cody asked,

"Officer Whitefeather, VPSO at Twasaan."

Cody O'Keefe punched the blinking button. "Tom, how the hell are you?"

"Not too good, Cody. We may have a problem."

"Just one?"

"This is pretty major. Word is coming back from Ketchikan that one of the victims is Tommy Harold. The council is pretty upset and asking a lot of questions. This is going to get pretty ugly if the troopers don't do some damage control."

"Damn it!" Cody exclaimed, "I'll get in touch with Lt. Blocker and see what can be done. There's going to be a press release in the morning. Maybe we can give you something to tell the council tonight."

"Thanks, Cody."

"No problem, I'll see what I can do." Trooper O'Keefe hung up the phone and walked down the narrow hall to the dispatch office.

"Marsha, can you get Lt. Blocker on the radio and have him call the office. I need to speak with him ASAP."

The dispatcher nodded her head and called the lieutenant, using his call sign, 5-A-1. A few seconds later, the lieutenant responded.

"This is 5-A-1, go ahead."

"5-A-1, 5-A-19 requests you contact him lima-lima."

"10-4, will do."

A few minutes later, the light began to blink on the squad bay telephone. The dispatcher announced, "It's for you, Cody, line one."

"Trooper O'Keefe here," Cody answered.

"Trooper O'Keefe, this is Lt. Blocker. What's going on?"

"Tom Whitefeather called from Twasaan. It seems like all hell is going to break out over there. They have heard rumors that Tommy Harold has been killed. The village council is asking Tom for an explanation. We were hoping that maybe we could tell them something since it is so late and there is going to be a press release in the morning anyway."

"Ummm. Don't know. I'll get in touch with our public relations person and find out. In the meantime, call Officer Whitefeather back and tell him someone from public relations will contact him directly and provide assistance."

"Thank you, sir. Will do."

Cody punched a different button and called the VPSO office in Twasaan. It was answered on the second ring.

"Officer Whitefeather, VPSO."

"Tom, this is Cody. I called the lieutenant. He said someone from public relations will be calling you shortly."

"Thanks, Cody."

"No problem. Talk to you in the morning." Trooper O'Keefe gathered his gear, jumped in the truck, and headed for his apartment.

CHAPTER TWENTY-TWO

Across town, Takqua, having abandoned the alias of Willem Tuttle and adopting the name of Edgar Abbott, sat alone, eating his meal at a small table on the edge of the spacious dining room of the Cape Fox Hotel. All around him were couples who were dining out, perhaps a birthday or anniversary celebration; obvious businessmen; and a few vacationers. A couple days of rest had done wonders for him. At the last minute, he had extended his visit for an additional day when he discovered that he was still too beat-up and sore to move. Now, though, with a hot meal, he was beginning to feel much better. Tomorrow morning, he would call on the tourist shops named by the Toddwells in their dying confessions and see for himself what Indian artifacts the proprietors had secreted for only their most favorite clients. Edgar's train of thought was interrupted by a young waitress. He judged her to be about college age.

"Is there anything else I can get for you?" she asked. He took the tone to be amiable yet disinterested in him.

"No, that will be all, thank you."

The waitress smiled. "Very well, I'll have your check in just a moment," and she walked around the corner of the dining room and disappeared from view.

Paying his check, Edgar walked about town for a little bit and soon tiring, retreated to his room, where he laid all his shaman talismans and Kushtikaw accoutrements on the bedspread and examined each closely. Maybe tomorrow he might have some luck at the antique shops. Edgar lay back on the bedspread next to his artifacts and turned out the table light.

Morning came early for Tom and Dot with a fist banging on the door of his trailer.

"Hey, Tom, hey. Get up and answer the damn door!"

Dot woke up first to the disturbance. "What the hell is go'n on? Tom, wake up! Someone is at the door."

Tom Whitefeather jumped out of bed and threw on his pants. Outside it was pitch-black. He opened the door to the trailer a crack. Standing illuminated in the light of the trailer was one of the village elders.

"You lied to us! We know Tommy is dead!"

"What? What time is it?" Officer Whitefeather asked.

"Time for you to tell me what is going on!"

"OK, come on in and let's see if we can sort this out." Tom opened the trailer door and let Jim Harold, a distant relative of Tommy Harold, into the living room. He had been drinking—a lot.

"How do you know Tommy is dead?" Tom Whitefeather asked, rubbing his head and trying to gain some thinking time.

"That's easy," the old man responded. "The coroner just called and asked if I could come to Ketchikan to identify the body. I asked if he knew it was Tommy, and he said yes, someone else who knew

Tommy in Ketchikan had already said it was him." Mr. Harold's eyes filled with tears. "You should have told me. He was here. I could have identified him right here. But of course, you didn't want to do that—because the troopers shot him in the head!"

"Mr. Harold, I'm sorry about all that," Officer Whitefeather replied. "I was asked not to say anything before they had a chance to sort things out. Once I was given permission to say something from the Department of Public Safety public affairs officer, I was going to tell you, but the person never called last night. I'm so sorry."

Dot had heard voices in the living room and had put on some clothes to join Tom Whitefeather and Jim Harold.

"Mr. Harold," she began, "I'm sorry about Tommy, too, but Tom has been worry'n about this all night. He was go'n to tell you as soon as he could."

Mr. Harold looked at both of them. "This is wrong. You hear me? Wrong!!! And this is just the beginning—it is going to get a lot worse. Tommy may be dead, but the troopers are going to pay. And, *you*," he glared and pointed a finger at Tom, "you better pack your bags because as soon as I can call a council vote, your ass is fired." With that, Mr. Harold got up and left, slamming the door behind him with such force it rocked the trailer.

Dot looked at Tom. She noted that he wasn't worried; but very tired of being pulled in different directions.

"I'll make some coffee," she said, walking to the stove. Tom just nodded, obviously distracted. She glanced at the wall clock in the kitchen; it was four-thirty in the morning.

An hour later, Cody rose to the clang of his alarm clock. He showered, shaved, and put on a clean uniform. Then he was out the door to find breakfast. The Ketchikan Café had just opened for business when he walked in out of a pouring rain and plopped down into the booth next to the window. He was the only customer.

"What'll it be today, Cody?" the old cook called from across the room.

"Same 'ol same 'ol," he replied.

"Coming up!" The cook turned and began putting together breakfast on the long stainless steel grill behind him.

"Say," he called over his shoulder, "it sure is a shame about Tommy, huh? He was a wild one but never deserved to be killed."

Cody was taken aback. "How do you know about that?"

"And *you're* an investigator? Hell, don't you even read the damn paper?"

Cody walked over to the rack of newspapers on the checkout counter. The headline read ***Multiple Murders, Suspect Shot***.

Oh, shit, thought Cody. He picked up the top copy and started reading. There were details in the article only an investigator would know. He began to strongly suspect that one or maybe more of the Criminal Investigation Division investigators had talked with the Ketchikan reporter off the record. Breakfast arrived just as O'Keefe was finishing rereading the story. It was all there: the homicides, thankfully without the gruesome details, and the apprehension of Tommy, including his fight to resist arrest. There were quotes from the charter pilot and the coroner to back up the more sketchy details and provide the story with a level of credibility. Cody ate breakfast and sipped his coffee. His next move was to call Tom and see what was going on in Twasaan. There was going to be hell to pay over this one.

At the Ketchikan Post, Lt. Blocker and the CID investigators were already hard at work and discussing damage control around the Saturday morning newspaper article.

"We're going to have to call the VPSO in Twasaan and give him a heads-up," Don said. "He is going to have to tell the council something. Tommy lived in Twasaan. We keep him in the dark, and the governor could hear about this before the end of the day."

"Well, let's keep his comments and involvement to a minimum," replied Bob Blocker. "We don't want to have to start plugging up leaks, especially before Internal Affairs and the Shooting Board have completed their routine investigation and cleared Jim, here," he said glancing around at the three investigators. "And by the way, which one of you idiots talked out of school to the reporter?" No one in the small group replied.

"Well, she better have been a hot piece of ass, because one of you idiots may just get fired over this stunt."

"How do you know it was one of us? O'Keefe or Whitefeather could have said something," said Skip Danski.

"I didn't get incredibly stupid when I put on the lieutenant bars. This has your fingerprints all over it."

None of the investigators said anything.

Half an hour later, Cody arrived in his pickup truck and entered the squad room through the side entrance. He wasn't quiet enough to escape the watchful eyes of the dispatcher.

"Lt. Blocker asked to see you as soon as you came in," she told him.

"Thanks, Jennifer. I'm on my way." Jennifer was a new hire, and he could sense a little chemistry between them. That is, if he had enough time to play with the chemistry set, he thought as he walked past her station.

Cody O'Keefe put the idea of calling Tom in Twasaan on hold and walked down the hall to the lieutenant's brightly lit office. He knocked on the door.

"Lieutenant, you wanted to see me?"

"Come in, Cody, we have a problem."

Trooper O'Keefe walked into the room and looked around at CID investigators Sergeant Jim Nichols and Troopers Skip Danski and Don Fletcher. He nodded to the group.

"Is it about the newspaper article?"

"Oh, you saw it too. Yes, we're going to have to do some damage control. It won't hurt the case, but we are going to take some hits on the public relations front."

"It will be the talk of the town for a while. What do you want me to do?" Cody asked.

"Keep a low profile. No talking to the press and call the VPSO and tell him the same thing."

"That's a tall order. We promised him that as soon as we heard something, he could tell the village council."

"I didn't promise him that, Cody. *You* did," responded Lt. Blocker heatedly.

"Sir, look, he's part of the investigative team. He gave us plenty of support. He's done everything we asked of him. If we don't give him something for the elders, they're going to eat him alive when they get a copy of the newspaper article."

"That can't be helped now. We need to focus on what is happening here. This blows up in our faces and the department will need to do some serious damage control before this is all over" the lieutenant said.

Then he added quietly "We all have to do what we can to get the investigation closed and move on as quickly as possible. Let this thing die down, Cody."

"Yes sir," Cody said disappointedly. "I'll call Tom now with the new instructions."

Trooper Cody O'Keefe did not have to tell the group that this problem was *not* going away. Everyone could read the tea leaves, especially Officer Tom Whitefeather. Cody picked up the black telephone and dialed Twasaan.

"This is VPSO Whitefeather," a voice said on the third ring.

"Tom, Cody. You doing OK?"

"Fuck you, Cody. That Public Affairs person never called last night. All hell's breaking loose over here."

"I didn't know; sorry, Tom."

"So what do you want me to do now? Do we have a new plan to hopefully get my ass out of hot water and keep my job?" Tom asked.

Cody explained the article in the morning paper and the repercussions to the investigation. Tom traded news with Cody, explaining the visit by Jim Harold, Tommy's distant relative.

"Oh, fuck. This is worse than we thought," mumbled Cody.

"A whole lot worse. I don't know what damage control magic your lieutenant is waving around over there, but it sure as shit isn't going to turn to magic dust over here," Tom said bitterly. "You know he's going to leave me high and dry."

"Tom, I don't know what to say. But my advice is to simply tell those folks that you've been instructed by the state troopers not to discuss any details for fear of compromising the investigation. As a professional law enforcement officer, you find that advice compelling. However, the citizens of Alaska have a right to know what is going on, and they should use their influence to get to the bottom of all this." Cody knew that he was exceeding any advice the lieutenant would have wanted him to give, but Tom was his friend and he couldn't see him abandoned as part of a public relations strategy. There was a long pause on the end of the line.

"I like it," Tom said. "It just might work. It puts the onus on the troopers to explain their actions to the politicos and highlights their attempts to quiet the VPSO. You're fucked now, but I'm looking good."

Cody O'Keefe rubbed his forehead and then responded, "We never had this conversation. I'll talk to you later."

He hung up the phone and then immediately dialed Ketchikan Motors. It was answered by a young kid on the second ring.

"Ketchikan Motors."

"Good morning, I'm Trooper O'Keefe. I'm conducting an investigation and found some type of identification tag belonging to your shop. If I give the tag number, can you tell me what the tag was used for?"

"Umm, donno. What color was it?"

"Red."

"Red is our repair tag color. Let me look in the repair records book."

A few minutes later, the voice was back. "OK, what's the number?"

"001064," Cody replied.

"OK, let's see, that tag is from 1981, that's from the 001 code number ... Here it is. The Sportsmen's Lodge in Craig. It was for a repair or tune-up job on a black four-horsepower Mercury outboard."

"Say you don't sell aluminum canoes there too, do you?" Cody inquired.

"Nope, not here. We just do engine repair."

"Could an engine like that be used on one of those flat-ended canoes?"

"Sure."

"Thanks, you have been a big help. Do you also have the telephone number for the resort written down somewhere?"

The boy gave Cody the number, and they hung up. He had to ponder this development a little. He had found the tag on Shakan River between the cabin and the old village. It belonged to a Mercury outboard which could be used on a flat-ended canoe. But the tag was for the Sportsmen's Lodge, which was near Craig and nowhere near Twasaan Bay. He pulled out the map of Prince of Wales Island and studied it closely. *Even if you couldn't take the canoe around the island from Craig to Twasaan, you could put a canoe in a truck and get pretty close by logging roads,* he reasoned to himself. Cody picked up the telephone and dialed the resort.

CHAPTER TWENTY-THREE

Gerta Freese heard the telephone ring in the kitchen where she was just finishing up from breakfast. "Good morning, Sportsmen's Lodge, how can I help you?"

"Good morning, ma'am, this is Trooper Cody O'Keefe."

"Oh, thank goodness," Mrs. Freese replied. "Are you calling about the stolen canoe?"

"A stolen canoe?" exclaimed Cody.

"Yes, we filed a report with the police officer in Craig about one of our canoes being gone."

"Excuse me, ma'am, exactly who are you again?"

"Gerta, Gerta Freese. I'm one of the owners here."

"And you think it was stolen?"

"Yes."

"How long has it been missing?"

"Not quite a month."

"And what color is it?"

"Red."

"Did it have a motor on it?"

"Yes, a black Mercury."

"Ummm."

At ten o'clock in the morning, Edgar Abbott, in fresh clothes and feeling much better, had checked out of the Cape Fox Hotel. A cab had taken him near the downtown Seamen's Home, a faded, chalk-blue structure with peeling white trim. He carefully got out of the cab and paid his fare, then looked about at his surroundings and made his way to a St. Vincent DePaul receptacle a short distance away. Standing under an eve of an old building while it rained, he pulled and separated his clothes from his bag, stuffing them individually into the wide mouth of a white metal box identified for charitable donations. Keeping only his small handbag, Edgar walked down the rain-slick cobblestone streets to the Sourdough Provisions Company. The sign on the glass door said that the store hours were 9 AM to 9 PM Monday through Saturday and closed in the winter on Sunday. It was almost ten-thirty when an older woman bundled up in a long, gray, wool coat with coordinated scarf and knitted cap arrived at the store and fumbled in her pockets for a set of keys. He noticed her short gray hair streaked with white perfectly matched her outfit.

"Sorry, I'm late," she said as she bent over to fit a key into the worn brass lock in the door. "We don't keep regular time in the winter. I'll have everything set up in just a minute ... and some fresh coffee. Why don't you come in and get warm?"

Edgar followed the woman into the store. The wispy older lady, Sandy, she called herself, went to the back of the store, flipping on the florescent lights and turning the power on to the cash register.

In the meanwhile, Edgar walked around the store, pretending

to look at all the curios but searching intently for Indian artifacts. He wasn't disappointed. Seeing him looking into a large glass showcase, Sandy walked over to him.

"Is there something you would like to see in the case?"

"No, nothing in particular. Why do you have all this used stuff in the case?"

"Used? Oh, no, not used. These are Indian artifacts, mostly trade beads and old handicrafts that we have purchased or traded with local Indians and Indian artisans over the years."

"Does anyone buy that stuff?" Edgar asked innocently.

"Oh, sure. Lots of it. The Indian antique market is very strong right now, and the Pacific Coast tribes like the Tlingit, Haidas, and Tshimsian are especially collectable."

"If I were to start a collection, where would I begin?" asked Edgar Abbott, looking bewildered.

Sandy perked up, realizing this may be an interested customer. "That depends on where you want to start. Some folks collect jewelry; some folks collect pots; other collect bent wood boxes or raffia baskets and bowls."

"If I wanted to start with something unusual and build my collection around that piece, what would you recommend for value and personal interest?"

"Well, for something like that ... it would be expensive, of course ... but I would recommend you talk to Edward, my husband. He's really the expert in the family. He has a very interesting collection of high-quality items, and he sometimes sells the odd piece to discriminating collectors." Then she added. "He's not going to be in this morning. But I can call him and have him meet you here this afternoon."

"The earlier the better."

"I'll call him." Sandy disappeared through a split curtain in the back of the store. A few minutes later, she returned to the showroom floor. "He says noon will be fine."

"Wonderful." Edgar checked his watch and left the store, turning down the street and walking past the gleaming lights of the Ketchikan Café toward the next curio shop located several blocks away, his bag tucked securely under his arm.

At the Ketchikan Post, Lt. Blocker was speaking to Captain Mike Evans, detachment commander in Juneau, while looking out the window at the snow shower. *At least it's a change from the rain*, he mused. The Public Affairs officer had called and complained that the news was leaked concerning the homicides and the escape and shooting of Tommy the Trapper.

"Somehow the newspapers got a hold of pretty sensitive information, sir," the lieutenant stated. "I asked the investigators, but they deny ever talking to the press. I'll keep my ears open and let you know what's going on."

"You'd better start doing a better job than you're doing now or this thing is going to get all fucked up. I want Sergeant Jim Nichols off the case; only officially, you understand. Have him catch the first flight to Anchorage today and tell him to report to the colonel when he gets there. He can run the investigation from Anchorage until this sorts itself out. The other two ... Skip Danski and Don Fletcher ... let them finish up and start writing their reports on the shooting. When they're done speaking with the IA investigators on the shooting, have them fly out as well. That can't take more than a couple of days at the most. Keep a tight lid on this thing, Bob."

"Yes sir."

"I'm counting on you."

"Yes sir."

Lt. Blocker hung up the phone and looked around the room at the three faces staring back at him. "Jim, they want you back in Anchorage ASAP. Officially you are off the case, but unofficially, you'll run it from Criminal Investigations Division in Anchorage. Catch the next flight north. I'll have dispatch call the on-duty trooper to give you a lift to the airport."

"I'll have to check out of my hotel and all."

"Go do it now. And Jim, don't talk about this to anyone, please. We're in a world of shit as it is, and we sure don't want to make it any deeper."

"Right."

Then glancing over at Skip and Don, he said, "You guys write up your reports on the shootings and get ready to talk with the IA guys who should be here anytime this afternoon. When they kick you loose, you're done. They want you back in Anchorage too. We'll handle the local stuff ourselves."

The two investigators said goodbye to Jim Nichols and walked down the hall to the squad room to draft their reports. Jim left shortly thereafter for his hotel, hitching a ride with an off-duty trooper.

Cody watched the two CID investigators come in and take two empty desks in the back of the room. They talked between themselves and rummaged around in their briefcases, finally extracting notes, blank paper, and pens. O'Keefe wanted to call Tom Whitefeather and give him the information on the Sportsmen's Lodge, but he didn't want to have that conversation in the presence of the investigators. He put the call on ice until later.

CHAPTER TWENTY-FOUR

Takqua, posing as Edgar Abbott, rounded the corner of Tongass Avenue and K Street and tried the door on the Totem Trading Post. It was locked. A handwritten note on the glass display booth next to the door explained the store would be closed until spring. Edgar cupped his hands around his face and peered into the dark interior but the inventory had been removed. He looked around and saw a flashing neon sign for Charlie's Totem Shop. A cardboard placard on the door announced it was open for business.

Edgar walked inside the store a minute later. The front of the shop was laid out in Alaska chic. Old harpoons, some handmade halibut hooks for the tourist trade, caribou parkas and mukluks graced the walls. Below those items of interest were rows of low end Alaskan souvenirs all for sale at ridiculously high prices. The sale of the day was a rack of XS T-shirts in awful colors with a message in bold black letters stating that *Grandma and Grandpa went on vacation, and all I got was this lousy T-shirt!* Over on the side were rows of key chains fashioned to look like miniature walruses. He picked one up and examined the artificial fur. They were cheap trinkets made in Korea. In fact, the Totem Shop was stuffed with tacky souvenirs. There were the ubiquitous magnetic stickers with painted flowers of Alaska for any refrigerator, tasteless greeting cards, ceramic mugs with fake Moose droppings in the bottom, and a rack of Alaskan delicacies like salmon jerky and caribou sausage. A pimply faced, high-school-aged kid was smacking on gum from behind the counter.

"What'cha need?"

"Do you sell Alaska native antiques or antiquities?" Edgar asked. The kid just stood there gawking at him. "You know, like trade beads, raw hide drums, and such?"

"No man, not here. None of our stuff is real."

"What about the native crafts on the walls."

"Well, sure, but that's just for show. They're not for sale, man." The kid scratched his crotch. "Just show."

"OK, just show. Thank you." Edgar turned around to leave.

"Hey, man," the kid said.

"Yes?"

"Nice ponytail, man. It looks awesome. I wanted one but my parents said no."

The bell jingled as the door closed behind Edgar Abbott.

Just before noon, Trooper Cody O'Keefe informed Jennifer, the dispatcher going off-shift, that he was taking a lunch break. She smiled at him in a way that made him wish he could ask her to lunch, but he just didn't have the time. He jumped into his patrol truck, started the engine, and putting the rig into gear, spun the tires on the slick pavement as he exited the parking lot. He called into dispatch that he was making a stop before going into town. He had one task first. On the way, he stopped by Blue Moose Marine.

"Ketchikan, this is 5-A-19. Please be advised that I will be 10-7 for a few at Blue Moose Marine."

"10-4, 5-A-19," replied the on-duty dispatcher.

When he was inside, he asked the proprietor if he could use his phone for a private call to Twasaan.

"Sure. As much business as you send my way, Cody, you bet. It's in the back. Help yourself."

Cody found the telephone next to an old pinup calendar and dialed Tom Whitefeather's office.

"Hello. What do you want?"

"Dot? Is this Dot?"

"Ya, I'm answer'n the phone now. He's get'n me trained."

"Gee, that's great. Is Tom around?" Cody asked.

"Ya. Right here, Cody. Nice talk'n to you."

The next voice was Tom's. "Hello, Officer Whitefeather, VPSO, how can I help you?"

"Hey, Tom, it's me, Cody. Can you talk?"

"Sure, what's up?"

"Tom, I tracked down that red Ketchikan Motors tag I found near the Shakan River. It belongs to the Sportsmen's Lodge in Craig. I called the place, and guess what?"

"I have no idea."

"The lady I talked to, Gerta Freese is her name, said she had a red, aluminum, flat-ended canoe with a black outboard stolen from the resort a little less than a month ago."

"Holy shit, the description sure matches the one I saw. And the time frame fits close too."

"Like a glove. I'm thinking this is a solid lead, and we need to check it out," Trooper O'Keefe elaborated.

"No point in stating the obvious. You know what else is obvious?" questioned Officer Whitefeather.

"What's that?"

"Tommy Harold didn't kill those people, and we may have evidence to prove it."

"It is shaping up that way. Keep this to yourself, OK?"

"Can I tell Dot?"

"Tell her what?" Cody asked. "Just kidding. Of course, you can tell her, but keep it between yourselves. Talk to you later," and Cody O'Keefe hung up the telephone.

Trooper O'Keefe arrived at the bowling alley about the same time Edgar Abbott walked through the threshold of the Sourdough Provisions Company. Edgar looked around as he approached the counter. He did not see Sandy. There was, however, a short, rotund man, with thinning red hair and gold, wireframe glasses who appeared to Edgar more of an accountant than a proprietor. His most distinguishing feature was a large, leather bolo with a southwest Indian motif, accentuated by a huge piece of irregular turquoise in the center.

"You must be the gentleman Sandy told me about," Edgar said.

"Yes, I'm Edward, Sandy's husband."

"Thank you for coming," Edgar replied. "I really don't have a particular interest in native artifact collecting. The concept just fascinates me. I was hoping that I might start my collection with something special, something ... well ... out of the ordinary ... the centerpiece of the collection. Something I could build around." Edgar could see Edward slowly begin to take the bait.

"We have some wonderful pieces in our showcases. Did Sandy show you any of those?"

"Yes, and she also explained that they were good, solid bargains but not at all uncommon."

"Well, let me show this piece," the proprietor said. "It is a trade bead necklace in excellent quality, good glass, European, and an affordable price." With that, he reached in and retrieved the item, setting it on the counter for Edgar to examine.

"It looks good, but mundane. Sandy said you had your own collection and that you sell pieces from time to time."

"That's true enough, but not for public display. I trade, buy, and sell only between a few friends and discriminating collectors. Most of my collection is museum quality," Edward replied proudly.

The store was empty and there was little foot traffic outside. Edgar prompted the proprietor to show him the collection. After all, he pointed out, he may become one of his discriminating clients. Edward, realizing that sales for the day would likely be dismal, agreed.

"Before I show you my collection, I should ask you, are you a cop or federal agent? The state and federal government frown on people having museum-quality collections, I guess. Maybe they think it all belongs in the Smithsonian. You know, the Antiquities Act and all that rubbish."

Edgar laughed. "No, nothing of the sort. Besides, do I really look like law enforcement officer with a ponytail?"

"No, I suppose not."

"I'm just a tourist poking around on the off-season. It's a nice town," Edgar lied.

Edward had to agree that Edgar looked nothing like a cop, or even sounded like a cop. Convincing himself that it was safe to show off his collection, the proprietor closed and locked the front door, placing an out to lunch sign in the window, and then escorted Edgar beyond the curtain that barred the entrance to the back offices.

"Where's Sandy?" Edgar asked. "I thought she might be back

here doing the books or ordering or something."

"I told her I'd work this afternoon, since I was coming to meet you anyway. No use having both of us here on such a miserable winter day," Edward responded over his shoulder.

Behind the dark brown curtain was the first office. On the far wall was a white door with the words "Janitor" printed in bold, black letters. Edward walked to the door, removed a towel draped across the doorknob revealing a cipher lock. He explained that the door stayed closed all the time. If he was in the room working on his collection, the towel was on the floor. When he was out, the towel was placed over the knob. He stood close to the cipher lock to preclude Edgar from seeing the combination. Soon, his pudgy fingers began rapidly pressing the stainless steel buttons. A second later a soft metallic click sounded. Then the white door popped open slightly, just an inch or two.

Edward looked back toward the front of the shop, then at Edgar. "You can't be too careful nowadays. If the government doesn't want your collection, thieves sure do. I'm the only one with the combination."

"And your wife, of course," Edgar added.

"Oh, no, this is my deal. She doesn't have the combination."

Inside the room were two massive chests, each containing about a dozen drawers. The furniture was heavy, built of stout rosewood and meant to last for centuries. Edward pulled the top drawer out and carefully set it on the large padded table which occupied the center of the room. Then reaching up to overhead light which was fixed to a mechanical arm, he pulled the device down toward the table so that the contents were well illuminated. Edgar could see that these were, indeed, rare pieces but not something from a shaman, and certainly not from a Kushtikaw.

Edward picked up each piece and told a short story of the object and how it came into his possession. Edgar pretended to be fascinated with the pieces in the collection. The second drawer came out to the table with the contents similar to the first. A half hour slipped by. It was all top quality to be sure, but not what he was hoping to find.

After explaining each piece, Edward would stop and ask if Edgar was interested. An hour had past. Finally, Edgar commented that the collection was the most interesting he had ever seen, but he needed to catch his plane shortly. The proprietor protested amiably that there was still more to come.

To save time, Edgar asked the proprietor what was the most unusual native antiquity he possessed. Edward smiled slyly and retrieved the bottom drawer. When he pulled back the green felt cover which protected the artifacts, Edgar let out a discernable gasp. There in the drawer were several shaman artifacts.

"Those are beautiful," Edgar exclaimed. "Where did you get them?"

"Oh, here and there. I have certain sources in archeology and academia who know the good stuff from the run of the mill. Smithsonian quality, eh?"

"I would guess so!" Edgar could feel his pulse increase and blood pressure rise. "What do you know about these artifacts?"

"Not as much as I should except to say that I have been assured on several occasions that these are the best examples of relics of the Tlingit clans' religious practices. Some of these items may, in fact, be priceless," Edward replied. He pulled up a nearby work chair to the table so he could examine the pieces under a microscope. "Beautiful, beautiful," he said totally absorbed in the examination.

"Uh, say, is there a bathroom around here? You know, nature

calls and all that," Edgar said.

"Sure, in the showroom on your right; can't miss it."

It was a human in the form of Edgar that left that small room, but it was Takqua who now took control of the situation. Instead of going to the restroom, he flicked out the showroom lights as he walked by the cash register and quietly turned the sign over on the door. It now read "Closed." He checked the street one more time for passersby, but no one was around. Swiftly he strode back to the secret room. He knew what he had to do; he knew what he was going to do. Now he even knew how he was going to do it. Entering the room, Edward was still sitting in the chair, bent over one of the artifacts with a microscope.

"Hey," he said, "come over and look at the carving on this jewel."

Takqua walked up behind him and reaching over, slid the large bolo tie around to the back of his neck while at the same time, twisting the braided leather strings around his hand. He pulled down hard! The effect was felt instantly. The bolo had become a garrote. Edward struggled to free himself, his glasses flying across the room. The pressure kept increasing. Waves of panic and adrenaline surged through his body as he fought to get his fingers under the thin, leather strings which were now buried deep in his flesh. Still, the pressure kept increasing. By now, Edward had been without air for 20 seconds. He tried reaching behind his head, his arms flailing. Now the leather bolo slowly began to cut off circulation. Edward started thrashing. Forty seconds. His legs kicked out involuntarily at weird angles against the table and his body convulsed in the chair. Two minutes. His face became beet red and bloodshot eyes moved around unfocused in their sockets. Three minutes. Finally, the body tired and then fell limp. Takqua kept the pressure on for 30 seconds more to ensure Edward was actually dead, not just passed out from a lack of oxygen. Then he slowly released the bolo. As he did, Edward's body slumped to one side and then fell unceremoniously to the floor with a loud smack as his head struck the seasoned oak planks.

Takqua located his handbag and began to systematically pillage the artifacts drawers. A small, folded note in the front of one drawer caught his eye. He quickly opened the letter to find it was from Professor Toddwell, explaining where he had found the accompanying artifacts on Dall Island and the likely presence of a Kushtikaw shaman. The ancient village, the professor wrote, used to reside on a protected beach on the west side of the island. The village was called Kagani, or Ka'gani, or perhaps Kaga'ni. No one knew for sure because so much of the language has been lost over the ages.

Kagani, another ancient village on Dall Island. He didn't know about its existence. Edgar needed to research Dall Island. He left the letter and unceremoniously began stuffing handfuls of artifacts into his handbag. He wished he could be respectful and say a prayer to give proper respect to the shaman spirits, but that would have to wait. He would perform a ceremony and a fast as soon as it was safe.

When Takqua calmed down, Edgar reemerged and surveyed the damage. It wasn't too bad he deduced. He closed the door to the secure room and draped the cloth towel back over the doorknob to make it appear as though no one had been there. Only then did he notice the light was still burning in the room with the Janitor sign on the door. He tried to reopen the door, but the cipher lock had already done its work.

Wasting no more time, Edgar picked up his bulging bag,

slung the straps over his shoulder, and slipped out the front door. Back on Tongass Avenue, he walked briskly in a wet snow shower over to the Tongass Hardware and Home Supplies, a general store, he deduced, much like Ace Hardware. There, he purchased some office supplies and several book-boxes. Carrying all his possessions, Edgar strolled two short blocks toward the nearest hotel. A few minutes later, he calmly meandered through the lobby toward the sign with an arrow which pointed to the elevators. He appeared as just another guest and went unnoticed by the busy lobby staff.

Once on the Otis elevator, he pressed the button for the second floor, got out, and found his way to the EXIT sign providing access to the emergency door. Once on the concrete staircase landing, he assembled all four boxes and carefully repacked his treasures. In the last one, he protected the shaman skull by wrapping it in the handbag. Then he addressed each of them to himself, care of the University of Washington, Department of Archeology and Ancient Civilizations, in Seattle, Washington. On the outside, he wrote "damaged auto parts."

Back out in front of the hotel, just a few minutes later, Edgar hailed a passing cab.

"Where to?" the driver asked.

"The ferry terminal," he replied. "I need to catch the ferry over to the airport to airfreight these boxes."

"Do you want me to drive you across?" the cabby asked hopefully.

"Not necessary, just drop me off and I'll walk on board."

An hour later, Edgar was walking through the Alaska Airlines Terminal. He was proud of his recent accomplishments and moved with confidence and natural athleticism. He congratulated himself on having the idea to airship his treasures to himself. The boxes containing the artifacts would arrive at the university in the morning. As he approached Gate 4, Sergeant Jim Nichols sat in seat 12D on the northbound Alaska Airlines Flight 62. Thirty seconds later he was on his way to Anchorage.

CHAPTER TWENTY-FIVE

At 10:00 p.m., when Edward didn't return home, Sandy became worried and called the store. Not getting an answer, she waited a couple hours more to see if he would show up at home. By midnight, she was concerned enough to call the Ketchikan Police Department. An officer on downtown foot patrol stopped by the Sourdough Provisions Company on a "welfare check" and found the front door unlocked. He called in the situation to the police department dispatcher, who called Sandy.

"That's not like him," she said. "Something has happened."

The officer stayed at his post in the front of the store until Sandy arrived. She walked through the establishment with the officer looking for anything amiss and found nothing untoward. Turning on the florescent lights, she and officer searched the store but everything appeared normal. Going outside, she saw her husband's car parked close to the trading post. She walked over to investigate the vehicle and found a parking ticket stuck under the wiper blade. Something was not right.

Sandy returned to the store and now approached the room

identified as the janitor's closet. The signal towel was carefully hung over the doorknob, but the light was still on in the room. Sandy knocked on the door. There was no response. Frantically, she screamed to the police officer.

"Call the fire station. They need to break the door down!" The officer hurriedly called 911. A few minutes, which seemed like an eternity to Sandy, drifted by before the officer and the now-distraught woman heard the piercing wail of the siren on "Big Red," Engine #2. The fire truck pulled quickly to the curb directly in front of the Sourdough Trading Company, and the crew of six exited the rig. The team leader ran to the officer. In no time, the expensive cipher lock on the door marked Janitor was beat into torn and twisted metal. When the door to the secure room finally gave way, they could see Edward lying on the floor, his precious collection of native artifacts scattered over him.

A team of paramedics rushed over to the body as the officer held the weeping wife in his arms. Edward lay on his side, his tongue slightly protruding from his mouth, his face swollen and discolored. One of the emergency medical technicians applied his stethoscope to Edward's neck but that was just protocol. The medic knew he was checking the pulse of a dead man. What they weren't prepared for was what came next. As the technicians rolled the body onto his back, they could see the forehead of his distorted face had been marked in blood with some type of symbol or design. Looking down, Edward's shirt had also been ripped open. Across his chest was carved the words "Thief."

Winter wore on, completely enveloping Southeast Alaska and turning much of the area into a quiet wonderland. Only the locals remained in the communities. Any establishments not open year-round had closed after Christmas. The rugged mountains, now white sentinels, stood stalwart at strategic points along the coast, a warning to the wayward traveler. The predominantly slate-gray skies formed the perfect backdrop for these granite guardians.

Along the edges of the old-growth forest, thick, sweeping branches of the fir trees housed hundreds of bald eagles which daily glided over the icy rivers in search of frozen salmon carcasses. On the forest floor, it was calm and quiet. Deer and small mammals moved gracefully and without noise, like parishioners at a church service. Only the ravens and crows appeared disrespectful to this environment. Their glossy black bodies contrasted against the pure white snow as much as their cawing feigned indifference to the imposed silence. Even the ducks and shorebirds seemed to recognize the transformation and went about their business with little fanfare.

Those months moved quickly for all concerned. Trooper O'Keefe and Lt. Blocker remained engaged in wrapping up odds and ends to the murder case. The Toddwells' bodies had been taken back to New York for burial by their daughter, Alice Toddwell. A grand jury came back without indicting Sergeant Jim Nichols in the death of Tommy the Trapper. The Internal Affairs investigation concurred with the grand jury findings. The Shooting Board, however, found that the sergeant should have exercised better judgment and been more cautious around the suspect. The report deduced that overconfidence had replaced officer safety procedures. Sergeant Nichols was given a three-week suspension and instructed to update the *Operating Procedures Manual*'s section on Use of Force and Non-Lethal Force. Glad to have just kept his position and rank, Jim poured all his time and effort into the mandate. The work was deemed exemplary by the brass, and he was now on the short list for promotion to lieutenant.

In Twasaan, Jim Harold, as promised, continued to make life miserable for Officer Tom Whitefeather, the Village Public Safety Officer. The tribal council voted not to renew his contract, but neither did they fire him outright. The logic of the elders being that winter was no time to start a recruiting effort. Tom was placed in limbo: neither working nor completely off duty. They called it "semi-administrative leave," and it would take effect for the remainder of his contract, which was approximately 6 months. Mostly, he was ignored by the village who felt betrayed by his close association with the troopers' investigation. Ignored, that is, unless or until some criminal activity occurred in the village and then he was expected to exercise his authority and perform his duty. He now half-heartedly was looking for another VPSO position in Alaska or thought he might go back to working for the Bureau of Indian Affairs. Mostly, though, he was in a funk.

Since he spent most of his time moping around his trailer these days, Dot spent more of her time in her trailer so as not to get underfoot. But there were a few sparks of the old Tom. Two nights ago, he had shown up at Dot's trailer wearing nothing but his parka and cowboy boots and carrying a six-pack of beer. Dot didn't drink anymore, but she enjoyed watching Tom in cowboy boots sitting naked in her living room with a can of Bud in his hand. After a while, she stripped down and sat with him, just talking. Talking, that is, until he ran out of beer and things to say and decided actions spoke louder than words.

Jumping off the couch, he began chasing her around inside of the small trailer whooping Cherokee war cries from the Dog-Soldier days. When she let him catch her in the kitchen, they made love. He called it counting coup with his war club. In addition to taking care of Tom in his current mental state, Dot continued to research shamans and Kushtikaws. By now, she had amassed quite a bit of information through her contacts, but discovered through an acquaintance at the Smithsonian that the real experts in this rarified field consisted of the staff in the archeology department at the University of Washington. They recommended she speak with one of the grad students, Edgar Abbott.

Edgar Abbott had picked up his packages without any mishaps and now had the relics, talismans, and Kushtikaw charms at his home. The Kushtikaw skull and ornate helmet were secure in an honored position on a prominent shelf in his living room, staring with empty sockets on all who entered the abode. He would frequently speak to the skull as though it were a family member. He felt his powers increasing every day and often dreamed of transforming into a large raven flying over the dark, primeval forests to secluded beaches. There, he scurried about on all four legs, transformed into a martin, mink, and, sometimes, even a wolf. On those nights, he would wake himself up with his own howling and, unable to return to sleep, would walk downstairs for another lengthy conversation with the Kushtikaw skull. As promised, Edgar had performed a smudging of his apartment, burned incense, and banned evil spirits with smoke and an eagle feather. He had fasted and prayed in thanks to the spirits for his good fortune. The spirits must have heard him, too, because he was now fully recovered and working on an excuse to his department head to return to Alaska, where he planned to divert to Dall Island and locate the ancient village of Kagani.

CHAPTER TWENTY-SIX

It was about midnight when Cody's phone began ringing next to his bed. He rolled over and picked up the phone, expecting to hear Jennifer's voice, the most recent dispatcher hired at the office and with whom he was beginning a relationship. She was attractive, young, the mother of two, and divorced. They had both decided to just keep things light for awhile and see how the relationship progressed. He pressed the phone to his ear.

"Hello, darling," he started saying.

"Hello, darl'n, back at you, han'some," the voice replied.

Cody shot upright in bed.

"Dot, uh, hi. I wasn't expecting you!"

"That's not what you said."

"Um, well, I was expecting it to be someone else."

"You mean I have competition?" Dot asked coquettishly.

"No ... yes ... no, I guess we should change the subject."

Dot laughed. "No use getting all hot and bothered, darl'n. I'm chill'n in Twasaan."

"I'm sleeping in Ketchikan," he said regaining his composure. "What's up?"

"I should be ask'n you the same thing."

"Why is that?"

"Why? Because of the murder at the Sourdough Trading Post, that's why."

"What about it?" he asked.

"What about it?" she mimicked. "Don't you read the papers?"

"Sure, I guess so. There was a murder at the Sourdough Trading Company, and the owner was strangled with his own bolo."

"No, not fuck'n *that*! The details ... he had native artifacts all over him, and his chest was carved with the word 'Thief.' Does that sound unusual to you?"

"How did you come by that information? Those details weren't in the newspaper."

Dot laughed again. "No shit. But they're true. I have good sources."

"When did you find this out?" Cody asked.

"Tonight ... about an hour ago."

"OK, I'll check in with the Ketchikan PD detectives in the morning."

"Good."

"Where's Tom?"

"Asleep in my bedroom ... he finally got tired chas'n me 'round and screw'n his brains out."

There was a long a pause. Cody didn't know what to say, but he had to come up with something. "Sure ... ah ... tell him hello for me, and I'll call you both in the morning. And thanks for the info."

"Which part?" she asked teasingly.

"About the details of the murder ..."

He heard her giggle. "Goodbye, Trooper O'Keefe."

Cody waited until he heard her phone click and then he put down the receiver. He had never known someone so uninhibited and so forward: like she had absolutely nothing to hide inside or out. *She must be an anomaly*, he thought.

As promised, the next morning, Cody stopped by the Ketchikan Police Department on his way to work and spoke with the case detectives. When he explained that he had heard specific details of their case, they were closed-mouthed but curious. After a few rounds of cat and mouse, Cody finally came out with his information. They were not surprised by the leak. The detectives were only surprised that it took so long for the details to get out. The most senior detective listed all the possibilities from the bereaved widow to the firemen, to the coroner, the funeral home employees, to their own policemen. Someone had to blab something sooner or later. Information that gruesome never has a shelf life, the detective explained.

Cody had asked the pair whether anything was missing from the collection. As they explained, no one knew for sure. He kept no records, only the inventory arranged in a specific manner. With the stone fetishes, glass-bead jewelry, and other carved artifacts dumped unceremoniously on the victim, there was really no way to know. They had, however, alerted the police agencies throughout Alaska and the Pacific Northwest to be alert to the sale of authentic Alaska native artifacts; especially, museum-quality pieces.

"Anything else?" he asked the detectives.

"No, not really. But guess what we *did* find," the senior detective said.

"No idea, what?" Cody asked.

"You remember the Toddwell murders? Well, our victim had a note from the professor in his collection."

"Really? What did it say?"

"Nothing much ... something about finding an artifact."

"Did the note say where?"

The two detectives looked at each other, the wheels turning. Then the junior investigator said he remembered. "Dall Island, wherever that is."

With the details of the Sourdough Provisions Company burning in his mind, Trooper O'Keefe stopped by the Blue Moose Marine. It had just opened, and the owner was pouring himself a cup of coffee.

"Miserable day, uh?" he asked as Cody walked into the dank shop.

"Yeah, maybe the weather will break soon and start warming up."

"And maybe ABBA will have a concert in downtown Ketchikan. It might happen, but I kinda fucking doubt it." As if to make a point of that statement, he dumped a load of sugar and powdered cream into his coffee mug and stirred the concoction with a lower unit bolt lying on the counter which was greasy, but handy.

"We don't have your new stainless steel propellers yet. The wholesaler is telling me that they had to order it from the factory. Two more weeks ... maybe ... if you're lucky. You ain't going out in this crap anyway, right?"

"Right. Say, can I use your phone a second to call Twasaan?"

"In the back, same place as always," the owner said, sitting down on a vinyl-covered stool and switching on the radio.

"Oh, and Cody? I got a new calendar. Check it out."

In the back of the shop, Cody found the telephone next to the new wall calendar advertising Rigid Tools with skimpily clad women in various suggestive poses holding big wrenches and such.

He quickly dialed Tom's trailer and getting no answer, tried calling Dot. It was picked up almost immediately.

"Hello, han'some."

"How did you know it was me?"

"Who said you were han'some? I might have been expecting someone else," she replied, laughing.

"I know who spilled the beans to you on the details of the murder in Ketchikan. What I don't know is why they didn't tell you about Tommy's death?"

"How do you know they didn't? And who do you think it is anyway, Mr. Detective?"

"The funeral home told you."

"Damn, you're good," she exclaimed.

"Well, those friends of yours sure stirred up a lot of trouble! They were probably the ones who talked to the reporters about Tommy the Trapper too. Not to mention, it may have cost your significant other his job," Cody admonished.

"That's all true ... sure enough ... but is it better we know or don't know? I want to know," she said with conviction, "even the bad shit."

"I agree with you there. Is Tom around?"

"Wait a second. Tom, it's for you ... Cody," he heard her shout.

Tom was on in a few seconds. "Hey, Cody. You caught me in the shower."

"You keeping banker's hours these days?" Trooper O'Keefe asked.

"Not keeping any hours at all, you know that."

"Sorry, Tom, I didn't mean it that way. Hey, I have something I was hoping you and Dot could run down for me." Cody went on to explain what he knew about the Ketchikan murder, the native artifacts, and the connection to Professor Toddwell. He also mentioned the letter and the reference to Dall Island.

"Tom, I think we need to know about the Tlingit history on Dall Island and any connection it may have to our Kushtikaw theory."

Tom was obviously excited. He wanted to redeem himself in the eyes of the elders and the only way that would happen is if he could prove Tommy Harold's innocence.

"Sounds like a break alright. OK, I'll get Dot to work on the history thing, and I'm going to see if I can catch a flight out there and snoop around."

Trooper O'Keefe concurred. "And Tom, be careful, OK? The guy tortured the Toddwells, remember? They may have told him all about Dall Island. Hell, he may be there now if it suited his purposes. And keep me in the loop."

"No problem, Cody. I'm just glad we're finally working on this investigation of the Kushtikaw theory again. I know Dot feels the same way."

"Me too. Talking about Dot, there is something I need her to do so I can get over to Craig on official business and unofficially speak with the owners of the Sportsmen's Lodge in Craig."

"Sure, I'll get her."

Half an hour later, Cody entered the doors of the Ketchikan Post. He noticed there was some unusual activity in the lieutenant's office.

"Cody," Lt. Blocker called, "can you come in here, please?"

Trooper O'Keefe walked to the big desk. "Yes sir?"

"Just listen to this recording that came into the Poaching Hotline, would you?" The lieutenant punched a couple of buttons on his telephone and put on the speaker. A female voice came on the line.

"Now, this is a Native Alaskan voice, no doubt about it. So, I'm thinking the information is legit." The lieutenant punched a button again. The female voice continued.

"You Troopers think you know so much ... well, let me tell you someth'n. When you come over to Prince of Wales Island ... we all know where you are and what you are do'n. When you are on road patrol, we go out in our boats and steal the fish. When you are out in your patrol boats, we know that too, and go shoot deer on the roads. That's why you never can catch us. Hell, some of us are go'n out right now!" The voice ended abruptly.

The lieutenant was angry. "Dammit, we cannot let that continue. Cody, go over to Prince of Wales and look around, would you? See what you can come up with. Let me know and we'll decide how to proceed from there."

"Yes sir. I'll leave today."

"I told Juneau we needed more people down here. They always want to send us support on temporary duty assignments. Why don't they just staff the damn post?" This last was said out of frustration and to no one in particular. Cody had already left the office and was making plans for his upcoming trip to Prince of Wales Island.

CHAPTER TWENTY-SEVEN

Less than 3 hours before dusk a craggy bush pilot with reddish gray hair and 2 days of white stubble covering the deep creases on his face sat nervously in the tight cockpit of the gold and white Cessna 206 seaplane. He was flying against the clock under gloomy, overcast skies. Officer Tom Whitefeather noted the pilot's discomfort, observing his gnarled, white-knuckled hands which tightly gripped the controls of the plane as he flew just above the remote forests and the snow-coated fir trees. Every now and then an especially tall tree would reach up to the heavens through the dense forest and the pilot would swerve momentarily. Tom swore to himself that he could almost hear the top of the tree scraping the belly of the aircraft. Normally a pilot would never fly so low. It was extremely dangerous, but nothing about this trip was normal. Failing to correct one minor mistake meant crashing into the waiting forest and certain death, perhaps never to be found. He tried to reason that the urgency of the moment justified the risk.

Tom was increasingly concerned about the ominous dark clouds pressing down on them from above, forcing them closer and closer to the forest. As the aircraft skimmed over the treetops, ravens, eagles, and lesser-winged creatures of the primeval forest would take flight at the last moment, all equally frightened by the roar of the oncoming plane. This added a certain element of danger since a bird crashing through the cockpit windshield or getting jammed into the engine intake would kill them both.

The pilot was clad in a distressed brown leather jacket and an old sweat-stained, yellow ball cap with "Alaska pilots do it in the bush" silk-screened in white across the front. Looking below, Officer Whitefeather's brow creased slightly as he wondered just how many hours the pilot had spent flying in Alaska. By reputation, the flying expertise of these famous bush pilots was only slightly eclipsed by that of the illegal big-game guides who were reputedly to be the best single-engine pilots in the world. Tom had to admit to himself that he was fortunate to even find someone willing to fly to Dall Island, much less into the fierce face of an oncoming storm.

The pilot, Rusty Middleton, was an old-time freelance pilot from the area with a mail delivery contract to a number of remote logging camps and fishing villages which dotted the lower coast of Prince of Wales Island. The old-timer was on his way to a small independent tree-thinning operation on Long Island carrying mail and winter supplies and Cape Muzon on Dall Island was on his route. Besides, he sure didn't mind picking up a few extra dollars in the process—so long as he didn't have to work too hard to get them, Rusty had explained to Tom.

Now he's working hard not to get both of us killed, Tom mused, looking out the side window of the aircraft. Officer Whitefeather could easily envision the pilot in his younger days running cocaine into Florida or Texas from some remote jungle stronghold in Central America. The pilot twisted to the left and right, checking for a clear path through the descending clouds. There was none; the weather had seen to that.

"This looks, bad," he said out loud, "real bad."

The storm was rapidly approaching from offshore, gaining strength in the vast waters of the Gulf of Alaska and heading directly for Cape Muzon.

"Yeah, I hear you, but you know the deal: no delivery ... no pay."

The pilot grumbled again, made another correction, and checked his gauges.

"We're gonna get stuck in this shit, you know that, don't you?" Rusty asked.

"Naw, you're going to drop me off, head out before the storm hits, and be toasty warm in bed tonight. I'll be the one freezing my nuts off."

That prediction wasn't far from wrong. Tom might be new to the area, but he knew weather, and he knew snow. He wondered how long he could realistically expect to be marooned when the storm finally did hit.

The Cessna continued to drop in altitude, the pilot skillfully keeping well above the treetops and below the turbulent clouds. To become lost in the clouds was tantamount to death. In the Alaska wilderness, there was no navigational system capable of returning a plane to a safe landing point. The clouds in the late-winter storms often blanketed both land and water, reducing visibility at ground level to nothing. Flying above the clouds meant seeing only the rugged peaks of the tallest of mountains thrusting up like spears through a blanket of impenetrable clouds. Both men knew that each year several private airplanes crashed into the sides of remote mountains due to pilot error and lack of good visibility. Visual flight rules, VFR, applied to all pilots ... all the time.

"Oh, shit," Tom heard Rusty exclaim as a seagull hit the wing of the aircraft.

"I keep hitting these damn birds, and I'll look like that fucking Greek bastard that put on bird wings so he could fly," Rusty mumbled to himself.

Tom tapped the pilot on his shoulder and pointed to his headset, mimicking that he needed to say something. The pilot looked over at him briefly, nodded, and pulled one of the ear pieces back from his head and leaned over.

"Yeah?"

"It looks like the weather isn't going to cooperate with us," Tom yelled into his ear. "Just get me to the tip of Dall Island and set it down. I'll get out wherever."

The pilot nodded and said, "I'll try, but from there, you are strictly on your own."

Rusty Milton cautiously maneuvered the white Cessna 206 with gold trim, staying less than 50 feet above the water until the first chips of ice mixed with rain began to slap the windshield. Then he nosed the aircraft up, making a sharp 180-degree turn to the left and started back down.

"I guess this is as far as I can get you," he shouted.

Tom acknowledged him. "OK, just set her down anywhere. I'll get out on the beach and pack in from there."

The plane gently set down on the rippling water, bounced a couple of times, and then sank softly until the pontoons buoyed the seaplane on the surface of the black muskeg water. Rusty turned the aircraft toward the rocky shore, gunning the engine. The propeller churned up a long cloud of wet spray as he cautiously guided the plane near the beach. When the pilot thought he was close enough, he shut down the engine. The silence rushed in to invade the moment. For a second, neither of them spoke, admiring the awesome beauty of this primitive land. Finally, Rusty reached up and pulled the black metal headset off his head and rubbed his face.

"OK, guy," he said turning to Tom, "we'll paddle the plane in from here. I don't want to puncture one of the pontoons on a rock in the middle of god-knows-where. We're going to have to hurry, too. The storm is right on my ass. I'll need to di-di-mau for Long Island as soon as possible."

"What's 'di-di-mau,'?" Tom asked.

"Fucking Vietnamese for 'haul ass.'"

With some degree of effort, he reached behind the seat into the cargo compartment and rummaging around in all the gear, miraculously produced two scarred and beat-up oak paddles, issuing one to each of them.

"Be careful now. Open your door and walk forward on the pontoon. It might be slippery, so watch out. I'll do the same on this side. Then we'll just paddle in to shore easy, like a canoe. Oh, and son, by the way, if you fall in, you're going to have to save yourself. I can't swim!"

"Thanks, I'll remember that."

Several minutes later, the aircraft pontoon lightly touched the sandy bottom at the base of a rocky beach. Instantly, Tom was unloading his gear onto the rocks and surveying his surroundings for a quick place to bivouac and get out of the weather.

"Remember what I said, I'll be back in 2 days to pick you up. Right here at high tide."

"I'll remember," Tom replied. "Thanks for everything. Say, how come you never learned to swim?"

"I can swim, OK," the pilot replied, "I just tell everyone that so they don't do anything foolish. I hate getting in this damn cold water is all."

"No shit. Does it work?" Tom said with an engaging smile. "You ever had anybody fall in?"

"Not that didn't save their own damn selves!" Rusty said with an air of authority. Then he added, "Tourists are the ones most impacted by my policy."

"What about women? Wouldn't you jump in and save a good-looking woman?"

"Especially not a good-looking woman," Rusty replied.

"Really? Why not?"

"You ever see a wet T-shirt contest where they use cold water?"

The thought of self-rescue by some hapless tourist, and women in cold water, made them both break out in laughter. Tom was laughing so hard he had to wipe tears from his eyes. Shaking his head in disbelief, he gave one of the pontoons a strong shove, sending the aircraft drifting backwards into deeper water. The pilot kept up the momentum, paddling the seaplane away from shore. Quickly negotiating the long, narrow aluminum pontoon like an acrobat, the old pilot jumped into the cockpit and cranked over the engine. Thirty seconds later, he was airborne. Tom watched him disappear over the quiet, snow-shrouded forest just minutes before the strong storm front rolled in.

Grabbing his gear, he moved into the old-growth forest. He wanted to be far enough from the beach and the landing site to at least feel some degree of security had anyone heard the plane land. After walking for almost half an hour through the woods carrying all his equipment, he finally found exactly what he was looking for. A thick cluster of cedar trees with low branches. Tom selected a particularly dense pine and crawled to the base, dragging his gear with him. In a matter of a few minutes, he had expertly built himself a shelter: almost a wikiup. It consisted of dry pine needles for a bed and his military-issued poncho for a roof.

Next, he took a small limb and brushing the area around the outside of his tiny campsite, eliminated any sign that might give away his position. As he settled in, the storm hit, sending large drops of rain down through the dense old-growth canopy to the forest floor, eventually hitting the poncho with a loud splat. A few tense minutes passed as Tom began to wonder if his new home would actually stay dry, but it passed the test of time. He planned to bivouac in the forest tonight, safe and dry, until the storm passed. With the dropping temperatures, he thought briefly about starting a fire and then dismissed the thought almost instantly. He would just have to tough it out. Until he was safe off the island, he would run a cold camp. The stakes were simply too great.

CHAPTER TWENTY-EIGHT

In Craig, Cody had checked into a rundown dingy hotel with the cheesy appellation of the Dew Drop Inn, owned by one of the local native corporations. After unpacking his bags, he called the Sportsmen's Lodge. The telephone was answered on the third ring by an obviously out of breath woman identifying herself as Gerta Freese.

"Hello, Mrs. Freese, I'm Trooper Cody O'Keefe. Remember me? I'm here in town to take a statement from you concerning the missing canoe."

"Oh, yes. I thought maybe you were calling to tell us you found it already."

"No ma'am. But I'm working on it."

"Good. When can we expect you?"

"What's a good time for you?"

"Well, we need to serve dinner shortly. How about anytime around eight o'clock this evening? We don't have many guests, and we should be through by then."

"Eight o'clock will be fine, Mrs. Freese. See you then." Saying goodbye, Cody hung up the telephone.

Later that evening, Cody drove several miles out of Craig in a truck borrowed from the Alaska Highway Department. The rain had turned to snow with the dropping temperature, making the roads icy and treacherous. It was 10 minutes past eight when the headlights of the truck illuminated the entrance to the building. Cody spent a few moments gathering his thoughts and a notepad before exiting the vehicle. By the time he reached the lodge, the door was opened by Gerta Freese.

"I saw the lights of your truck and thought that might be you," she said by way of introduction. "Please come on in to the dining room. I'll get Johann. We really appreciate you coming out here so late." Cody found himself a comfortable chair at the long table in the expansive dining room of the lodge. Turning around, he stared at his reflection in the large onyx black windows, which, during the day, provided a picturesque view of the ocean. He couldn't help thinking about Tom on Dall Island, roughing it in this weather. He was worried about him. He knew that Tom could take care of himself, but he would have felt more comfortable if they had both gone to Dall Island together. He had an uneasy feeling.

As night settled in on Dall Island, Tom turned over a couple of times on his pine needle bed, getting more comfortable and familiar with his surroundings. Relaxed, he adjusted his shoulder holster and retrieving his weapon, jacked a round into his Colt .45 semi-automatic, carefully positioning the weapon next to the tree trunk at his head. Feeling a couple of accessory pockets on his pack, he reached into one of the outer pockets and drew out his dinner ... some tough old jerky and a chunk of fry bread. Passing the time eating, Tom thought about other things: the universe, nature, the sea, the forest, his life. He thought about the isolation and solitude of late winter in this remote corner of Alaska. He inhaled the clean, crisp smells from the sea and forest and felt lucky to be alive. He could hear the ravens finding sanctuary in tops of the majestic old hemlocks for the night and soon the sounds faded. As the blackness of a winter night invaded the forest, all Tom could hear was the tapping of the rain on his poncho. He drifted off in a light sleep, his right hand never far from his pistol.

Gerta Freese interrupted Cody's thoughts.

"Would you like tea or coffee or something Trooper O'Keefe? We have both. Johann will be here shortly."

"Water would be just fine thanks."

"So, Trooper O'Keefe, you are here to take my statement concerning the canoe," Johann said as he walked up to the table and extended his hand.

Shaking his hand, Cody replied, "Yes sir, that's right. How long has it been missing?"

Johann made himself at home at the head of the table. "Well, let's see, about 4 months or so I guess."

"When did you first notice it was missing?"

"Didn't my wife tell you we filed a report with all that information?"

"Sure, but I want to hear it again from you in your own words."

"Ummm," Johann said rubbing his chin, "it was outside; it was just before or after that big snowstorm we had. Remember the big one just after Christmas? Well, I was outside and saw it was gone."

"Was it locked up or anything?"

"Oh, no. Not around here. At first, I thought someone just borrowed it, but it never showed back up."

"Why would anyone want to borrow it in the middle of winter?"

"I don't know. People are like that, you know."

"OK," Cody said, making a note in his diary, "you said it was a square-ended aluminum canoe?"

"Right, a red canoe with a black motor," Mrs. Freese replied, setting the glass tumbler full of water down in front of him and sitting down in a high-backed chair next to Mr. Freese.

"Right. How many of them do you own?"

"Just a couple now," Johann stated. "We used to own about half a dozen or so, but we slowly sold them off and replaced them with rafts. More durable, easier to store and repair. The new rafts have superior construction and can withstand far more than a rigid hull boat, much better for hunting. And they can easily handle up to twice the cargo with greater stability." With that, he lit up a cigar and leaned back in his chair.

"In fact," Gerta added reaching over and touching Johann's hand lightly, "we sold one of our older ones to that Mr. Harold last year. Terrible what happened to him and the poor Toddwells."

"You *what*?" Cody said surprised. He could see Mr. and Mrs. Freese jump back in fright.

"We sold one to Tommy," Johann stuttered hesitantly.

"What color was it?"

"No color, just aluminum. He didn't want any color because he was using it for trapping. I really think, though, he thought that the colored ones would be more expensive."

"And you didn't call when we broadcasted a request for information during the investigation?" Cody didn't want to say it, but in his view, if they had come forward in time, Tommy might still be alive. "Why?"

"We thought we were too far away to be part of the investigation, dear," Gerta replied patting his hand and nodding to Johann, who readily agreed.

“Too far away …,” Cody mumbled aloud as he scribbled in his diary, trying to control his anger.

Then he continued in a calmer tone, “So the stolen canoe never showed back up?”

“That’s right,” Johann said, sweating a little and beginning to wring his hands.

Cody saw the protective body language and knew he must be getting close to something, but what?

“Anyone in the area ever borrow one of the canoes without asking?”

“No, not really. The Thompson boy did once, while we were out. That was about 3 years ago. His dad made him return it and work for us for free for a month as a punishment.”

“Sounds like a bargain to me.”

Gerta nodded, “Yes, it was. Not too many parents would do something like that.”

“Yah,” Johann added, “now anyone will do almost anything to make money.”

“Make money? Did the boy make money on the canoe?”

“Oh, no, that’s not what we’re saying. Just that people seem more dishonest nowadays,” Johann said, sweat now visibly breaking out on his forehead.

Where the hell do I go from here? Something is up, but I can’t get hold of it, Cody thought, looking at the intent faces of both Greta and Johann.

“Well, let me see the hotel register of the people that stayed here during the time the canoe turned up missing. Maybe they might have seen or heard something.”

Johann looked aghast. “You’re going to contact our guests?” he stammered.

Cody smiled to himself. *BINGO! Right on target ... something is going on here after all.*

"That's right, Mr. and Mrs. Freese, a guest can be an excellent source of information. I can start calling them tonight."

Now Johann was visibly upset, and Gerta appeared worried.

"Oh no, that's not a good idea at all, disturbing our former guests like that. It would be terrible for business, word of mouth and all that. No, if that is what you intend to do, we just won't file an insurance report. We withdraw our request for a police report to support the insurance claim."

"You can't."

"We can't? And why not?" Johann asked plaintively.

"Because the crime has already been committed, and I am already here. Now, let me see the register, please."

Gerta looked across at her husband and held his hand tightly, saying, "Trooper O'Keefe, we need to tell you something. We've made a terrible mistake. We're sorry. One of our guests lost the canoe and paid us for it. We just wanted to file an insurance claim on the item, but our insurance only covers theft."

"So," Cody said completing the thought, "you reported the canoe stolen. That way, you could collect from your customer *and* the insurance company."

"That's right, Trooper. We're very sorry," Johann said almost in tears.

"And we've never done this before," Gerta added.

"Who was the customer that lost the canoe?"

"His name was Willem Tuttle, a very quiet photographer," Gerta volunteered. "He lost the boat and motor north of here on a river while out photographing some bears."

Johann chipped in, "The experience almost killed him, I think.

When he came back, he was all bruised and beat up."

"Really? What did he look like?"

"His injuries?" Johann raised his eyebrows. "I ... we didn't call a doc ..."

"No, a physical description," Cody snapped. He regretted his impatience immediately. Then calming himself after a second or so, he went on. "Please tell me what he looked like."

"He was taller than average," Gerta said, "and very muscular. Strong, but not like the weight lifters you see on television like on Wide World of Sports."

"Race?" Cody asked. He was taking all this down in his diary.

"Oh, white, probably. White skin with black eyes and long black hair."

"Could be Indian though, Mamma," Johann added. "He had a strong lean face and a thin scar across his nose. Not so that you would notice."

"Long black hair? How long?"

"To his shoulders. He kept it in a ponytail," Gerta replied.

Johann got up from the table. "Sorry, I need to use the restroom. I'll be back in a minute."

When he had left, Cody returned to his line of questioning. "Go ahead, Mrs. Freese, as you were saying?"

"Yes, well, I remember that he looked and dressed like he was a professional photographer."

"What kind of clothes?"

"Oh, you know the type: the Woolrich or Filson heavy wool coat with corduroy slacks and penny loafers or hiking boots. Rumpled but educated. Shabby but sophisticated."

"Could you describe the coat," Cody asked, remembering the one in the evidence locker which had been found at Tommy's campsite.

"No, I don't … I really don't recall. It just seemed to me he had one."

"Did he have it with him when he left? He must have been wearing something. It's been awfully cold."

"No, I don't really remember."

"Could you identify the coat if you saw it again?"

"Sure. Well, maybe. Actually I'm not sure about that either."

Johann walked over and sat back down at his place at the head of the table just as Cody was finishing.

"Any unique characteristics? Did he limp, have tattoos, things like that?" Cody asked.

"Well, he was limping a lot when he left here, but the thing I remember the most is just the thin scar that ran across the bridge of his nose," Johann concluded.

"Where did he go when he left here?"

"Well, let's see. He left here saying he was going to stay in Ketchikan for a few days."

"Is he in some kind of trouble?" Gerta queried. She rose from the table to fix some tea at the service bar in the far corner of the dining room.

"I'm not sure. This could all be coincidence ... nothing for you to worry about though."

Johann was still concerned. "Are you going to file some sort of report on us, Trooper O'Keefe? We really didn't mean to do anything wrong."

"No, I'm not going to file a report on your insurance scam, but this better not ever happen again, OK?" He didn't have the heart to tell them he was there with absolutely no authority and was scamming them out of information.

"Never again, Trooper O'Keefe, promise," Johann said and

shook Cody's hand as though they had reached some agreement.

"Thank you, Trooper," Gerta added.

Cody left the lodge and sped back to Craig in the borrowed truck, the vehicle sliding around the turns in slow motion as it lost traction on each turn. His mind was carefully pondering each of the details he had uncovered from the Freeses. Most of all, he worried about calling the lieutenant with this information. It was well past ten p.m. when Cody arrived back at the Dew Drop Inn. He could hear the Country Western music emanating from the smoky lounge all the way out into the parking lot. *Loggers must be in town,* he thought.

He walked into the lobby of the motel, wondering what it would be like trying to sleep. As he opened the door to his room, he saw that the dull red message light was blinking rhythmically on the telephone, which sat on the side table adjacent to the sagging double bed. He picked up the receiver and dialed the motel operator. She apparently had already gone home for the night. He would have to wait until morning to ask for the message.

CHAPTER TWENTY-NINE

Dawn couldn't come early enough for Tom. Several times during the night, he had awakened with a start; tensing immediately and instinctively touching the cold steel of his pistol. Straining his ears, listening for any sound in the forest indicating an intruder, he stared into the black void. Tom would stay in that state of hyperawareness until his mind began to relax with the night sounds of the forest animals. After a while, he would begin to drift off into a state of semiconsciousness—then it would happen all over again. By four a.m., Tom was mentally tired, chilled to the bone, stiff, and eager to get started, but it was still pitch-dark outside. He rolled from side to side trying to stay warm and comfortable, keeping his mind occupied until first light.

CHAPTER THIRTY

It was still dark outside at exactly fifteen past five when the radio alarm clock went off next to Cody's head with an annoying buzz. He reached over and with an open palm, smashed his hand across the button on the top of the plastic device, hoping to eliminate the low-intensity torture. It worked. He had activated the snooze button on the electric timekeeper. Cody hated alarm clocks, most often just waking up on his own. He never carried an alarm clock with him on patrol. He had found that after years of practice, he never overslept by more than a few minutes and more often than not, he would wake up a few minutes early. But he wasn't in the bush now. He was in a motel in Craig, Alaska. Turning on the light, he stretched, jumped out of bed, and started his morning exercise routine of sit-ups and push-ups. He finished the routine in a few minutes and rose sweating from the smelly, burnt-orange shag rug carpet patterned with periodic cigarette burns. Grabbing a fresh change of clothes from his brown rucksack, he started the water for his shower. In was cold outside so it would take some time before the water was suitable for bathing.

Then the telephone rang, halting his progress.

"Hello?"

"Cody?"

"Yes."

"Hi, this is Dot. Sorry to call you so early, but I got some strange news ... uh ... information. I called last night, but you weren't there. Did you get my message?"

"I got back to my room too late to do anything about it. I have some news of my own."

"Really? What is it?"

"No, you first. Yours sounds more interesting, and it's your dime, after all."

"Well," Dot began, "you know how over the past several weeks I have been work'n closely with the some of the graduate students at the University of Washington and University of Alaska who are help'n me research the history and locations of the old villages and all. There was one person at the University of Washington in particular who has been very helpful. He's not really a student. He graduated several years ago, but he spends a lot of time with the graduate students doing research ... said he was writing a book about the history and rituals of the Tlingit shaman. I was surprised at what he knew. It was all very strange. You could almost feel him breathe into you as he spoke. There is something ... a power ... you can feel from this person. I have never met anyone like him. He probably knows as much about the old ways as any tribal shaman, maybe more. He certainly seemed to know more about Kushtikaws and shape-changers than I did."

"Really? I find that hard to believe."

"Yes, really," she replied firmly. "Anyway, when I called yesterday, one of the students told me he had left a few days ago on another trip."

"Do you know what he looks like?" Cody asked.

"They said he is tall with long black hair and a scar on his face."

"Damn. That sounds a lot like the guest at the Sportsmen's Lodge. Did you get a name?"

Dot paused. "Yes, wait a minute. I'm get'n it now. Edgar Abbott. The Smithsonian even knows this guy."

"Jesus!" Cody exclaimed.

"What's the matter? Did I do something wrong?"

"No, nothing wrong. Just one hell of a coincidence. Dot, you aren't going to believe this, but that description sounds like the same person the lodge owners described to me as the guy using one of their canoes."

"What?!"

"Yep, it seems that it wasn't theft at all. One of their clients borrowed a red canoe and didn't return it. He paid them for it, but they wanted to collect insurance on top of it. Only thing was they had to file a theft report. Anyway, when I finally got the bottom of the whole thing, the guest that took the canoe matches your description. And there's more," he added quickly. "It seems that the Freeses sold Tommy one of their old used canoes."

"So what are we go'n to do?"

"Well, first, let's go over the facts. What was the name your suspect used?"

"Edgar Abbott. What about yours?"

"Edgar Abbott, right. Mine was Willem Tuttle. So there's no match there."

"That doesn't mean it wasn't the same guy."

"I know, Dot. I just putting similarities together for now. Let's go on." Hearing no objection, he moved forward. "Tom saw a red canoe, and Tommy Harold had a plain canoe. No matter what, there was a canoe seen in the vicinity of the murders. Now, assuming Tommy was innocent, the only other canoe was red, the same color as the one borrowed by my guy, Willem Tuttle, who didn't return it to the lodge. You found out that someone matching this description, including the scar, works with the grad students at UW and is very knowledgeable about Indian mythology and Kushtikaws." Cody paused suddenly. "Dot, how much does he know? What did you tell him?"

"Almost everyth'n we know, Cody. Noth'n about the murders or anyth'n, just mythology and ancient rituals. He was certainly interested in Kagani. We talked about that a lot."

"What about Sha'te?"

"Not much. I'm still work'n on that one, too, but he knows about the existence of Kagani and Sha'te. Hell, he told me more about Kagani than I knew." Then she added suddenly, "Cody, he knows we are trying to find Kagani and Sha'te so he probably figures we are looking for a Kushitkaw too."

"That means that Tom may be in trouble. Since no one knows where Sha'te is, and if he hasn't been to Kagani yet, he might try to beat us to it. If that's the case, then Tom may run into him on Dall Island. We're going to have to find Tom quickly."

"Cody, he might be killed!" With that, her emotions gave way and she began to cry softly.

Cody tried to calm her growing fears. "Don't worry, Dot, I'll call Ketchikan right away and see if I can get the troopers to help. I'll take care of Tom, you just keep working on the location of Sha'te and keep me posted." But he wasn't so sure. Dot hadn't seen the gruesome murders at the cabin. He couldn't bring himself to think of Tom as a victim. *He's too smart, strong, and knows woodlore. Sure he'll be OK ... maybe.*

Cody hung up and then pensively dialed the Ketchikan office of the Department of Public Safety. He had an awful lot of explaining to do. The call was answered on the third ring by Marsha Johnson.

"Alaska State Troopers and Fish and Wildlife Protection, how may I address your call?"

"Marsha, hi, it's me. Say, is Lt. Blocker in today?"

"Well, he won't be in for a couple of hours, Cody. Is this an emergency?"

"Could be ... I don't know for sure, but I think I need some help."

"Where are you?"

"I'm in Craig, and I need to get to Dall Island as soon as possible. The VPSO for Twasaan is at Cape Muzon and needs help."

"What were you doing over in Craig with the VPSO?"

"Looking for the person who killed the Toddwells. We may have found him, if we hurry."

"OK. Let me see if I can track down the lieutenant. Where can you be reached?"

Cody gave her the number to the motel.

"I'll get right back to you," she said and then hung up.

Minutes passed like hours waiting for Marsha to return his call. When it did come through, the tone of the ring shot like adrenaline through his body. He instantly picked up the telephone.

"Marsha?"

"It's me, Cody, who's Marsha?"

"Dot, Marsha is a dispatcher in Ketchikan. What's up?"

"I just wanted to see if you found out anything yet?"

"I'm waiting for the call from Ketchikan now."

"Oh, sorry," she said, realizing she had interrupted. "Call me and tell me what's happening."

"I will, promise," and with that he hung up the phone.

The receiver had just touched the cradle when the telephone rang again.

"Marsha?"

"No, it's me, Cody. What the fuck are you up to now?"

"Lt. Blocker!" he said, somewhat taken aback by the response.

"That's right, Cody. You called us, remember? Now, what is it you're up to? I want everything—all the details. And so help me, Cody, if you have screwed up even one iota, I'll have your badge for this."

Cody realized this would probably be the end of his career, but he put aside his own concerns, explaining to the lieutenant everything in minute detail, including Tom's whereabouts.

"So you see, Lieutenant, there really was someone else at the Twasaan cabin, or at least we have a strong suspicion and a motive to go along with it."

"What you have is a bunch of jumping to conclusions and three people who don't want to see what really happened because an Indian was involved."

Cody blew up. "Oh, bullshit, Lieutenant! That's crap, and you know it. I thought the idea of law enforcement was to get the bad guy. Well, guess what, Lieutenant? I think CID blew it, and now you're covering it up. Ever since I've been on this investigation, I've been stonewalled and given crap. I've come across a real suspect here that deserves to be checked out, and all you can say is that I'm jumping to conclusions? What was Tommy, except handy? We both know he didn't do it, Lieutenant."

There was silence on the line for several seconds. Then Lt. Blocker's voice came across slow, angry, and menacing.

"Cody, you are out of line. I'll tell you how it is. CID did their work, and you are doing your dead-level best to fuck it up. Do you know what would happen if the native community even suspected that Tommy was not the real murderer? Do you *know* how much trouble you can cause here, Cody, without the least bit of hard evidence? Everything you have is hearsay and circumstantial."

"What about the canoe, Lieutenant?"

"What about the canoe? Let's talk about the canoe, Cody," he hissed. "You can't even put your suspect at the murder scene, for chrissake! Have you even *looked* at a map? How would he get from one side of the island to the other by canoe? It would take a month of paddling."

"He had access to the truck at the lodge. He could have driven a logging road and found the closest point of approach," Cody countered immediately.

"OK, let's just say he did. Even if your suspect, and I use the term lightly, did use a logging road to launch the canoe to get to the cabin, it would have been at least a day before he reached the Toddwells ... in dead winter. And don't forget, we would have found it in our search, which, of course, we didn't. We found Tommy's canoe instead."

"Not exactly right, sir. The canoe had an engine. Just like on Tommy's boat. He didn't need to paddle. He could have motored over in a few hours. The missing canoe is red. The same color, same shape, and the same type engine that Officer Whitefeather observed in the days prior to the murders. And Lieutenant, don't forget we have a description now," Cody argued.

"Of what? A description of *what*, Cody? Of a guy who used a canoe and some college kid in Seattle that matches the description? Good work, Trooper," the lieutenant said sarcastically. "Really good work. We can take that to court for sure."

"Look," Cody said, "I am more convinced than ever that we are on to something, and if we don't get Tom off Cape Muzon, he may be the next victim. This guy is good, real good, and he's very, very dangerous. The reason we only have circumstantial evidence is because the guy is so cunning. He doesn't even think twice about killing."

"That's boogeyman talk, Cody, pure and simple. That imaginary crap doesn't wash with me."

"You don't have to believe me, Lieutenant. You saw the Toddwells, yourself. They were butchered, and taken apart piece by piece. Tommy could not have done that ... ever. Not to mention not one single drop of blood was found on Tommy or in his camp. I bet you haven't even checked the blood in the canoe to see if it was human or animal, but if you checked it, it would be animal blood. And chances are the blood I found on the beach is human."

"That's Monday morning quarterbacking, Cody, and doesn't change anything. You have nothing but mere suspicion at best! CID found their man. You just can't let go."

"No, Lieutenant, you just can't admit to yourself that the wrong person died in this investigation because CID jumped to conclusions—and this killer is one hell of a lot smarter than all of us combined!"

"That's just bullshit, Cody; pure and simple. We're sitting on a powder keg with the native community, and you're trying like hell to light the fuse. If they even suspected for one moment that we thought Tommy wasn't the murderer, there would be hell to pay. I just can't let you continue to screw up our investigation. You get your ass back here and report to me immediately!"

"Sorry, I can't do that, Lieutenant. I have to find Tom first. I'd like your help—"

"My help? *My help*? Cody, the fact I even listened to your shit is help enough. I want you back here *now*! That's an order, Cody."

There was silence on the line, then Cody spoke softly. "So I guess the answer is no, huh?"

But the telephone line was already dead.

"Shit! Shit! Shit!" Cody slammed downed the receiver and stormed around the small room.

CHAPTER THIRTY-ONE

At first light, Tom rolled up his bedroll and securing his gear, hoisted his pack and adjusted the load. Then he jumped up and down a few times to make sure everything was balanced, secure, and quiet. When he was confident he could be quiet, he checked his weapon and extra magazines and reholstered his pistol. The precautions, as far as Tom was concerned, were essential. The thought of a killer stalking the same woods trying to locate Kagani was never far from his mind. He checked himself over one last time and moved out, heading south toward Kagani. By his estimation, he couldn't be more than 2 miles from the abandoned village ... 3 miles at the most. Walking through the woods, he guessed that he would probably be there within the hour. He was wrong. It was much harder than he ever thought possible.

Tom glanced at his watch. It was almost eight and he still had a ways to go. He kept fighting the devil's club and small dormant berry bushes as he forged ahead. The snow had changed to rain. It finally stopped, but he was soaked to the bone. Mostly his pants and socks were wet. Not wanting to risk hypothermia, he found a good place to rest, stopped, and retrieved a fresh set of clothes from within the depths of his pack. Putting on his dry set of clothing, he had an eerie feeling he was being watched. He looked around him. There was only forest, the trees around him gradually fading into the foreboding darkness of the old-growth forest as far as the eye could see. Trying to shake off the uncomfortable feeling by staying alert, he started down a gentle but slippery slope which was punctuated by more devil's club and thick clumps of alder. At the base of the hill he eventually picked up a big-game trail which headed into the forest, making traveling across the hostile terrain easier.

Limited vision was one of the first problems he encountered when entering the old forest. More than once he thought he saw human movement and instantly went into a combat pistol stance. Each time this happened, Tom would curse under his breath. Once, he even crouched behind the closest tree for cover, only to find out moments later that he had alerted a Sitka black-tailed deer. He watched the animal trot off in the woods. Tom realized he was scaring up too many animals. *If this continues,* he thought, *the whole forest will know I'm trying to reach Kagani.* A thought which rested in the back of his mind slowly began to take form. He began to wonder if any of those animals were a Kushtikaw in disguise, luring him further into the darkness of the vast island wilderness.

At the top of the hill looking down at his progress, Takqua crouched naked and motionless behind a fir tree adorned in full-body paint of black stripes. Patiently, he watched Tom work his way through the underbrush leading to the forest, his unblinking eyes set in large black circles drawn on his face. The only portion of his body visible was a single eye which peered out from around the tree trunk. He knew from this distance it would have been impossible for anyone to spot him.

Takqua first became aware of Tom yesterday when he had heard the plane flying at treetop level. Just the curiosity of another interloper had forced him to immediately abandon his worksite at Kagani. Angry that someone would even be in these woods, he set off in the direction of the airplane. He was cognizant that sound traveled on water and that perhaps the seaplane had simply dropped off a hunting party on the island, but after he gave that some thought, he dismissed that idea as improbable. It was too early for black bear season and too late for deer season. No, whoever it was had other motives. *A forest survey crew perhaps?* He had to know as quickly as possible and return to his work.

Under the cover of darkness, he wandered through the cold and rain until he found the cold camp, well concealed under a large fir tree. Takqua had almost missed the campsite at first, it was so well concealed. But the musty smell of nylon and rubber made him stop until he could finally distinguish the carefully constructed lean-to beneath the tree. He sat there for awhile in the blackness of night, watching the person beneath the tarp. Then, quietly, he left and found an observation point on higher ground, waiting patiently until first light. Now, from his vantage point looking down at Tom, he could see clearly that this person was not an animal hunter at all; he was a man hunter. And he was hunting him! He marveled at the hunter's skill. How deftly he moved through the woods. How did he find him? How much did he know about him? Takqua was determined to find out.

As Tom slid silently through the forest like a large bear, the animal instincts in Takqua took over and like a dangerous animal, he began to stalk Tom. He was never far behind—moving quietly, quickly, from tree to tree, always staying in the outer perimeter of the woods, yet always keeping the man in sight. He would watch amused as Tom periodically stepped off the trail and crouching down, checked to see if anyone was following him. Each time, Takqua anticipated Tom's move and sat down behind a large tree, one eye constantly exposed, watching Tom, his lips turned in a cruel grin. Over the next hour, the fatal game of hide-and-seek continued to play itself out in the heavily wooded forest as Tom slowly approached the ancient village of Kagani.

A pale, winter sun had risen above the trees and a dim light shown through the forest by the time Tom reached the ruins. He had never seen one of the ancient villages before, and it impressed him, even in this advanced state of disrepair. The place was smaller than he had expected. Most of the ornate longhouse was destroyed, its huge timber siding lying rotting on the ground. The totems guarding the village, however, were still standing upright and facing the sea, something that immediately surprised him since they bore the constant prevailing southeastern winds from the Gulf. Beyond the totems, on the far side of the village, he could smell the salt air and almost make out the horizon and the gray, white-capped waters of the Gulf of Alaska.

Tom turned and surveyed the ruins, looking for any signs of human occupation, but found none. He was relieved. As he picked his way through the ruins of the antediluvian village, the thought of confronting a possible Kushtikaw, or even a person who thought they were a shape-changer bothered Tom. It wasn't that he really believed in Indian legends, it was just that he had heard enough about the power of the real shaman that he didn't want to confront one. *Not here, not now, not ever,* he reasoned. The thought made him look around quickly, weapon in hand. Seeing nothing, he holstered his gun and resumed his search of the village and the accompanying burial grounds.

Takqua had followed the intruder to the ruins and was now circling him from somewhere in the murky depths of the forest. To kill him, he needed the element of surprise. It was painfully obvious that Tom would eventually find signs of where he had been working—it was only a matter of time. Takqua was glad he had taken the singular precaution of hiding his gear and equipment in the woods, well away from the village, but still in near proximity to the burial grounds. Nevertheless, he realized a good tracker like Tom would eventually find the shallow impressions of a footprint in the moist soil and become alerted. While he was thinking about that, he watched as Tom stumbled across the first desecrated grave.

In an instant, with his senses heightened, Tom picked up on the tracks leading off into the woods. Drawing his pistol and checking to make certain the magazine was secure, Tom dropped his backpack gear and headed off into the woods, weapon at the ready.

Takqua, stalking Tom as though he were an animal, now acted swiftly and decisively to intercept him. Moving quietly within striking range over a period of 20 minutes, he had remained concealed from view by keeping several large fir trees between him and Tom. Takqua was unarmed except for his ceremonial knife with beaded handle that he kept on a thin leather belt. As he approached, he drew his knife and prepared to attack. Takqua felt no fear. *The gods will help me on my sacred quest; they always have. I will be protected.* The confidence returned to his face just before he let out a chilling scream and rushed forward, the razor-sharp knife raised menacingly above his head. Tom spun instantly, identified his target, and fired, but he was too late. In an instant, the two bodies collided, and the knife blade buried itself deep in Tom's shoulder from the downward thrust. The brut force of the impact sent Tom flying backwards, knocking his pistol from his hands. He tried to roll and recover, but it was too late. Takqua was all over him, sending smashing blows into his face. Tom tried to fight him off, but the body paint wouldn't allow for a hand hold. After a brief struggle, he mercifully blacked out. Once Takqua realized that Tom was no longer conscious, he reached down and pulled him up off the forest floor, throwing the body over his shoulder like a sack of sand. He headed back to the village with his prize. There was much to do.

When the attendant for the Craig floatplane terminal opened later that morning, her first customer was Cody.

"Sorry, all flights are cancelled this morning due to weather. The best I can do is to try and get a flight for you this afternoon, but you'll have to check back. There's a front coming in later on, and if it brings cold air, it may help clear this stuff out of here."

Cody looked out the window of the small log cabin structure at the damp dismal weather. He could see the smoke emanating from the chimneys curling around; it didn't look promising. All he could do was to wait and see.

Tom woke up to the smell of smoke. He was suspended upside down, disoriented, and scared. Just inches beneath him was a small fire. Straining around in his bonds, he spotted Takqua in full-body paint squatting by the small fire, staring back at him unblinkingly through large, black-painted circles.

"So the enemy awakens."

"Who are you?" Tom choked out, tears in his eyes from the smoke.

"Who are *you*?" came the reply.

"I'm Tom Whitefeather, the officer in Twasaan. Now put out the fire and get me down, dammit; you've had your fun."

"I will, when I've had my fun. Promise."

His words sent chills through Tom. "What do you want with me?" But Tom already suspected what he wanted.

"I want to know what you are doing here and why you were hunting me. By the way, you hunt poorly. The entire forest knew when you arrived on the island. The only thing that didn't run away was me."

"I wasn't hunting you," Tom lied.

"Are you sure?" came the question from the painted face. "Let's find out. You know fire is the great cleanser in nature. I wonder if it can cleanse your soul."

With that, Takqua reached down beside him and gently put on a handful of tree moss onto the smoldering fire. Energized by new fuel, the flames shot up immediately, catching fire to Tom's hair and licking his scalp. Tom howled in pain and jerked frantically around the ropes that securely held him above the fire. After a minute or two of screaming, he calmed down, resigned to his fate. He could not escape.

"You're going to kill me, aren't you?"

The face stared back impassively. Then after a moment, Takqua spoke. "First things first. Why were you hunting me?"

"I wasn't hunting you ... *ahhhhhhh!*" he cried. Pain soared through him as another handful of moss was thrown on the ritual fire.

"Why were you hunting me?" the voice asked again. His words were as cold as ice.

"We-I- thought you might have had something to do with some

murders. I want to ask you some questions and clear things up."

"Who is we?"

"'We?' What do you mean by 'we'?"

This time, a larger handful of moss was thrown on the fire. Tom screamed and cried, jerking around in his ropes. All the hair had been burned off the top of his head, revealing a red and white and black mass of smoldering flesh. The flames had been high enough to burn off his eyebrows and singed his eyelashes. Tom breathed heavily and choked on the smoke from his own burning flesh.

"Three of us ... a trooper from Ketchikan, a native woman from Twasaan, and me; that's all. Please, no more. I'll tell you everything."

"What are their names?" the icy voice asked.

"Cody .. .Cody O'Keefe, he's a trooper, and Dot, Dot Green. She lives in Twasaan."

"Ah, and the three of you were simply trying to find me to talk to me. I don't think so." Another handful of moss went on the fire. Again, Tom howled in pain, gasping for breath and struggling in his bonds. Sweat poured from his face and tears ran from his eyes. Tom's face was already blistered from the heat. Patches of burnt flesh were appearing on his forehead, eyelids, and cheeks. The tips of his ears were already burned into black, unidentifiable lumps.

"We thought you killed the Toddwells. We found your necklace! Please, no more." Tom was crying, begging for the pain to stop.

"Ah, the necklace, of course. So you figured out I killed the Toddwells?"

A response wasn't necessary.

"So what about Kagani and Sha'te?"

"What do you want to know?" Tom gasped almost losing consciousness.

"I want to know about Sha'te. Have you found Sha'te?"

"No, not yet. Dot thinks it is somewhere along the Canadian border."

"Where along the Canadian border?" the face asked again.

"I don't know really, somewhere south, I think, maybe toward the Nass River. I don't know really! Please don't hurt me anymore."

"Well, I believe you. In fact, I know where Sha'te is, but I needed to come to Kagani to see if I could find the Kushtikaw talisman and shaman artifacts. I couldn't find anything. This place has been searched and everything of value taken years ago," he said disgustedly. "Now all that remains are rotting totems and the empty hulk of a once-great village. What a sad commentary for a proud people." Takqua stood up.

"By the way, you must be wondering how I knew you would be here. Well, your girlfriend gave you away. That silly bitch told me everything, and then some. Oh, and about cutting you down before I go? I lied. I just wanted you to have something to think about as you die."

With that, Takqua added more fuel to the fire, including some dried pieces of cedar log. When the fire died out, he knew Tom would be dead. He left Tom there crying and pleading for his life as the flames slowly engulfed his face and head. As Takqua walked through the woods, he could still hear his screaming almost a half mile away.

CHAPTER THIRTY-TWO

Back in his motel room, Cody waited impatiently for the weather to clear. A feeling of hopelessness and frustration came over him, and he dialed Twasaan.

"Hello."

"Dot, it's me, Cody."

"Did you call Ketchikan?"

"Yes, but they're not going to be much help on this one. I think we're on our own from here on in."

"What about Tom?"

"Tom will be OK, I promise. Don't worry. As soon as the weather lifts here, I'll charter a flight on my Visa card, even if I don't have a job."

"Is that supposed to be funny?" Dot inquired.

"No, just sarcastic. Never mind, Dot. I'll be in touch."

"Goodbye, Cody."

"Goodbye, Dot."

Dot gently set the telephone down on the cradle. She was worried. If they didn't get to Sha'te before the murderer did, he could find whatever it was he was looking for and disappear forever. She looked out at the mixed rain and snow and shuddered to herself. Something was wrong. Something was terribly wrong. She could feel it in her bones.

It was the late afternoon before Cody could finally catch a flight to Dall Island. Earlier in the day while walking around Craig, he had run into Rusty as he came out of a local bar. Rusty, who had taken Tom to Cape Muzon, was concerned about Tom's welfare because of the weather. Cody asked if he could go along for a fee, and the old bush pilot, never one to turn down a fare, readily agreed. Now Rusty saw Cody coming down the slick wooden floatplane dock just as he was finishing his preflight check.

"She's good as ever and ready to go."

"Alright, let's get started then."

Within minutes, they were airborne and island hopping to Cape Muzon.

Rusty pulled back his headset. "I don't know how close we can get. I told him I'd meet him where I dropped him off yesterday afternoon at high tide. Hopefully he'll be there."

"What if he's not?"

"If he's not, we'll have to decide what to do. No use worrying about the what-if's until it happens, though."

They both fell silent for the remainder of the trip.

Their plane was with 20 miles of the island when they picked up a crackling on the radio.

"What are they saying?" Cody asked Rusty.

"Don't know," Rusty said. "It sounds like we are picking up aircraft transmissions from Canada ... happens out here a lot."

"Do Canadian planes come out this far?"

"Sure ... sometimes. It is well within their fuel range from Prince Rupert. Some of the pilots resupply the troll fleet or bring out fresh crews. It happens."

The Canadian pilot turned around in the cockpit and addressed Edgar. "Good weather in Prince Rupert, eh? Now when we get there, you tell them we were in the Queen Charlotte Islands, eh? And don't forget the increased fee. The bloody Alaskans get pissed over violations of their airspace."

Edgar Abbott nodded his head in agreement and sat back in the Canadian DeHavilland. It had picked him up earlier, and they were headed back, an hour out of Prince Rupert. He knew he was safe.

Rusty guided the gold and white Cessna around the island, banked gracefully, and turning into the wind and drizzle, eased down onto the water with full flaps on and little fanfare. Spray blew across the brackish water as the pilot maneuvered the plane to shore. They motored as close as he could, then he cut the engine and gave Cody the same lecture and admonitions he had given Tom. Then the two paddled the aircraft to shore. No one was there to meet them. Cody sensed the eeriness of his surroundings and became alarmed. He remembered the same sensation of being watched before at Naha and at the cabin on the Shakan River. He turned to the pilot.

"This is a matter of life and death. I want you to stay here until I come back, got it? Not actually on shore but out in the bay. You'll be safe there. I'll return as soon as I can, even if it's after dark."

"Hey," Rusty said complaining, "I agreed to bring you here, but I don't get paid to get killed. I'm not a peace officer, I'm a pilot, for chrissake."

"You leave me here, and you'd better leave Alaska, too, understand? I'll pay you your standby fee. Just be here is all!"

As soon as the tip of the pontoon of the Cessna touched the beach, Cody bounded into the woods carrying only his .44 Marlin rifle. He scrambled around until he found Tom's campsite under the big fir tree and checked around to pick up his sign. Once he was sure of the tracks, he headed south toward Cape Muzon. Cody unzipped his jacket to stay cool as he ran through the woods, taking whatever game trail afforded him the best route. Even so, the branches from the fir trees and the scrub brush tore at his clothing and whipped his face. After almost 2 hours of running, slipping, and fighting the brush, he stopped to catch his breath. That was when Cody first picked up the smell of burning flesh in the air. Instantly he froze. Keeping the wind to his face, he let the smell guide him to the village, now just a short distance away. Nearing his destination, Cody sat in the dark in the forest staring toward the village, his ears straining for sounds of life. He could tell someone was there because of a small fire which glowed neared some large decayed beams which, he thought, once must have supported the village longhouse.

Cody crawled on his hands and knees through the woods to get closer to the campfire. Then he stopped, waited, and listened. He heard nothing. Saw nothing. Only the acrid smell of burned flesh flooded his senses.

After being fully satisfied that whoever started the campfire was nowhere around, he moved in closer; this time, within only a few yards of the smoldering fire. The stench was much stronger and almost made him choke. Cody could barely make out through the underbrush something or someone suspended over the smoldering fire. He watched the area for a few more seconds, his eyes straining to make out the shape when he suddenly recognized that the shape, trussed upside down, was Tom's body.

With a loud cry of disbelief and anguish, Cody jumped up from his hiding place and ran to him. Although the head of the corpse was little more than a charred lump of black coal, there was no doubt in his mind that it was Tom. Cody screamed in rage as he hugged the suspended corpse. Then slowly, carefully, he cut the body down and placed it next to the fire. He knew that he shouldn't do that. To cut down the body was disturbing evidence which investigators needed to see, but that thought was buried deep inside his subconscious.

Tom was a friend and a law enforcement officer. He deserved better than to be left hanging upside down swaying in the wind. Taking off his brown parka, he covered the victim, sat down beside Tom's body, and cried like he hadn't cried in years. Cody had no idea how long he had been there sitting next to Tom, talking to him, until the faint glow of day turned the blackness of night into a living forest. He looked around and realized the time. He grabbed his rifle and headed back to the plane.

Rusty was catnapping when he looked up from the cockpit and saw a solitary figure standing on the shore. At first he didn't recognize Cody. He was expecting two people on shore, not one. He grabbed the binoculars and looked at the person carefully. Satisfied that it was Cody, Rusty grabbed a paddle and slowly the aircraft made its way to shore. Even before the pontoons touched the beach, Cody had waded out and climbed aboard. Rusty saw the look on his face. Cody was exhausted. His eyes stared without focusing, streams of sweat, dirt, and blood filled the creases in his face, making him look years older. He smelled like smoke, woods, and earth.

"Hey, where's Tom? Will he be coming back with us?"

"Tom's dead," Cody said tersely.

"Dead? What happened?"

Cody didn't respond.

Rusty tried again. "You said he was dead. Are we going to leave him here?"

"For now ..." came the quiet response. Cody turned to Rusty and stared at him. Rusty could see the look of deep hatred in Cody's eyes, and it scared him.

"I did what you wanted, I stayed here all night ... I won't even charge you!"

"Just get me back to Craig as quickly as possible, and I'll take care of everything ..."

"Sure, right. Anything you say."

The rest of the trip was spent in silence. When the Cessna finally did tie up at the float dock, Cody retrieved his rucksack and rifle and headed for the motel. Turning to Rusty he said, "I'll see that you get paid for all your time. Thanks for everything," and walked away.

Once in the musty motel room, Cody threw his gear down on one the twin beds, stripped down, and took a long, hot shower. When he was done, he sat at the desk, wrote down what had happened to the best of his ability, and then reached for the telephone.

"Ketchikan Dispatch."

"Linda, this is Cody," he said, recognizing her voice.

"Cody, where are you? Are you alright?"

"No, I'm not alright. Is Lt. Blocker there?"

"Sure he is, Cody, but do you want to talk to him?"

"Yes."

A few moments later, a voice came on the line. "Lieutenant Blocker here."

"Lieutenant, this is Cody," he began in a slow, quiet voice. "I want to report the murder of Tom Whitefeather, the VPSO for Twasaan. His body is at the old village of Kagani. He died yesterday after—"

"Whoa! Hold everything, Cody. Are you telling me that VPSO Whitefeather is dead? Killed after you both decided to see what was going on at Dall Island?"

"I told you it was dangerous. I asked for help, Lieutenant, and you refused. I don't know if you had sent anyone if they could have gotten there in time. The weather was crappy all day. All I know is by the time I got there, he was dead."

"How did he die?"

"It was a slow, horrible, and lonely death. The bastard hung him upside down and then tortured him with a small cooking fire just beneath his head. He left him there alive, upside down to burn slowly to death, his head cooking while he was still alive. The pain must have been excruciating. Chances are ... chances are ..." Cody fought to gain control of his emotions. "Chances are it took Tom a long time to die. You could smell his burned body a quarter of a mile away." Large teardrops were silently rolling down Cody's face.

"Oh, my God!" There was a long, awkward silence on the line. Then the lieutenant spoke again. "I'll call CID and the FBI and report this. They can probably all be here by tomorrow morning."

The lieutenant's mind was now racing, trying to determine the possibilities of a second murderer. He felt trapped.

Cody responded sharply. "The CID, Lieutenant? Don't you think they've fucked this thing up enough already?"

"Cody, calling CID and the FBI is protocol, and that's what I'm going to do. We'll sort the rest out later. Where can you be reached?"

Cody was having difficulty thinking. He needed rest and to work things out. "I'm at the motel in Craig. Marsha has the number."

"Hummm, it might be simpler if you just came back here in time to brief everyone, then you can guide them to the murder scene at Kagani, Cody."

"OK. It'll take a little time to get everything together and catch an afternoon flight back. I'll be in Ketchikan before sundown."

"Call me when you get here. By the way, have you written down what you experienced and observed at the murder scene?"

"Yes, Lieutenant. I've followed the fucking protocol. I've written everything down in detail ... everything."

Cody's response sent a chill down the lieutenant's spine, but he answered calmly, "That's good, Cody. That's good. Call when you get in. I'll take it from here."

Cody hung up the telephone and thought to himself, *This sounds a lot like what he told me when I found the bodies of the Toddwells at the cabin on the Shakan River.* The thought made him angry all over again.

After he hung up the telephone, the lieutenant walked over and quietly closed the door to his office. He sat down at his desk and rubbed his head. He needed some time to think. *Could Cody be right? Could there actually be another murderer, an accomplice? What if Tommy was simply in the wrong place at the wrong time like Cody suggested? If that were true, then CID blew the investigation, and he was an unwitting participant in a major cover-up. No.* He still couldn't believe that a mistake like that had actually occurred.

The lieutenant reached for the phone and dialed Anchorage.

"Sergeant Jim Nichols, please."

"Who may I say is calling?"

"Lt. Blocker, Ketchikan Post, Fish and Wildlife Protection."

"One moment, please."

There was silence on the line. After what seemed like an eternity in waiting, a voice spoke. "Bob, this is Jim Nichols. How the hell are you doing?" he said in a jovial tone.

"Not good, Jim, not good at all. Cody just called from Craig, over on Prince of Wales Island. You remember Cody was convinced that Tommy might not have acted alone or that he may, in fact, be the wrong suspect?"

"Yeah, I remember. So what?"

The lieutenant could tell there was a distinct change in the sergeant's voice.

"Well, Jim, he has been investigating something he calls the Kushtikaw theory. He and the VPSO Tom Whitefeather started working some of their leads, which seemed to indicate that whoever killed the Toddwells was actually looking for something—"

"Yeah, to rob them."

"No, not to rob them, to reclaim lost property. Something to do with the old Indian villages, grave robbing or some such."

"Oh, yes, I remember now. A mystery man, the bushy-haired stranger and all that ... maybe even a shaman ... I thought he gave all that up." The voice was cordial but icy. The lieutenant could feel the apprehension.

"They didn't give up, Jim. In fact, they figured that the village of Kagani was somehow involved and the VPSO went to check it out."

"So what did he find?"

"He didn't find anything. It found him and tortured him to death. This time with a small cooking fire."

There was a long silence on the line. The lieutenant broke in. "Jim, are you there?"

"Yes, I'm here. I'm trying to piece this thing together. How do we know the two are connected? Maybe it's just a coincidence."

"It may be a coincidence to you, but it's not to me. Do you know where Kagani is? On a remote island called Dall Island. You ever heard of Cape Muzon? The cape is at the southernmost end of the island. Have any idea how many people would be in the woods there this time of year? Not fucking many. Anyway, figuring these things out is your job, so get your god damn team together and get down here. Cody will be here by the time you arrive, and he can brief you on all the details including anything he and Tom Whitefeather were working on together before the VPSO died."

"OK. The team will be in Ketchikan by late this afternoon."

"Fine. Let me know when and I'll make sure you have transportation."

"Bob?"

"Yes."

"We're all professionals in this for the long haul. Let's not jump to conclusions here before we have all that facts, OK?"

"Jim, you just don't get it, do you?" Bob Blocker exclaimed. "No one is jumping to any conclusions. There is a maniac on the loose out there, and if we don't catch him soon, someone else is going to die."

CHAPTER THIRTY-THREE

After Cody finished his shower, he sat down at the small wood table with cigarette-burned edges in his motel room and dialed Twasaan hoping to reach Dot. He was not looking forward to telling her about Tom. He let the telephone ring for the preset number of times before hearing a recording come on. Cody listened. He thought it was eerie hearing Tom's voice and knowing that he was dead. He didn't leave a message. Instead, he tried Dot's home number. The telephone just rang unanswered. Cody leaned back in his motel chair. It was just as well. He would have had a difficult time explaining to her how Tom died. Suddenly, he felt old, tired, and worn out. Slowly, Cody laid the phone back in its cradle and closed his eyes in a futile effort to stop the tears. He would try calling her later.

By the time he caught the afternoon flight to Ketchikan, he had tried calling Dot a number of times without any success. As the yellow DeHavilland floatplane lifted off from Craig Harbor, Cody could barely make out Fish Egg Island and the native community of Klawock through the light foggy gray mist and wet drizzle that blanketed the area. Cody was the only passenger that afternoon and barely noticed the pilot as he boarded the small commercial aircraft. Now as the operator read through the "do's and don'ts" preflight safety warning, he looked over at him closely. Cody hadn't seen this one before. He didn't look old enough to drive much less fly a plane. Cody tapped the young pilot on the shoulder, who responded by pulling away the earpiece on his communications headset.

"Hey, how long you been flying in Southeast?" he asked.

"Not long, about a month."

"A month? Where did you come from?" He was trying not to be too concerned.

"Phoenix," came the reply.

"Phoenix? You got all your commercial hours in the flat land? How'd you get float rated?"

The kid looked over angrily, eyes flashing. He perceived this as a challenge to skills ... and his manhood. "Who are you anyway, the fucking FAA?"

"Hey, I didn't mean to cross-examine you," Cody said innocently enough, "I just was asking. You look a little young to be flying out here. Or maybe I'm just getting old."

"Well," the young pilot replied with a laugh, "it really doesn't matter if you're young or old. I'm flying this tub, and you got in it. No one put a gun to your head. So sit back and relax, or pray, hell, I don't care. Just don't bother me. This ride is going to be bad enough to make old men out of both of us." With that, the kid pulled the earpiece forward covering his ears, checked the instruments, and headed straight for a thick cloud bank.

Cody tapped him on the shoulder again.

"Now what?"

"This plane isn't equipped with radar."

"Thank you, Mr. Spock, is that all?"

"No, that's not all," Cody said testily. "You're getting ready to fly into a narrow winding mountain pass in zero visibility with no radar, that's what."

"That's right. The mouth of the pass is obscured by a heavy cloud layer," the young pilot replied.

Cody looked him straight in the eye. "So what's going to keep us from crashing into the mountainside, Captain Kirk?"

"The very latest technology," the kid replied sarcastically.

"And what might that be?"

"This!" The kid held up a stopwatch.

"A stopwatch?!"

"That's right. We start into the pass on a heading of zero-seven-two flying directly over the Klawock fish hatchery, then over the Johnson logging camp, which is just about now, and I hit the stop-watch like this." With that, the young pilot pressed the start button on the watch just as the plane buried itself in zero visibility.

"Shit, we can't see! We're going to crash."

"Not just yet. We have about 20 seconds before we're in danger of impact. I'll turn the plane around on a reciprocal heading if we're not out of this thick fog in 10 or 12 seconds."

"Holy fuck!" Seconds ticked by slowly. Cody sat there speechless. All he could do was look out through the window at the blinding gray mist that covered the windows. A feeling of claustrophobia was beginning to set in, his whole body tight as a drum. Then, about the time the kid would have to turn the plane around, they broke through the cloud into a clearing blue sky with high clouds and several miles' visibility.

"Jesus, where did you learn that trick?" Cody said, wiping the sweat from his forehead and eyes.

The kid smiled. "Pretty cool, huh? The other day I was sitting in the Hilltop Bar there in Craig and started talking to some old fart named Rusty Middleton who claimed to be a pretty good bush pilot. We got to talking, and he said that the old bush hands would use that trick to fly through the passes up north, so I thought, hell, I'd give it try. It works. Just like the Pony Express, I get through."

Cody exploded. "You dumb sonofabitch, you almost got us killed back there. When we get to Ketch—"

The young pilot held up hand for silence and listened intently, then said something into the mike. Next, he turned to Cody. "Hey, you Trooper O'Keefe?"

Cody nodded solemnly, still cross.

"Yep. He's here. Got a message for him?" Using his right hand, the kid pressed the earpiece to his head, presumably to hear better.

Although he was listening intently, Cody only got snatches of the conversation.

"Yep."

"Sure ... OK. Right, I'll tell him. NZ2772 out."

The pilot turned to Cody. "That was your office calling. They want me to drop you off at the barge dock so you can meet some investigators coming in about the same time from Anchorage."

Frowning, Cody nodded that he understood and forgot all about the stopwatch business. Thirty minutes later, the yellow floatplane made a wide bank at Guard Island and flew right down Tongass Narrows into the prevailing wind. A minute later, they taxied up to an old float dock where Lt. Blocker was waiting to catch the mooring lines from the taxiing airplane.

The pilot flagged him off with a wave of his hand. Then he leaned out and yelled through the partially opened cockpit door, "That's OK, thanks. We're not going to be here that long!" The kid maneuvered the long aluminum floats of the DeHavilland aircraft close to the dock and then jumped onto the platform, catching the strut from the left wing and hanging on. The plane stopped in about 6 feet.

Cody opened the side door to the aircraft and climbed out. Then he retrieved his gear stashed next to the door. Turning around, he almost bumped into a stern-faced Lt. Blocker.

"CID just landed at the airport. One of the troopers is picking them up now. We should meet up with them at the office in about 15 minutes," he said in a low voice.

Cody didn't say anything, but instead, picked up his gear and followed the lieutenant to the black-and-white patrol car parked at the top on the steep ramp. *Just my luck that the tide would be out and I'd have to climb this damn ramp loaded down with gear*, Cody thought as he negotiated the slippery wooden walkway.

By the time he arrived at the patrol vehicle, the lieutenant had opened the trunk and was already starting the car. Cody threw his gear in and slammed the lid, then sat down beside the driver. It was time to find out what was on the lieutenant's mind.

"Lieutenant, I know you're pissed. I disobeyed a direct order and now a good police officer is dead because of my unofficial investigation. But I'm not apologizing for doing my sworn duty, you have to understand that."

"What I understand is that this whole thing somehow got screwed up, and I ended up in the middle of it. I don't know who I'm more pissed off at right now, you or CID! Neither one of you guys were giving me the straight story and—"

"Don't even start that shit with me, Lieutenant. I tried pointing out from the start that there was more to this investigation than just Tommy, but no one would listen. You supported CID—"

Lt. Blocker cut him off in midsentence. "Oh, bullshit! I was following the rules, Cody, pure and simple. And looking out for the department." Cody could see the lieutenant was red-faced and angry.

"That's good, Lieutenant," Cody said quietly. "But if everyone is looking out for the department, who is looking out for the public? We *are* the Department of *Public Safety,* aren't we?"

Lt. Blocker blew up. "Don't get smart with me, Trooper. You know damn well what I meant by that statement. I was following protocols."

"Since when do we have a protocol that say we let murderers get away? That we don't do good investigations? That we pin the crime on whoever is handy? That's not in any book I've read," Cody replied testily.

"Trooper O'Keefe, this investigation was never black and white. I know that much. CID called it like they saw it, and there wasn't much else to show them—"

Cody cut him off. "Well, Lieutenant, there damn sure is now, so let's see just what the hell the great CID is going to do about it." Cody had decided that the lieutenant was just posturing for a safe political stance in this whole affair. While Lt. Blocker appeared genuinely concerned about apprehending this murderer, whoever he was, Cody couldn't help thinking that the lieutenant was more concerned about his career than anything else. In that regard, Tom's death was only a political turning point with little meaning, he thought bitterly. It was becoming clear that Lt. Blocker wasn't interested in justice, just his job.

As it turned out, they didn't have long to find out about CID. The investigators arrived at the Ketchikan Post just as the lieutenant parked his car.

"Hi, Bob ... Cody," Jim Nichols, the CID sergeant, called out. Both Cody and the lieutenant waved back, but not enthusiastically, noted Don Fletcher, one of the original CID investigators on the team. Jim Nichols, Don Fletcher, and Skip Danski gathered their briefcases and followed Cody and Lt. Blocker silently past the dispatcher into his office.

Cody turned and held the sleeve of the lieutenant's brown patrol jacket. "Where's the FBI?" Cody asked.

"We haven't called them yet. We'll call after we've had a chance to look over the murder scene."

"Shouldn't they at least be informed?"

"Later."

"Go ahead and sit down, all of you. Close the door, please, Jim," Bob Blocker said. Then seated behind his wooden desk, the lieutenant looked at everyone in his office and said, "We've got a hell of a mess on our hands. What are we going to do about it?"

The two CID investigators looked over at Jim Nichols, dressed in the law enforcement standard of blue blazer, gray slacks, white shirt, and maroon tie. Jim shrugged his shoulders and looked over at Cody.

"Tell you the truth, I'm still not sure we have a problem. There is a good possibility that the murders were not connected except by an inexperienced investigator looking to make something sinister out of something simple. Cody, tell us about Tom's murder at Kagani, is it? Don't leave out any details."

"Sometime things aren't as we perceive them to be," the lieutenant added. He was amazed how Jim Nichols could turn something around and make it harmless. Cody stared at the lieutenant in disgust.

Over the next hour, Cody told them everything in detail, including how he had found the body, but cut it down and covered the corpse. When he had finished, the room took on an eerie silence.

Cody spoke back up. "This isn't about looking for the boogeyman, it's about looking for a shaman. And it isn't simple, it's complex. At least, I think anytime three people are murdered by one assailant over a 4-month period and a distance of 300 miles, it's complex."

"You *would* see it that way, Cody, because you painted it that way. But let's look at the two crime scenes as though they were separate scenarios. Would you agree that the same murderer would have a common motive and that experience has shown that multiple murders by the same individual have unique characteristics?"

"That's what I've been taught," Cody replied.

"So there should be some similarities between the two crime scenes, right?" Jim queried.

"Should be."

"Not *should* be ... *must* be," Jim corrected. The other two investigators were smiling. They knew Jim Nichol's reputation for interrogation. They could see he was just warming up.

"So, what do these murders all have in common that would tie the two together?" Jim asked.

"They were committed by the same person," Cody replied.

Jim came out of his seat and stood over Cody. "You really are a piece of work, you know that? You can't prove these murders were committed by one person. Get real! There isn't one scintilla of evidence, not *one* from what I understand, that connects these two cases together. The first murders happened in a cabin, the victims were skinned and decapitated. The second murder happened in the woods near an old abandoned Indian village, and the victim was burned and not decapitated. Robbery was the obvious motive in the first crime, and we'll know tomorrow what the motive was in the second murder. What the fuck is similar about that?"

Cody slowly rose from his chair, flushed with anger. He put his face so close to the investigator's that all the two men could see were each other's eyes. He stared into the set of nervous eyes as he spoke, slowly, calmly, and logically. "I'm not here to do your fucking job for you or get your asses out of a jam. But I will tell you this. Where your investigation got all fucked up is when you began assuming you knew what the motive was. As it happened, you were all wrong. Like I have said, this case isn't simple, it's complex. This isn't about robbing cabins for food and clothes, it's about some highly intelligent, very clever psychopath in the pursuit of spiritual power. What do these murders have in common? How about the close proximity to ancient villages whose shamans, in the past, were very powerful. Now if you take that motive—"

"Cody you're so full of shit—" Don Fletcher began saying. Jim Nichols, still looking Cody in the eye, raised his hand. Don became quiet.

"Trooper, can you prove what you just said?" Jim spit the words out in a precise fashion.

"I'm close, but not that close. The site at Kagani needs to be investigated still, but—"

Jim cut him off. "So this is pure speculation then?"

Cody didn't budge. "I wouldn't call it speculation. I would call it a theory. I know what he looks like, what he does, and why he does it. I have a name, Willem Tuttle. And I have three victims, one of whom was a better police officer than any of you could ever hope to be. He died proving this theory because he believed you all were flat-wrong. That's not speculation, that's physical and circumstantial and certainly tangible evidence. Now, you can use your investigative skills to try and discredit me here in front of my supervisor, but I'm fairly confident that he'll tell you I don't give in to intimidation and could really give a shit about you fuck-heads right now. Or you can get your groupies together and we can go over to Kagani, tear the village apart, and try to figure out where this guy is and how to stop him before he kills again. This psycho had to come from somewhere, and he had to get to Dall Island somehow. My suggestion is we start working on getting this guy before he kills again."

The room was silent. Jim looked away from Cody and sat back down, glancing over at Lt. Blocker, and shrugged.

The last sentence jogged Cody's mind, and he realized that he still had not talked to Dot. He broke his gaze and looked over at the seated troopers and the lieutenant.

"Is there anything else?"

Investigator Skip Danski spoke up first. "OK, Cody, let's say that you were right. Have you told anyone about this ... this ... Kushtikaw theory of yours?"

"If you are asking if the native community knows about my investigation, the answer is no. If you are asking if any American Natives know about my investigation, the answer is yes."

"So someone else besides Tom is helping you on this case?"

"That's right. This investigation ... my investigation ... is important to the native community aside from the fact that the wrong person was arrested and died. These crimes are centered in their religious beliefs, ancient customs, and the desecration of their burial grounds. Now, with the second death of a Native American within the past 3 months, there is absolutely no way this case is going to stay covered up."

"Cody's right," said Bob Blocker from behind the large desk.

"This investigation has all the earmarks of a political time bomb waiting to explode."

"So who is this other person helping you, Cody? What's his name?" Don asked innocently enough.

Cody didn't know where this was leading, so he responded carefully. "The name is not as important as the fact that this person is an expert in the field of native cultures and has contributed much to piecing the case together."

"Surely we will have an opportunity of interviewing the person as part of the investigation?"

"Surely. But in due time, not now."

"Well, can you at least assure us that this person is keeping good records and following some rudimentary precautions as far as evidence goes? The last thing we need is to arrest someone and lose it in court because of bad evidence."

"That's not an issue at the moment," Cody said.

"Alright, so where do we go from here?" Sergeant Nichols interrupted.

Don spoke up. "It seems like we need to take a look at the homicide in Kagani two ways. One as a separate incident totally disconnected from the murders at the cabin, and then a second look as though they were connected, using Cody's Kushtikaw theory and see where we are."

"That seems reasonable to me," the lieutenant followed.

"I can go along with that for now, provided that no one starts jumping to conclusions," Jim cautioned. "So when can we get started?" he said, looking over at the lieutenant.

"As soon as you like. How about just before first light?" Looking around the room he said, "OK, let's meet here at 0500 tomorrow morning. We'll go from there. In the meantime, I'll see to it that we have a charter flight available. I tried calling Juneau to see if we could use the Grumman Goose, but the governor's got it for the weekend."

Cody could see the meeting was essentially over. With Dot still on his mind, he wanted to try to call her again. "If you don't mind, I need to use the restroom. I haven't had a chance since I left Craig this afternoon." Cody left the office for the restroom. On the way back, he tried to call Dot again, but still no answer. He looked out the window. It was cold, pitch-black, and raining. *Where the hell could she be?* he wondered.

By the time he returned to the lieutenant's office, some of the oncoming shift were talking to the CID investigators and Lt. Blocker was on the telephone. Cody took the opportunity of going back to his desk to check his in-basket. Since he hadn't been to the office for over a month, it was overflowing with paperwork. As Cody worked his way through the stagnant paperwork, sorting, triaging, and eliminating, he was unaware of the office revolving around him. By the time he looked at his watch, it was well after eight in the evening. He got up, stretched, and headed for the door. Then he noticed that someone had taken his gear out of the lieutenant's car and piled it up neatly in front of the dispatch counter. Jennifer was on that night, and Cody stopped by to say hello.

"How is everything going, Cody?" she asked. "You look like death warmed over."

"Oh, as well as could be expected. You heard about Tom?"

She nodded. "It's terrible, Cody. How could anyone do that? It's so savage!"

Cody found himself fighting back the tears again. He found a place to sit down in dispatch and lowered his head. It somehow felt like the world was closing in on him.

"Cody, it will be alright. It has to be. You'll get through this as time moves on."

Cody silently shook his lowered head. He wasn't so sure.

There was an uncomfortable silence for a few moments. Jennifer changed the conversation. "Cody, I see you haven't picked up your messages yet."

"That's because I thought that you guys would likely reassign my cases and redirect my calls since I was AWOL."

"Oh, we were instructed to do all that, but this one is personal so we just kept it."

Cody looked at the pink message slip. It was from Dot. Through welling tears, Cody read the note. The words hit him like an ice-cold dagger. He reread the note again.

"Jennifer," he said jumping up, "I have to go right away. This is really important. By the way, did the lieutenant tell you that I won't be going to Dall Island and Kagani tomorrow?"

"No, he didn't."

"Yeh, I guess he wouldn't. The FBI will be going in my place. I'll call their office in Juneau now." Cody returned to his desk and dialed the Juneau office of the FBI. They were closed. The recording said, "If this is an emergency, please call 907 566-7676 for assistance." Hastily, Cody dialed the number which was answered by a service.

"Hello. This is 566-7676, can I help you?" a female voice asked.

"Yes, I'm trying to get in touch with Special Agent Darcy, is he available?"

"Is this an emergency?"

"You bet it is!"

"Hold on, please, and I'll try to call him."

After a few minutes, the operator was back. "I'm sorry, I'm not able to contact him right now. Can I take a message?"

"Sure, tell him that a village police officer has been murdered and that the Alaska Troopers in Ketchikan are investigating the case. They will be leaving for Kagani, the site of the homicide, at approximately 0600 tomorrow, by charter plane. He needs to be in the Ketchikan office no later than 0500 tomorrow morning if he intends to go. Lt. Bob Blocker is in charge of the overall operation, but CID Sergeant Jim Nichols from Anchorage is the lead investigator. They are looking forward to his expertise on the case."

"OK, I have it. Let me read it back to you once more."

Satisfied that the message at least would get to FBI Agent Darcy, Cody returned to the dispatch counter and gathered his gear.

"Jennifer, please leave a message for the lieutenant that I'm on my way to Sitklan Island. I'll keep in touch. Oh, by the way, is my truck around? I'll need the keys."

"I think it is next door at maintenance. The keys should be in it."

"Thanks. Don't forget to give the lieutenant the message, please."

"I won't," she promised.

Cody threw his gear into the front seat of the truck and headed for the boat harbor. If he got underway before midnight, even in this weather, he should be at Sitklan Island by dawn.

CHAPTER THIRTY-FOUR

The damp, prevailing, southeasterly winds off the Gulf of Alaska carried a soft, gray drizzle toward the mainland, catching him as he neared the obscure island. Cody knew how these ocean winds often disguised the coming of rougher seas. Skippers of small fishing trollers, caught off guard in the open waters off Cape Chacon, Cape Muzon, and Cape Fox, would be sent scurrying into protected inlets and obscure harbors with names like *Very Inlet,* and *Hole in the Wall* to wait out the storm.

Cody surveyed the approaching beach once, then threw the twin throttles of the gray patrol boat into neutral. Hydraulically raising the outboard engines, he allowed the backwash from the wake to push the boat onto the pebble-strewn, northern shore of Sitklan Island. To a commercial fisherman, this island might appear similar to hundreds of other verdant guardians standing watch over the rugged and treacherous southern coast of the Alaskan panhandle. It had the same ubiquitous pines, the same rocky shoreline. But as far as Cody was concerned, that is where the similarities ended. This island was different; he could feel it.

Dot's telephone message had relayed that on the eastern side of Sitklan Island was the abandoned village of Sha'te. Because of the close pronunciation of both words in her earlier research, she had somehow confused Chief Shakes' village in old Wrangell with this village. *There was little doubt in her mind now, however, Shakes and Sha'te were two different villages and Sha'te, not Shakes, was the last known village to have a powerful shaman reputed to be a Kushtikaw ... or so the Tlingit legend went. It was good enough for Dot to leave Twasaan and fly down here on her own—and maybe to her death,* he thought, then quickly dismissed the gruesome idea.

"This place *looks* like a Kushtikaw could live here," Cody murmured under his breath.

Even now, over a hundred years later, it still appeared mystical. The ominous, high, snow-covered peaks were shrouded in a thick mist. The tall hemlocks and cedars reached to the sky, supporting the clouds as though they were the roof of the old-growth rainforest.

Cody's topographic map of the area indicated that the only modern structure in use on the island was an old trapper's cabin some miles away. He knew these were typically rented out by the Forest Service to sportsmen wishing to fly into a remote area of Southeast Alaska to hunt black bear along the deserted beaches or fish for trout and salmon in the numerous mountain streams. He considered the possibility that the cabin might be occupied, but dismissed that thought. It was already late in the season for winter steelhead runs and too early for salmon fishing or black bear hunting. Likely the cabin would be vacant, unless Dot was already there.

Cody knew the murderer, or Kushtikaw, would come to the island eventually. He couldn't resist, the bait was too strong. But was he here now, at the cabin, or would he wait until sometime later, remaining hidden in one of his lairs? He considered the murderer as dangerous as any rogue brown bear. He had to be careful. As a precaution, Cody chose to stop on the northern side of the island, some miles from where Dot said the old village was located, and hike in. He was hoping to arrive undetected. The twin engines of the powerboat made a high-pitched whine, and he did not want to alert the Kushtikaw of his arrival.

As the boat gently edged against the shore, he hastily unloaded his equipment and grabbed the rifle and scabbard he kept in the bow compartment of the boat. Throwing his gear ashore, he quickly set the rifle on top of his pack, then, seconds later, set up his standard mooring system. That completed, he carefully pushed the boat out into the calm, chilly water. Cody watched patiently as the boat slowly glided away from him. After the boat was well away from shore, he forcefully pulled on the line connected to the ground tackle and the base of the 20 lb. Danforth. The anchor, chain, and mooring line slid from the deck, plunging into the dark water with a loud splash. The noise resonated loudly around the cove. Cody instantly reacted to the sound by turning around once to see if he had been spotted. Somehow he couldn't shake the eerie sensation that even now, the Kushtikaw was watching him. He swallowed his fear as quickly as it surfaced, dismissing the feeling as being overly apprehensive. Taking the yellow half-inch line, Cody ran up the beach to an old snag standing prominently near the edge of the forest. After securing the mooring line around a sturdy limb with a bowline hitch, he returned to the sandy beach to retrieve his equipment.

He slung his brown Cordura rucksack over his smooth nylon parka, making a conscious decision not to cinch the padded waist strap. Then he unzipped his parka. Cody didn't want anything to restrict quick access to his revolver. As he had learned in Vietnam, he would want to be able to access all his gear quickly in the event of an ambush. Finally, he adjusted the shoulder straps on the rucksack then picked up the rifle and scabbard. He carefully unwrapped the plastic Visqueen which protected his rifle, stowing the plastic sheeting and scabbard under a rock at the tree line. Turning the weapon to the side, he worked the lever action on the blued .44 Marlin carbine to make sure the weapon was fully loaded. Satisfied at last, he started off into the old forest. The hunt for the Kushtikaw had begun.

CHAPTER THIRTY-FIVE

As near as Cody could tell, the old village of Sha'te, or later called Ka Shakes, Dot had written, was about 4 miles away. Between him and his destination was a heavily wooded hill, much of it old-growth forest. Like the jungle, the old forests provided some distinct advantages and noted disadvantages. The tall trees and sweeping boughs, for instance, were spaced far enough apart to provide a walker with a clear path. The pine needles that littered the forest floor forming thick mats cushioned the walker and dampened any noise. Noise that the Kushtikaw might otherwise hear, or as Cody reminded himself, noise he might otherwise hear. He put that discomforting thought quickly behind him. *With any luck, he would find Dot and get her to safety before the killer arrived, then ...* he didn't finish the thought.

Cody moved his shoulders to readjust the load on his back and headed quietly into the dark woods. The forest was much as Cody expected ... open and easy to travel. The natural canopy formed by the majestic trees even helped to reduce the rain. He examined the individual trees in the forest, taking note of the fact that each was mossy only on the northernmost side of each trunk. Then setting off in a slow, but consistent pace, he started up the steep hill using the mossy side of the tree trunks as a navigation guide. It was almost noon before he finally managed to break out of the woods near the summit of the hill. Walking into a small muskeg clearing, he strode over to a nearby rocky bluff which commanded a view of the island. From this position, below and to the right, he could make out the dense forest near a wide, graceful bay. *Somewhere in the forest Dot believes is the location of Sha'te,* he thought.

On one side of the dense forest was a broad silver stream. Even from this distance, he could make out the white frothing waters of the rapids which churned the cold water almost from the time it spilled from a small lake to the time it entered the expansive bay. Cody carefully surveyed the lake. He could barely make out the small trapper's cabin nestled in the tree line at the entrance of the river.

"That must be the Forest Service cabin," he mumbled. He propped his rifle against his leg. Then, sliding out of his rucksack, Cody unzipped one of the two outer compartments of the pack which held his 10 X 50 power binoculars. He checked the setting on the binoculars and then raised them to his eyes. Carefully, he covered the terrain below him in small overlapping quadrants, his eyes missing nothing. Ultimately, he focused in on the cabin. Smoke was coming from the black metal chimney! *Is that Dot or the Kushtikaw?* he thought. Remembering the Toddwells' cabin and the fire which consumed Tom, he hoped the killer had not arrived on the island yet. He could feel his pulse quicken. Cody mentally calmed himself down. He needed to be careful not careless.

Cody secured his binoculars and replaced his rucksack, working the wrinkles out of his parka. His mind was thinking about the weather, rain, wind, and how to approach the cabin when he glanced over and saw it. The lean-to shelter with a pine-bough roof stood half concealed in the trees. Seeing the shelter and its near proximity surprised and startled him. He instinctively raised the rifle to his hip, scanning the forest around him, expecting an eminent attack from the Kushtikaw. He remained frozen in this position for several minutes, closely watching the forest around him, his nose testing the air currents for traces of human presence. Satisfied he was alone, he cautiously moved toward the lean-to, rifle at the ready.

Cody somehow sensed the abandoned lean-to was made by the Kushtikaw. The pine boughs were all fresh and poles showed signs of being recently cut. He checked the view from the lean-to. It was carefully positioned so that the murderer would have detected his presence the moment he approached the island in his boat. This scared him. The Kushtikaw had already anticipated Cody's first move. *The first rule in hunting is to understand and think like your quarry,* he mused. The ramifications of that thought were not pleasant. *So, Edgar knows I'm here. So much for the element of surprise. From here on in the battle is enjoined.*

Cody systematically searched the lean-to and the immediate area around the shelter in ever-widening circles, but found nothing. The entire area was clean and devoid of sign; another indication in his mind that the Kushtikaw had been there. His hand moved carefully over the front of the lean-to for signs of footprints but he neither saw, nor felt, any. He tried to catch a shadow to indicate even a slight depression in the ground, but there was nothing to see. Marveling at the woodsmanship skills, Cody turned and started down the rugged hill toward Sha'te, Dot ... and the Kushtikaw.

Working his way carefully beneath the rocky bluff, Cody slipped into the overgrown depths of a steep ravine which almost completely blocked out available light. Ordinarily, he might have chosen a different approach, but the ravine afforded him the most direct route to the bay and Sha'te. Devil's club plants tore at his parka and tried to scratch his face. Cody used his rifle to push the wet vegetation aside and to help him keep his balance on the slippery slope. One false move and he would likely tumble hundreds of feet through the thickets before stopping. Convinced more than ever his suspect was on the island, getting to the village and making sure Dot was safe was all that mattered now.

The farther he descended down the hill, the heavier the vegetation and the more daylight he lost. Even in the early afternoon, the forest seemed bathed in an eerie gray iridescence. The trees didn't even form shadows but rather presented pockets of varying degrees of darkness. Suddenly, the thought of the Kushtikaw on the island, maybe even stalking him, almost made him run through the woods toward the village. However, he knew that was exactly the wrong thing to do. He stopped and sat for a few minutes ... he forced himself to keep control. Cody recalled how seals, safely seated on rocks, would panic at the sight of a killer whale passing by their lair and hurtle themselves into the ocean, in hopes of escaping ... only to be crushed in the jaws of the Orca and eaten.

To Cody, the Kushtikaw was just as dangerous as any wild animal. He obviously was an expert woodsman, a survivalist, and a psycho with incredible strength who had, so far, anticipated his every move. In Cody's book, this made him unpredictable and lethal. The thoughts of what the killer was capable doing if he had half the chance made him slow down. Cody didn't know enough about the Kushtikaw, but what he did know scared the hell out of him. He knew that if he were going to survive this ordeal at all, it would be because he either was lucky enough to avoid contact, or because he had the element of surprise. He didn't dwell on the alternatives.

After 2 hours of pushing hard and continuously slipping down the steep bank of the ravine, he stopped again to rest. A gentle mist had begun to fall, soaking everything in tiny droplets. Sweat streamed down his face. He discarded his pack next to a large forest fern, then draped his parka over the top of the bush to protect the interior of the garment from getting wet. Thirsty, Cody walked over to a small clear stream. He knelt down, placing his rifle on the narrow bank next to him. He was alert to any possible ambush.

Dipping his hands down into the cold water which was fed from the snow peaks high above him, he clasped his hands together to form a natural cup. As he brought his hands to his mouth, his eyes searched the forest for signs of movement. Suddenly, a bolt of terror shot through his body! Out of the corner of his eye, he could make out small movements in the thick underbrush. He froze. Then confirming in his own mind that the underbrush was moving, he rolled to one side, grabbed his rifle, and swung to the left, pointing the gun up the hill above him in one continuous movement. At the same instant, a huge black bear exited the foliage a few feet from him. For what seemed like an eternity, the two stared at each other eye to eye, neither blinking; Cody, his heart pounding, tried to remain perfectly still, his finger slowly tightened against the trigger. In that split second, the big bear caught the human scent, and in a loud "woof," wheeled about, running through the forest, breaking devil's club plants and small saplings.

Cody remained in that position awhile longer. He was about to exhale when he was shocked for the second time. Just beyond where the bear entered the forest, he thought for an instant he could make out a face with black circles around the eyes watching him through a clump of forest ferns. In a split second, the realization came to him that the Kushtikaw must have been the apparition he saw at Naha Cove. He was the one who tried to smother him in the open grave!

Cody carefully kept his eye on the spot where he had last seen Edgar, his .44 Marlin rifle at the ready. Slowly he approached the place where he had sighted him, prepared to kill him instantly if he were attacked. The thoughts of the Toddwells' mutilated bodies and Tom's charred and burned body flooded his mind and clouded his thinking. Almost automatically, he brushed the thoughts aside. He forced himself to stay focused.

As he approached the area, Cody almost thought it was his imagination playing tricks on him. On the ground in front of him he spotted a large depression and human footprints in the soft ground behind large, green, forest ferns. *So it was the Kushtikaw after all! He is here.* He turned round quickly in an anticipated attack. No one. He looked around once more, but he was alone. Cody searched the area for more clues. The initial tracks which were clearly visible near the bushes began to disappear the further into the woods he went. Finally, he gave up. The bare footprints were impossible to track. It was then that he remembered his rucksack and parka next to the stream. He ran back to where he had left them. His gear was gone! *The Kushtikaw not only knows my moves, he knows how I think!* That thought scared the hell out of him. Cody knew that he had lost the element of surprise, and worse, the killer was in control.

At first light, hours before, Dot had departed the Forest Service cabin after dampening the woodstove and stocking the firebox with large chunks of dried cedar. *That should burn all day*, she thought, closing the door on the cabin. Then she walked to the lake and surveyed the tranquility around her. A floatplane had brought her to the lake a day earlier after she had called the Forest Service in Ketchikan and ask permission to rent the cabin. She thought it ironic that she had to ask permission to use a cabin that was built on land once taken away from her ancestors. To her, the cabin was an insult and an illegal trespass. But her thoughts that morning were on the ancient Indians that had once lived and died on the beautiful island.

Walking along the shore of the lake, her eyes continued to scan the landscape until she found the depression in the topography she was looking for ... the tumultuous river which, according to history, flowed by the old village as it traveled the last hundred feet to the bay. *It's a shame they aren't still here*. She turned the collar up on her faded canvas jacket and headed off into the woods toward the river.

After a few minutes, Dot picked up the noise of the wild river, and shortly thereafter, it came into view. Volumes of cold water and bits of ice chunks from the lake cascading over huge ice-encrusted boulders created as the freezing mist which rose above the tumultuous rapids settled on the rocks. Keeping the river to her right, Dot worked her way downriver. Periodically, when she thought she might have seen something of interest, she would venture into the forest, looking for signs of the archaic village, always making sure to stay within sound of the river. It was midafternoon before she was rewarded. Dot found something left by the Indians who once inhabited the area.

Between the tailing end of the forest and the river was a large stone. On it was carved a beautiful petroglyph made by the early inhabitants of the village. The design, etched into the flat surface of the rock, was the face of a bear with human hands clutching what was obviously a salmon. A tear formed in Dot's eye as she ran her hand across the surface of the carving, thinking about her ancestors who once lived in this idyllic location.

Dot, now convinced she was close to discovering the location of Sha'te, turned and began following the tree line into the old-growth forest. It was dark in the woods. As her eyes adjusted to the light, her heart soared. She could barely make out a totem pole long since fallen over and appearing more like an old decayed tree trunk than the sentinel of a once-proud village.

Running over to the fallen totem, she began to pull away the olive-colored moss and small ferns which now covered the carving, hiding and disfiguring the story cut into wood. When she had cleaned a significant amount of debris and growth from the totem, Dot ran her hand gently over the carved faces as though she were reading Braille. She cried as she read the totem which told of a powerful and successful village that had merged both the bear and raven clans.

Wiping a tear away, Dot paused to look around. She could now see that the forest floor was littered with rotten totems, their ancient faces lay deformed and overgrown with moss and ferns. Seeing another totem close-by in a similar condition, Dot ran over and frantically began working on the carved faces, pulling the soft, green vegetation from the crevices of the faces and exposing the rotten, bleached cedar beneath. As she worked on the totem, she started to interpret the story, this time of a shaman, the spiritual leader of the village. Dot had not seen a totem like this before, and her interest in learning more about this village peaked. *This has got to be Sha'te. It must be*, she thought elatedly, using her sleeve to wipe another tear from her face.

She was so totally engrossed in her discoveries that it was some time before she began to feel a strange presence come over her, as though she were being watched. She turned around quickly, expecting Cody, but no one was there. Turning back to her work, she gasped. Before her, as if he were an apparition, stood the Kushtikaw. The evil one was naked, with bands of black stripes starting at his neck and running down the length of his body. On his head was an ornately carved wooden headdress depicting a raven's head with its long, curved beak. Peering out beneath the helmet were the spirit's eyes, painted in circles of black which covered his eyebrows and extended beyond his cheeks. Instinctively, Dot threw her hands up in front of her face and screamed, instantly losing bladder control.

"Are-are-you-a Kushtikaw?" she managed to stammer.

"I am Takqua. Prepare yourself to die."

"No-no, please, I haven't done anything ... I never hurt you ... please ... pleeeeease—"

Her final pleas were drowned out by a high pitched war cry. Suddenly a sick sound like a ripe watermelon splitting filled the air as Dot's body flew backwards. Takqua had struck a blow with a double-handed upper cut from a heavy wooden war club. Blood and teeth spewed from her mouth as she hit the forest floor, rolled twice and did not move, the right side of her jaw caved in from the force of the blow.

CHAPTER THIRTY-SIX

Cody had heard the piercing scream from across the river. He tore off his wool shirt and leaving his revolver behind, jumped into the frigid waters of the fast-moving river, his rifle carried over his head. As he fought to wade and swim across the icy-cold river, the current pulled at his wool pants, slowing him down and making traversing almost impossible.

As he approached the opposite bank, he was met with total silence and then, an overwhelming sense of danger. Adrenaline coursed through his body with every heartbeat as seconds ticked by like years. After what seemed like an eternity, he reached the shore. Throwing his rifle between two boulders, he pulled himself from the suction of the ice-cold current. Ignoring the dragging weight of the wool pants clinging to his body, Cody scooped up his rifle and chambering a fresh round on the run, sprinted into the woods.

For several seconds he was almost blind until his eyes adjusted to the dark depths of the forest. Then he got his bearings. As his eyes became accustomed to the reduced light, he could make out the black apparition he saw at Naha Cove pick up a war club and wave it over his head in mocking defiance above Dot's body. Cody brought the rifle up to his shoulder and fired once at the figure. The rifle bucked and the 44 Magnum round went high, striking the tip of the ancient weapon and splitting the shaft. Wood splinters flew everywhere as the Kushtikaw dropped the remains of the club and ran into the woods.

In an instant, Cody worked the lever action expelling the hot, spent, shell casing and chambering another round. He shouldered the rifle fired again but the Kushtikaw had disappeared into the underbrush. O'Keefe dashed after the shape shifter, jumping over fallen totems and running through the forest, simultaneously working the lever action on the Marlin rifle, and loading another fresh round. As he ran past Dot's still form sprawled across the ground he glanced down; her entire head nothing but a bloody mass. The trooper felt a moment of pure hatred for the villain. Dodging around a nearby cedar tree, he thought he had another clear shot and fired from the hip. This time the bullet went wide, striking a tree limb next to the fleeing killer. Cody cursed aloud and worked the lever-action again but by this time the Kushtikaw had simply vanished. Cody, out of breath and livid with himself for letting the killer get away, returned to the last point he had seen the shape shifter. He sat down and looked at the partial print left in the crushed pine needles and soil. "Heel-toe depression," he mumbled to himself. "If this is an Indian he sure walks like a white man."

Cody found an old rotten snag and broke off a fairly straight 5-foot section. Then using his sheath knife, he quickly laid the wood branch down next to the Kushtikaw's tracks and created an improvised tracking stick. Now he could track him even in poor terrain, the marks on the stick helping to indicate where to find the next footprint.

At first it was easygoing. The Kushtikaw had run along a small game trail which was parallel to the bay. Here, the soil was softer and although covered with pine needles, the killer still left good tracks. After almost an hour, however, the trail cut into the woods, away from the water. Here the terrain was much firmer and the pine needle beds much thicker. Cody's progress was also slowed by the decreasing daylight. Suddenly, he broke through the woods and found himself at the edge of the lake, the sun just peering over the mountaintops. In that split second, Cody realized that the Kushtikaw had led him into a trap!

As he turned to meet his assailant, the killer let out a shrill cry and dropped from a tree limb above him. He hit Cody hard, and the rifle flew from his grasp. The trooper tried desperately to recover his balance, but the Kushtikaw was all over him, biting him and clawing him with his long fingers. Cody tried to fight back, but the oily body paint made it impossible for him to get a firm grip. Then suddenly, the Kushtikaw had a gleaming knife in his hand! O'Keefe struggled desperately trying to defend himself, but in one quick swipe, the shape-changer had cut him deeply across his face and shoulder. In a final effort at survival, Cody bucked his assailant to one side and ran for the safety of the lake. He never made it. With a loud roar, the Kushtikaw was already on Cody's back, the weight of his body driving him headfirst into a large log next to the shore.

Cody awoke with a sudden jolt, suspended upside down from a beam in the ceiling in the trapper's cabin. He hurt all over. His face was throbbing and left eye was either burned or swollen shut, he couldn't tell for sure. He sensed his arms were securely tied or handcuffed behind him. Blood from the cuts on his face was running into his other eye, but he looked himself over as best he could. He had been stripped and hung like slab of beef waiting to be butchered. The thought of the Toddwells' last moments sent an icy panic through his body. He could see that just beneath him was a large metal bowl. Drops of his blood had already covered the bottom in a thin coat of bright red. A burning lump was beginning to rise in his throat. Panic was beginning to take over. *Control yourself or you'll die. Control yourself or you'll die*, he silently repeated over and over.

As he pivoted around on the end of his rope Trooper O'Keefe could make out a woodstove in the far corner of the room. A large, foul-smelling cast iron pot sat on top. And, not far away, he could make out an oil lamp which burned brightly on the countertop in front of a small, dingy glass window.

O'Keefe continued to slowly pivot around, dangling from the coarse manila rope. He was alone now, but for how long was anybody's guess. He could feel that his legs were lashed together by a rope from the knees to his ankles. A tingling sensation told him that the weight of his body was beginning to cut off the circulation to his legs. Looking past his feet he could see the end of the rope ran to a large wrought iron ring on the center beam of the cabin. "Probably used for skinning large animals in the winter," he said half out loud. How much time he had left before he blacked out again was just as guess at this point. He knew he had to do something, time was running out.

Controlling his panic ... but barely ... he started to swing at the end of the rope in an attempt to break free. Cody had nothing to lose. As he picked up momentum, the rope creaked and he thought he could feel the old metal ring give way—just a little.

It was just after sunset as the Kushtikaw knelt down beside the calm waters of the small lake and watched the rising of a crisp, full moon. Beams of pale-yellow moonlight glistened off the ripples of water. On the other side of the lake he could see the faint glow of the oil lamp marking the position of the cabin. He prayed to the ancients to honor the upcoming sacrificial ceremony and for allowing it to take place. He reached over and lightly kissed the old green skull three times and placed it to the side. It was almost dark now. He struck a match to the kindling and the little bundle erupted into flames. He continued to add twigs and dried moss to the fire as he began his macabre ritual. Reverently, he displayed the items of all he had taken from the desecrated grave: burial beads, gold amulets, and jewelry. Next to his small treasure trove was his knife with the colorful beaded hilt stuck blade-first in the ground. He spoke to the shaman's skull, apologizing for desecrating the graves and removing the artifacts. The Kushtikaw prayed that the slave he sent next would be accepted by the spirits as repayment for all he had done.

"Please don't be angry," he asked of the spirits. "It will be a fair trade. I need your powers, and you can certainly use a slave."

He brushed away debris and smoothed the earth around him. Then the killer scratched out some ancient symbols and placed the verdigris skull in the center of this circular design. Four small candles were lit and placed in the exact quadrants of the compass: north, south, east, and west. To the exterior of the circle he placed four small sticks representing the elements: earth, water, wind and fire. Next, he busied himself in stirring blood and hair he had taken from Cody with blood, meat, and bone from a freshly killed otter, chopping the contents into fine pieces and mixing the ingredients together. Then, he sprinkled the mixture around the outside of the drawing as he danced and sang an ancient chant. Edgar was so deeply engrossed in the ceremony that he almost missed a brief movement out of the corner of his eye. It was small, inconsequential really, but it was enough to make him stop what he was doing and become alert. At first he couldn't place it. He looked around. He was alone. Perhaps it was only his imagination. Then he saw it again. Something was moving across the window at the cabin. The trooper was trying to escape!

"Nooooo!" he yelled, startled and angry. He reached down and grabbing his sharp ceremonial knife, began sprinting barefoot toward the log cabin. The underbrush tore at his face and body as his ran through the forest but he ignored the pain from the whipping branches. He stumbled and fell head first, attempting to negotiate the old fallen snags and slippery rocks along the shoreline. Still he ran on. Along the shallows at the edge of the lake, he ran even faster, the cold water splashing up around him. Clear of the woods and lake at last, he howled a long war cry as he raceded up the grassy knoll toward the log cabin, his knife gripped tightly in his hand!

Inside the cabin, Cody had heard the awful, bloodcurdling scream and pure panic took over. Swinging harder and faster, he tried frantically to wear through the rope or snap the iron ring. He began measuring his life in galloping heartbeats. Sweat dripped off his body. A stench of fear, sweat, and stale blood mixed with the heat of the wood stove and permeated the small, closed room. The trooper heard the killer's footsteps resounding off the planks of the wooden porch as he approached the cabin door at a full run. Then it happened! The timing of the cabin door bursting open coincided with the wrought iron ring suddenly pulling free from the support beam with a loud crack. Cody, at the apex of the swing when the ring gave way, was thrown through the air, causing the full force of his body to slam against the door just as the Kushtikaw was at the threshold. A split second later, his body crashed to the dirty cabin floor, wedging him between the wall and the door.

Sometime later he came to. He was still tied and disoriented. Pitiful little cries escaped from his dry, crusted lips in sobs and choked squeaks. He felt the fear of the moment all over again, and vomited. After crying a while, Cody gained some composure and control over his emotions. He painfully rolled onto his back and looked around. Everything was so dark and quiet! He could feel his body throbbing as though on fire, marking time with his heartbeat. Still, he sensed that he was alone in the cabin. Edging himself up to the wall, he carefully pulled himself into a sitting position. He didn't know where the Kushtikaw was; he didn't want to know. Cody just wanted to be free.

Slowly, he began working his swollen, bleeding hands under his bare buttocks and legs. The blood seeping from his wounds created a slippery surface, and after great difficulty, he managed to bring his hands in front of his body. He was still handcuffed, the metal biting into his flesh at the wrists. He rested for a while longer, then attempted to untie his legs. It was futile. His hands were too numb from the restriction caused by the tight handcuffs. It was too dark to see the rope knots anyway.

Cody looked over toward the counter and could make out the outline of another oil lamp hanging on a large hook near the stove. He carefully stood up and pulled the lantern down from the wall. Holding it in both hands, he shuffled closer to the stove and sitting back down on the floor, worked open the firebox door. Finding a half-burned piece of wood kindling from the interior of the firebox, he lit the oil-soaked wick. The lamp sputtered to life, and the room flooded with light.

Cody looked around quickly for something to cut the thick

manila rope wound tightly about his legs. His mind raced as he considered the possibilities. He carried the lantern to the kitchen counter. Hurriedly, he pulled open the counter drawers and thrust his hands into each, searching the interiors. He found nothing. "Perhaps in the sink," he muttered to himself.

He was working his way down the wooden counter past the window when he saw it. Peering through the glass pane was the most horrifying sight he had ever witnessed. The Kushtikaw's head was tilted, face pressed against the window. Painted in black with large circles around his eyes, his face reflected pure hatred in the glow from the lantern contrasting with the blackness outside. The effect was terrifying. The face slowly glided up and down against the windowpane. His mouth was pulled back in a tight grimace. Bright red blood dripped from his nose and dribbled from the corners of his mouth, smearing the glass, leaving a long, bloody streak. Suddenly, with a piercing scream, the Kushtikaw thrust both arms through the window, shattering the glass, and grabbing Cody by the throat. The trooper could see his adversary's face contorted with rage, his eyes bulging as he squeezed harder on his throat. His body was so close Cody could smell the stench of his breath ... hot and putrid on his face. The Kushtikaw's arms were cut and bleeding, shards of glass protruded from his flesh.

Cody began weakening and feeling his life being slowly squeezed from him. Black spots appeared before his eyes, and he began to feel dizzy, while his hands searched frantically for a weapon—anything—he could use to defend himself. Finally, his fingers touched something solid on the countertop. He grabbed the object and swung it as hard as he could at the Kushtikaw's head.

It all happened in a flash, yet Cody's mind recorded it all in slow motion, every detail seen in clear relief, as though it were captured on a surrealistic videotape. The force of the blow sent glass fragments of the lantern flying across the tiny room. Simultaneously, in a blinding flash, the oil from the lantern exploded! Instantly his assailant's hair and face were covered in flames. His head lit up like a torch. The room filled with light and the awful fumes from burning hair and flesh. The Kushtikaw tried to put out the flames engulfing him, then panicked and screamed. The shape changer jerked back from the window, embedding large glass shards in his back and shoulders and slicing off large pieces of flesh. He turned and staggered back down the grassy slope toward the lake, trying to extinguish the flames now engulfing his head and torso.

In the cabin, the lamp oil from the lantern had spilled everywhere. The fire on the countertop had spread to the front porch of the cabin. Cody found a large shard of glass and cut the rope binding his feet. He sliced himself several times with the glass, in his haste to be free, but he didn't care. What mattered now was staying alive at all costs. The ropes finally parted and Cody pulled himself across the floor to the cabin door. He barely escaped the inferno. He could see the flames licking the walls hear the fire crackle as it ignited the interior of the tiny cabin. The intense heat radiating from the fire drove him off the end of the porch, where he landed next to the wood pile.

In the moonlight, Cody could make out the silhouette of the Kushtikaw at the edge of the lake, howling in pain. Then suddenly the screaming stopped as the killer turned toward Cody and stumbled back up the hill. O'Keefe frantically searched for a way to escape or defend himself from the maniac, then he saw it. A large ax embedded in the chopping block next to the wood pile. He cringed in pain as he tried to work his way over to the rounds of stacked wood next to the chopping block. Reaching the ax, Cody slowly pulled himself to a standing position. He felt faint. Pain was everywhere—in every breath he took, in every movement he made. Slowly, he began working the shaft of the ax back and forth, desperately trying to free the heavy blade from the grip of the wood block. In the brilliant orange glow of the cabin fire, he could see the Kushtikaw clearly now, hair burned away, his face black and charred. Patches of cooked skin had peeled back to reveal the pink tissue and meat beneath it. Cody watched with morbid fascination as the killer, contorted in pain, continued to advance toward him. Closer now, the Kushtikaw stretched out his good arm and pointed his index finger at Cody and mumbled something unintelligible.

With a sudden yell and a final burst of anger, Cody freed the heavy double-bladed ax from the block and swung it in a wide arc toward the hand that was about to touch him. The swing was so forceful that the weight and momentum of the ax spun Cody around. The Kushtikaw's arm, severed at the bicep, hit the ground with a heavy thud. The shape changer let out a shrill cry of pain through his enlarged blackened lips, his eyes reflecting pain and surprise. Cody continued the circle, the momentum adding force to the swift arc of the ax. The broad blade struck the side of the Kushtikaw's neck, instantly decapitating him. The lump of charred flesh that once was Edgar's head flew from his shoulders in an eruption of blood, then bounced and rolled down the grassy hill until it came to rest on its side in the water at the edge of the lake, the eyes staring vacantly up at the night sky. Cody looked down at the headless body twitching at his feet. With a sigh of relief, his trembling hands slid down the bloody ax shaft and he sank slowly to the damp earth.

"That which does not kill us makes us stronger," he half mumbled through swollen lips—and passed out, still holding the ax.

CHAPTER THIRTY-SEVEN

At first light, the U.S. Forest Service, receiving reports of a possible forest fire in Misty Fiords National Monument, sent a helicopter out to check on the column of black smoke rising above the forest. The pilot stared in disbelief at the burned-out cabin and the bloody bodies lying on the ground. He didn't land, couldn't land—he didn't dare to. Swallowing hard, he called the air field dispatcher at Ketchikan and reported what he saw.

"Ketchikan District, this is November 2719, over."

"2719, this is Ketchikan Ranger District, over."

"Ketchikan, this is 2719. I checked out the smoke as requested. It is coming from the cabin on Sitklan Island. Be advised this place has bodies everywhere. There are two corpses here and another near the beach by the bay. I don't know what happened here, but it was bad. We need the paramedic and the troopers here ASAP, over."

"Copy 2719, stand by while I call the forest ranger."

The pilot made a gentle bank and swung the helicopter wide over the lake.

Two hours, later a blue DeHavilland Beaver on floats with the gold emblem of the Alaska State Troopers on the tail made two passes, banked slowly, and came in for a landing. The aluminum pontoons cleanly cut the water, sending spray out the sides of the pontoons as the plane gradually reduced speed. Finally, it turned, increased rpms and headed toward the beach in front of the burned-out log cabin. Just before it reached the shore, the pilot, wearing a state trooper uniform and ball cap, cut the engine on the plane. It coasted up on the soft sandy shore, then he opened the cockpit door and jumped out, securing the plane with a temporary anchor line. An FBI agent, an Alaska State Trooper wearing lieutenant bars, and a paramedic surveyed the scene. Seeing the bodies, the paramedic raced over to check one of the victims.

"My God, what happened here? Where's the head? Oh, shit! Lt. Blocker, it's Cody. The sonofabitch is still alive!" The sentences all rolled out at once.

SEATTLE

After months of care, Cody was physically healthy enough to leave the hospital and was anxiously awaiting release from the psychiatric ward. The burns on his face, side, and buttocks were almost healed. A bandage covered one eye, but the doctor had assured him that barring an infection, he would not lose his sight in that eye. The minor cuts and scrapes were almost gone. Only the stitches and nightmares remained—vivid, terrifying fragments of color and emotion. Dr. Wang, the young psychiatrist, had told him those scars were very deep but that they would eventually heal too. Something about post traumatic stress disorder but Cody was not so sure.

He was reading in his room one afternoon when someone knocked on the door. He could see Dr. Wang through the glass window and waved him in. He was not elated to see his other visitor, Skip Danski.

"Hello, Cody, how are you doing?"

"Skip." Cody nodded, "Well enough, I suppose."

Skip Danski turned to his left and introduced Lt. Julie Sykes of the Washington State Police.

"Glad to meet you, Julie," Cody O'Keefe acknowledged.

"Good to see you up and around, Cody. The sergeant has told me a lot about you."

"Sergeant?" Cody looked over at Skip Danski who was beaming.

"Yep, a few months ago. Reassigned to IA."

It slowly dawned on Cody that Skip was there in a formal capacity. "So, Sergeant, what brings you to Seattle?"

"You, Cody. We're trying to sort out what happened."

"Nothing happened, everything happened, it's over," Cody replied.

"This is serious, Cody. There are a few loose ends leading to a few bodies, and we need some answers."

"I don't have answers, Skip, I only have questions."

Dr. Wang stepped in. "Cody, if you can remember what happened or can help in some small way, it will likely help with your release."

"*If* we don't arrest you," Sergeant Danski added.

Cody shot Skip a cold glance.

"Can you remember anything at all, Cody?" Julie asked, putting her hand on his arm.

"Not much. It just comes and goes in short mental flashes."

"Can anyone help with your story?" she asked.

"Sure, where's Dot?"

"Dot?" Julie asked.

"Dot is the name of an unreliable witness from Twasaan who got herself mixed up in this thing and almost killed," Danski responded bemused.

"Has she been interviewed?" Julie asked.

"No, like I said, she was classified as a troublemaker and unreliable. We didn't think she had anything credible to add."

"Really?" Lt. Sykes asked surprised. "Where is she now?"

"Back in Twasaan."

"Do they have telephones there?"

Through repeated visits from Lt. Sykes, Cody learned most of the news. Dot had survived. The Native Health Clinic in Ketchikan had her medivaced to Harborview Hospital for extensive reconstructive surgery and psychological analysis. It took several operations to put her back together and reconstructive surgery to repair her jaw and mouth. Even with that, she would never be able to fully smile again; the doctors were unable to repair the nerves controlling the right side of her face. But at least she was alive and back in Twasaan, and that was all that mattered to Cody. Tommy's death was seen as a tragic miscarriage of justice which was exacerbated by cultural differences. Julie told him Tommy's closest relative was an executive on the Native Corporation board, and the governor had received a substantial amount of political pressure over the hasty accusations, arrest, the shooting, and what they considered to be a department cover-up which was instigated by CID.

A few weeks later, the union representative called him at the hospital from Anchorage to see how he was doing.

"You're a lucky SOB, my friend. That Lieutenant Sykes put together an outstanding investigation report, which clearly showed you had nothing to do with the murders and that you even tracked down the killer when no one else would believe you. That Indian maiden in Twasaan was a big help too, filling in the background information. You must have a way with women. We have been closely monitoring the investigation on your behalf, of course. We have your back. But around Anchorage Headquarters, I gotta tell you, you are a persona non gratis with the brass." he warned. "You crossed the line and embarrassed the department. They will never forget this. On the positive side, the native community was thankful you found this psychopath and cleared Tommy's name. And, by the way, get this: the murderer was a nonnative too! They *especially* liked that. Oh, and your union dues are in arrears."

"Fuck'em. Fuck you."

CHAPTER THIRTY-EIGHT

It was a damp and dreary day as Cody, dressed in his formal Fish and Wildlife Protection uniform, checked out of the Executive Hotel in Ketchikan and waited under the narrow carport for his ride. He would have stayed in his own apartment, but the investigators had secured the premises with a new lock to protect whatever evidence they thought was there. He hadn't had many well-wishers either. It seemed as though he had lost all his friends. Nothing really mattered to him now except that he was alive.

"Let them think what they want," he said out loud to himself. He looked down at his uniform and straightened his tunic, giving himself the once-over. His brass was polished, boots shined, and the brim of his brown Smokey Bear hat pulled down slightly, resting gently on top of the Band-Aid on his forehead.

Just then, a black-and-white patrol vehicle, Lieutenant Blocker's personal patrol car he observed, pulled to the curb. It was being driven by a young rookie trooper who nodded at him to get in. Little was said, but Cody could see that the rookie was watching him out of the corner of his eye.

He doesn't have to feel uncomfortable for very long, Cody mused. It was a 4-minute ride from downtown to the Post on the Tongass Highway. Trooper Cody O'Keefe entered the double glass doors for the last time and said hello to the duty dispatcher, who nodded back and smiled. Everything was quiet. The air was thick with suspense and pent-up emotion. He calmly walked to the lieutenant's office and in military fashion, knocked loudly on the door. Lieutenant Blocker, dressed in his service uniform, looked up from his desk and motioned him in. Cody noticed immediately that the lieutenant did not make eye contact. In the room were Sergeant Jim Nichols, investigator Don Fletcher, and, of course, Skip Danski, from Internal Affairs.

Cody stood at attention while the lieutenant began. "Internal Affairs went over the scene at the cabin with a fine-tooth comb. Their report was written and turned over to the Ketchikan District Attorney, but, fortunately for you, based upon additional evidence, testimony, and the report of Lt. Julie Sykes from the Washington State Police, the Grand Jury refused to indict you."

"Yes sir. Thank you."

"Don't thank me. I told the colonel that as far as I was concerned, you're history in this organization. You violated enough rules in the Standard Operating Procedures manual that they may need to rewrite the damn thing! On the other hand, the Public Safety Commissioner told the colonel the governor was receiving quite a bit of mail from the native community on your behalf. Oh, don't get your hopes up here, the commissioner spoke at length with the governor. The commissioner has assured the colonel that he would not stand in the way of a dismissal hearing. Internal Affairs is far from through with this and charges keep piling up. Oh, and in the course of their investigation, they located your unauthorized weapons. Holy shit Cody, I sure had you figured wrong."

Cody looked straight ahead but was beginning to tire. "Yes sir," he managed.

"Furthermore, Sergeant Danski has provided an in depth briefing to the colonel and the commissioner. Isn't that right?" he said as he looked to his left.

"That's correct," Danski responded smugly.

The lieutenant continued. "Their intentions to fully support this adverse action are clearly elaborated in this report I will now give you. The Department of Public Safety simply cannot have a vigilante with law enforcement credentials running all over Alaska."

"Yes sir, is that all?"

"No goddammit, that's not all!"

The diatribe continued for almost half an hour more; much longer than Cody had expected. Finally, the lieutenant read the charges, itemizing the various violations. Cody said nothing, neither confirming nor denying anything. Then the lieutenant read two separate memorandums, one to the commissioner and the other to governor, requesting a dismissal hearing date as soon as possible.

"It's over, Trooper O'Keefe. You're history. I expect you to turn in your weapon and credentials now. We will retrieve your equipment as soon as we close down the investigation and allow you access to your apartment. You can fight this, of course, but you'll lose."

"Of course."

Finally, Sergeant Nichols handed a large, pale-blue envelope to Cody. On the cover was written *"From the Office of the Governor, EYES ONLY, Trooper Cody O'Keefe."*

"I'm instructed that you will read this in our presence, Trooper."

Cody reluctantly tore open the side of the envelope and pulled the official letter out and read it aloud. Tears filled his eyes, and his hands trembled as he came to the part which said "… therefore, Trooper Cody O'Keefe is hereby reassigned to the Governor's Office in Juneau to serve at the governor's pleasure in the position of Special Agent."

"Sonofabitch!" The lieutenant looked around the room in disbelief. Everyone was stunned. Cody looked from one person to another, then folded the governor's letter and secured it in the breast pocket of his tunic. Lt. Blocker crumpled up the dismissal request and supporting documents and threw the wad across the room.

Cody shrugged and smiled. "Will there be anything else, Lieutenant?"

Silence filled the room. There was nothing more to say.

As he walked out past the dispatch desk, Jennifer said softly, "I heard what went on in there, Cody. Congratulations on your new assignment. It's probably for the best anyway. By the way, this was left for you."

Cody took the small letter from her. It had been postmarked from Twasaan. Slowly opening the envelope, he read the contents. It was short and to the point. "Cody, stay well. I miss you, Dot."